THE ADVENTURES

OF

VALENTINE VAUX;

OR,

THE TRICKS OF A VENTRILOQUIST.

BY

TIMOTHY PORTWINE.

LONDON

PRINTED AND PUBLISHED BY E. LLOYD, 44, HOLYWELL STREET, STRAND; AND
AT 30, CURTAIN ROAD, SHOREDITCH.

1840.

PREFACE.

In bringing the Adventures of Valentine Vaux to a conclusion, the Editor cannot refrain from expressing his sincere thanks to the very numerous subscribers who have encouraged him with their patronage during the period occupied by the publication of this work. From the commencement the greatest success has been the cheering reward of his humble efforts to please ; and so delightful had his task become, that nothing' but ill health would have induced him to bring the work thus soon to a conclusion.

And now, having said thus much on his own part, he takes the present opportunity of informing his friends that the Publisher of Valentine Vaux has purchased from one of the most popular writers of the day, *an entirely new and original Romance*, which, for general interest, will be found to exceed anything that has appeared since the days of Sir Walter Scott. Engravings of a costly description are in active preparation ; the paper has been expressly made for the work, and, in short, the whole getting up will be attended to with that care which will ensure for it a most extensive circulation amongst all classes of her Majesty's subjects.

It is expected that the first number, (to be issued in the same cheap form as Ela, the Outcast), will be published on Wednesday, the 3rd day of June.

May 30th, 1840.

VALENTINE VAUX,

OR THE
TRICKS OF A VENTRILOQUIST.

BY TIMOTHY PORTWINE.

CHAPTER I.

A BRIEF INTRODUCTION!—OUR HERO'S
EARLY MISFORTUNES;—UNCLE SAM
AND HIS PECULIARITIES;—A JOUR-
NEY INTO THE COUNTRY.

THE father of Valentine Vaux was
one of those unfortunate individuals
whose excessive good nature is their
ruin. To serve a friend he would go
almost any length, but as those friends
were not equally accommodating in
their turn, he often found himself
minus sundry odd pounds, through endeavouring, as he termed it, "to help
a lame dog over the style." In fact,
he lent money till his own exchequer
began to get very low, and then, as
is too frequently the case, his acquaintances cut him to look out for
some other easy fool who they might
victimize in the same manner. Upon
this the father of our hero waxed exceedingly wrathful, but as his former
friends were now *non est inventus*, his
anger was not heeded, and he was
suffered to vent his ill humour upon
all those who, unfortunately, could
not get out of his way.

In truth, this unhappy victim of his
own good nature, was now doomed to
give up many of the luxuries he had
once been able to enjoy; his handsome house was changed for a very

No. 1

diminutive cottage; his establishment was reduced, and instead of keeping half a dozen domestics, he was compelled to put up with the attendance of one female servant, who resolutely refused to leave him in his present altered circumstances.

Luckily for him he had only one child, the hero of our present narrative; but the thought of leaving him penniless was a trouble that bore heavily upon his heart. In fact there were times when people said he was certainly going mad, but as his uncomplaining wife took care always to contradict such rumours, the neighbours wisely thought the matter was no business of theirs, and accordingly in time very little notice was taken of his somewhat eccentric vagaries. By and bye, however, there was good reason for supposing the report to be true, for, to the great consternation of every body, it was one morning spread abroad that the unfortunate gentleman in difficulties, had put an end to all his cares at once by cutting his own throat! This was an awful blow to the widow, but luckily, her husband had bequeathed her and our young hero to the care of his brother Sam, who generously resolving to fulfil the trust, took Valentine into his house, and, at the same time, allowed the widow an annuity sufficient to make the remainder of her days smooth and comfortable.

Uncle Sam was, to use his own expression, "a man well to do in the world." His father had been a steady plodding tradesman, who after amassing a handsome fortune, died, as is our common lot, leaving the bulk of his property to his eldest son, the father of Valentine, and a flourishing concern in the grocery line to Sam, whose business habits seemed to be more steady than those of his first born. Sam, as in duty bound, followed his parent to the grave, and his grief for the loss he had sustained seemed to know no limits. He however returned home from the funeral with a determination to put in practice all the resignation he could muster, and having ascertained to a farthing the value of the property he had thus become possessed of, his heart became lightened of half its troubles in the cheering prospect that lay before him. He moreover wore a sad-coloured suit for the time prescribed by immemorial custom; mixed but little in company, and applied himself diligently to business. Vaux senior had been a lucky man in all his transactions, and the luck of the father descended as by heirship to his plodding successor. In a few years Uncle Sam found himself the master of a very handsome fortune, which he wisely enough determined to enjoy in peace and quiet, before old age with sorrows and vexations stole upon him. He therefore sold the business for a good round sum, funded the proceeds, and having purchased a pile of bricks and timber, (miscalled a villa!) in the Brixton Road. retired thither, to pass the remainder of his life in the same dignified way that many a worthy citizen had done before him. Here he would now and then have our hero to spend a few days with him; for Valentine was now regarded as his heir, but as the boy was rather too rackety for the nerves of an old batchelor, these treats were seldom of very long duration, and generally ended to the satisfaction of both parties.

Yet, it may be observed, amidst all the comforts that surrounded him, there was still one draw back to his perfect enjoyment:—Uncle Sam lived of celibacy! This at first was a subject of deep regret. but after a short time he learnt to bear his misfortune with the composure of a stoic, and thus may the resignation be accounted for. At the next house lived a couple whom Sam had often envied for their apparent happiness; they seemed so fond, so attached to each other, that their harmony was really quite delightful. One evening, however, the picture that had hitherto looked so fair and beautiful was on a sudden tarnished. Uncle Sam was walking in his garden admiring the rapid growth of his hollyoaks and dahlias, gradually a murmering sound came upon his ear. He listened, and the voices of his much envied neighbours might now be distinguished. The husband was calmly remonstrating—the wife angrily replying. As a storm waxes strong from the gentlest breeze, so did the tongue of the lady rapidly proceed from the sweetest *piano* to the most furious *forte*. The husband was roused and retaliated; the wife screamed and spoke daggers. Charges and recriminations succeeded, the lady shouted with absolute rage, a scuffle was heard, and then a sound followed very much like that which might be supposed to proceed from the sharp contact of a poker and a human skull. Sam shuddered, shrugged his shoulders, and hastening in doors, vowed with a dreadful oath never to get married.

It is needless to say the old batchelor kept his word, but I have heard him relate in confidence that he was once very nearly becoming a victim to matrimony. It appears that shortly after commencing business, fortune, or rather *mis*-fortune, threw into his household a very pretty girl who took upon herself the rather onerous duties of maid of all work. Whatever Susan did was pleasing in the sight of her master; the house was always in apple-pie order; his bed was made with the nicest care, for he was very particular in that respect; his dinners too, were delicious under her culinary management, and above all she could cook potatoes to a turn! The heart of Uncle Sam was in flames; he absolutely fell over head and ears in love with the girl, and was about to tell her so, when an unforeseen event nipped his young hopes in the bud, At the precise moment when he had made up his mind to pop the question Susan was nowhere to be found. He rang the bell, but no maid of all work answered the summons; he searched the house, but no Susan was there! Sam went to bed, but not to sleep, and on the following morning he learnt to his inexpressible horror that she had eloped with a neighbouring potboy, and half a dozen of his best silver tea spoons. But this is a digres-

sion, and it is now time that we return to our narrative.

In the snug retirement of Brixton our worthy batchelor was, in every sense of the expression, a happy man. Domestic jars never disturbed his serenity, nor did many friends annoy him with their impertinent visits, for he had taken the precaution in early life to keep the circle of his acquaintance within as narrow bounds as possible. The "buss" seldom stopped at his door, and when it did, the party alighting from it, came by special invitation. On these occasions he was a jovial host—gave good dinners and choice wines,—cracked a joke with the spirit of a *bon vivant*, and sent his friends home well pleased with his hospitality.

The amusements of uncle Sam were not of a highly intellectual order, Reading, it must be confessed, he was not very partial to, and the only books that formed his library were the ponderous folio tomes, in which he used to keep his accounts. These were ranged in the recesses on each side of the fire-place, and—such is the force of habit, his chief enjoyment was found in gloting over the folios of his old day books and ledgers. These afforded pleasure at all times, for few were the accounts therein that had not that pleasing monosyllable " PAID" placed conspicuously against them. Sam read —gave an occasional grunt of satisfaction, and always rose from his studies a happy man.

Vaux-Hall, for such was the name he had given his retreat, was pleasantly enough situated, considering its proximity to London. By clambering three pair of stairs to the back attics you might obtain a glimpse, provided the fog was not too thick, of Norwood and its vicinity. When tired of this scene you had only to pass into the front and a panoramic view of Clapham, Battersea, and Wandsworth lay before you, with a rich fore-ground of chimney pots and slated roofs. Sam often gazed upon these scenes through the medium of an eighteen-penny two-slide telescope, and to his mind no place in all the world possessed so many charmes as did the place where he had set up his rest. Happy and contented he wished for no other change, but looked forward with pleasure to the blessings of a serene old age.

But troubles—though none of his own seeking—he was doomed to endure. In fact the letters he occasionally received from his sister-in-law described Valentine as giving way to idle and mischievous habits, and even hinted that unless he was shortly removed from the place where he now was, some trouble would ensue from the tricks he was continually playing upon the people, who were not inclined to put up with them. Among other elegant accomplishments, she said he had learnt the art of ventriloquism, with which he had almost frightened half the people of the town not of their senses, and there was very little doubt but he would get severely punished if they could only find out to whom they owed all the mischief that had lately taken place. Uncle Sam was sorely perplexed when he heard this, for he really loved his nephew, and feared lest any evil should befal him in consequence of his youthful indiscretions. As for ventriloquism, it was a hard word that he knew nothing about; it might be robbery or murder for aught he could tell, and not doubting but that it must be somethig very bad indeed, he resolved upon a journey into the country in order that he might concert some scheme or other to save the youth from the consequences of his errors. Full of this resolution, he determined to summon his housekeeper, Mrs. Deborah Dawkins, in order that she might pack up a few things in his carpet bag, preparatory to his setting off on his meditated journey. He therefore applied himself to the bell rope with such vigour that he stopped not in his operation until the terrified old lady rushed trembling into his presence.

Now it so happened that at the very moment of this summons, the worthy housekeeper was in the act of enclosing a codling with a wall of dough to form an apple dumpling for her master's especial eating. Deborah was alarmed, for she thought some direful calamity must have occurred, and rushing from the dresser up the short flight of stairs, she stopped not until she stood in the presence of her master, who was still occupied with the bell-rope, which he had pulled till his face had assumed the hue of vermilion. There, holding fast by the handle of the lock with one hand, and grasping the apple dumpling in the other, Deborah stood for a moment or two to recover breath. For the first time in her life, Deborah Dawkins—(a woman be it remembered) was speechless! She had expected some dreadful catastrophe—that her master was dying, or that the house was on fire, and yet there she found him exercising himself in the manner described.

" In heaven's name what do you want, sir?" at last gasped the affrighted woman.

" Two clean shirts and a nightcap," was the laconic reply.

" Now these few words were not, it must be admitted, very explanatory, and the poor woman naturally enough supposing her master had gone mad, started back as if she had been electrified. Her face, that just before had been so pale, now became flushed — her very nose assumed a coppery hue, and she was just going to rush with terror from the room, when the loud horse-laugh from uncle Sam arrested his retreating footsteps, and filled her with irrepressible rage. Her master now saw that he had offended a faithful old domestic whom he esteemed, and foreseeing the possibility of having to look out for a new housekeeper, he prudently soothed her indignation by a well-timed application of that commodity which is aptly, though perhaps rather inelegantly termed " soft soap." He smiled and uttered a few words intended to be complimentary—what female heart, even though as in this case, could withstand the honied expressions of the good man? At any rate Mrs. Deborah Dawkins appeared—she smiled, and uncle Sam had conquered.

A few words sufficed to explain the meaning of those few ominous words, " Two clean shirts and a nightcap." He mentioned the necessity of his immediately proceeding into the country, and ere another half hour had elapsed, everything was declared to be in readi-

the dark, by way of saving the expense of candles, I planted myself opposite the window, and assuming a mysterious tone, desired him to prepare for an immediate visit to the infernal regions. If you had seen the old man you must have laughed, for he at once supposed he had been addressed by no less a person than his Satanic Majesty himself, and jumping up from his seat, he overturned the table in his haste to reach the door. This, however, in his flurry he was unable to open, and whilst he was trying to force his exit, I continued to terrify him more and more, by promising all sorts of tortures when he reached the place that must not be mentioned to ears polite."

"Ha! ha! ha!" shouted Uncle Sam, who entertained a thorough hatred for all lawyers, "this must have been a rare bit of fun, indeed, nephew. The scoundrel deserved it, I'll warrant you, and I dare say it will serve to make him a little more honest in future."

"Why, to tell you the truth, it has done some good already, I believe," replied Valentine. "He had taken out a writ against an unfortunate client, and the poor devil would have been in prison by this time; but my trick has had the effect of frightening him into reflection, and the consequence is, that the man is still at liberty."

"Excellent!" exclaimed uncle Sam with delight.

"Do you call it excellent, brother-in-law?" asked Mrs. Vaux with a mixture of surprise and vexation.

"To be sure I do," replied the old gentleman. "A great good has been effected, and it's not for us just now to look at the means by which it has been brought about. Here's a rascally lawyer been frightened into an act of mercy, and if ventriloquism can do so much for the benefit of mankind, hang me if it ought not to be taught in our universities as one of the most useful branches of education."

"Then you would encourage my son in his foolish pranks?" cried the widow despairingly.

"There you mistake me altogether," replied Uncle Sam. "I would have him see the trouble an indiscriminate exercise of his talents may bring him into, but at the same time would not altogether check him when the object he has in view is harmless. However, I hope soon to see him engaged in some respectable employment, and then I dare say he will scarcely ever give a thought to that which now fills you with so much uneasiness."

"I wish it may turn out so," replied Mrs. Vaux.

"Bah! you take the thing too seriously by half," exclaimed the old gentleman. "Valentine is young at present, but I dare say he'll be steady enough when a few more years have been added to his life."

"I dare say I shall, uncle," laughed Valentine; "so as you and my mother may perhaps like to talk the matter over together, I'll leave you for the present, while I just run down to the Town-hall."

"And what the devil have you got to do down at the Town-hall?" demanded Uncle Sam.

"Some mischief, I'll answer for it," replied Mrs. Vaux:—"there's to be a meeting held there to day, and depend upon it some mad trick or other is running in his head."

"I only want to see the fun that's going on," replied Valentine. There is to be an election for common crier at the Town-hall to day, and I should like to be an observer of the absurdity."

"And what is there to see after all?" asked his mother.

"A great deal of amusement, if I am not mistaken," replied the young man. "There are two candidates in the field, one is to be proposed by the whigs, and the other by the tories, and the chances are that there will be warm work among them. Already the town is in a state of ferment equal to that which takes place during the election of a Member of Parliament, and I shall be much surprised if some of the opposite parties do not come to blows."

" At any rate, I hope you will not do any thing to set them together by the ears" exclaimed Uncle Sam. "It's dangerous to meddle with such rabid animals as your whigs andtories are, and for my own part, I should say you would act most wisely by staying at home."

" Do you doubt my prudence then?" exclaimed Valentine, in a tone of heroic ardour.

" To tell you the truth, I do for one," replied his mother.

" And I can't say but what I do for another," chimed in the old gentleman. " However, boys, I know are not easily to be restrained against their will, so go about your business, and remember, if you get into any scrape you must manage to crawl out of it the best way you can."

Valentine only laughed at the fears of the two elderly folks, and snatching up his hat he ran out of the room determined to enjoy himself as much as possible at the expense of his neighbours.

CHAPTER III.

TRICKS OF VENTRILOQUISM — BLACK AND WHITE, OR A CONTRAST VERY STRANGELY EXHIBITED--VALENTINE VAUX MAKES HIS APPEARANCE IN A CERTAIN ASSEMBLY, AND THE MISCHIEF HE OCCASIONS THERE.— A VISIT TO LONDON PROPOSED.

LIKE a school boy, released from the studies of the day, Valentine bounded off, and having indulged in a hearty laugh at the expense of his mother and Uncle Sam, took his way down the High Street, towards the Town-hall. In his mind's eye he could already see a rare field for amusement in the scene he was about to visit, and chuckling at the idea, he went gaily onwards without stopping to speak with any of the old acquaintance he met with in the course of his

way. At last he perceived a chimney sweep trudging on a little in advance of him, while nearly at the same distance, but on the opposite side of the way, was a baker, who, with a heavy basket at his back, was going the usual round among his customers. To Valentine this immediately offered a rich prospect for putting his peculiar talents into practice, and speaking in a feigned voice, he bawled out "sweep!" accompanied with a loud "ha! ha! ha!" that was anything but pleasant to the lad of soot.

" Vos that ere meant for me, spooney?" cried the sweep, showing his white teeth with rage.

" In course it was. blackee," answered Valentine in the same voice as before, and concluding, as on the previous occasion, with a loud laugh of scornful defiance.

This was too much for the patience of our chummy, who, jerking the bag a little higher upon his shoulder, set off at a running pace, and then crossing the road, he purposely brought himself in contact with the baker, who, by the violence of the shock, was very nearly sent into the kennel.

" Now, my fine fellow," exclaimed the enraged cleanser of foul flues, " p'raps you'll know how to treat 'spectable people ven yer meets 'em agen."

" What do you mean by running against me, you ugly man's child?" demanded the indignant baker,

" Vy I means to hinsult yer, as yer hinsulted me jist now," replied chummy, poking his nose so near to the baker's mouth that it was in evident danger of being snapped off.

"Who insulted you?"

" You!"

" When?"

" Vy jist now! Didn't yer call across the road arter me, and didn't yer set up a grin that would have frightened even a Cheshire cat?"

" It's a lie!" vociferated the baker.

" You hear vot he ses, gemmen?" exclaimed the sweep, appealing to the bystanders. " He ses it's a lie, and if that aint enough to aggerawate a saint I'm blessed if I know vot is."

VALENTINE VAUX,

OR THE

TRICKS OF A VENTRILOQUIST.

BY TIMOTHY PORTWINE.

But p'raps you'll be purlite enough to say that agen, vill yer?"

"It's a lie!" exclaimed Valentine, who stood close by enjoying the sport, and at the same time imitating the baker's voice so exactly that it would be impossible to detect any difference. This was enough for the hero of the brush; down went his sack upon the pavement, off flew his jacket in a jiffey, and then throwing himself into an attitude of attack, he lent the baker two or three such smart taps upon the face, that he was obliged to throw down his basket and act upon the defensive. A regular fight now took place, and before many minutes had elapsed it would be almost impossible to say which was the baker or which the sweep, so completely had they mingled complexions. In the midst of the struggle that now ensued, the two combatants rolled into the kennel, and in this desperate plight Valentine left them both, whilst he pursued his way towards the Town-hall.

On reaching the place where the important election of a common-crier was to take place, our hero found the greatest bustle prevailing in all directions. Small knots of persons were to be seen in various parts, keenly arguing among themselves the superiority of their favourite candidate.

No. 2.

The Tories were for electing Abel Squeak, on account of his high church principles, and the fact of his having once been heard to declare it as his solemn opinion, that all reformers were destructives. These were qualifications that ought not to be overlooked, and the consequence was, that Squeak became the pet of all those who had the good of their country at heart.

As for Mr. Brownrigge Bullman, he stood well with the radical portion of the community, because in all things he was diametrically opposite to his rival in the present contest. Squeak was a conservative to the back bone. Bullman, a thorough-going, restless, whole-hog man, who had vowed never to rest satisfied, till the country was governed in a fashion exactly according to his own rather peculiar notions. He gloried in being the very reverse of his antagonist in all things, and as if to carry this feeling to the utmost bounds, he grew as corpulent as a fatted bullock, while Squeak dwindled away in size, till he became not much larger round the waist than a farthing rushlight in the dog days. Bullman's friends exulted in this, because they knew that the dignity of the office to which he aspired, would be enhanced by his majestic proportions; whilst, on the other hand, Squeak's supporters looked with no inconsiderable alarm upon a circumstance that they were well aware would operate so seriously against their cause. Then their voices too were so different that no one who was not biassed by party frenzy, could for a moment hesitate as to the overwhelming superiority of the one over the other. The tones of Brownrigge Bullman were a rich diapason that might be heard from one extremity of the parish to the other, whilst his rival could utter nothing but a wheezing sound, that was scarcely audible at the distance of half a dozen yards.

But this was a physical defect that the tory supporters could easily overlook, and regarding only the principles of their favourite candidate, they cared not if their future Town-crier was *dumb*, so that he professed those political principles which they themselves admired. As for the result of the election, that at present was wrapped up in mysterious uncertainty, for it so happened that the two parties were nearly balanced, and the hopes of both sides rested on the chance of gaining a few deserters from the ranks of their opponents. Bullman himself felt pretty confident of success, in consequence of certain whisperings he had sent abroad, of a determination to exterminate his rival in the event of matters going against him. He supposed Squeak might be terrified into a resignation, but in this he was sadly disappointed, for when the morning of election came, the little man presented himself on the hustings, to the no small chagrin of Bullman, and his enthusiastic supporters.

When Valentine entered the Hall, the high bailiff and other dignitaries of the parochial government had not yet arrived, and the hubbub that reigned throughout the assembly shewed the deep interest that was taken in the day's proceedings. Now and then cheers were heard from each party, in honour of their favourite candidate, and these were followed by the groans and hisses of those, who, having nothing better to do, kicked up all the noise they could, by way of passing away the time. So far Valentine took no part in the bustling scene that was going on; he had formed his own plans of operation, and did not choose to hazard their success by commencing till the proper period arrived. For the present, he was content to remain a passive spectator of all that was going on, occasionally, it is true, indulging in a hearty laugh at the wit and humour of those who surrounded him.

At last a movement was observed on the hustings, and presently afterwards the high bailiff made his appearance, followed by all the chief dignitaries of the town. Then came the two candidates, each attended by numerous supporters, and when the hooting had subsided, the bailiff had kindly informed the assembled multitude of what they knew before—namely, that they were assembled together that day for the purpose of electing by their votes an efficient man to fulfill the important and arduous duties belonging to the office that had unfortunately become vacant by the recent demise of Barnaby Snuffle, their lately respected and never-to-be-sufficiently regretted common crier. Having delivered himself of this short speech, the high bailiff backed himself towards the chair, and took his seat amidst the loudest acclamations from sundry charity children who had been ranged on either side of the hustings for the purpose of adding further importance to the proceedings.

The business being thus opened, Mr. Nicholas Nail, the parish undertaker, advanced with great solemnity, and having bowed three times to as many distinct portions of the hall, gave a loud hem, and thus addressed the assembled multitude :—

"Ladies and gentlemen, unaccustomed though I am to public speaking, I could not, on so *grave* an occasion as this, remain *mute*. A great duty is to be performed; an office of trust and responsibility is to be filled, and I have *undertaken* to propose Abel Squeak as a man in every way fitted to shed lustre and renown upon the dignity of common crier. It is not for me to re-*hearse* the numerous qualities that render him so peculiarly fit for this situation of honour, or to point out to your recollection the many *black jobs* in which his adversary is well known to have been engaged. I *plume* myself upon the justice of my cause, and all I hope is, that when the election is concluded, all ill nature may be *shrouded* in oblivion, and that our animosities may be *buried* in the *tomb* of all the Capulets."

"Bravo, Master Nicholas Nail!" exclaimed all the Tories in raptures at his oratory.

"Bravo, old screw-'em-tight," cried Valentine in a feigned voice, which seemed to proceed from a different part of the hall.

"Gentlemen," exclaimed the bailiff, rising with much dignity and looking unutterable things towards the place from whence the sound was supposed to come;—"Gentlemen!" he repeated, violently striking his right fist into the open palm of his left hand—"this is truly dis-grace-ful!"

"It was a rascally radical," shouted one of Abel Squeak's supporters.

"It's a Tory!" cried Valentine, in a tone that seemed to issue from just in front of the hustings.

"Who says it's a *story?*" furiously demanded the preceding speaker. "Only let me know who it was, and I'll pulverize him into absolute nothingness."

"Order! order!— chair! chair," vociferated a hundred or two of voices in as many different tones.

"Gentlemen!" roared the bailiff most energetically—"I am—"

"An infernal ass!" interrupted Valentine, throwing his voice into a distant part of the meeting.

"Tom Pips, the farrier," answered a little man who happened to owe the aforesaid Tom Pips a grudge, and who took this method of revenging himself.

"Tom Pips is a radical, and knows no better," retorted one of the conservative friends of the bailiff.

"If any body says as how it was me again," growled the farrier, "I'll shove my fist down his throat and turn him inside out!"

This threat seemed to have some effect, for order was presently afterwards restored, when, taking advantage of the temporary calm, Mr. Snoxall, the hatter, rose to second the nomination of Abel Squeak.

He *felt* assured, he said, that his conservative brethren would convince their radical townsmen that they (the Tories) were made of good *stuff*. He should be proud to see Abel Squeak at the *top of the poll*, and in order to *crown* that wish a little exertion would serve to give his opponent a *finisher*.

"You had better take a NAP, old boy," exclaimed Valentine, who was determined to have a spree with the assembled burgesses.

"Really, gentlemen, this is too bad," remonstrated the bailiff; "who is it that persists in disturbing the meeting in this scandalous manner?"

"The man with the spectacles," answered Valentine.

"Then let him he brought before me and I'll punish him," cried the high bailiff, pompously; bring him here, I say, and we'll soon see whether this uproar can't be put an end to."

In an instant every unfortunate devil who happennd to wear spectacles was laid hold of and dragged towards the judgment seat of his worship the bailiff. It was a ludicrous sight to see no less than fifteen of these purblind gentry ranged in front of the great man, and yielding to the merriment it occasioned, the whole assemblage burst into a tremendous roar of laughter.

"Now, fellows," exclaimed the indignant bailiff, "which among you was it that disturbed the business for which we are assembled?"

No answer was given to this question, and his worship was rather perplexed how to act, when Valentine, sending his voice among those who surrounded the chair, shouted:—

"If they are obstinate, teach them to behave better in future by sending the whole lot to prison!"

"Mr. Tomkins, I thank you for the hint," exclaimed the bailiff, bowing to a podgy little cheesemonger who stood by his side.

"I'm blessed if the hint came from me," responded the aforesaid Mr. Tomkins.

"Then I thank the gentleman, whoever he was," replied the high bailiff. "The idea is an excellent one, and I shall act upon it. Mr. Headborough, have the goodness to bring your men here, and carry these riotous individuals o prison, till I have more time to sift the matter to its very bottom."

"I am not the person you have to complain of," remonstrated the elder of these traitors in spectacles.

"Nor I," chimed in the whole fourteen of his companions in misfortune.

"I don't care for that," cried the bailiff; "as a magistrate I am bound to act impartially, and I don't know how I can better prove my wish to deal out equal justice than by ordering you ALL to be locked up till the real offender is discovered."

The fifteen gentlemen in specs looked woefully chap-fallen at this announcement, and as many of them as happened to be provided with sticks or umbrellas, threw themselves upon the defensive, and bade defiance to the officers who were advancing to carry the orders of the high bailiff into effect. Nor was this act of open rebellion without its effect upon the crowd, many of whom ranged themselves on the side of the weaker party, and in a jiffy the demon of discord reigned triumphant throughout the assembly. It was in vain that the bailiff endeavoured to restore order by the exercise of his stentorian lungs; nobody appeared to heed him in the least, and as for Valentine, he took advantage which the opportunity afforded him of fanning up the flame of strife and disorder.

In the midst of this confusion the election of common crier was of course forgotten, but the two parties, radicals and conservatives, gladly seized the opportunity which it offered to vent the spleen they had so long fostered against each other. Separating themselves therefore into two bodies, the factions seemed determined upon trying their strength, and at it they went pell mell, as if the fate of an empire depended upon their exertions that day. At length, however, a reinforcement of constables arrived at the door of the Town Hall, who after dealing out broken heads in abundance, succeeded in forcing their way among the combatants, who they soon managed to disperse by means of the vigorous blows with which they saluted all those who happened to fall within their reach. At this moment the scene of confusion utterly baffles all description; for as every one was anxious to take care of himself, a general rush was made towards the door, and as all could not get out at once, they squeezed, jostled, and thumped away at another with such hearty good will that the air was filled with sounds that might remind a spectator of bedlam broke loose. In the course of time, however, the belligerents contrived to force their way from this scene of tumult, and as all, by this time, had had enough of it, every man, as he issued from the Town-hall, returned to his own house, fully determined in his own mind never to get into such a scrape again, as long as he lived.

Having watched this affair from the commencement to its conclusion, Valentine Vaux, the originator of the disturbance, hurried home, where, finding his mother and uncle Sam anxiously waiting his return, he related all that had passed, confessing his own share in the business, and describing accurately the whole affair which had terminated so disastrous to all parties. Mrs. Vaux listened to his narrative with fear and trembling, for she dreaded a discovery of his participation in the mischief which had ensued, and the consequent punishment that would be sure to fall on him.

"It's just what I was always afraid of," she said; "you are a foolish wilful boy, Valentine, and by and by, you will carry this folly so far that you will be made to smart for it."

"Aye, if they find me out," replied her son, "but let me tell you it will puzzle them to do that. Besides, in the present instance, it serves the stupid fellows right, for they met to elect a common crier, and must needs turn the matter to political purposes."

"And what had you to do with it if they did?" asked Mrs. Vaux.

"Ah! what indeed?" exclaimed uncle Sam; "but you are a giddy, thoughtless fellow, sir, and that's the truth of it."

"Nay, sir, I hope you are not seriously angry ——"

"Angry!" interrupted the old gentleman; "no, no, I'm not angry, Valentine, because I know striplings like you are always prone to mischief. But your mother seems to be alarmed lest any evil consequences should ensue, and as I am somewhat of her way of thinking, it is absolutely necessary that immediate measures should be concerted for your safety."

"Valentine must leave home directly," cried the mother, "for I'm convinced they'll not be long in finding out who it was that set them all together by the ears."

"Would you have me fly like a coward, mother?" asked Valentine.

"I would have you go away with as little loss of time as possible?" replied the lady. "Here you are not safe for an instant, and though I am sorry to part with you under such circumstances, the sacrifice must be made, and I will e'en submit to it."

"And pray where would you have him go to?" asked uncle Sam.

"To London," replied Mrs. Vaux, after a moment's consideration.

"Is the woman mad?" exclaimed uncle Sam with astonishment; "would you send a gay young fellow like him up to town, where every temptation and folly will be thrown in his way?"

"If I would do so," replied the mother, "it is because I know he would there be in some respects under your eye. You would be able to watch over him and ——"

"To tell you the truth I don't want to have the duty imposed upon me," exclaimed the old gentleman. "I have lived a bachelor all my days, Mrs. Vaux, and it's hardly likely that at my time of life, I should choose to undertake the bringing up a harum-scarum fellow who will be getting into one scrape just as fast as he gets out of another. No, no, if Valentine likes to play off his tricks upon travellers, he must answer for the consequences, for hang me if I'm going to look after him."

"You hear, Valentine, how much trouble you are likely to bring yourself into," cried the widow. "Even your best friends turn their backs on you, and all through that unfortunate love of mischief that seems inherent to your nature."

"Really, mother, you are too severe with me about what, after all, is a mere trifle," answered Valentine. "If I love a joke there is no great crime in it, and most likely I, like other people, shall grow tired of it all in good time."

"I'll tell you what it is, young man," said uncle Sam, rousing himself from a brown study: "I don't altogether like the idea of suffering you to take your chance without putting out a hand to save you; so I'll tell you what I'll do—you shall go up on a visit to my friend Mr. Bramstone, and I have no doubt, under his eye, you will be perfectly cured of all these whims and oddities that at present threaten to disturb not only your own peace but that of your mother."

" Does Mr. Bramstone live in London, sir?" asked Valentine.

" He does."

" Then I'm a lucky dog after all," exclaimed the young man. " I wanted of all things to pay a visit to town, and this affair that I have been engaged in has served to forward my views very considerably."

"Aye, aye, sir," answered his uncle, "but you must remember it will not do to play off your merry pranks there. People will not put up with it quite so quietly as they do in this dull place, and if you should be found out in any of your tricks, broken bones will follow to a certainty."

" Don't you think, sir, it would be better that Valentine should be under your own roof? that is, if I may be so bold as to suggest it," asked Mrs. Vaux, in a tone of submission.

" You must allow me to have my own way, madam, in this affair," exclaimed Uncle Sam. " The boy would be apt to think he had a right to do as he liked in my house, and very likely I should not have the heart to call him to order for it, but if he goes among strangers, the case will be altered; there he must be upon his best behaviour, and who knows but it may serve to steady his too volatile nature, and make him the pride and ornament of society."

" That indeed would be delightful," cried Mrs. Vaux, rapturously.

" Well, I'm very glad the thought struck me," returned Uncle Sam; " so, if you can trust to your own resolution, you shall immediately become an inmate of Mr. Bramstone's house, where you may be as happy as the days are long."

" I agree to give it a trial, at any rate," answered Valentine; " that is," he continued with hesitation, " if he is not too straight-laced in his notions for a young man of twenty."

"On the contrary, you will find him a very nice, agreeable fellow," replied the old gentleman. " He is as steady as old Time, but is considerate enough to make all due allowances for the occasional outbursts of youthful folly."

" You must give up your ventriloquism, my dear," observed our hero's mother gravely.

" That is to say, he must gradually give it up," returned Uncle Sam. " We must not expect too much at one time, you know, my dear madam, for fear of disappointment. Valentine, I dare say, will endeavour to amend his folly, but if he should occasionally indulge in this habit of his, we must look over it, in hopes that he will be ultimately cured."

On this understanding, our hero agreed to become an inmate of Mr. Bramstone's house, and it was then further arranged that he should start for London, by the coach, on the following morning. With this understanding they parted for the present, mutually well pleased with an arrangement that was likely enough to terminate so well.

———

CHAPTER IV.

PREPARATIONS FOR A JOURNEY, WITH A DISSERTATION UPON ROADSIDE ABUSES—VALENTINE TAKES HIS DEPARTURE—TRICKS UPON TRAVELLERS—HOW A CERTAIN PERSON GROWS RUSTY, AND THE MEANS HE TAKES TO BE REVENGED—A CAPSIZE.

VALENTINE, his mother, and Uncle Sam, were up by times on the next morning, and the busy note of preparation was to be heard from the top to the bottom of the house. Mrs. Vaux was particularly active on the occasion, and her tongue ran nineteen to the dozen as she gave orders, and then countermanded them, as some new notion or other entered her teeming brain. As for Uncle Sam, he was contented with doing the looking on part, now and then venturing to give a little bit of advice wherever he thought it requisite. But the busiest of all was our hero, to whom the idea of a journey to London was most inspiring. Boxes were packed and corded, parcels made up, and a large store of ham sandwiches, together with a small bottle of wine, for refreshments on the road, were stowed away into a basket, so as to be handy whenever hunger or thirst might induce the traveller to partake of either one or the other. Amidst all this bustle, it was refreshing to see the vivacity with which Mrs. Vaux issued her commands, and assisted in their execution. At one moment she was at the top of the house bawling and squalling to know where this, that, and the other article was; then she came down stairs, and away she went trudging from room to room to see that nothing had been forgotten that ought to be remembered.

Now it must be confessed that Uncle Sam was terribly out of sorts at all this clatter; as an old batchelor he loved quiet, and the uproar that at present surrounded him was not very pleasant to his somewhat irritable nerves. In his despair he had thrown himself upon a sofa by the breakfast table, in hopes that the others would follow to do honour to the good things that had been spread thereon. But even in this he was doomed to be disappointed, for Mrs. Vaux was too much engaged just then to bestow a single thought upon breakfast, and as for Valentine the idea of the journey had taken away his appetite, and instead of devouring a roll with his usual avidity, he was every minute jumping up and running to the window to see whether the horses were being put to.

" Now there's a good fellow, do sit down and eat heartily," exclaimed Uncle Sam. " Remember, my boy, you've got a long journey before you, and the keen air will give you a tremendous appetite before you get half way to London."

" That may be very easily remedied, by partaking of a good dinner upon the road," answered Valentine.

" A dinner on the road, indeed !" exclaimed the old gentleman peevishly " and are you aware, sir, that what you call a good dinner on the road, costs a great deal more than it is worth ?"

" Somewhere about three and sixpence, I believe," answered Valentine, with remarkable composure.

" And that is just three shillings too much," exclaimed his uncle petulently. " No man, to my certain knowledge, can eat a dinner in ten minutes, and that's all the time the rascally coachman ever allows his passengers to fill their empty stomachs."

" Did I ever," cried Mrs. Vaux, in astonishment; " but I suppose it's done because people shall not eat too much."

" Why of course it is," answered Uncle Sam, nearly choking himself with a huge lump of roll, which, together with his indignation, he was scarcely able to swallow. " It's an infamous conspiracy, entered into between the coachman and the innkeeper to starve her majesty's faithful subjects. They just give you time to run into the house and sit yourself down 'to a well-spread table, but no sooner than you have swallowed your third or fourth mouthful, than the guard blows his horn, and you must either submit to go without the dinner you have paid for or be left behind."

" Infamous !" gasped forth Mrs. Vaux, " and is there no law to punish such roguery ?"

" None," replied Uncle Sam, striking the table very hard with his clenched fist; nor has any patriotic member of parliament yet been found possessed of humanity enough to bring a bill into the house for the better regulation of passengers' dinners."

" If such a man were found, he would deserve the everlasting gratitude of his country," observed the lady.

"However, I have taken care to provide against such a robbery in the present instance, for yonder little French basket contains sandwiches enough to last for a week at the very least," interrupted Valentine, laughing heartily at his mother's excessive zeal, in her care to preserve him from the horrors of starvation. Mrs. Vaux would have liked to box the ears of her son for his impudence, but quickly swallowing her indignation, she was about to revert to the former subject, when a remarkably dirty-faced girl thrust her shaggy-looking head in at the door :

"Please ma'am, Dick the hostlar has just runned over to say, as how the horses is put to, and the coachman's began swearing like anything, because the passengera ain't ready."

"Zounds! Valentine, my boy, you'll be too late after all, if you don't look sharp," exclaimed Uncle Sam, jumping up from the table, and seizing hold of a half dozen packages at once, as if he had a serious intention of making himself useful. But then recollecting that there were plenty to do that sort of work, he threw the parcels down as quickly as he had taken up, and laying hold of Valentine's arm dragged him by main force into the street, after having desired Mrs. Vaux and attendants to follow with all possible expedition. On arriving at the inn yard, the passengers were all seated, and of course in no very good humour at having to wait three minutes and a half beyond the time when the vehicle was announced to start. One old gentleman in particular, growled most vehemently as he saw the quantity of luggage that was to be stowed away, and at last, when he perceived a basket with a sucking pig handed up and placed just behind him on the roof, he fairly raved out, declaring that they were going to make a menagerie of the stage coach.

"Very likely," replied Valentine, " and an excellent one it will be, if we may judge from the fine specimen of a living bear, they seem to have got here already!"

"Young man, did you mean that remark for me?" demanded the crusty passenger in a threatening tone.

" I did, sir," replied Valentine, scrambling up the wheel and seating himself exactly opposite his antagonist.

"All right !" shouted the coachman, smacking his whip, and in a moment afterwards they were rattling down the High Street, at a pace very little short of railroad speed. The old gentleman whose temper had been so much ruffled now grew much calmer, or at least he appeared to be so, and to the gratification of those who began already to look upon him with dread, as likely to turn out a very disagreeable sort of travelling companion, he soon fell into a deep sleep that it would not be very easy to disturb.

So far, Valentine had refrained from exercising his powers of ventriloquism, but as he owed the crusty passenger a trick or two for the ill nature he had given utterance to, he resolved to take the first opportunity that offered to carry his mirthful propensity into execution. Now it so happened that our hero occupied a seat at the back part of the coach, and over that receptacle for all sorts of things called the " boot." So far this suited his purpose well enough, and having arranged his plans he took an opportunity, when the crusty old gentleman woke up, to introduce the subject of mad dogs, and the great danger to be apprehended at a time when they were said to be remarkably numerous. Then particularly addressing himself to the person he wished to terrify, he enquired whether it had ever been his misfortune to see an animal labouring under the dreadful effects of hydrophobia.

"No," was the laconic answer of the person spoken to.

"Then you are very lucky sir," exclaimed Valentine, " for you have no idea how viciously they attack every object that comes in their way ; their fury is absolutely terrific."

"Well, and what have I to do with that?" asked the old gentleman.

VALENTINE VAUX,

OR THE

TRICKS OF A VENTRILOQUIST.

BY TIMOTHY PORTWINE.

"Oh, nothing particular," replied Valentine mysteriously, "only, between ourselves, there is a dog in this very coach, and—"

"You mean a *puppy*, sir," exclaimed the crusty passenger, looking full in the face of Valentine.

"You may, perhaps, in the simplicity of your heart, flatter yourself that you have for once in your life said a good thing," replied our hero, without being in the least disconcerted. "Your age, sir, screens you from my indignation, and you may therefore be as insulting as you please, without running any risk of destroying that happy equanimity for which

No. 3.

I am conspicuous among my friends. The hint was given in good part, and you can therefore either accept or reject it as you think fit."

"And pray, young gentleman, where may the dog be?" asked the other, in a tone of affected carelessness.

"In the boot, beneath where we are sitting."

"God bless me! how very wrong of the coachman to take such a creature!" said an old woman, who till now had remained a passive auditor of all that was passing.

"It was very wrong, doubtless," replied Valentine, "but the dog is intended as a present from a gentleman belonging to our town to a friend in London. To do the coachman justice he did refuse to take the animal, but the gentleman was so importunate with the hostler that the man shut the creature into the boot without saying a word about it to the driver."

"Then the coachman is not aware of the dog being here?" "Certainly not," answered Valentine.

"And does the animal appear to be a very vicious one?"—"Remarkably so," replied our ventriloquist, and at the same moment a sullen growl was heard issuing from the place over which they were sitting. This had an instantaneous effect upon all the passengers occupying that part of the coach, and whilst an exclamation of surprise escaped their lips, Valentine stamped with his heel and in an authoritative voice commanded the supposed dog to "lie down." But this only seemed to exasperate the animal the more, for immediately so violent a barking and snapping succeeded that it appeared as if the infuriated beast would break out from his place of confinement and make an indiscriminate attack upon the legs of whoever he could get at. Upon this the old gentleman grew more and more alarmed, and as they happened at this moment to be passing a portion of the road that had been inundated by a recent flood, Valentine exerted himself to the utmost, and with so much effect that the terrified victim of his hoax started from his seat and prepared to make a desperate leap.

"What are you going to do, sir?" exclaimed our hero with an appearance of alarm.

"What am I going to do?" retorted the other;" why jump from this confounded coach to be sure; anything to escape from that enraged animal that seems every moment as if it would force a way through to where we are."

"But do you see what an awkward situation we happen to be in?" asked Valentine. "We are surrounded on every side with water which already reaches up to the axletrees of the coach?"

"So much the better," exclaimed the old gentleman; "rabid animals have a horror of water, so that there will be very little chance of this dog following me."

"For goodness sake, sir, don't jump!" cried the elderly female as she saw her fellow traveller preparing for a leap; "your foot may slip, and if once you lose your balance it will be all over."

The old gentleman seemed to be of her way of thinking, for he paused and then drew back a step, but at that juncture Valentine recommenced his imitations of the infuriated dog with more vehemence than ever. This decided the fate of the crusty passenger, whose dread of hydrophobia was so excessive that, regardless alike of consequences and the entreaties of his fellow passengers, he took a desperate leap, and the tremendous splash that followed announced the completion of the design. At this period the coachman stopped his horses, and with the assistance of his passengers succeeded after some difficulty in rescuing the old gentleman from his perilous situation. Unfortunately it so happened that the inside of the stage was completely filled, so that the poor fellow, soaked and drenched as he was, was compelled to take his seat on the roof of the coach, and at a respectful distance from those who were not by any means anxious to have him too near their persons. As to the driver the whole matter was to him involved in the profoundest mystery, and addressing himself to Valentine he enquired whether the affair was the effect of accident, or whether the poor gentleman had attempted to make away with himself.

"The fact is it was neither one nor the other," replied the ventriloquist, putting as much gravity as possible into his countenance. "Terror, I believe, was the cause of all this mischief, and no wonder either, seeing that you or some of your people have thought fit to take a mad dog as a passenger to London."

"A mad dog!" vociferated the astonished coachman.

"Oh, I dare say you know nothing at all about it," sneered the old lady passenger who had just recovered from a fainting fit on purpose to give the driver a severe rating for his conduct.

"You pretend to be ignorant of what sort of a neighbour we have got in the boot. But we happen to know all about it, sir, and if I dont get you discharged from you situation my name is not Penelope Pawks, that's all!"

"Gentlemen," exclaimed the bewildered coachman, "will any body have the kindness to explain what all this means?"

"The dog! the dog!" shouted all the passengers in a breath.

"What dog do you mean?"

"In the boot," answered the chorus.

"I know of no dog in boots," exclaimed the coachman with indignation, "but one thing I'm pretty well satisfied with, and that is that you are all mad together. Dog, indeed! I should like to know how sich an animal could get into the coach without my knowing it."

"You doubt our words then?" said Valentine.

"Why in course I do," responded the Jehu.

At this moment the barking and growling was again heard; upon which the coachman's countenance grew very long and the elderly lady made preparations for going off in another fainting fit.

"Are you convinced now, sir?" demanded the crusty passenger, who sat all this time shivering in his wet clothes, "do you think we are all mad now, eh, sirrah?"

"No, but I think that animal is," replied the driver, though hang me if I can make it out how he ever got a place by our coach without being booked. However, you needn't be afraid of him; he's safe enough where he is, when we get to the end of the next stage we'll give him something for himself what he wont like."

So saying he applied the lash of his whip to the two leaders, and once more the vehicle was in motion. But the fears of the outside passengers were far from being allayed by the coachman's promise of retributive justice; they were by no means convinced that the supposed dog was quite as safe as had been represented, and our hero took care to keep their terrors on the *qui vive* by occasionally continuing the barking and snapping that had so greatly terrified them during the latter part of their journey.

"Dear me! what a very unpleasant situation to be sure!" exclaimed the crusty gentleman whose teeth were chattering through the combined effects of fear and the ducking he had received. This is the first time I ever happened to travel by this coach, and I'll take good care it shall be the last;—oh dear! oh dear! I shouldn't at all wonder if the soaking I've had should be the death of me."

"Not quite so bad as that, I hope," cried Valentine; "however, thanks to the forethought of my worthy mother I happen to have some brandy which shall be very much at your service. There, sir," he continued, handing a glass to the person he had been addressing,—"drink that off, and if you change your clothes at the next in where we stop, there will be very little fear of taking cold."

The old gentleman was too good a judge to refuse this offer, and after he had swallowed the contents of the glass, a dram was offered with similar success to the lady upon whose nerves terror had had so remarkable an effect. The other passengers were of course treated with similar courtesy by our ventriloquist, and by the time the bottle was emptied of its contents the vehicle arrived at the road side inn where the horses were to be changed. Here the crusty gentleman took his portmanteau, and being shewn into a private apartment he quickly stripped off his wet clothes and presently afterwards he appeared as trim and as sleek as if no accident had happened.

"Now, Bill," said the coachman as soon as he had brought his unwieldly body to the ground, "we've got something to do as will require an uncommon deal of care; so in the first place just run into the house and bring out your master's gun."

"Why, what d'ye want a gun for?" asked the yokel.

"To shoot with, to be sure," replied the driver;—"we've got sum-mat alive in the boot, and I'm blessed if I don't give him what he wont like before I'm done with him."

"What can there be alive in the coach except the people you're a driv-ing?" demanded the hostler.

"A dog," responded the other—"at least it sounds like one, and if it aint that it's neither more nor less than the devil."

"Why I'm blessed if you aint goin' mad!" muttered the fellow.

"No I aint, Bill, but the animal is, I'm afraid," replied the coachman. "He's been barking and growling all through the last stage, and now I'm going to see how he'll like a belly full of shot."

"I'm thinking he wont get it here then," returned Bill.

"And why not?" asked the other with surprise.

"'Cause we don't happen to have either powder or shot in the place," replied Bill. "Master keeps a gun over the fire place to frighten the thieves, but we haven't had any thing to put in it for the last two years."

"Well, then, have you got such a thing as a pitch-fork?" asked the coachman impatiently.

"Aye, a dozen on 'em if you want 'em."

"Then fetch one and open the door of the boot a little way," exclaimed the whip; "you can finish him with the prong you know, and if the job's cleverly done, dang my buttons if I don't give you five shillings besides what you'll collect among the passen-gers."

This was enough for Bill, the door was carefully opened a little way and the before-named weapon introduced and thrust about in every direction, so as to pin the imaginary intruder upon one of its points, and thus de-stroy the source of the last hour's uneasiness. But the more Bill poked the pitch-fork about the more vehe-ment became the growling and snap-of the supposed animal within, for Valentine was standing close y, and of course he could not resist such an opportunity of keeping up the alarm

he had already occasioned. At last, however, the sound had become weaker so that it was evident to those who were standing about, that the dog must have been severely wounded and that it only required another thrust or two to bring the matter to a speedy conclusion. Presently after-wards all was still and quiet, and when they had waited, as it was sup-posed a sufficient time, the door was thrown wide open, and a search com-menced after the mangled body of the unfortunate tyke. But as may be imagined, all this labour was thrown away, for the only thing that could be found which had ever possessed life was a fine goose that had been plucked of its feathers, and which it was therefore very evident could not have been killed by Bill in his late murderous attack. Upon this a gene-ral laugh burst from the by-standers, and the ostler scratching his head, declared that the thing altogether passed his comprehension; unless witchcraft had had any thing to do with it.

Luckily, however, a rustic who was standing by declared that he had no doubt the dog had somehow or other contrived to run away, and as this explanation was the best that could be offered, it was eagerly ac-cepted by Bill, with a further sug-gestion that no doubt the creature would die in the first ditch he came to. With this he marched boldly up to the coachman, and demanded the reward that had been promised on the completion of his contract. But our whip was never without an ex-cuse when one was required, and ap-plying the thumb of his right hand to his nose, he enquired with a cun-ning leer what he had the impudence to ask the reward for."

"Why, for killing the mad dog to be sure," replied the ostler.

"Show me the dog and you shall have what I promised," exclaimed the driver. "If you've killed him pro-duce his body, and the money shall be yours in less than no time, old boy."

"How can I if he's run away?" asked the disappointed ostler.

"You can find him somewhere about, by to-morrow or the next, day," replied the other, "and my word's good till then, I should think, Bill."

"Pay me now and I'll find him," returned the ostler.

"Oh no, we dont do it that way," retorted coachee with a knowing wink. "Prove to me that the job's done and I scorn to be worse than my word, but you ain't going to convince me that the dog's killed, when you can't show us his carcase."

The ostler now applied himself to the passengers for any subscription they might be pleased to make, but as they also happened to think he had not performed the service he boasted of, they gave him nothing but jeers and a promise to remember him the next time they happened to go that way. This breach of contract was a source of sore displeasure to Bill, and as he was determined upon having revenge somehow or other, he took an opportunity to remove the lync-hpin from one of the wheels, and then walked off to watch from the road side the effects of his infamous manæuvre.

Of course no one suspected the trick that had been played upon them, and when sundry glasses of brandy and water had been swallowed and paid for, the passengers took their former places, whilst the coachman resumed the reins preparatory to a fresh start. At length when every thing was ready, the smack of the whip was heard, and away they went at a steady pace down hill, though little did any of them dream of the imminent peril in which their lives had been placed through the mischievous act of the disappointed ostler. Now it frequently happens that a coach will travel some distance in this condition, provided the pace is not a rapid one, and the road tolerably good. In the present instance the vehicle had proceeded three or four miles on its journey without any accident taking place; but at last they came to a place where fresh gravel had been thrown down, and a greater strain being caused thereby, away went the treacherous wheel, and

almost at the same instant, over went the coach, pitching the whole of the outsiders to the other side of a hedge, where, luckily for themselves, they were received on a dunghill, the softness of which preserved them from broken bones and contusions. To be sure there was a tremendous shouting and screaming, but when the electrified passengers found that no serious injury had been inflicted upon any one, they rose from the uncomfortable position they had taken, and lent their assistance towards restoring the coach to its usual upright condition.

Upon this there commenced a general bluster in order to effect the much desired object—but either from the awkwardness of those who had volunteered their assistance or some other cause which we cannot stop to explain, the ponderous machine refused to stir a jot, and our disappointed travellers therefore found themselves under the necessity of repairing to an inn which they could descry at no great distance off, and where they must of course wait till the coach could once more be put in a proper order for continuing the journey. This was a mortifying alternative to those who had important business to transact in town; but there was no help for it, and as no means of conveyance was to be obtained, the only way was to put the best complexion upon the matter, and to resign themselves to the misfortune for which there was now no remedy.

This being agreed upon, the whole party followed the coachman towards the place where they hoped to find a shelter, and some of them even began to crack their jokes at the unforeseen accident that had so suddenly put a stop to their journey, but which had fortunately been attended with so little injury to any body. The crusty gentleman, it is true, inveighed bitterly against what he was pleased to term the carelessness of the driver, and the old lady vowed that if ever she got safe to London, she would never again intrust her precious person in so much danger. But these were the only exceptions to good humour; and on reaching the inn, the hearty welcome they met with, afforded some consolation for the inconvenience they were much obliged to put up with.

———

CHAPTER V.

HOW TO GET A SUPPER FOR TWELVE AT ANOTHER PERSON'S EXPENCE; THE CRUSTY OLD GENTLEMAN IS TAKEN IN, AND THE AWKWARD DILEMMA THAT ENSUES—THE DISPUTE, AND A SHORT WAY OF MAKING A MAN PAY AGAINST HIS WILL —THE JOURNEY RESUMED.

LEAVING the watchman and Timothy Tap, the landlord of the house, together with half a dozen stout countrymen, to raise up the vehicle and put it into proper travelling condition, the passengers resolved to make themselves as comfortable as they could during the time they were compelled to stay beneath the roof of the "Marquis of Granby." As for the crusty gentleman, he appeared to be in especial ill humour with himself and every body else, and as he happened to have heard that the coach could not possibly be got ready in two hours, and as the darkness of night was already setting in, he went to bed, as much perhaps to avoid the expence of a supper, as to escape the society of those who he believed were laughing at him in their sleeves for the accident he had met with in the early part of their journey.

Valentine soon guessed the reason of the old gentleman absenting himself, and in his own mind he resolved to have a bit more fun at his expense. With this determination he suffered him to remain quiet until a loud snoring announced that he was fast asleep, and then taking his station in a closet that happened to be in the passage, he assumed the old gentleman's voice, and called lustily for the landlady. In an instant her feet were heard ascending the stairs, two at a time, and then applying her mouth to the key-hole of his chamber door, she enquired what he was now " pleased to want."

" I want my supper," exclaimed Valentine, imitating the voice of the person he intended to hoax.

" Very good, sir, what will you like to have.

" Veal cutlets and ham to match," replied Valentine.

" How much shall I cook ?" demanded the landlady.

" Enough for twelve people," replied the ventriloquist. "I intend to treat my fellow passengers, so that when you go down you can inform them that I shall expect the pleasure of their company to supper."

" It shall be done directly, sir," and so saying, the landlady was turning away to take her departure, when the same voice was heard desiring her to stop.

" Did you call, sir ?"

" Yes, I forgot to mention one thing; tell your husband to make a couple of crown bowls of punch to come in afterwards, and let the bill be made out to me."

Satisfied with this order, and blessing her stars for the lucky accident that had overturned the coach, the good woman bustled down stairs and presently afterwards the cheering sound of the frying pan might be heard mingled with most hunger provoking odours from the delicious dish she was preparing. At the same time her husband might be seen busily occupied in squeezing lemons, and adjusting all things in their proper proportions for the punch that had been entrusted to his making. In fact the whole scene was a most refreshing and delightful one to persons who were in every way qualified to give a good supper a hearty and whol some salutation. In the mean time an intimation had been conveyed to the remainder of the passengers, and when the cloth was laid, each person took a seat at the table, where they manifested their impatience by occasionally sharpening their knives, or relieving the tedium by wiping the dirt from between the prongs of the forks on the clean table cloth. At last the savoury dishes made their appearance, and when every thing was placed in order a message was sent up to the crusty gentleman announcing that his fellow travellers were anxiously expecting his arrival. This summons was quite inexplicable to the person to whom it had been sent, but as he supposed the coach was about starting again, he bustled down stairs and bolted into the room where the company was anxiously awaiting his arrival. As he popped his bald head into the room, a buz of stifled admiration might be heard, and at the same moment Valentine jumped up and handed him, though not without a good deal of resistance, to a chair at the head of the table.

Now whether it was through being taken by surprise, or from what other cause it might be, we cannot explain—but strange as it may appear, the old gentleman actually resigned himself to the situation into which he had been forced, and it was remarked by every one present that he performed the arduous duties of a chairman with uncommon ability. The fact is, it never entered his mind that he should be called upon to pay a farthing towards the expense; and as the veal cutlets and ham exactly suited his appetite, he set to with the vigour and resolution of a man that is determined to make the best use of a good opportunity. He therefore eat himself into remarkable good humour, and, when the cloth was removed hailed the appearance of the two bowls of punch with an enthusiasm that he had never before been known to exhibit. But, alas ! the happy vision was soon to be dissolved, and the now happy man was to learn the expense at which all this pleasure had been purchased. In fact when bumpers had been filled round, Valentine rose, and in a neat speech proposed the health of the worthy chairman who had so liberally and handsomely provided the substantial repast of which they had just partaken. This toast was of course heartily responded to, and when the cheers with which it was received had subsided, the crusty gentleman stood up, and declared there must be some mistake in the matter, for that he could most solemnly aver he had nothing whatever to do with it.

" Really," exclaimed Valentine, with an appearance of the greatest astonishment, " this is one of the most remarkable, and I may add, most disagreeable situations that I ever found myself placed in. It appears then that we have been regaling ourselves in this sumptuous manner, as we supposed, at the expense of the gentleman who has kindly taken the chair, and yet when the supper is over, he solemnly declares that he knows nothing at all about it, and in fact, that it was not ordered by him !"

" Shameful ! scandalous !" vociferated all the company.

" You may call it shameful and scandalous if you please," exclaimed the old gentleman, jumping up in a towering passion, " but I'm not going to be imposed upon in this way I can assure you."

" Then you mean to say that you will not pay for it ?" cried Valentine, with every appearance of indignation.

" That's exactly what I do mean, sir !" retorted the crusty passenger. " The supper was none of my ordering, and what's more, I don't intend to pay for a single mouthful beyond what I have eaten."

" And pray, sir, who is to pay for the punch?" demanded our hero.

" Those that thought proper to order it, of course."

" That was yourself then."

" How ! I order punch !" exclaimed the old gentleman. " I, that always avoid extravagance, and who could have no earthly reason for treating a parcel of people that I never saw in my life before, and who, I dare say, I shall never see again."

" But, sir, we have proof that you did order it."

" Produce it, then—produce it, sir !" cried the crusty gentleman, casting a glance of triumph round the room— " produce your evidence, and if any body can swear that I gave orders for this supper, I'll pay for it, and the punch to boot."

Valentine rang the bell, and immediately afterwards the landlady came bustling into the room with the bill in her hand.

" Did you ring, gentlemen !" she enquired with a curtsey.

" I rang to ask you a question of some importance," replied Valentine. " It appears, madam, that you have provided us with a very excellent supper and these two bowls of punch. I need not say that we are very well satisfied with the manner in which you have catered for our appetite; but an important question remains to be answered:—Pray who was it that ordered it all?"

"The gentleman that sits at the head of the table," replied the hostess.

"There, sir, what have you to say now?" asked Valentine, very exultingly.

"That it's a most abominable falsehood!" roared the old gentleman. "I was asleep up stairs, and I would ask any one whether it's very likely, under those circumstances, that I should do anything of the sort."

"I'll take my oath you did," cried the landlady.

"You will!" exclaimed the old gentleman, "then pray have the goodness to explain it to the satisfaction of myself and this company."

"Well, sir," replied the hostess, "about an hour ago I was scolding our Dolly about half a dozen plates thatshe had been breaking, all of a sudden I heard somebody upstairs a calling me. Ho, ho! thinks I, that's the nice looking old gentleman that's gone to lie down and rest himself, poor soul. So up I goes—for I knew it was his voice, and putting my mouth to the keyhole, I says, say—I, "did you call sir?' 'To be sure I did,' says he, 'I want to have my supper.' 'Very good, sir,' says I—just so—" what will you like to have?' 'Veal cutlets and ham to match,' bawls he—these were his exact words as I'm an honest woman. 'How much shall I cook?' says I. 'Enough for twelve people,' says he, 'because I mean to treat all my fellow passengers, so when you go down you can inform them that I shall expect the pleasure of their company,' which I accordingly did as you are all aware."

"Yes, yes, you did," responded every body.

"Now, sir," exclaimed Valentine to the crusty passenger, "you have heard this good woman's plain unvarnished tale, and I should like to know whether you can deny a single word of it. But I perceive you are conscience-stricken and dumb-foundered so, I shall just ask her one more question, and then leave you to reconcile it with your conscience whether you ought not to be ashamed of yourself for raising such a paltry objection to so reasonable a demand."

"Pray proceed, sir—pray proceed!" exclaimed the accused.

"I would now know madam," continued the ventriloquist, "who it was that ordered this liberal allowance of punch?"

"The same old gentleman that told me to get the supper ready," replied the hostess. "I was just coming down when he called me back, and 'landlady,' says he, 'I forgot to mention one thing—tell your husband to make a couple of crown bowls of punch to come in afterwards, and let the bill be made out to me; so accordingly I've brought this little account with me for the gentleman to look at."

"Two pounds five shillings!" exclaimed the crusty gentleman throwing the bill upon the table, and sinking back in his chair in a rage that he could not conceal.

"And a very moderate charge too, in my opinion," observed Valentine, "so allow me sir, to pledge you in a bumper, and may the difference of opinion never destroy friendship."

"Damn the toast and the punch too!" roared the choleric gentleman thrusting away his glass, and spilling the contents upon the table. "I'm an ill-used individual sir; you are all making a laughing-stock of me, but I'll not put up with it, The landlord has not got his money yet, and never will if he looks to me for it."

"Stop, stop, stop!" exclaimed Valentine, "you forget my dear sir, that we are all against you in this matter, the sense of the company is on the side of reason and justice, and if you refuse to pay a just debt, thank God we have laws in England that will make you—Not pay it indeed;— a pretty declaration forsooth, for a respectable-looking elderly man like you to make."

"You may say or do just as you please," replied the other, "but when my mind is thoroughly made up, as is the case in the present instance, it's no very easy matter to talk me into

VALENTINE VAUX,

OR THE
TRICKS OF A VENTRILOQUIST.

BY TIMOTHY PORTWINE.

doing the contrary. I have said that I won't pay it, and I won't."

"Come, come, what's all this bother about?" exclaimed the landlord, who having heard the nature of the dispute from his wife, now bustled into the room to enforce his demand.

"The bother is about a disputed account," replied the crusty gentleman indignantly. "Twelve hungry persons have sat down to a supper, and they expect me to pay for it as well as for a couple of bowls of punch that came in afterwards."

"And since you ordered it you can't refuse to pay for it," returned the landlord.

No. 4.

"But I did not order it, and therefore I do refuse to pay for it," exclaimed the elderly gentleman in high dudgeon.

"Really this is most unreasonable and ungentlemanly conduct," interposed Valentine. "Here is a person who we all took to be respectable, orders a supper and its usual accompaniments, and yet when the time comes for payment, he shirks the question, and tries to get off by paying his own share. For my own part I have,—thank heaven !—enough in my pockets to pay for what I have and so I dare say has every other gentleman present; but it is the principle of the thing I look at, and on that sense alone I do think it nothing more than right that we should insist upon the contract being fulfilled."

"Aye, and it shall be fulfilled too !" exclaimed the landlord, " or else hang me if he don't go into our horsepond. To him I look for payment, and I'll have it too before he goes out of my sight."

"Come, come," interposed one of the passengers, who had taken his cue from Valentine, " pay this money like a man, and don't go out of our company with the character of being a mean, shuffling fellow that won't do as he has promised."

"I tell you I'll not pay it," exclaimed the other resolutely ;—" I have made up my mind not to be imposed upon, and I shall stick to it to the last."

" But remember what my husband said about the horsepond just now," whispered the hostess in his ear.

"I care for no horsepond, ma'am," returned the old gentleman sharply. "Let him do it if he dares, and I'll bring my action against him for assault and battery. No, no, if he wants it he shall have my card, and he may summon me for the amount, and then if the court gives it against me, I'll go into a prison and pay him off that way."

As he said this he jumped up, and seizing hold of his portmanteau was making his way towards the door, when the landlord interposing himself declared loudly that he should not leave the room till his demand was satisfied.

" I warn you to keep off, fellow !" exclaimed the old gentleman, " keep your distance I say, for not one farthing beyond my own expences will I ever consent to pay."

" You won't ! then we'll try that however," cried the host, and seizing hold of one end of the portmanteau he tried to wrench it from the grasp of his adversary. But the other was too resolute for him, and then they began pulling and hauling with a degree of rigour, that was highly amusing to the spectators. But the landlady it seems could not see quite so much fun in it as the others did, and no sooner did she find how matters were going, then slipping out of the room she returned in a few minutes afterwards, armed with a basting ladle which she applied so vigorously to the back and shoulders of the crusty old gentleman, that he was at last fain to leave go his hold and cry out for quarters.

" Now, sir," exclaimed the landlord, " will you settle your account, or must I keep this portmanteau till you think fit to do so ?"

"Why I suppose I must do so," replied the vanquished party, because you have got the advantage of me in obtaining possession of my goods and chattels, but mind I call all these persons to witness, that I do so from compulsion, and that you must afterwards expect to take the consequenees of your illegal proceedings. I'm an injured man, sir, and the host of the " Marquis of Granby shall find to his cost that he has found a customer who will not be imposed upon with impunity."

" I only want my money, " replied the landlord," and surely there's no great harm in that. You know you ordered the supper, or else my wife wouldn't stick to it as she does, and that being the case, who am I to look to for it except yourself."

" Well, well," exclaimed Valentine, who now began to think the joke had gone far enough, " I'll be my half the expense, and then perhaps matters may be satisfactorily compromised. What say you to my suggestion, old boy."

" That I'll have nothing at all to do with you, or any of you," growled the crusty gentleman thrusting back the offered money. I suspect I have been made the victim of some infamous hoax, and if I only find out that it is so, every one engaged in it shall smart severely enough I promise you,"

With this threat he paid the bill, and having once more got possession of his portmanteau, bustled out of the room. and taking his place upon the coach, wrapped himself up in a great coat with a determination to hold no further conversation with his fellow-passengers during the remainder of his journey. In a short time afterwards Valentine and the rest had resumed their several places, and once more they were proceeding on their way towards London.

CHAPTER IV.

SOME INSIGHT INTO THE FAMILY AF-FAIRS OF MR. SEPTIMUS BRAMSTONE, —THE AFFECTIONATE BROTHER AND DUTIFUL NEPHEW ;—VALENTINE'S ARRIVAL IN TOWN, AND THE FRIEND-LY RECEPTION HE THERE MET WITH, —A WAITER'S QUANDARIES ; — AN ALARMING INCIDENT WITH A LUDI-CROUS TERMINATION.

MR. SEPTIMUS BRAMSTONE, to whose care Valentine was for the present consigned. was a respectable middle-aged gentleman, who having made a considerable fortune by trade, and thought proper to retire at the ripe age of sixty-five, in order that he might pass the latter years of his life in that tranquillity which all men so eagerly covet. He was a widower without family, having lost his wife some twenty years previously to the date of our narrative, and as at that period he happened to be particularly engaged in commercial affairs, he had few opportunities of looking out for a successor to his late worthy and ever-to-be-deplored rib. At last his increasing age and infirmities admonished him that he had more need of a nurse than a wife, and abandoning all matrimonial projects, he wisely resolved to pass the remainder of his days in that delightful calm which he might in vain look for in the connubial state. This was exactly what his brother and nephew, the only relation he had in the world,—most anxiously desired, for they had long entertained hopes of becoming the heirs of Septimus, and of course looked with a jealous eye upon any female whom the old gentleman chanced to regard with any thing approaching favour or esteem. They were, how-ever, artful enough to disguise their real feelings, and whilst flattering and fawning upon their unsuspicious relative, they took care by every means in their power to make him believe that they venerated him as a superior being.

But this was only before the old gentleman's face; behind his back they spoke of him in the most dispa-raging terms, and wondered how in the name of fortune it was that death had not long ago laid claim to their wealthy relative. But of one thing they felt pretty confident, for know-ing the deception with which they had treated the old man, they thought there could not be much doubt about his leaving all his property among them whenever he died. Still nei-ther Harry Bramstone nor his son Arnold ever suffered him to be with-out their company for any long time, lest any body else should awaken him to a knowledge of their real character, and thus frustrate a plan which they had taken so much pains to concoct.

Under these circumstances it may be supposed that it was with no in-considerable feeling of alarm that our two worthies heard of Valentine's pro-jected visit to their relative. They at once foresaw that their own reign of infamy would speedily terminate un-less they could devise means to coun-teract any influence he might happen to obtain over Mr. Septimus Bram-stone. They dreaded his arrival, and as neither of them stood very nice upon trifles, it was resolved to pre-vent the visit taking place by any means that offered. It was, however, some time before they could hit upon a method which would be perfectly se-cure, nor was it until various plans had been proposed and rejected, that they at last agreed upon an expedient which they had little doubt would be crowned with complete success. Their plan was to take a hackney-coach and drive to the inn where the stage by which Valentine was expected would put up, and then for the elder conspirator to represent himself to our hero as Mr. Septimus Bramstone. Nor was this likely to prove a very difficult task, for Valentine was unacquainted with the person he was about to visit, and of course could not discover the cheat until it would be too late. Once in their power they intended to take him through various by-ways towards Wapping, and upon their arrival there, to betray him into the hands of a crimp who would speedily lure him on board any of the vessels that were about to sail immediately for foreign parts. Such was their plan, and it was only through the coach having been delayed so much beyond its usual time, as we have seen, that Valentine escaped the snares of his insidious foes. In fact, they waited at the inn till their patience was completely exhausted, and then, not doubting but that the vehicle had been overturned somewhere on the road, they sullenly made their way home with a pious wish, that if such an event had occurred, Valentine might have had his neck broken in the fall.

Whilst the father and son were impatiently pacing up and down the inn yard, Mr. Septimus Bramstone was in the coffee-room of the tavern enjoying himself over a glass of brandy and water till the expected arrival of his young friend. It is true he thought the time rather long, but he was an experienced traveller himself, and knowing the numerous causes of delay on the road, he waited with tolerable patience till nearly three hours over the usual time of arrival had passed. Then, to be sure, he began to grow a little uneasy for the safety of his expected guest, but just as he had looked up at the clock for about the fiftieth time, the vehicle was heard lumbering down the inn yard, and in an instant he was upon his legs, and the next moment he was standing by the long expected coach. Still he was uncertain which of the passengers was the person he was in quest of, but as most of them were either too old or of the opposite sex, he at last decided upon addressing himself to a young man who at the moment descended from his place above, and whose scrutinizing eye showed that he was looking about for some one among the motley assemblage by which he was surrounded.

"Pray sir," he said, "may I be so bold as to ask whether your name is Valentine?"

"It is, sir," replied the person he had addressed, "and your question assures me that you are Mr. Septimus Bramstone, who I expected to meet me here."

"Aye, aye," replied the old gentleman, shaking our hero cordially by the hand," you have made a shrewd guess of it this time at any rate. But the coach is so much over its usual time of arrival, that I almost began to be afraid that some accident must have happened to delay you. However, you are heartily welcome to London, sir, so step into the coffee-room, where we can partake of some refreshment while you relate the cause of this extraordinary delay."

This proposition was readily acceded to by Valentine, and having given directions as to the disposal of his luggage he followed the old gentleman, and shortly afterwards they were comfortably seated in the public room. Here a good many people were congregated in numerous small and distinct parties, but by carrying on their conversation in a subdued tone, they contrived to pass without exciting any particular observation. In this brief time Mr. Bramstone heard all that the other had to relate, and when his young friend had arrived at the conclusion he burst into a roar of laughter that somewhat startled the company, as each person happened to imagine that he was the particular object which had called forth this demonstration of mirth. This notion was, however, quickly dispelled by the old gentleman begging pardon for his boisterous conduct, and when it became evident that his apology had been accepted, he whispered to Valentine:—

"And so all this delay on the road was occasioned by your powers of ventriloquism. I have heard from your uncle that you possessed the faculty in an extraordinary degree, but as I never happened to witness an exhibition, I thought in all possibility he must have been deceived."

"My uncle," replied Valentine, "is, I believe, afraid that my practical jokes will some day or other get me into a scrape that it will not be very easy to get out of. He, however, does not recollect that it would be difficult to fix the perpetration of a bit of mischief upon a ventriloquist, and that I am therefore tolerably secure as long as I act with my usual prudence and caution."

"A joke is a joke, as long as it is not carried too far," observed Mr. Bramstone, "but it unfortunately happens that few people have command enough over themselves to resist the opportunity of amusing themseves whenever it occurs. Hence a man may always be in hot water, though possessing a gift that he has not the power to keep within proper limits."

"Nay my dear, sir, you wrong me if for an instant you suppose I would exercise my talent, to the injury of any one."

"You would not do so willingly perhaps," replied Mr. Bramstone, "but the question is whether you can always restrain your inclinations when they are powerfully excited. I could not forbear laughing just now, at the tricks you played the crusty passenger, and yet upon consideration it appears that the matter was carried far beyond a joke. In the first place he got a severe ducking in the water, and in the second he was compelled to pay tavern expences, for which he was not liable."

"Why as for that," answered Valentine, the ducking he received turned out to be of no serious consequence, and as for the supper and punch, it must be remembered that I offered to pay for it, when matters began to wear a serious aspect. Besides, from what I have ascertained, he is a wealthy old miser, and it therefore appears that he has only been rightly served, for giving way to such penurious habits."

"Well, well, we won't argue upon that subject," returned Mr. Bram-

stone, "because it's most likely that after all we should both continue to maintain our own opinions. There is one favour, however, that I should like to ask of you, only that I am half afraid it might lead to disagreeable consequences."

"What is it my good, sir?" asked Valentine.

"To test your abilities in the peculiar line that has obtained for you no little degree of celebrity," replied the old gentleman.

"I understand you," exclaimed Valentine ; "you would like to be convinced of the power I possess, and yet fear lest the indulgence of your curiosity should involve us in any trouble. But you shall see, sir, that I can exercise my talent, without ill-nature, and that by a right effort I can raise a smile in the countenance of even the morose."

"Have a care what you are about Mr. Vaux," whispered the old gentleman. "The people here are all strangers to us, and may not be disposed to put up with our jokes, without resenting them."

"Trust all to me," replied Valentine. "I am only going to bother the waiter a little, and as he seems to be not over civil, there can be no great harm in having a laugh at his expence."

At this moment the waiter alluded to, entered the coffee room with a mutton chop, and a glass of stout, for an exquisite that was seated by himself, in a box at the further end of the room. Valentine watched his man, and as soon as he had put down the aforesaid articles, he threw his voice to a box near the fire-place, and in a sharp voice called out, "waiter."

"Coming, sir," answered the hero of the napkin, gliding swiftly across the room, towards the place from whence the summons seemed to have issued. There, however, he found three gentlemen engaged in earnest conversation, who deeming his presence a great piece of impertinence, angrily demanded what he stood looking and cringing there for.

"Beg pardon, I'm sure gen'l'men,"

stammered the waiter, " but I thouht one of you called, and—"

" Dont talke to us, fellow, but go along about your business," exclaimed the most indignant of the party—" Do you hear, sir, leave us uand don't let's have any of thts impertinance agaiu."

" Waiter, where's that bottle of wine I ordered half an hour ago ?" vociferated Valentine in another voice, and apparently from a different part of the room.

" What wine did you order, sir ?" asked the waiter bustling up to the table, and addressing himself to a very surly looking old gentleman, who was engaged in poring over the columns of a newspaper. To this query, however, he deigned no reply, and after waiting what he deemed to be a reasonable time, the question was repeated in rather a louder key.

" Beg pardon, sir, but did you order port or sherry ?"

Neither," grouled the otd fellow, without condescending to raise his eyes from the journal, he was so intently perusing.

" Very odd ! very odd indeed !" thought the waiter ;—" somebody called for wine, that's certain, and it came from this part of the room, too, or I'm much mistaken."

As he was thus cogitating within himself, he sailed along at his usual rapid pace, but scarcely had he reached the door when Valentine once more changing his tone, called out—

" Glass of warm brandy and water, Thomas."

" Yezzir," replied the waiter, and disappearing from the room, he returned a minute or two afterwards with the smoking beverage which he placed before an effeminate young puppy who was smoking a cigar over the solitary four pennyworth of gin and water that had lasted him the whole evening.

" What the devole do you mean by bringing me this, sar ?" lisped the dandy angrily.

" Because you ordered it," replied Thomas sulkily.

" I'm demmed if I did !" exclaimed the exquisite, endeavouring to look very fierce. " I tell you, fellow, I never drink brandy and water. I've an utter abhorrence of the vulgar liquor, and if I have any more of your demmed impertinence, I'm demmed if I don't kick you, demme !"

" Will you !" exclaimed Thomas rather exasperated by the broad hint conveyed in the last threat ; " it's all very well, sir, for you to talk of kicking a man that's about four times your size, but if you come any of this nonsense with me, I'm —"

" What's all this noise about, Thomas ?" asked the landlord, attracted to the spot by the loud tones of his official. " Tell me, sir, why do I hear this disturbance ?"

" I don't know, sir," replied the waiter, " but to speak a bit of my mind, I'm almost certain the devil is lurking somewhere or other in the coffee room.

" Thomas, you are drunk ?" exclaimed his master reproachfully.

" Then I'm sure I don't know what I've got drunk upon," replied the waiter. " Howsomedever, sir, I've had no less than three orders from different parts of the room, and yet I can't find out who it was that gave 'em."

" He's a demmed impertinent rascal !" drawled the exquisite who had turned up his nose at the brandy and water.

" He ought to be kicked out of the house !" growled the old gentleman, raising his eyes for an instant from the newspaper.

" He's infernally drunk !" chimed in the three gentlemen whose conversation had been interrupted.

" He must be drunk !" exclaimed the landlord emphatically. " It's a clear case, and the best thing he can do is to go to bed and recover himself as well as he can."

While this was going on Valentine had, unperceived, turned the lock of a closet door, and putting the key into his pocket, he gave his friend Mr. Bramstone a hint that he was going to change his tactics, and by means of his ventriloquial powers to make the persons present believe there was a thief concealed in the cupboard. Seizing his opportunity, therefore, he directed his voice towards the closet, and exclaimed in half smothered accents :—

" Let me out ! good luck to you let me out, or I shall be stifled in this infernal close place. Open the door, I say,—do, there's good christians, and I promise to confess all."

" Why, what in the name of fortune is the matter now !" cried the landlord with amazement.

" The matter is that I shall die if you don't let me out," replied the mysterious voice.

" Where the devil are you ?" asked the landlord.

" Here, in the corner cupboard that aint big enough for a good sized dog."

" And pray how came you there ?"

" I'm ashamed to confess it," replied the supposed delinquent, " but the truth is, I crept in here to conceal myself till the family were gone to bed."

· " And what did you mean to do then ?"

" Rob the house, and if any body disturbed me, murder all the blessed inhabitants."

" Villain ! you shall be hanged !" exclaimed the horrified landlord, " you shall swing for this, depend on it. You hear his confession, gentlemen, he continued, addressing himself to those around him. Here's a ruffian who acknowledges that he intended nothing less than robbery and murder, and I call upon all of you that are men, to assist in capturing him."

' Mercy ! mercy !" shouted the voice from the closet.

" Oh yes, you shall have mercy," cried the host,—" just as much as you meant to show me and my poor wife and family. I'll send you to Newgate, you ruffian, and if the judge don't order you to be hanged there's neither law nor justice in the land."

So saying he snatched up a poker, and was going to break open the clo-

set door when Valentine, who began to think the fun would end too soon if the discovery of the hoax took place just yet, jumped up and laying hold of the weapon. remonstrated against the folly of irritating a man who was in all probability armed to the very teeth.

" Gad ! I forgot that !" ejaculated the host lowering the weapon as he spoke ;—" in my wrath I never recollected the danger of facing a man that thinks no more of murder than he would of braining a mad dog."

" Bah ! you are a coward, landlord !" exclaimed the old gentleman, who had been poring the whole of the evening over the newspaper. " Here are enough of us to eat the scoundrel, and if you all promise to back me, I'll drag him out of his lurking-place in about a minute.

" Will you ?" growled the voice from the cupboard ; " I should like to see the man that would dare to lay his hands upon me, that's all ! Remember, gentlemen, I'm well armed, and if I must be made a prisoner, it shan't be till I've killed about half a dozen of you at least."

" Did you ever hear such a bloodthirsty villain !" gasped the landlord, retreating a few paces, and nearly upsetting all those who happened to stand in his way.

" If I were you," said Valentine, in his own proper person, " I would try what fair words will do. You hear how resolute the man is, and if we drive him to desperation there's no knowing how soon he may fulfil his sanguinary threat.

" I'll try him at any rate," answered the host with a knowing wink, " and then, when he least expects it, we'll all pounce upon him and make the scoundrel our prisoner." Hereupon the worthy man cleared his throat with a very loud hem, and assuming a more gentle tone, he demanded upon what terms the prisoner in the closet wished to treat."

" In the first place I must have this door opened," replied the voice.

" Good ! that I agree to."

"In the next place you must promise not to prevent my escape from this house."

"Well, I promise that too," replied the host after a brief consultation with his companions.

"And in the third place you must agree to pay me the sum of fifty pounds in a way that I shall afterwards point out," continued the mysterious voice.

"Zounds! I'll pay you with a vengeance!" exclaimed the enraged landlord; you shall have your reward in Newgate, you infernal jail-bird, you shall."

"You'd better mind what you're a-doing on," replied the supposed robber." I've already told you that I'm armed, and I'm blest if I'm going to be sent to quod without making some of you suffer for it."

"Thomas," exclaimed the landlord, addressing himself to the before-named waiter," run out and fetch a policeman;—be quick, or we may all be murdered before you get back."

"You had better fetch three or four while you are about it," squeaked out the dandy despiser of brandy and water. "One may not be enough to capture this demned horrid fellow!"

"Twenty won't do it when my blood's once put up," exclaimed the voice from the closet; "I'm determined not to be taken to-night, so if any of you happen to catch a bit of cold steel, or to have a hole made through his body with a bullet, don't say it was for the want of fair warning. Fair play is a jewel, my lads, and if you don't mean to give me that, you must take what falls, that's all I know about it."

"I'ts no good argifying the topic," observed the landlord to those around him, "because I'v made up my mind the rasca lsharnt escape, and so that's the way to say it."

"We shall get killed!" groaned half a dozen of the company.

"There's no occasion for any thing of the sort," returned the worthy host, "I've sent for a policeman, and if one won't do we'll have a whole division of them."

"I'll bet a crown some of 'em gets what they wont like!" exclaimed the voice.

"That's no business of ours," replied the master of the house. "The police are paid for what they do, and if a few of 'em should happen to get killed, there's some consolation in knowing that the rascal will get hanged for it."

"Now master, what's the row?" exclaimed a lanky-looking policeman, who at this moment came bustling into the coffee-room.

"There's a thief in that closet, and I want to have him apprehended for being found concealed in my house," replied the host.

"Now, young fellow, come out of that, will you?" exclaimed the policeman rapping hastily at the door with his knuckles.

"I shant!" vociferated the voice.

"Oh, you won't, won't you!" exclaimed the officer —" then we must see whether we won't make you, that's all;—where's the key of this closet, Mr. What's-your-name?"

"I'm sure I don't know;—have you seen any thing of it, Thomas?" said the landlord, appealing to his waiter.

"It aint in the door, and it aint on the nail where I always hang it up," replied the functionary; "so I shouldn't be at all surprised if the feller's got it inside along with him."

"If he had he'd have let himself out long before this," returned the host.

"Well, never mind the key, we can do without it," exclaimed the policeman, and then addressing himself to the imaginary culprit, he enquired whether he meant to walk out quietly, or whether he intended to put him to the disagreeable necessity of compelling him to surrender.

"I sharnt do nothing at all in the matter," answered the voice, "so if you want me you must just take the trouble to come arter me;—that's all about it."

"I'm blowed if I don't come then!" exclaimed the policeman furiously, and snatching the poker from the landlord's hands, he commenced an attack upon the door that threatened speedily to lay the expected prisoner at his mercy. Upon this the whole party retreated to

VALENTINE VAUX,

OR THE

TRICKS OF A VENTRILOQUIST.

BY TIMOTHY PORTWINE.

the farther end of the room, where they could witness the future proceedings with equal satisfaction, and at the same time with more safety to themselves. At last the door began to give way to the repeated attacks that had been made upon it with the poker, and whilst all were looking on with breathless expectation, it suddenly flew open, and lo !—nothing appeared!

"I'm blest if there's anything here !" exclaimed the policeman, after a brief examination of the closet had satisfied him of that fact. The place is empty, and what's more, no one's been here, after all the fuss that's been made about it."

No. 5

"That's as much as to say we're all liars !" returned the host, venturing to come forward. "Luckily, however we've witnesses enough to prove that somebody was there, and as you've thought fit to let him escape why I shall complain to the commissioners and get you discharged.

" I'm certain no one's gone out since I've been here," replied the policeman, somewhat alarmed at this last threat.

"That's a lie !" shouted the same voice from the farther end of the passage;—"I'm free now, so let the best man catch me if he can !"

" Follow ! follow !" shouted the policeman, rushing towards the place from whence the sound came, and followed by all the company, who ran helter-skelter into the street—some of them glad to escape on any terms, and others anxious to witness the capture of a ruffian who had so successfully set them all at defiance.

Mr. Septimus Bramstone could not forbear laughing at the successful trick that had been practised by his young friend, and taking advantage of the opportunity, they both left the tavern, and calling for a coach, were speedily conveyed to the house of the elder gentleman, where they found Mr. Harry Bramstone and his son Arnold waiting their arrival in no very good humour. As may be expected, our hero was not very cordially received by either the father or his son, and in fact their coolness was so pointed that Septimus could not forbear taking the matter up rather testily.

"I don't know whether you are aware of it, brother," he exclaimed, " but this young gentleman is the nephew of my much esteemed friend, Sam Vaux."

"I guessed as much," growled the elder of the two.

"And so did I," chimed in his equally disappointed son.

"Then having guessed it, I should have supposed you would greet him with cordiality," answered the other, reproachfully.

"A very likely thing, truly !" exclaimed both father and son, with a sneer of marked contempt.

"Upon my word gentlemen, you both appear to be strangely out of sorts this evening, I think," ejaculated Mr. Septimus Bramstone. " I introduce my visitor as a friend, and for some unaccountable reason or another you treat him as you would a foe."

"And it's not to be much wondered at if we do," retorted his brother. " You can be vastly civil to a stranger it seems, whilst your poor nephew, here, is neglected and passed by."

"Really, brother, I don't know what you may think about it, but in my opinion this is carrying matters a little too far," returned Septimus, with evident tokens of displeasure. " This house is my own, I believe, sir, and I should like

to know who has any business to interfere with my arrangement.

"Oh, certainly—certainly—you have every right to make a fool of yourself if you please," returned the other, " but at the same time you cannot wonder much at my feeling jealous that you pass over a nephew to shower favour upon a stranger."

" If my presence here is likely to cause any ill-feeling, I'll instantly look out elsewhere for a lodging," exclaimed Valentine, snatching up his hat and preparing his departure.

" You will do no such thing, sir, unless you wish to offend me," answered Septimus, rising and interposing himself between his visitor and the door. " I have invited you here, Mr. Vaux, and here you shall remain in spite of all the brothers and nephews in the whole world."

" At any rate neither I nor Arnold will trouble you with our presence, whilst that young man is your guest," replied the other. " We thought you had not so far forgotten yourself as to prefer strangers to your own relations, but since we have found out our mistake, we will leave you till you come to your proper senses again."

" Very well, gentlemen, you can go as soon as you please," retorted Septimus, angrily; " you are of course at liberty to do as you may think fit, but remember I shall not require your company until it may be perfectly agreeable to yourselves."

" This is scandalous by Jove !" exclaimed his brother—" most infamous, upon my soul ; and I should suppose such conduct can only proceed from downright madness. So we will leave you, sir, with your newly found friend, and I expect the very next thing we hear, will be that you are going to make a still greater fool of yourself by marrying some woman young enough to be your daughter."

With this ebullition of anger, Mr. Harry Bramstone and his son strode out of the room, and by the loud slamming of the street door it was pretty evident that they departed from the house in high dudgeon. Septimus was evidently disconcerted at the little fracas that had occurred between himself and his relatives, but quickly recovering himself, he bade Valentine take no heed of a quarrel which after all would soon be made up.

"The fact is," he said, "my brother and nephew are jealous of every one to whom I pay the least attention. They perhaps naturally enough have looked forward to a handsome addition to their fortune whenever death shall think fit to remove me. But they forget that I am still a hearty man, and waiting for dead men's shoes is often a very tedious affair you know."

"I should hope they are not so selfish as you imagine, my dear sir," replied Valentine, endeavouring to remove the unfavourable reception.

"When you know them as we' as I do, you will alter your opinion,' answered the old gentleman. "You heard what was said about my marrying some woman young enough to be my daughter, and egad it's put a notion into my head that they may both be heartily sorry for."

"Then you mean to look out for a wife, sir?"

"Nay, I have one already in my mind's eye," replied Septimus, drawing himself up proudly. "Not—be it understood—a young woman though, but a female about my own age, and one who seems in every respect exactly calculated to render the remainder of my days happy and contented."

"You have known the lady some time I presume?" observed Valentine hardly able to suppress a laugh at the old gentleman's expense.

"I have been acquainted with the widow Maxwell for the last twenty years," replied Septimus. "Her husband and I were upon the most intimate terms of friendship, and when he died, I more than once thought of taking pity upon his forlorn relict."

"But do you think the lady is come-at-able?" asked Valentine.

"I certainly do think so," replied the other; "in fact we have kept up a friendly intimacy for some years past, and I am proud to say she regards me with more favour than any of her other acquaintances. Nay, as good luck will have it, I am to dine with her to-morrow, and if my present resolution holds good till then, I'll take the opportunity of popping the question."

"You will?"

"Aye, as surely as my name's Septimus Bramstone," exclaimed the old gentleman. "My brother's taunt just now has put me upon my mettle, and he shall be made to repent it till the latest day he has to live. However, enough has been said upon the subject at present, and as I dare say you are fatigued with your day's journey, the sooner we go to bed the better. So good night Valentine, and over the breakfast table to-morrow we will talk more of this subject. Harry and his son have thought proper to insult me, but it shall not be long before I make them bitterly repent their insolence."

So saying, they both proceeded up stairs, and Valentine being shown to his bed room, soon forgot the various incidents of the day in the deep slumber which had been produced by fatigue.

CHAPTER VII.

AN ELDERLY GENTLEMAN TAKES RATHER AN EXTRAORDINARY FREAK INTO HIS HEAD—A MATRIMONIAL PROJECT IS SET ON FOOT—BILLING AND COOING BETWEEN A PAIR OF ANCIENT TURTLE DOVES—TRIVIAL CIRCUMSTANCES GIVE PLACE TO GREAT EVENTS—THE KISS AND ITS CONSEQUENCES—THE DISMISSAL AND UTTER DESPAIR OF MR. SEPTIMUS BRAMSTONE.

ACCORDING to promise the subject was introduced again the next morning at the breakfast table, and to Valentine's surprise the old gentleman was still resolved to pursue his matrimonial project. He launched forth with all the ardour of a younger man, in praise of the widow whose heart he had resolved to take by storm, and dwelt with much satisfaction on the prospect of connubial happiness that had just dawned upon him at the ripe age of three score and five. Our hero listened to his rapturous discourse with profound attention, but he was aware that the ground he was treading on was extremely dangerous—and having no wish to offend either the old gentleman or his relations he wisely forbore giving any opinion either one way or the other.

This was quickly perceived by Mr. Septimus Bramstone, but as he guessed the cause of Valentine's silence, he readily forgave his apathy, and then turning the conversation into another channel, soon drew from his young companion a narrative of the many curious adventures that had befallen him through his proficiency in the art of ventriloquism. At all these Septimus laughed heartily, and his visitor began to entertain hopes that he would abandon his matrimonial scheme; but in this respect he was doomed to be disappointed, for no sooner were the breakfast things cleared away and a few letters written, than the old gentleman rose from his seat declaring that he was now going to dress himself in his best, so as to make a befitting appearance before the lady whose hand he aspired to. Nor was this any inconsiderable labour, if we may judge from the time it took to complete his toilette—for three hours elapsed before Mr. Septimus Bramstone emerged from his dressing-room. To be sure, when the worthy bachelor did make his re-appearance, he was vastly improved by the great pains he had taken to adorn his person, and appealing earnestly to Valentine, he enquired whether he thought he would do. This question was of course answered in the affirmative, and having desired his visitor to make himself quite at home in his house, he took his departure with a promise to return at as early an hour in the evening as he possibly could.

Entering a cab at the first coach-stand he came to, our elderly Adonis desired to be driven to the suburban retreat of the widow Maxwell; and then throwing himself back on the seat, he began to rehearse over in his own mind the various pretty sayings he intended to give utterance to, and also to plan out a favourable opportunity to broach the subject which was the immediate object of his visit. But this was not quite so easy as he had expected—a thousand excellent conceits floated through his brain; but no sooner were they though tof, than for some reason or other, each one in its turn was rejected, as not being exactly the thing.

All this was provoking enough; but Septimus Bramstone was a philosopher; and as fast as one fabric tumbled down, he sedulously set himself about constructing another, which was doomed in like manner to be abandoned for some fresh scheme that intrusively enough popped itself into his teeming brain.

At last he was roused from his dreamy reveries by the sudden stopping of the cab; and on raising his eyes he discovered that he was already at the end of his journey. This was perplexing to a man who had as yet formed no plan of operations; but this case was a desperate one: and discharging his driver, he skipped as lightly as age would let him, to the door, which had been already opened by Peggy Dingle, the faithful domestic of widow Maxwell.

"Please to walk into the dining-room, sir, and missis will be with you directly," said Peggy, leading the way into the place she had named.

"Is Mrs. Maxwell expecting any other company to-day, besides myself?" asked Septimus.

"No, there isn't another soul that I know on," replied the abigail; and then burstling out of the room, she left the visitor to indulge in solitude the pleasing vision that rose to his view.

"Egad, this is lucky!" he said to himself. "Of all things, I wished to be by ourselves: and as good fortune will have it, the widow appears to be exactly of my way of thinking. Every thing seems to befriend me, and it will be my own fault if I don't secure a tolerably easy victory."

As he said this, he viewed himself in the chimney-glass; and by the time he had brushed up his brutus and arranged his neck-cloth, the door opened, and the widow walked with a majestic air into the apartment. Then followed sundry compliments which we shall leave the reader to imagine; and while they were engaged in bowing and curtseying to each other. Peggy Driugle and her little understrapper placed the various dishes upon the table. Upon the completion of this necessary preliminary, the lady and her visitor seated themselves; but the conversatiou that now took place between them, was limited to common-place subjects, because Peggy was in close attendance; and it was easy enough to perceive that she was greedily devouring every word that was said, as if she expected what was to follow. At length, however, the meal was dispatched—the dishes were cleared away, to be succeeded by the dessert; and when all this had been satisfactorily arranged, Peggy Dingle left the room.

This was the moment most anxiously desired by Mr. Septimus Bramstone—and yet, strange as it may appear, he felt uneasy at the novelty of his situation. In truth, he knew not how to commence the wooing he had set on his mind; and for want of something better to say, he remarked that the weather was uncommonly fine for the time of year.

"Delightful!" exclaimed the widow, rapturously.

"And then your cottage, too, is so charmingly situated," rejoined Septimus—such beautiful prospects,—such ——"

"Yes," interrupted the widow—"the place is well enough, I believe—in fact, I dare say it is, as you observe, very pretty—but, like all other things in this world, it has its drawback."

"Impossible!" ejaculated Mr. Bramstone—"to me this place is a perfect little paradise: in fact, my dear madam, I never enjoy myself so completely as when sheltered beneath this roof."

"Really, sir, you are pleased to be complimentary," replied the blushing widow:—"howsoever, as I was saying nothing in life is without its drawbacks, and well as you seem to think of my cottage, I can assure you, that I find it nconsiderably dull."

This appeared to be the very opportunity our venerable lover had so anxiously sought—did the widow intend it as a hint for him to declare his passion? and if so, ought he not to seize hold of the chance which she had so kindly given him—Septimus thought he ought; but at the same time it was his opinion, that he should proceed with the greatest caution. He therefore swallowed a glass of wine to give him courage; and then looking earnestly at his fair hostess, he said in a tremulous voice—

"Do you really find this place so very dull, madam?"

"I do indeed, sir," replied the widow—"nor is it to be wondered at, when you consider that I am buried alive here, as it were. Peggy Dingle, poor faithful createur, is almost my only companion; and I mope away year after year of my life, without seeing a single soul except yourself."

"If my visits are agreeable, they shall be paid more frequently, my dear madam," exclaimed Septimus, who now began to think the awful moment was at hand.

"Mr. Bramstone is always a welcome guest," simpered the lady; "and come whenever he may, he will ever find me glad to see him. Indeed, your society is the only change I see—and believe me, sir, I——"

"Well, madam—proceed I beg of you."

"Excuse me, my dear sir, but I had almost forgotten what I was saying.—You men are such sad fellows, that if a female gives but half a word of encouragement, they are pestered to death forever afterwards."

"Well, madam, I'll not urge you any further upon that point," exclaimed the complaisant Mr. Septimus. "We will therefore, with your permission, recur to a former part of our conversation.—You said just now that you found this place very dull."

"Very much so, sir, I do assure you."

"And has it never struck you, that the fault might be very easily remedied?"

"Never."

"And yet society would make it pleasant."

"That may be, sir," answered the widow; "but I am not fond of a great deal of company—indeed I should very much dislike it."

"Again you mistake me, madam:—I don't mean that you should keep a great deal of company—one person would be enough; and that person should be ———"

"Who, or what, sir ?"

"A husband !"

"Mr. Septimus Bramstone !"

"Aye, madam; I have been trying a long time to come to the point; but the truth is out at last—and now you know exactly what I mean."

"Indeed, sir, I am as far from knowing what you mean, as ever I was:—will you have the goodness to explain yourself ?"

"It is very easy, my dear madam, to bid me explain myself," replied Septimus—"but when a man has lived to my time of life without declaring himself, it's not so easy to shape his tongue to the fashioning of fine speeches. I spoke plainly, as I believe, widow, and if you won't understand me, why———"

"It's not that I won't understand you, sir," answered the widow Maxwell; "but the fact is, your whole conduct is involved in so much mystery, that I must really request an explanation of your meaning."

"Well, if I must, here goes !" grunted Septimus—and then collecting all his firmness, he added:—"the truth is, my dear lady, that I have for a long time past been thinking what a fool I must be to lead a single life, when so many blessings attend upon matrimony. Upon this I began to look round me for one who I thought would be a suitable match; and when at last I had made up my mind upon that subject, who think you was the object of my tender regards ?"

"Lord, Mr. Bramstone, how should I know ?" simpered the widow.

"Yourself, ma'am !"

"Oh, sir this is too much !" said the widow Maxwell—"you have been too abrupt in your declaration—indeed—indeed you have !"

"You are not offended, I hope ?"

"No—not absolutely offended, replied the widow; "you are pardoned, sir, but I must have time to consider your proposal. It is a weighty affair, Mr. Bramstone, and must be duly pondered over before I can possibly give an answer."

"Name your own time my dear madam, and I will wait your reply with all patience and resignation."

"Will three months be too long ?" asked the widow.

"Three months ! 'tis an age to a man of sixty-five;" exclaimed the old gentleman.—"Say three days, and I'll endeavour to curb my impatient hopes within those bounds."

"Really, sir, you are too urgent;"

"Believe me, not at all too urgent." replied Septimus. "If I'm to marry I would do so immediately, but if you should unhappily determine to reject my suit, I will pass the remainder of my days in some out of the way place where—"

"Why you wouldn't turn hermit, Mr Bramstone."

"I would turn any thing out of spite," replied the old gentleman emphatically.

"But perhaps after all there may be no occasion for it."

"Certainly, if you are not unkind."

"And after mature consideration I may not be, you know," answered the widow with an encouraging smile.

"Damn it, madam, you have raised my hopes above par," exclaimed the worthy citizen with delight.

"Mr. Bramstone," you forget yourself," mildly observed the widow; this language to a lady is unpardonable !"

"It certainly is," replied Septimus with visible confusion—"In my rapture I forgot myself it must be confessed but here, upon my knees I beg your forgiveness. You will not—can not—must not—shall not, hold me longer in your displeasure."

"For this once, sir, you are forgiven," replied the widow Maxwell.

"Thanks ! dear madam ! a thousand thanks !" exclaimed Septimus jumping once more upon his legs. To the widow it really appeared that he had gone mad with joy, but if her astonishment was great before, how much was it increased when the old gentleman advanced his own lips towards hers and actually stole a kiss ere she had the power to resist this act of daring impropriety! at this moment, too, Peggy Dingle opened the door and popping her head into the room, asked if any body had called her.

"Begone, huzzy!" exclaimed the indignant lady, and then addressing herself to the delinquent she continued; "as for you, sir, I am surprised how you can dare to look me in the face after so great a violation of propriety as you have been guilty of. But it is well, sir, I have found you out, and disregarding all former friendship, I command you to leave my house for ever!"

"You don't mean that, madam surely?" faltered out Septimus.

"But I do mean so, sir," continued the lady," and if you would not wish to add to your insult, you would not delay for one instant to obey my commands."

"My fault has been great, I admit," replied the other, "but surely, when all things are taken into consideration, it is not unpardonable."

"Don't expect ever to be forgiven, sir," exclaimed the indignant dame. "I have been disgraced before my own servant—she was a witness of your presumption, and what will the girl think of me if I suffer it to pass without showing a proper degree of resentment?"

"May I not hope then for forgiveness?" asked Septimus timidly.

"You may not hope for any thing from me," replied the widow.

"I have been insulted in my own house, and in the presence of my servant."

"But she is prudent, and will never say any thing that would injure the reputation of her mistress."

"Unfortunately, sir, Peggy Dingle has a chattering tongue, and in all probability this scandalous affair will be spread over the neighbourhood before many hours have passed over my head."

"But hear me, madam—"

"I'll hear nothing, sir, from your lips!" exclaimed the still indignant widow—"Leave my house, Mr. Bram-stone, and never dare to enter it again!" Septimus found that it was in vain to remonstrate just then, and taking up his hat he slowly departed, though not without forming a resolution to venture back on the following day, in order that he might plead for forgiveness when the widow's anger was somewhat modified by time.

As for the lady, she called for Peggy Dingle, and having lectured her upon the duty of keeping her mistress's secret inviolable, dismissed her from the room, with a command that she should on no account mention the affair of which she had unfortunately been a witness. This of course Peggy faithfully promised, but the following chapter will show her utter incapacity to keep a secret, even though her mistress's reputation depended upon it.

CHAPTER VIII.

AN EXPEDITIOUS METHOD OF CIRCULATING A SECRET;—THE WIDOW MAXWELL'S UNEASINESS AND PEGGY DINGLE'S COOL METHOD OF TREATING SERIOUS DIFFICULTIES;—HOW TO PUNISH AN OFFENDER;—A SURPRIST, AND SOMETHING LIKE AN APPARITION.

The next morning by seven o'clock, Peggy Dingle might have been seen peeping with nervous anxiety near the brick wall that divided the garden of her mistress from that of her next door neighbour. The truth is, she was bursting to tell all she knew about the surprising events of the preceding day, and was looking for Betty the housemaid, in order that she might relieve herself by imparting the story of the kiss and her mistress's virtuous indignation thereat. Luckily for her, Betty in a few moments afterwards made her appearance, and then, after some complimentary speeches had passed between them, they as a matter of course, entered into every minute particular they could rake together relative to the private affairs of each other's families.

As may be expected, Peggy Dingle was full of the preceding day's adventures, and having first of all exacted a very solemn promise of secresy from the other, she told all that she knew concerning the stolen kiss, and the subsequent dismissal of Mr. Septimus Bramstone; of course, not standing over nice for a shade or two, and exaggerating a little here and there to heighten the effect of her glowing description. The other giggled and enjoyed the joke amazingly, and Peggy having thus unburdened herself, and afterwards extorted another promise not on any account to tell what she had heard even to her dearest friend, withdrew to complete her numerous little domestic arrangements.

But, alas! human nature is frail, and it happened unfortunately enough that Betty Higginbottom could not keep a secret any better than Peggy Dingle. Not, be it understood, that the aforesaid Betty wished to make any mischief, but happening at the time to see her very particular acquaintance, the nursery maid at the next house, walking in the garden, she just popped her head over the wall and told, with a few embellishments, the affair that had happened between the widow Maxwell and Mr. Septimus Bramstone. As in the previous case, the nursery maid was particularly requested not on any consideration to mention it any farther, and a promise to that effect was given.

"Now promises, like pie-crust, are made to be broken, and a pretty bit of scandal like that which she had heard was too good to be kept to herself, so the nursery maid thought there could be no great harm in telling it to the cook next door. From the cook it passed onwards with amazing celerity, so that by eight o'clock, just one hour after Peggy had first set it afloat—the little act of gallantry between Mrs. Maxwell and Septimus Bramstone was known and laughed at through the entire row in which the widow's residence was situated. As may be supposed, however, the story had lost nothing by passing through so many mouths.

Peggy Dingle was still busying herself in the kitchen when the parlour bell rang, summoning her into the presence of her mistress. Having finished what she was about, and not till then, Peggy answered the bell. On entering the breakfast-parlour she found the widow Maxwell looking all the worse for the flurry into which she had been thrown by the adventure of the preceding day. Peggy, however, did not wish to revive unpleasant recollections, and affecting to take no notice of the poor lady's discomfiture, she waited in profound silence to receive whatever orders were to be given. But the widow Maxwell remained mute for some time, as if turning over some weighty matters in her mind. At last she seemed to recollect herself, and smiling languishly, she said with the greatest earnestness:—

"Peggy Dingle, I have an idea—"

"A what, ma'am?"

"An idea, Peggy—"

"Lar, ma'am!" again interrupted the girl," why what in the name o' fortin be that? An idea, did you say?—Why, if you'll believe me, I never had such a thing belonging to me in all my born days."—"I mean Peggy," answered the widow,—"that I have been thinking"—"Ah, is that all!" returned the girl without surprise; well then, for the matter of that, so have I."

"Indeed!" exclaimed the lady; "and pray girl, may I ask what has been the subject of your thoughts?"

"Oh yes, to be sure you may," answered Peggy in the genuine simplicity of her heart; "I've been thinking about that nasty disagreeable fellow, Mr. Septimus Bramstone, and the 'liberty he took with you yesterday, and how I'd have served him if he dared to have kissed me as he did you!"

"Peggy!" exclaimed the widow in a tone of reproach.

"Well, ma'am."

"Never mention that subject again as long as you live," exclaimed her mistress.—"Don't even allude to his name in my presence, for I have found him out, Peggy, and have made up my mind that he is a good-for-nothing, false-hearted brute."

"Why in coorse he is," replied the submissive abigail. "Haven't I told you so long and long enough ago, and didn't you deny it and threaten to turn me away if ever I dared say much again. But now you've found him out

VALENTINE VAUX,

OR THE

TRICKS OF A VENTRILOQUIST.

BY TIMOTHY PORTWINE.

yourself, and a very nice old gentleman he is, I don't think !''

"Enough of this, Peggy," exclaimed Mrs. Maxwell ; " I have indeed discovered that he is not worth a single thought, and from this time I shall take care to banish him from my memory."

"Well, for my own part, I should think you would never forget him," returned the domestic with an arch leer. "Didn't he take advantage of a woman's weakness, and kiss you whether you liked it or not ?"

"He did !" exclaimed the widow Maxwell emphatically, and she seemed to be in a towering passion as she

made the acknowledgment. Peggy Dingle remained silent for a few moments, and then giving utterance to a sound something between a sigh and a groan, she said, wrathfully :—

"Ah, ma'am !" as I said just now, I only wish the imperant fellow had attempted to kiss me, that's all !—see if I wouldn't have made him remember it as long as he lives !''

"Why you surely don't mean to say that you wish Mr. Bramstone to kiss you ?'' exclaimed the widow with astonishment.

"Yes, but I do though," replied the girl; " I do wish it, ma'am, and if I didn't scratch his eyes out, say my name aint Peggy Dingle. I'd make him remember kissing folks against their will, I warrant you. Oh! he should have such a beautifully clawed face that he should not be able to show it again for a whole month at least. I would, ma'am, and no mistake."

"And yet, after all, Peggy, I am thinking that would be but a poor revenge for so grievous an affront," observed Mrs. Maxwell. "Men, you know, don't suffer from these scandalous reports as we poor women do, and I dare say by and by he would enjoy the joke, as he calls it, and join in the laugh he has raised at my expense!"

"Then I'd punish him for it in another way," said the girl.

"And pray what new method does your wisdom suggest?" enquired her mistress.

"Oh," replied Peggy, clenching her fist and looking as red as a turkey cock; "I know how I'd serve him out; I'd carry him before them old chaps at Union Hall."

"What!" exclaimed the widow; "take him before the police magistrates?"

"Ah! that I would," replied Peggy, "and so would you too, if you'd got half my spirit in you."

"And expose myself by so doing," cried her mistress. "Why the thing would be madness, and I should be laughed at and pointed out in the streets for ever afterwards."

"Well, and what of that?" asked Peggy; "suppose they did, do you think I should mind it a bit?"

"At any rate I should," exclaimed the lady thoughtfully, and then after a brief pause she said:—"Do you think, Peggy, there is any fear of Mr. Bramstone's excessive rudeness being known to any of our neighbours?"

"Why, between our two selves; ma'am, I should think not," replied the girl with some hesitation.

Poor Peggy Dingle felt very sorry that she had mentioned the little bit of scandal to the servant at the next house, but then she consoled herself with the recollection that she had made her promise to keep the matter very secret, so she thought there could not be much to fear on that score. In truth the simple girl little thought that by that time the news had run like wildfire throughout the whole neighbourhood, and was at that moment the subject of general conversation and laughter. She had not however much opportunity to think of the matter, for almost immediately afterwards Mrs. Maxwell resumed the conversation.

"If by any unlucky chance this affair should be known," observed her mistress, "I should never be able to hold up my head in safety."

"Dear, dear! how very shocking," cried the girl.

"All this would be the result of this scandalous story being known," said Mrs. Maxwell; "but of course, Peggy, I can rely upon your prudence?"

"Oh, to be sure you may, ma'am," replied the girl trying all she possibly could to conceal her confusion.

"And the cook—do you think she is to be depended on?"

"She's a good soul, and wo'nt say a word if I only give her a hint."

"And Dick, the footboy!"

"Will be mum as a mouse, I can answer for't," replied Peggy. "Only promise to raise his wages, ma'am, if he holds his tongue, and he'll know which side his bread's buttered. Dick's a 'cute chap, and ever since he took to following my ways it's surprising how he's altered for the better."

"He shall have two pounds a-year added to his present wages," said Mrs. Maxwell. "You can tell him so, Peggy, and at the same time let him know that if he suffers the least hint to drop, I'll discharge him on the instant. You understand me, Peggy?"

"Of course I do," returned the wench; "Dick's to have two pounds added to his wages, and I'm to tell him not to say nothing to nobody about that kiss that Mr. ———."

"Hush! interrupted the widow,' not a word more upon that subject, Peggy, but tell me whether you think the lad will be faithful to me."

"Lor' bless you!" exclaimed the girl; "why Dick would be as mute as a mackarel for half that money."

"Well, never mind," returned her mistress, "if he will only be secret the trifle will be well bestowed. The cook, too, shall have an addition made to her wages besides a new gown at Christmas, and as for yourself, Peggy, I'll give you ———."

"Just nothing at all, ma'am, if you please, interrupted the girl, cortseying with evident confusion.

"Psha! but I insist!" exclaimed the lady resolutely.

"It's no use your insisting, ma'am, because I wont have it," returned the abigail. "When I says a thing I means it, and what's more I've got a partic'lar reason for being obstinate."

"Peggy!"

"Ah! missis, you may stare as much as ever you like," cried the domestic, "but I've made up my mind all about it, and won't take so much as a brass farden!"

The fact is Peggy's conscience pricked her sorely, for in her own heart she knew well enough that she had no claim whatever upon her mistress's liberality. The secret had been already divulged, and she began to entertain sundry uneasy suspicions lest the person she had told it to might be no more trustworthy than herself. In short Peggy Dingle knew the frailty of her sex in that particular; so that we cannot wonder at the apprehension she now felt, and the delicacy that induced her to refuse the kindness her mistress was about to insist on.

The widow Maxwell sipped her coffee, and fortunately for her attendant observed not the uneasiness and guilt her countenance but too plainly exhibited. Her mind, too, was filled with her own unpleasant reflections, and the worthy widow manifested pretty evident, symptoms of being the owner of a heart very ill at rest. She sighed very deeply at times; occasionally applied a white cambric handkerchief to her eyes, and then sighed again!

In this expressive pantomime the morning's meal was dispatched, and breakfast being at last finished, the widow Maxwell desired Peggy to clear the table, with all possible haste. The domestic prepared to obey the commands of her mistress, though very slowly, for it seemed she wanted to say something or other, and was waiting for an opportunity to do so. First she took up one thing, then another, then she put them down again exactly in the same place, and looked at her mistress, but still not one word could she utter. It was an embarrassing moment to Peggy, and she was just wondering how she could broach the subject, when a violent double rat-tat at the street door startled her, and huddling the breakfast things on the tray, she was proceeding to leave the room with them when the parlour door suddenly opened, and who, of all other persons in the world, should stalk in like a ghost but Mr. Septimus Bramstone himself!

Now had this been in reality an apparition it could not have inspired the girl with more terror than was occasioned by the visit of one who had so recently and so grievously offended. At the sight of so desperate a monster Peggy could no longer restrain her feelings. She screamed outright—started back a pace or two, and then down went the tray and its brittle contents upon the floor; roused by the crash, Mrs. Maxwell turned round to scold her domestic for such an act of carelessness, when—oh, horror of horrors!—her eyes fell upon the pale-visage of Mr. Septimus Bramstone. It was now her turn to scream, and she did so most lustily, for she verily believed that the cadaverous-looking object before her could be no other than the ghost of the wretched man who had so grossly insulted her on the preceding day. In this bewilderment of the moment she supposed that in his despair he had committed suicide, and was now come to reproach her for the harshness with which he had been dismissed.

As for Mr. Septimus Bramstone, he stood confounded at the noisy reception he had met with, and it was some little time before he could sufficiently recover himself to utter a word. At last, however, he succeeded by a violent effort, and solemnly advancing one step nearer to the widow, he pronounced in a tone of awful hollowness, the single word :—

" Madam !"

He would have said much more, but the agitation of the moment prevented him, and having proceeded thus far, he stuck as if he had been in the middle of an Irish bog.

As for Mrs. Maxwell, she found herself in an equally awkward predicament, and being excessively indignant at the intrusion, she merely answered his salutation with the cold monosyllable " Sir !" which was uttered in such a way that the blood froze in his veins. Mr. Septimus Bramstone was perfectly electrified, and " more in sorrow than in anger," he stood gazing before her for some time in speechless amazement.

Peggy by this time had come to her recollection, and having bestowed a very meaning look upon the broken fragments of china that lay scattered around her, she thought—having done enough mischief for the present—it was high time to withdraw in order that the necessary explanation might take place between her mistress and Mr. Bramstone. She therefore scrambled the broken pieces together, and having uttered sundry maledictions upon the evil fortune that had occasioned such a fearful smash, left the room to tell the cook and footboy all that she knew, together with a few trifling additions of her own.

As soon as the widow Maxwell found that she was left alone with Septimus, she rose with all the dignity she could command, and was going to leave the room, when her elderly admirer took her hand in his, and pressing it with becoming fervour, besought the indignant lady to stay and hear his apology for the imprudence he had been guilty of the day before. But though his tones might have softened a rock, they had no effect whatever on the angry feelings of the widow Maxwell, and she was just going to flounce out of the room, when thinking better of it, she suddenly paused

—and whilst her eyes shot forth terrible lightning, addressed him in a voice far from being remarkable for good temper :—

" Mr. Bramstone," she exclaimed haughtily, " what insult is this you intend to offer me ? Leave me, sir, and never dare to enter my house again, or I shall be compelled to take more violent means for your expulsion !"

" Hear, me, Mrs. Maxwell," cried the old gentleman ; " hear me, madam, and then be cruel if you can."

" I will hear no apologies, Mr. Bramstone," replied the widow, still endeavouring to make her way to the door; " and after your outrageous conduct yesterday, sir, I am surprised at your insolence in making your appearance here."

" Nay, madam, you are too severe with me," remonstrated Mr. Septimus. " That I offended almost past all hope of forgiveness, I must needs confess ; but no female can ever shut her heart against mercy, and I came to apologise and ask pardon for what, after all, is only a venial offence : Nay, my love—"

" Don't love me, sir !" exclaimed the irritated lady, " but be a little more respectful in your behaviour, if you please. Love, indeed ! I wonder what insolence we shall have next."

" Believe me, madam, you are too hasty—"

" And believe me sir, I am not half hasty enough. If I did as I ought, Mr. Bramstone, I should order you to be thrust neck and shoulders out of the house, and it is only because I do not wish the whole neighbourhood to be disturbed that I have not desired it to be done before this time. But I'll tell you what, sir, I'll not bear this any longer ! Let me go—I insist upon leaving the room !"

" Not till I have your pardon, Mrs, Maxwell," returned the old gentleman obstinately retaining possession of her hand. " Say I am forgiven, and you are instantly free."

" Forgiven !" cried the widow scornfully ; " and do you really imagine, sir, that I can ever forgive a wretch like you ? Do you remember the occasion of my just indignation, sir?"

"And how dare you, sir, take so great a liberty?" demanded the lady with still increasing anger. "What possible excuse have you to offer for it, Mr. Bramstone?"

"Love, my dear madam, is my only excuse," replied the old gentleman sentimentally. "Love—all-conquering love!

"Methinks your age, sir, might have cooled your ardour."

"How can that be, widow, "cried Septimus, "when your charms have fanned it into a blaze?"

"Really, sir," exclaimed the widow indignantly, "your insolence is beyond all bearing. Your conduct yesterday has completely opened my eyes to the infamy of your ways, and from this time I desire we may never meet again."

"Yet before I go," cried the unmoved Septimus, "I would just ask you where is the harm of an innocent kiss?"

"There is a great deal of harm in it," answered the widow. "When the late poor dear, departed. Mr. Maxwell paid his addresses to me—his conduct was beyond all reproach, so mild—so subdued—so amiably respectful. During the whole of our courtship, sir, he never so much as once hinted that he wished for such a thing as a kiss."

"Perhaps his passion was not so ardent as mine," observed Mr. Septimus, "or at any rate it don't argue much for his gallantry."

"He was a most excellent creature," returned the widow, "and on no occasion was he ever tempted to forget himself as you have done. In our courting days, when he came to visit me, he used to sit himself down on one side of the table, while I took my seat as far off as possible on the other. At that respectful distance we used to converse of love, and when he rose to depart—which he always did at an early hour—a warm shake of the hand was sufficient to assure each of us that our love was as genuine as it was exalted."

"Well, there's no accounting for taste, certainly," replied Mr. Septimus Bramstone. "It, however, appears, madam, that we differ somewhat in our notions of love-making, but as the difference of opinion should never be suffered to lessen friendship, I do most sincerely hope you will pardon my first transgression.

"Never, sir!" was the prompt reply of the widow.

"Nay, but I have seen my error, and came here purposely to confess it, and likewise beg your pardon," cried Septimus.

"A most impertinent visit it was, sir, let me tell you," exclaimed the widow Maxwell; "and pray, sir, who was it let you into my house?"

"Who?—Why your own footboy, to be sure!"

"What!—Dick!"

"Upon my life, I believe that's the very name you call him by."

"A little villain!" exclaimed the lady furiously, and then muttering to herself, she continued :—" But he shall smart for this! It was only just now that I proposed to raise the urchin's wages—and this is the return for the kindness I meant to do him! But the two pounds a year extra shall not be his—nay, as I live, I'll this very moment give him notice to quit my service at the end of a month! I'll teach him not to let in a parcel of worthless people whether I like it or not!"

"My dear widow, you seem agitated," exclaimed Mr. Septimus Bramstone, as he watched her varying countenance with a sad foreboding, that his own errant was perfectly useless.

"I am agitated, sir," answered Mrs. Maxwell; "leave me Mr. Bramstone, and never let me see you again :—Do you hear sir, leave this house directly, or—"

"Say that you forgive all that is past and I will leave you, madam," replied the old gentleman. "Let your lips pronounce my pardon, and I go that instant. Nay, upon my knees I ask for one kind word before I go.

How long Mr. Septimus Bramstone would have remained in this humble attitude at the widow's feet we know not, but while he was still kneeling a loud knocking at the door alarmed him, and in an instant he started on his feet. Septimus was at all times a nervous man ;—conscience in the present instance had perhaps made him still more so, and darting out of the room he nearly knocked down the visitor as he passed him in the hall. When the old gentleman once more found himself on the outside of the house, he walked briskly towards home, thoroughly convinced in his own mind that all hope of obtaining the widow Maxwell's hand was now gone for ever.

CHAPTER IX.

IN WHICH CERTAIN PARTIES TALK OVER CERTAIN MATTERS THAT ARE PECULIARLY INTERESTING TO THEM-SELVES, AND WHICH WILL REVEAL SOMETHING WHICH THE READER OUGHT TO KNOW.

AFTER the arrival of Valentine Vaux at the London coach office as narrated in a former chapter, Mr. Henry Bram-stone and his son Arnold hastened homewards in no very good humour at the cordial reception our hero had met with from their relative, whose property they expected to enjoy when-ever the old gentleman should take it into his head to leave this world for a better. It was mortifying enough to see the kindness with which the youth was welcomed by Septimus, and al-ready they began to entertain mis-givings lest their kinsman should so far forget them as to alter his will and make a new one in favour of the much dreaded stranger.

With thoughts like these agitating them, it may be supposed they were not very communicative with each other as they trudged on together. Indeed it was not very often that they spoke at all, and the little they did say, only had the effect of increasing their growling propensities—so that

on their arrival at home neither of the gentlemen were in very good humour with their wives, who were by this time anxiously expecting their re-turn.

"Well my love," cried the elder lady, taking the hand of her lord and master as he shuffled sulkily up to the fire-place—"is he come yet, or has the coach fortunately overturned in its way up to town, and broke his neck ?"

"Humph !" growled Harry Bram-stone; "he is come, and the coach wouldn't overturn to please us. Curse him, he's a lively-looking young fel-low enough, and for my own part I don't think there's any chance of his dying for some years to come, and the consequence will be that my fool of a brother will give away all his fortune to a stranger that has no right to a farthing of it."

"Heaven and earth must be moved to prevent it," cried the elder Bram-stone, emphatically. "My brother Sep., may be a fool, but d—n me if he shall do as he likes with us;—my mind is made up, and something des-perate must be done."

"Something ought to be done, at any rate," observed Mrs. Lucretia Bramstone, venturing for once to put in a word. "Uncle Septimus don't seem to know what's right, so of course it's our place to teach him. Arnold, dear,"—she continued, ad-dressing her husband, "do you mean to be cut out by this young fellow after all the pains you have taken to make yourself agreeable to your rich re-lation."

"Bah !" interposed the elder gen-tleman, "Arnold never went the right way to work, or he might have made everything as right as need be. If he'd have coaxed his uncle a little more he'd have got on the blind side of him, and then Valentine Vaux would never have had a chance of doing us."

"What could I do more ?" asked Arnold, taking a huge pinch of snuff, and thrusting it up his nostrils with prodigious violence ; "didn't I order my last suit of clothes of his tailor, and in the most obliging manner leave him to settle the account? Wasn't that a circumstance that should make the old buck regard me as a lad of spirit and fashion?"

" I don't know what it ought to have done," replied Mr. Harry Bramstone, " but I am perfectly well aware that the result was quite the reverse of what you expected."

" Why he paid the bill, did he not?" exclaimed Mrs. Bramstone.

" Certainly, he did, my dear," answered her husband with provoking ironry;—Septimus paid the bill, as you observe, but not without a very strong remonstrance and a strict command to his nephew to offend in a similar way no more.

" Nor have I, sir"—

" True," resumed his father, " but you have in other ways—in the first place you poisoned his favourite spaniel for some trifling offence or other, and in the second you set fire to your uncle's wig under pretence of holding a candle to him while he was reading a letter."

" The latter was an accident I assure you, sir," replied Arnold;—"Nay, I made the best apology I could, and the old buffer seemed so satisfied with it, that I have been to visit him several times since without experiencing any coolness from him."

" To say the least, Arnold, your conduct has been extremely foolish," cried his mother;—"those little things together have given your uncle a very different notion of you, and now the consequence is, that a stranger seems likely enough to cut us all out."

" Heaven and earth must be moved to prevent it," again exclaimed the elder Mr. Bramstone in a tone of decision.

" That's just what you said before, sir," observed Arnold, taking another huge pinch of snuff. " You said heaven and earth must be moved to prevent this young shaver from chousing us out of our rights, and at present not a single proposition has been made as to what is to be done."

" The magnitude of the business must plead my excuse," answered Harry Bramstone sinking into a brown study, from which he was roused by the giggling of his son and daughter-in-law who were amusing themselves by tickling each other as if they had not been married for a period of at least six months from the date of this veritable history. At this the old gentleman glanced angrily towards his son, and after two or three expletives, which we shall not repeat, desired them to remember that they were not mere children, and that in fact they were just then engaged in " raising heaven and earth to prevent the long expected property of their relative from falling into the hands of a stranger." This seemed to have the desired effect, for the fair Lucretia seated herself silently by the side of her mamma-in-law, whilst Arnold, beating the devil's tattoo on the table with his fingers, waited patiently for any thing else the old gentleman might have to say. But the last-named personage chose to remain indignantly silent, whilst his better-half resumed her questions as to the business they had just been engaged upon.

" Is this Valentine a decentish-looking young fellow?" she asked.

" Why for that matter, the least said the soonest mended," answered Arnold brushing up his whiskers and trying to look remarkably fierce;—"the cove aint so much to be grinned at as far as looks go, and yet I can't think how uncle Septimus could ever have the heart to countenance him when he's got a nephew who, to speak without vanity, is not such a bad looking chap after all."

" Stuff and nonsense!" exclaimed his father indignantly, " think less of personal appearance and more of what we have got to do;—haven't I said that heaven and earth must be—"

" Moved to prevent this youngster from doing us out of our birthright," interrupted Arnold, and at the same time finishing a speech which he by this knew by heart." " True, we have got our work cut out for some time to come, so the next question we have got to consider is, how we are to proceed in an affair that I don't exactly see my way clearly through."

" I have it!" exclaimed the old man after a pause, and then slapping his son on the back with a force which seemed to rival that of a blacksmith's hammer.

"I have it, my boy," he continued ;—"this Valentine is raw from the country, a trifle, I dare say, will frighten him out of his wits, and I have a plan in my head that will send him scampering out of town a good deal faster than he came to it."

"Elucidate, most worthy sir," said Arnold with a drawl that threatened to last till the middle of the following week; "proceed sir, I beg ;—your plan, sir,—your plan ?"

"In few words then, Arnold, you must challenge this Valentine."

"I challenge Valentine !" exclaimed the younger Bramstone.

"My husband send a challenge !" half screamed Mrs. Lucretia with inconceivable terror.

"Our dear son challenge that insignificant country booby !" chimed in the elder Mrs. Bramstone ;—"are you mad, husband—or is this only a joke to try us with ?"

"I never was less inclined to joke in my life, madam," replied Harry Bramstone mopishly ;—we have got an awkward customer to get rid of, and upon Arnold must rest the duty of doing it."

"But supposing I should get killed?" suggested the young man—"Suppose, I say, I should get killed,—what would be the use then of my uncle Septimus making his will in my favour !"

"And we married scarcely six months! sobbed his wife in a paroxysm of alarm ; —"would you make me a widow, sir, and see me in one of those ugly looking caps that always make the wearers look like—like perfect frights !"

"Nonsense !—you none of you understand me," exclaimed Mr. Bramstone peevishly.—"Arnold has only got to challenge this interloper, and I'll answer for it he will not have to put his courage to the test in the way of fighting."

"You think he's not got much pluck then ?" observed the son.

"At any rate I'll be bound he's not one of the fighting sort," answered old Harry. A few big words will serve to frighten him out of the little senses he has, and no doubt he'll be glad enough to get away from London if you only play your cards tolerably well. Send him a challenge, my boy, by all means,

and if that won't do we must find some other way to get rid of him, that's all I know about it.

"But suppose this Valentine should not happen to be quite such a coward as you take him for ?" exclaimed Arnold—" suppose, dad, he should take it into his head to accept my challenge ; how should I be able to get off after bouncing him into it ?"

"Ah ! suppose he should insist upon fighting !" cried Lucretia reproachfully ; "I might lose a husband by it, and who knows that I should ever be able to get another as long as I live ?"

"Well, then," returned the old gentleman, "the best way, perhaps, will be to let the matter stand as it is for the present. But mind you, I have got a plan in my head that will set every thing to rights in no time."

"And pray, my love, what may this wise plan of your's be ?" asked the senior Mrs. Bramstone, with the confidence of one who thinks she has a right to make such a demand. "What notion has taken posse▩▩ of you that is likely to secure for ourselves the old man's property."

"Oh !" exclaimed Arnold—" that's coming to the point, dad—how do you propose to make sure of the old chap's tin ?"

"Do tell us, there's a dear," cried the younger lady, "Arnold is, I know, in a terrible fever about the money, and besides that"—

"You are in a terrible fever as well, I suppose you mean to say," interrupted the old man. "Aha ! I see how it is, you all want to worm out the secret, but you shan't though, till every thing is rife for action. The notion is hardly formed yet, and wants a deal of thought to bring it to perfection, but when every thing is properly arranged, something strikes me you will all acknowledge that there is nothing like the old head after all. Ha ! ha ! ha ! it will be a capital joke for us as long as we live—brother Septimus will be defeated when least he expects it, and as for that impertinent, interfering, money-wheedling infernal scoundrel, Valentine Vaux, why the sooner he makes himself scarce the better, for I can tell him he will never have

VALENTINE VAUX,

OR THE

TRICKS OF A VENTRILOQUIST.

BY TIMOTHY PORTWINE.

a farthing of the old chap's money, that's to say, unless my plan fails, and between ourselves I must say it's hardly likely it will, seeing that everything will be so cutely managed."

Having delivered himself of this rather lengthy oration, Mr. Harry Bramstone gave a pretty broad hint that it was time all steady people were in bed; upon which the others began to think so too, and then began the usual preparation of taking off boots and putting on slippers, together with the bringing in of chamber candlesticks, and the bidding each other "good night;" all of which operations took some little time, so that the hour of midnight had passed before all of them were in that happy dreamy state in which men—aye, and women too—forget the cares of the world, and imagine themselves all and everything, but that which they really are.

No. 7.

CHAPTER X

VALENTINE AND HIS FRIEND PAY VISIT TO THE HOUSE OF LORDS;—THE STRANGE SCENE THEY WITNESS THERE, AND A CLEAR VIEW OF FOLLY AS IT FLIES.

The day following Valentine's arrival in London, was rather a dull one to him; for it so happened that his friend,

Mr. Septimus Bramstone, was obliged to leave home on business of importance, in which his young friend could not very well accompany him. As a stranger to town too, he did not choose to venture abroad without his friend, so that the only alternative that remained was to stay at home and write a letter to his mother; after which he amused himself with a book till the old gentleman came home again to dinner—a meal which was scarcely over, when Septimus began to sound his young friend as to the way he would like to amuse himself in during the remainder of the day. The theatre was named as one source, the billiard table as another, and a stroll through the west end of the town as a third; but somehow or other Valentine happened to be very difficult to please on that occasion, so that the old gentleman found that in undertaking to gratify his guest, he had volunteered a task that was more easy in imagination than it was in reality.

Thus circumstanced, Mr. Septimus Bramstone began to think whether it was worth his while to venture any more propositions, but happening just then to recollect the two Houses of Parliament, he hinted that excellent sport was to be seen in either of those places, and concluded by begging Valentine to accompany him to one of the houses, as there was generally something going on that made it worth while to pass a few hours in listening to our legislators, even at the risk of afterwards being accused of keeping late hours and bad company.

Valentine willingly enough consented to accompany his friend on a visit of this kind, and on being pressed to say which of the two houses he would prefer going to, he named the Lords, as being the most likely place of the two where amusement might be obtained. He had often wished for an opportunity to see our noble legislators at their work of law-making, and having frequently heard that capital sport was to be found there, he anticipated no small treat in his projected visit to the House of Peers.

We will now suppose the formula of an introduction got over, and accom-pany Valentine and his friend into the gallery, where they arrived just as a learned lord was reading the minister of the crown a pretty severe rebuke for the large professions they had made, and the little or nothing that had been done in the course of an unusually long session. To be sure, the noble lord forgot that he had been the chief cause of several excellent bills being thrown out;—that he, in fact, had violently opposed everything which would have been in the least way advantageous to the country; and consequently that if there was any blame at all, it rested entirely with himself. Nor were those on his side of the house more mindful of that fact than he was himself, for the more personal and insulting the learned peer became in his language, the more vehemently did his friends cheer him on, till Valentine began to think a serious outbreak must be the consequence between him and the premier. At length the charges against the minister became so heavy, that our hero, who had previously heard the attacked party speak, threw his voice in the direction of the first Lord of the Treasury, and imitating him exactly, exclaimed with startling earnestness:—"That's a lie!"

Upon this, up jumped we know not how many rabid gentlemen, who all and individually looked as if they should like to swallow the Prime Minister for daring to assert that any body possessing their line of politics, could utter such a thing as an untruth. As for the minister himself, he was too much amazed at the circumstance to offer any contradiction; and whilst he sat dumbfounded at the inexplicable event, his antagonist motioned his friend to remain quiet whilst he gave the noble lord at the head of the government such a setting down as he had never received in his life before. Hereupon the Lord High Chancellor thought it his duty to interfere, and as all Lord High Chancellors are supposed to act with perfect impartiality, he spoke in such a way that both parties might very naturally wonder whether the rebuke was intended for himself or his adversary.

Matters now appeared to take a more

pacific turn, and the peer who had commenced the attack, changed his system, and instead of abusing his foe after the elegant style of a Billingsgate fishwoman, he tried the powers of sarcasm, with which he succeeded so well, that it soon became evident that not only the prime minister, but that his colleagues in office, shrunk under the infliction that seemed to give so much satisfaction to their adversaries. Cheers and laughter now resounded through the house, and so indecorous did they become in their mirth, that at last Valentine, who was rather a liberal in opinion, gave vent to his indignation in an exclamation of "shame!" This, as our readers will easily enough suppose, was sufficient to set the whole house in a ferment, and in one instant every peer was upon his legs demanding the cause of so scandalous an interruption to the important deliberation which had called them together. Upon this the speaker again interposed, declaring that the privileges of the house had been violated, and promising to pursue the culprit with his heaviest displeasure, provided any body would in the first place point out the offender. But this was a task of no very easy accomplishment; for though enquiries were made in the gallery to ascertain whether any body there could give a clue to unravel the mystery, every one maintained strongly that the offending party was not among themselves; and that in fact the cry appeared to them to have proceeded from one of the peers. But this was altogether incredible; for of course an hereditary legislator could never have forgotten himself so far, and therefore strangers were ordered to withdraw while the house went into deliberation as to what course should be adopted under such very peculiar circumstances.

This ordering of strangers to retire was perhaps intended as a punishment to those who were so unceremoniously turned out, but candour obliges us to confess that Valentine and every body else thought it a very happy release to find themselves once more on the outside of the walls, within which they had beheld a scene that would have disgraced even a bear-garden. As for our hero, he was perfectly astonished at what he had seen and heard, for he had been used to suppose that there was some little order in an assembly that consisted of men who ranked among the highest and noblest in the land; instead of which he had witnessed a scene, of which the lowest portion of the community would have been thoroughly ashamed. But Mr. Bramstone surprised him still more by assuring him that such noisy proceedings were by no means uncommon; and that the very men who were assembled night after night to frame laws for the good government of the state, were themselves frequently the first to offend against the very acts which they had been assisting to pass.

Valentine shrugged his shoulders as he heard this; and hoping that fortune might never be spiteful enough to make a lord of him, he returned home with his friend to partake of a supper which was doubly welcome to him after the dry business which for the last few hours had occupied his attention. A cigar or two and a glass of brandy-and-water, however, served to produce a forgetfulness of the past; and just at that hour when day and night separate, Valentine gladly retired to his bedroom, and throwing himself down upon his couch, he dreamed away the rest of the night in visions of home that seemed to transport him once more amidst the happy scenes in which his earliest years had been passed.

CHAPTER XI.

IMPERTINENT INTRUDERS, AND THEIR MYSTERIOUS CONDUCT—MR. SEPTIMUS BRAMSTONE IS RATHER PUZZLED, AND IS IN DANGER OF FALLING A VICTIM TO THE VILLANY OF HIS RELATIONS WHEN UNEXPECTED SUCCOUR ARRIVES.

Valentine slept so well and so soundly on the following morning, that after waiting a reasonable time Mr. Septimus Bramstone thought he might as well begin breakfast, and thus leave his young friend to enjoy his slumber as long as he thought fit. Unfortunately, however, his own quiet was not to be undisturbed for any long time, for scarcely had he finished his last cup of tea when the door was opened, and a servant announced that two gentlemen were in the hall who wished to see him immediately.

"And pray, Betty, what are their names?" asked her master.

"Lord, sir, I declare I've quite forgot," answered the girl, "but I know they were very funny ones though for all that."

"What sort of persons are they?" again demanded her master.

"Queer looking chaps enough," replied Betty;—"one's partic'larly short, and tother's partic'larly tall; so that perhaps between 'em they'd make two decent sized chaps."

"What do they look like?"

"I should say they're either doctors or undertakers," replied the girl;—"there's something mysterious in the look of 'em though; and if I was you, sir, I wouldn't let 'em any furder into the place till they gave a proper account of themselves."

"At any rate I shall not see them till they have sent in their names," exclaimed Septimus;—"so go to them from me and ask the gentlemen for their cards;—and do you hear, Betty, take another good look at them, and then report to me what you think of them."

Betty left the room to execute this mission, and returned again shortly, saying that the second view had not at all improved her opinion of the strangers; and that in fact, from their whispering so much together, she was more than ever convinced that they were up to no good. Mr. Bramstone listened to the girl's narrative, and then having made up his mind that she had greatly exaggerated the whole affair, he enquired whether she had asked for their cards as he had desired.

"Why in course I did, sir," replied the girl; "but as they neither of 'em happened to have got sich a thing, why it stands to reason that I couldn't bring t you not by no possible means whatsomdever."

"Did you ask their names then?" interrogated her master. "Oh yes, I asked 'em what their names were," answered Betty, "and one of 'em told me that he was a professional man, and that his name was Dr. Dundizzy."

"Dundizzy, eh?—and pray who may the other gentleman be?"

"Dr. Slop, at your service," replied a peculiarly sepulchral voice, and looking up, Mr. Bramstone saw the identical tall and short gentlemen of whom he had just been speaking. He was about to ask them to be seated, but ere he could do so, the gentlemen—who appeared to make themselves quite at home—plumped themselves upon a sofa with as much freedom as though they had the honour of being among the most intimate associates of the owner of the house.

"I believe, gentlemen, you wished to speak with me," said Mr. Bramstone, as soon as he had partially recovered from his surprise. "Perhaps you will have the kindness to come to the point at once then, for I happen to be particularly engaged this morning, and shall consequently be obliged to leave you again before many minutes are over."

"Indeed!" exclaimed Dr. Dundizzy, in a very gruff voice, and—"

"Indeed!" cried Dr. Slop, in a very squeeky one.

"Really, gentlemen," said Septimus, "your conduct appears to be rather strange, to speak in the mildest terms. You have thought fit to honour me with a visit without any invitation, and I would know your business in order that I may be relieved of your company as soon as possible."

"To come to the point then," exclaimed Dr. Dundizzy, "my friend and myself have just called in to see how you are to-day. We heard that you have been ill, and out of the purest and most disinterested friendship, we have taken the liberty of calling in to see how you are to-day."

"You are extremely kind, sir, I dare say," replied Mr. Bramstone; "but the fact is, I have never had much the matter with me, and even if I had, it is most likely I should have sent to my own medical attendant. You will therefore excuse me, gentlemen, if I say good morning to you both, as I happen to be particularly engaged in an affair that requires my immediate attention.".

"We can't help your engagements my good sir," returned Dr. Dundizzy, "for the fact is our business is more important than any you can have got in hand, and what is more, we shall not leave this place till we are fully satisfied about the matter that has brought us here. We'll neither of us stir just yet, will we, Dr. Slop."

"Most assuredly not," returned the other bowing solemnly.

"Upon my word, gentlemen," exclaimed Mr. Bramstone indignantly. "this is very pretty conduct certainly. First of all you introduce yourself into my house in a most impertinent manner, and then refuse to leave it when I have told you our business is ended."

"And if we do so, sir, it is for your own good," returned Dr. Dundizzie pompously.

"The devil it is!" exclaimed Septimus with amazement.

"Most certainly it is," returned Dr. Slop, grasping the hand of the old gentleman and proceeding to count his pulse with the utmost coolness and deliberation. "In fact, sir, we have been sent here by an anxious friend of yours in order to inquire into the state of your health, and if necessary to take immediate steps for your recovery."

"What! whether I will or no, I suppose?"

"Of course," responded Dr. Dundizzy," for it unfortunately happens that patients suffering under your particular malady are not aware of any thing being the matter with them, the consequence of which is that their complaint gains ground and reaches to an alarming height, so that all medical skill proves unavailing."

"And you have the impertinence to assert that any thing is the matter with me?" exclaimed Mr. Bramstone. "You, I suppose, are a couple of needy practitioners in want of a patient or two, and I am to be victimized in order

that you may obtain a patient who you believe is able to pay your exorbitant fees."

"We are guided by a perfect conscientiousness in the discharge of our duty, I assure you," squeaked out Dr. Slop; "nay, it is the nature of your complaint to be suspicious, but I dare say after a short time we shall be able to restore you to your former healthful condition."

"What do you mean to say ails me?" demanded Mr. Bramstone.

"I would rather not say too much at present," answered Dr. Dundizzie; "but perhaps you'll excuse me forasking after those great relations of yours, the sun, moon, and seven stars?"

Mr. Bramstone looked unutterable things as this question was put, and then drawing himself up to his full height, he demanded in a tone of excessive indignation what the other meant by so impertinent an observation.

"Pray be calm, sir," exclaimed Dundizzie with provoking coolness. "I have a great and most important duty to perform, and it is therefore highly necessary that I proceed in this affair according to my own peculiar system, which has never failed in soothing even my most refractory patients. You are very much excited, sir, and let me tell you, sir, that unless you are a great deal calmer, sir, it will be my duty, sir, to order severer measures to be taken, sir!"

"Are you a tailor, sir, that you talk about taking measures?" answered Mr. Bramstone with contempt.

"Hush! cried Dr. Slop coaxingly, "hush, my good friend, and don't oblige us to proceed to coercive measures."

"Coercive measures be hanged!" vociferated Septimus in a towering passion; "who is it I should like to know, that talks about coercing a free-born Englishman in his own house. But I see how it is—you have been sent here to insult me, and as I don't feel inclined to put up with any more of your impertinence, I give you fair warning that, unless you both disappear in about a brace of seconds, I shall *take measures*, as you call them, to kick you both into the street."

Upon hearing this, the two worthy disciples of Galen consulted with each other, and, if we might judge by their oft-repeated glances at the door, they were evidently arguing upon the prudence of making as hasty a retreat as possible. But a stronger motive seemed to impel them to stay where they were, and after some little preparation, Doctor Slop—assuming his blandest smiles—approached Septimus with a degree of humility that might have disarmed a savage of his ferocity:

"Excuse us, my dear friend," he said, "but you appear to be much excited, and as anger, in such cases as yours, only serves to increase the severity of the disease, I would like to try the effect of my never-failing and all-powerful soothing system. It has done wonders, my good sir, I can assure you, and, in cases of the most desperate madness, has——"

"Madness!" exclaimed Mr. Septimus Bramstone, seizing the poker and brandishing it with a vigour that made his two opponents skip to the farther end of the room. "Have you come here to talk to me about madness, when all my friends know that her majesty has not a more sane subject in the whole of her dominions."

"But it so happens that your friends have a very different opinion about the matter," returned Dr. Dundizzie; "in fact, sir, they have sent us to see what is to be done under such unfortunate circumstances, and as I have no longer any doubt of your madness, it only remains for us to sign a certificate, in order to procure you an asylum in one of the numerous places provided for persons afflicted with your unhappy malady."

As he spoke the doctor made a sudden spring upon his patient, and ere he was aware of his intention, the poker was wrenched from his grasp, and hurled to the further part of the room. To describe the rage of the old gentleman would be utterly impossible; he absolutely roared himself hoarse in the abuse he heaped upon them, and then rushing upon his adversary with the fury of a tiger, he strove with all his might to hurl his ponderous antagonist to the floor. In this, however, he was disappointed; for Dr. Slop hastened to the assistance of his friend, and between them they were in the act of fastening the old gentleman's hands behind him, when the door was burst violently open and Valentine, darting into the room, flew upon the two doctors with such vehemence that they were glad to make their escape by fleeing to two different corners of the apartment.

"How is this, sir?" exclaimed our hero as soon as he had seated his friend in a chair; "what means this outrage? Speak, and if these intruders prove to have insulted you, I swear to punish them in a manner that will prove a lesson to them for the remainder of their lives."

"The villains have come to swear that I am mad," cried the old man in alarm. "They have been sent to take me away to some lunatic asylum. and if it had not been for your fortunate arrival, I should have been sacrificed to the accursed avarice of my relations."

"Is this true?" demanded Valentine of the trembling culprits; "must I indeed believe that men can be found so base as to sacrifice an old man merely because there are those who are thirsting for his gold?"

"I don't know who you may be, young man," stammered Dr. Dundizzie, "but I would have you know that a respectable physician is not to be brow-beaten and bullied when he happens to enter a house in the execution of his professional duties. I am here. with my friend Dr. Slop, to inquire into the state of this person's mind, and as we are both of us of opinion that he requires closely looking after for the future, we were about to sign a certificate that would have procured him admission to a place where he would have been carefully attended to till he was considered capable of again taking his affairs into his own hands."

"And this kind consideration, I

suppose, proceeded from his relatives?" observed Valentine. "I have heard something of them, and perhaps they may hear something of me before I have done with them."

"Excuse me, sir, and we will confess all," cried Dr. Slop, venturing to leave the corner in which he had sought shelter; "the fact is we, both of us, came here by order of—"

"Hold your fool's tongue, Dr. Slop, I command you!" exclaimed his friend in a frenzy of rage. "The fact is, we came here to perform a great public duty, and what is more, I mean to perform it too, before I leave the house."

"If you are wise men you will quit the place before any further mischief come of it," returned Valentine, threateningly. "I am a friend of Mr. Bramstone's, and if any further violence is offered, I may, perhaps, take you in a manner that your infamous conduct so well merit."

"But you will please to remember that there are two of us to overcome," answered Dr. Dundizzie, elevating his cane, and then trying to look as long as possible. "We are in this house to make enquiries relative to the sanity of Mr. Septimus Bramstone, and as he has given ample proof of his mind being in a state of derangement, we consider it to be our duty to give him into the hands of those who will know how to take care of him for the future."

"And so you believe my friend to be out of his senses!" exclaimed Valentine in a tone that betrayed the rage that was beginning to overpower him. "For a paltry bribe you would consign him to a madhouse, even though you well enough know that he is more in his senses than you are at this present moment."

"We know our duty, sir," answered Dr. Dundizzie, with solemn gravity, "and what is more, are prepared to perform it."

"What do you mean?" exclaimed our hero; "that you are both cold-blooded villains, I can readily conceive, yet I cannot imagine that you would so far forget the dictates of humanity as to consign a fellow-creature to the dungeons of a mad house merely for the paltry reward that has been offered by those who have an interest in getting him sent out of the way."

"We have no time to talk with you now," replied Dr. Dundizzie;—"the truth is we have a couple of keepers waiting for us in the street, and at a word they will both be here to take the old gentleman to the asylum."

And so saying he was walking towards the window for the purpose of beckoning to the fellows, but Valentine foresaw the design, and rushing forward, he seized the doctor in his arms—dragged him towards the window, and both by words and actions, gave very significant hints that he intended to pitch him without much ceremony into the street. Upon this, Dr. Slop advanced in double quick time to the assistance of his companion, but as Mr. Bramstone saw his intention, he darted upon the man of physic, and in an instant laid him sprawling upon the floor, where he held him whilst Valentine proceeded with the affair he had undertaken.

Fortunately for Dr. Dundizzie, the window was not a very high one, and happening to alight upon his legs, he went scampering off at a pace that promised quickly to carry him out o the reach of harm. As for Dr. Slop, he no sooner saw the fate of his companion, than, naturally enough anticipating a similar fate for himself, he made a violent effort to get free from the old gentleman, whose turn it now was to triumph over his prostrate foe. Indeed so strenuously did he exert himself for this purpose that at last contriving to jump up from the floor, he made a desperate rush towards the door, which fortunately for him, happened to be open, and then making one leap down the stairs gained the street without further interruption. To say that the terrified son of Esculapius made the best use of his opportunity would be unnecessary; our readers will no doubt conceive the celerity of his movements in such an exigency, and all will no doubt believe us when we declare that neither Valentine nor his friend, thought it worth their while to pursue the enemy any further. For this time, therefore, both the doctors got off better than they deserved, and now that all danger was past, their conquerors enjoyed a hearty laugh at the expense of their frustrated enemies.

CHAPTER XII.

AN AQUATIC EXCURSION PROPOSED—THE START—MR. SEPTIMUS BRAMSTONE FINDS HIMSELF IN QUEER HANDS—MATTERS BEGIN TO LOOK RATHER MYSTERIOUS, AND OUR HERO FINDS HIMSELF INVOLVED IN A DILEMMA.

HAVING got rid of their two disagreeable visitors, Mr. Septimus Bramstone thought fit to ring for the lunch. over which the friends began to discuss the propriety of doing something extraordinary to pass away a day that had been broken into in so very disagreeable a manner. Numerous little projects were named, all of which were abandoned with the same rapidity that they had been proposed, until Mr. Bramstone happened to recollect that he had a very particular friend residing at Richmond, who he knew would be very glad to see them both, and who, of course, they were bound to honour with their company, just by way of assisting him in emptying a few bottles of wine to the good of his health, and that of all his amiable family.

To Valentine this proposition was particularly enticing, for he had frequently heard the scenery about Richmond praised as being the most delightful and fairy-like in the whole kingdom, and being besides a bit of an enthusiast in those matters, he quickly agreed to the proposal—swallowed his lunch with the avidity of a half-starved man, and finished the refreshment almost before his more elderly companion had begun.

But patience is a most convenient blessing to those who happen to be endowed with it, and so Valentine discovered in the present instance, for Mr. Bramstone some how or other thought fit to be longer than usual, and it was not till he had picked his teeth and talked over an immense quantity of unimportant things, that he at last rose from his seat and declared himself ready for the start. Yet, even then there was the ceremony of squeezing himself into a particularly confined great coat, which, with the assistance of Valentine, was accomplished in something less than a quarter of an hour, and then it was announced that he was ready to start to Hungerford Market, from which place the steam-boats started for the place they were desirous of reaching.

After pushing and jostling through the busy streets of London till they were both pretty well tired of being elbowed about by every one they met, our two friends found themselves in the Strand. Here, however, Mr. Bramstone happened to recollect that he had a little business to transact with a brother-trustee, and as the affair was a private one, Valentine was requested to walk slowly towards the place of starting, where his friend promised to join him in the course of half an hour at the most. Now our hero had no idea of suffering business to interfere with pleasure, and, to confess the truth, he heartily wished the aforesaid co-trustee at the devil; still he could not very decently give utterance to the thought, and merely asking his companion to cut the affair as short as possible, he went his ways muttering his displeasure in terms that we shall not repeat for fear of shocking the nerves of our lady-readers.

As for Septimus, we must do him the justice to say that he did not very greatly exceed the half hour, and having finished what he had to do, he took his departure from the house of his friend, and then bustling on with all the speed he could, was just turning down into the Adelphi when some one laid hold of his arm, and

VALENTINE VAUX,

OR THE

TRICKS OF A VENTRILOQUIST.

BY TIMOTHY PORTWINE.

turning round to see who it was that had interrupted him, he beheld a square-built, rough-looking man, covered from chin to heels in a shabby-looking wrap-rascal, that gave him more the appearance of a bailiff than of anything else under the sun. Mr. Septimus Bramstone stared at the man in mute wonder, upon which the other burst out into a peal of vulgar laughter, and slapping him familiarly on the shoulder, enquired whether he was inclined for a ride a little way out of town that fine afternoon.

"I certainly do, and what's more I mean to have one," answered the old gentleman, wondering what all

No. 3.

this was to end in, and trying to persuade himself that the man was the driver of one of the short stages about town.

"Vy that's the werry ticket," exclaimed the other with the same familiarity he had used before; "I've got a coach wot's been vaitin' for you ever so long, so jump in and I'll take you to von o' the nicest places yer ever vas in in yer life."

"I am much obliged to you, my friend," replied Septimus, "but the fact is I have made up my mind to go by water and my friend is now waiting my arrival to go on board one of the Richmond steam-boats."

"Sorry to say yer can't go on board a Richmond steam-boat to day," exclaimed the man. "The water couldn't do yer no good, not whatsomdever. Besides I've orders to take you some'ere else, and it's more nor my life's worth to let yer go except by my conweyance."

"Nonsense, man, there must be some mistake in this," returned the old gentleman, endeavouring to release himself from the grasp of his insolent tormentor; "let me go, sirrah, or I will call the first policeman that passes to my assistance."

"And vot do yer think the police vill care for any thing yer may say?" demanded the fellow insolently. Them chaps never interfere when they ought, and besides, if they did, I've got a chap here to help me, and ve'd pretty soon show 'em wot's wot, and no mistake."

"What mean you by having some one else to help you?" asked Mr. Bramstone, growing more and more alarmed.

"Oh, I'll soon shew yer vot a rum 'un he is," exclaimed the other, and then beckoning to an equally villanous-looking ruffian, he shouted:—"I say, Bill, come here and show yerself to the gen'l'man, vill yer!"

On this the before-mentioned villanous looking ruffian approached with a swaggering air, and nodding with all the familiarity of an old acquaintance, asked Septimus whether he found himself any better.

"I really don't understand what you mean," cried the person he had addressed; "I am very well, and have been so, for aught I know, for a long time past."

"Oh! that's vhere it is, yer see," exclaimed the first speaker, "yer thinks yerself werry vell I dare say—but then there happens to be people as knows you ain't well, and yer ought to be werry much obliged to 'em for looking arter yer so kindly."

"Fellow!" roared Septimus, "if you go on in this way much longer you'll drive me mad."

A loud horse laugh followed this speech of the old gentleman's, and when the two shabby-looking fellows had had their grin out, the principal of them said, with an impudent leer at his companion:—

"The gen'l'man says as how ve shall drive him mad, Bill, but somehow or other I've a notion that ve shall be troubled to do that, seeing that he's as mad as a March hare already."

"Insolent scoundrel, how dare you talk in this way to me?" cried Septimus in a towering passion. "Besides, you see what a crowd of people your conduct has already brought about us, and I now give you fair warning that unless you immediately go away, I will call somebody to my assistance who will compel you to retreat a little faster than perhaps you may like."

"Oho! if it comes to that 'ere," retorted the ruffian, "it's high time to show my authority for vot I'm doing. This little bit o' writin' is signed by two doctors named Dundizzie and Slop, and the meaning on it all is that you are mad, and consequently must go along with us to a place vhere they'll know how to take proper care on yer."

"Good heavens, what treachery is this!" exclaimed Mr. Bramstone, turning deadly pale as these words were uttered.

"I knows nothin' about treachery, 'cause you see it aint at all in my line," answered the man. "All I does know is that you must be mad, cause this here bit o' paper says so, and therefore I'll thank you to jump into that coach, for fear I should have the trouble of makin yer."

"I'll not go," shouted the old gentleman, starting back and preparing to make a start in the vain hope of escaping from his tormentors. Both the men, however, perceived his intention, and darting upon him, they, with all their strength, began lugging their victim towards the vehicle which was waiting for them close by the curb. But Septimus still resisted with all his power, until finding that he was as nothing in their hands, he turned towards the by-standers, and in piteous accents implored them to assist him against the violence ef his persecutors.

" I'll tell yer vot it is, gen'l'men," exclaimed the man, as he perceived that the appeal was not entirely thrown away upon the crowd—" this here unfort'nate creature having been taken queer in his upper story, and his friends having taken pity on him, have purwided him vith a comfortable lodging at our master's house, vhere he'll be treated like a lord, and then be sent home agin as soon as ever he's vell enough to be trusted."

" Aye, aye, my poor fellow," said a compassionate looking old gentleman in green spectacles; " it's all for the best, no doubt, so go with these good men quietly and I dare say it will be all the better for you."

" Will nobody assist me ?" cried Septimus, despairingly—" is there no one among you that will save me from the hands of these infernal villains ?"

" There !" exclaimed the man, " you hear how he's a going on—he calls us infernal villains, and if that aint a proof of his madness. I don't know vot is. So come along, vill you, old gen'l'man, and when ve gets yer home see if ve don't give you summat as vill make yer better in less than no time !"

And as he said this, he and his companion, still resisting their victim, into the coach, which had no sooner received its load than it was driven off amidst the laughter of the thoughtless and the pity of those who really believed the old gentleman was as mad as the keeper had declared. The elderly man in the green specs shook his head as the vehicle disappeared; and heaving a deep sigh, he fervently prayed that he might never lose his senses or be subjected to the tender mercies of such men as those who had just driven off with their victim.

All this time Valentine had been impatiently waiting the arrival of his friend, and was wondering what in the name of all that was provoking could have kept him so long. The half hour had passed some time since, and he had even wearied himself with making ducks and drakes in the water, with all the oyster shells he could find near the spot where he was standing. Then he watched the different steam-boats that were constantly arriving or departing from the pier; and as he saw the last Richmond vessel leave the place, he could not help expressing his indignation in " curses not loud but deep." Every moment he kept turning about to see whether there were any signs of his friend's arrival; but when at last he had been waiting no less than two long weary hours, he resolved upon turning home, imagining, as a matter of course, that Mr. Septimus Bramstone must have been somehow detained longer than he had expected; and that in all probability he should find him anxiously waiting his arrival.

With this notion he left the esplanade at Hungerford Market; and hurrying onwards as fast as he could, reached the house of his friend in about half the time that he expected it would have taken him. When Susan opened the door, his first eager enquiry was whether Mr. Bramstone had yet returned; and upon that faithful domestic answering in the negative, he stood aghast for a moment or two as if some sudden conviction had struck him that an accident must have been the occasion of so unaccountable a circumstance.

But to his surprise Susan appeared to think nothing at all of it—in fact she told him that her master sometimes took it into his head to dine out, and as he had not kept his appointment with Valentine, why the natural supposition was, that he had been detained by business and would return as soon as he could conveniently get away. With all this our hero was obliged to appear perfectly satisfied—though to say the truth, he still had his misgivings upon the subject, and a thousand disagreeable surmises rose in his mind, all of which were wide enough of the mark, as our readers may readily enough suppose.

Still he knew it was in vain to go out in search of his friend, since it was impossible for him to guess in what direction he might have gone when they last parted. Susan saw his perplexity, and laughing at his fears, hinted that his wisest plan would be to go into the drawing-room, where he could amuse himself over a glass or two of wine, till the return of Septimus. This suggestion was not thrown away upon our young gentleman, who accordingly hurried up stairs and employed himself in the pleasant manner advised by Susan, and fell into a brown study, from which he was aroused by a thundering rat-tat-tat at the street door, that frightened half the neighbours, and sent poor Susan panting with terror to see what could be the occasion of such a rumpus. Upon this Valentine jumped up and ran to the window, but all he could see were a dozen or two of female heads peeping through the area railings of the houses opposite, whilst at the different drawing-room windows the heads of their mistresses might be seen peering with anxious curiosity, to see what could be the cause of such an unusual noise at the door of their usually quiet neighbour Bramstone. At any other time Valentine would have moralized upon this scene, but even if he had been inclined to do so on the present occasion, it would have been abruptly cut short, for almost immediately afterwards the door was thrown open; and who should enter the room but Mr. Arnold Bramstone, who, hailing our hero with all the familiarity of an old acquaintance, enquired, first, most affectionately after his own health, and then after that of his uncle, at whose absence he expressed, or rather effected considerable surprise.

"I am waiting his return home," replied Valentine; "and indeed was just considering within myself whether it might not be as well to call at your house to enquire whether you have seen any thing of him to-day."

"Why, you don't mean to say the old buffer is absent without leave," exclaimed Arnold, with well-affected astonishment.

"I will not say anything about his being absent without leave," answered Valentine, "because I presume he has a right to do exactly as he pleases without asking any body. That he is not at home, however, you are by this time perfectly aware, and can perhaps quiet my apprehensions by saying where he is likely to be found."

"Well, that's the rummest go I ever heard of," cried the other;—" uncle Sep. has walked himself off it seems, and you expect me to know as much about him, as if we had met together in the course of the day."

"Humph!" retorted Valentine, "perhaps I had very good reason too, for what I said."

"Why as for reason," answered the other, "that, very likely, is best known to yourself. The old file, I suppose, can go out or come in just when he pleases without my having anything to do with the business?"

"I suppose he can," replied Valentine, tartly; "but it happens that a couple of impertinent fellows came here to-day and annoyed Mr. Bramstone in a manner that produced for them both a castigation at my hands, that they will not be likely to forget in a hurry."

"Indeed!" ejaculated the other; "and pray my very good friend what in the name of fortune have I to do with that?"

"A great deal, unless I am very much mistaken in my suspicions," answered Valentine. "They told Mr. Bramstone that they had been sent here by some of his family; and as they turned out to be a brace of mad doctors, I thought it not very unlikely but that you and your father had taken some unfair means to get rid of a relative who was in your way."

"Upon my soul, young fellow, I can't possibly help your unaccountable thoughts," replied Arnold, indifferently. "Uncle Bramstone is a good sort of elderly chap enough, and I dare say will cut up pretty well when he's dead and gone; but as to doing anything to injure him in his lifetime, why its clean out of the question, and not to be thought of for a single moment by any one that has not taken leave of his senses."

"Then you positively deny having any thing to do with the mad doctors as well as with his unaccountable disappearance at this present time?"

"Of course I do; but what made

you think I had anything to do with his absence from home ?"

" To be plain with you," replied Valentine, " I have heard the old gentleman say that both you and your father were jealous at his having taken notice of me—fearing, most probably, that he may leave me a part of that property which you have a right to expect. Now instances have unfortunately been known of persons sending their relatives to a mad-house when they have wanted to secure their money; and since the singular visit of this morning, I cannot help thinking that it is likely enough there has been some unfair play in the present instance."

." Upon my word, sir, I am very much obliged to you for your high opinion of both my father and myself," exclaimed Arnold, biting his lips with vexation.

"If I have wronged you, I shall cheerfully ask pardon for it hereafter," returned Valentine. " So far, however, things look very suspicious, though I certainly cannot bring the matter home without further and far more satisfactory evidence."

Arnold Bramstone appeared to be much vexed at those words, but he knew it would be useless to fly in a passion, as that would only make matters worse. He therefore swallowed his indignation as well as he could, and resolving to put the best complexion upon the matter, said with affected composure :—

, " It strikes me, young fellow, that you have brought rather an ugly charge against two persons you know very little about. It's devilish hard, as you must acknowledge, to have such things said; and I could almost find it in my heart to fly into a passion and challenge you according to the fashion of all persons who rank themselves as gentlemen."

" Which would be very useless, seeing that I have made up my mind never to accept or give a challenge," returned Valentine. " It is for fools to throw away their lives in a ridiculous quarrel; but for my own part, I would sooner be branded with the name of a coward than have to answer hereafter for the blood of a fellow-creature."

" Will you believe me, then, if I deny knowing anything about that which you have just now charged me with ?" asked Arnold with earnestness.

" In the absence of all proof I certainly would," answered Valentine ;—" nay, I will say further, that nothing in the world would afford me more satisfaction than to believe that you are guiltless of the charge."

" Then let your suspicions rest on me no longer," cried Arnold; " for I here solemnly declare that I have nothing to do either with the visit of the two doctors this morning, or with the old gentleman's disappearance now. Nay, for my own part, I think you have needlessly alarmed yourself on his account, for I dare say he is engaged somewhere or other on business, and that he will return home again in the course of the evening."

" Have you any notion where he may be ?" asked Valentine.

" Why that is a matter that is beyond my power of answering," replied Arnold; " but my old dad happens to have a party of his friends to-night, and I shouldn't be at all surprised if uncle Sep. has taken it into his head to drop in unexpected. He's a queer chap sometimes, is uncle Sep. and nobody ever knows what he is going to be up to next."

" Would it appear intruding if I was to accompany you home ?" asked Valentine. " My anxiety must excuse my presumption; but I really should feel much more easy if I could but assure myself that my kind friend is safe from the harm I feared had befallen him."

" Why, for that matter, my old dad will be glad to see you I know," replied the other. " He's a rum 'un sometimes, as you will find out if ever you know much of him, so if you like to go along with me we'll go home, and then afterwards there's a place that I should like to introduce you to, just by way of showing a jokel, like yourself, what queer scenes are to be witnessed in London."

Valentine willingly enough agreed with this proposition, and after waiting a little longer to see whether Septimus returned, he accompanied Arnold towards that part of the town where his father resided.

CHAPTER XIII·

ARNOLD BRAMSTONE LETS VALENTINE INTO A SECRET OR TWO WORTH KNOWING—A CIRCUITOUS ROUTE, AND AN ADVENTURE, IN WHICH OUR HERO TOUCHES THE CONSCIENCE OF A JEW.

WHEN Valentine and his companion left the house, they proceeded down sundry by-streets and lanes till they came to the Angel at Islington, from whence they passed through a number of other darkish-looking places, till they arrived at White Conduit Fields, across which Arnold Bramstone prepared to conduct his rather unwilling companion. In fact Valentine brought himself to a dead standstill, and pointing to the mud through which they had to wade their way, he enquired whether there was no better road by which to reach their place of destination.

" Better road ?" exclaimed Arnold, affecting surprise at his friend's want of confidence in him ; " are you such a coward then as to be afraid of a little bit of mud, when we are almost at the end of our journey."

" Why, as for mud," replied Valentine, " I believe I can make my way over this filthy place as well as yourself, but when I happen to know that there are much better roads to your father's house, I cannot help feeling surprised at your choosing such a one as this appears to be."

" And yet, between ourselves, there's a very good reason for what I am doing," replied Arnold. " The fact is, my dear boy, I happen just now to have a number of mad dogs looking after me, and—"

" Mad dogs !" exclaimed Valentine, " and pray what in the name of fortune do you mean by that ?"

" Creditors," replied Arnold, won-

dering at his friend's simplicity ; " fellows that have the insolence to dun people for a settlement of their accounts, and who would clap an unfortunate chap like myself in a prison with as little remorse as they would condemn a troublesome blue-bottle to death."

" And it is not to be much wondered at either," returned Valentine, " seeing that these poor devils must either go to prison themselves or insist upon their customers paying their bills."

" The fact is, my dear fellow," cried Arnold, " that none of us dashing young dogs ever think about paying bills till the time comes when they can be put off no longer. It's an unpleasant reflection, and only serves as a damper when we ought to be gay and light-hearted ; besides, who ever cares for a vulgar shopkeeper, seeing that the rogues take care to make a good profit of us while they can, and if now and then some of them make a smash of it, why they have a ready way to wipe off all their incumbrances at once, and to become better men than ever."

" And you can laugh at such conduct !" exclaimed Valentine, shocked at the levity of his companion.

" Why, crying would do no good," answered the other, " and as the thing is done every day, why of course there can be no great harm in it. For instance, my dad keeps me short in money matters, and, as a fellow of spirit, it naturally follows that I look out for some other means to keep the game alive."

" Which you do by making other people suffer for your own extravagance ?" observed Valentine reproachfully.

" Psha ! everybody does it," retorted the other with impatience ; " it's a sign of good breeding, my dear fellow, and depend upon it, a man is never so well respected as when he cuts a dash."

" What ! at the expense of other people ?"

" To be sure," answered Arnold ; " man is a selfish animal, and what care I, or any body else, who stands so that the thing can only be done comfortably? However, it don't seem that you and I shall agree very well upon this subject, so suppose we change it for another till you have learnt a few more of our London ways, and then I'll warrant me you will look at these things less squeeamishly than you seem to do at present."

"Not unless I grow so foolish as to disregard the consequences."

"Nonsense!" interrupted Arnold; "what in the name of all that is ridiculous, has a man to do with consequences? Unpleasant reflections should at all times be avoided as long as possible, and then when a man does fall—"

"The consequences are extremely unpleasant!" shouted our hero, bursting into a loud laugh as his companion made a false step, and fell sprawling in the mud through which he had been trying to steer his way, so as not to soil the exquisite polish of his boots. Valentine, however, soon changed his tone for one of commiseration when he saw the plight in which his companion rose from the ground, and then lending his assistance, he endeavoured as well as he could to wipe off the mud with which Arnold was liberally plastered. To this operation his friend submitted with no little impatience, but as the accident had happened there was no help for it, and at last regaining some of his former good humour, he burst forth into such a peal of laughter that Valentine could not forbear joining him in full chorus, till both their sides ached to such a degree that they were fain to stop from utter exhaustion. From this condition Arnold was the first to recover himself, and then affecting to be a little indignant at the merriment of our hero, he exclaimed:—

"Zounds, man, there is not much to laugh at either, in a poor devil slipping down in such a dirty, filthy place as this is! You see what a pretty pickle I am in, and yet there you stand grinning at me like a Cheshire cat."

"And if I do" replied Valentine, "my laughter may be excused, seeing that it was partly provoked by your own merriment on the occasion. Besides, the fault was entirely your own, for had you not come this out-of-the-way road to avoid meeting any of your creditors, we should have been at the end of our journey long ago without any fear of meeting with such a disaster as has now befallen you."

"It's all very well for you to preach," exclaimed Arnold, "but the fact is it might not prove very pleasant to meet one of those fellows, considering that some of them have been ill-natured enough to get execution against me, and if I should happen to be seen, the consequences might prove extremely disagreeable."

"Why, you don't mean to say that you are in immediate danger of being dragged to a prison?" exclaimed our hero in a tone of the deepest concern.

"But I do mean to say so," answered the other;—and what is more there is no doubt but such will be my fate unless my old dad chooses to come down with the ready."

"Which he will do of course rather than see his son the inmate of a jail?" cried Valentine.

"Ah! so you may think, my boy," returned Arnold, "but, between ourselves, I see very little chance of it. The old man is not very rich, you must know, and as my debt happens to be rather heavy, I don't see how he can do the amiable upon the present occasion without making a sacrifice that I cannot very well expect of him."

"But there is your uncle Septimus," observed Valentine, "he has a kind heart I know, and depend upon it he will do all that he can to rescue his nephew from the hands of the harpies of the law."

"Don't mention the old man whatever you do, exclaimed Arnold impatiently; "he is as worthy an old brick as ever lived, but as to coming down with the ready on an occasion like this, I believe it about as hopeless as that I should find compassion among my stony-hearted creditors."

"At all events you might try him,"

replied Valentine, "and as I happen to be a bit of a favourite with him, I will do all in my power to back your petition."

"Damn it, man! don't say any thing more about it," exclaimed Arnold with impatience. "I tell you it would be no go; Uncle Sep. knows what a rattling life I have led, and wouldn't give a sixpence towards saving me from a jail."

"Surely you don't know him as well as I do, or you would not say that of him," cried Valentine. "His benevolence is unbounded, and I am very certain he could not rest in his bed while he knew that any one belonging to him was lying in a jail for the want of his generous assistance."

"Aye, aye, I know he's a trump," replied Arnold, "and that he would not like to see a poor devil like me in trouble. But then you see I have behaved like an ungrateful scoundrel to him, and hang me if I could ask him to put out his hand to serve me even though I might be starving for want of a crust."

"Nay," exclaimed Valentine, "perhaps you are labouring under some mistaken notion. Your uncle has never told me that he thought you ungrateful, and the only thing that seems to vex him in your conduct is that he considers you are more extravagant than your means will allow of."

"If he knew of something I could tell him though," answered Arnold, "his opinion of me would most likely be considerably changed. I have injured him beyond my power of making amends, and——"

"Stop!" exclaimed Valentine interrupting him, "remember, I am almost a stranger to the family, and would therefore rather not hear any of your secrets. There is one thing, however, which I wish to observe, which is that it is never too late to make reparation for injuries; and further, that Mr. Septimus Branstone would be the last man to resent them after he saw that you repented you conduct."

"Would you have me beg his pardon like a cringing slave!" demanded the other with a gesture of impatience.

"By no means," answered our hero, "and yet on the other hand, there is no disgrace a in man acknowledging his errors to those whom his own conscience tells him he has injured."

"I was a confounded jackass to say anything about it," exclaimed Arnold; "if I had kept my own counsel, you never would have known what you very likely guess before this time."

"I guess nothing, and therefore the less you say the better;" answered Valentine, anxious to check the other before he said that, which he might afterwards wish recalled. "To be sure I did at one time fancy that you played some trick or other with Mr. Bramstone, but since I have your most positive denial, of course the suspicion has been altogether removed."

"You no longer believe then, that either myself or my father have done anything to the old gentleman?"

"I sincerely hope you have not," replied Valentine; "because I have fancied there was no cause why you and I should not be very good friends, and I should be very sorry that any thing should arise to disturb the feeling I have entertained towards you during the time we have known each other."

"You don't absolutely hate me then?" cried Arnold.

"Hate you!" exclaimed our hero; "and pray, why should I entertain so illiberal a feeling against one who has never injured me?"

"Ah! there it is!" responded Arnold; "you have been brought up in a very different way to what I have. My old dad can't bear the idea of any one cutting him out of his chance of having a good place in uncle Sep's will, and somehow or other, the moment he heard you were coming up to stay with the old gentleman, he took such a dislike to your very name, that I believe nothing would have given him half so much pleasure as to have heard that the coach had turned over and broken your precious neck."

VALENTINE VAUX,

OR THE

TRICKS OF A VENTRILOQUIST.

BY TIMOTHY PORTWINE.

"Indeed!" exclaimed Valentine with surprise.

"It's a fact, I assure you," replied the other, "and what is more, he took no little pains to make me look upon you as an interloper, that would by and by be living in splendour upon what ought to be mine, whilst I should be left to die a beggar and an outcast."

"And yet you are now taking me to the house of the very man whose hatred I have so unconsciously obtained!"

"Well, and suppose I am," returned Arnold, "what harm is there in that, pray? The old man knows better how to play his cards than to let

you see his petty spite, and I'll answer for it, he will receive you with as much apparent civility as if you were one of his most esteemed friends."

"At any rate you give him the character of being a hypocrite," exclaimed Valentine.

"And if I do, it's only a true portrait I have drawn of him;" returned the other. "He is an artful old chap as ever you would wish to meet with, and would cringe to the very shoe-tie, even to his worst enemy, if he only happened to think anything was to be got by doing so."

"But, as he has nothing to get out of me," replied Valentine, "there is no reason for supposing he will do so great an honour as to confer his gracious favour upon me. For that reason I will defer my visit to him till another opportunity, lest I should have the misfortune to quarrel with the only brother of my best and most esteemed friend."

" Fiddlesticks !—and pray what need you care about anything of the sort ?" exclaimed Arnold Bramstone. " Besides, you forget what you were going home with me for ; recollect yourself, will you, or I shall fly in a passion presently, and if I do, it will not be so easy to calm me again I can tell you :—the old gentleman is perhaps at our house, and if so you can walk home with him you know, and in that manner make up for this dull walk across the fields with a harum scarum fellow that would avoid his creditors."

As he spoke, they turned into a sort of lane that ran direct for the part of town they wanted to go to, and scarcely had they gone a dozen paces when, by the light of the full moon, they saw a Jew clothesman seated on a bank by the side of the lane, and looking over the contents of his bag, which were strewed about in the shape of innumerable articles of clothing which he had collected from various houses in the course of that day's perambulation. As Valentine perceived him, he withdrew Arnold behind the trunk of a tree, and then speaking in a very low tone, pointed out the object which had thus engaged his attention. At this sight Arnold could scarcely forbear laughing aloud, but he was prevented by his companion, who whispered in his ear that if he would be quiet they might have a little amusement at the expense of this swarthy son of Israel.

"Then go it, my boy," answered Arnold in the same subdued tones ; " frighten him if you can, and if you want any assistance, there's a fellow at your elbow that will not be backward in lending his best aid towards sending away this Jew collector of rags and rubbish, a little faster than ever he ran in all his life before."

" Hush !—he will hear us," whispered Valentine, and then pointing with his finger, he continued :—" you perceive where he has thrown his bag over a bush ?—superstition will convince a man of anything, however improbable it may be, and I will see whether we cannot make him imagine that the object now before him is a ghost."

" And it don't look so much unlike one either," observed Arnold, looking towards the place which the other had pointed out. " There seem to be a couple of outstretched arms, and as the moon shines down upon it, the whole assumes pretty much the appearance of an awful apparition."

" At all events the old man does not appear to have noticed it at present," whispered Valentine. " He is engaged, as you see, in rummaging over the cast-off apparel he has collected, and little imagines that a couple of mischievous fellows are looking on with an intention of enjoying a little bit of sport at his expense."

" And that," answered the other, " is about the only thing a Jew will let you enjoy at his expense. So now let's begin, and by way of directing his attention towards the horrible figure he has so unconsciously formed, suppose I give him an halloo to rouse him from his interesting occupation."

" By no means, or you will spoil the sport," returned Valentine ; " he is now deeply engaged in examining the rubbish he has bought in his day's rounds, and if you will only have patience for a few moments, I will make him believe the gaunt-looking figure before him is gifted with the faculty of speech."

This Arnold Bramstone thought not very likely, but yielding to the persuasion of his friend, he listened, and soon a low, sepulchral voice was heard as if proceeding from the place where the imaginary ghost was standing. Upon this the Jew in the utmost terror raised his eyes, and perceiving the horrible figure before him his teeth chattered, and whilst his eyes seemed ready to start from his head, he exclaimed with alarm—

"Avaunt! thou spirit of darkness!—avaunt, I say, and leave a poor old sinner like me to get a living as well as I can by cheating these christian dogs, whenever I can do so without being found out. Leave me, I say, or by Father Abraham I swear I shall never be able to leave this cursed spot alive."

"Thou art an old rogue and deserve no pity," cried Valentine, in the same hollow tones as before, and throwing his voice so that it appeared to proceed from the figure which had so greatly terrified the Israelite. Upon this the old man became more alarmed than ever, and making a feeble effort to rise, he fell rolling among the rags and rubbish which but a few minutes before had been the object of all his thoughts.

"Spare me!" he cried—"spare me, for I am a wicked wretch, and unfit to die till I have had more time for preparation. Grant me but another year and I will promise never to cheat any one again, but will turn my thoughts towards better deeds than those I have been used to commit."

"Ha! ha! ha!" laughed the same hollow voice; "I have watched you through life, thou man of sin, and would have spared thee had I not seen the hardness of thy heart towards all mankind. Of a verity thou art an old and a hardened sinner, and must prepare to go with me."

"Where?" demanded the Israelite in an agony of terror.

"That you will find out soon enough," returned the voice.

"Shall I not rest in Abraham's bosom?"

"Thou wilt rest in a sea of burning brimstone," answered the supposed apparition. "There is a place prepared for thee hotter than all the other hot places put together. In it thou must remain as in a bath, so rise and follow me, for I have many other sinners to visit, though none that are tobe at all compared with thee for diabolical villany. Follow, I say, or I shall seize thee by the hair of thy head, and drag thee to thy place of punishment."

"Mercy!—mercy!—spare me, good Mr. Beelzebub," cried the terrified dealer in worn-out apparel. "That I am a sinner I do confess, but if thou wilt forgive me this time I promise never to do the like any more."

"Old man, thou liest!" exclaimed the voice, as if in a terrible passion. "Thou hast often sworn to lead a better life, and yet, forgetful of all thy vows, thou returnest again to the filthy ways of thy degraded tribe. Again I say unto thee, rise, for I am grown impatient and will no longer brook these delays."

At this moment the wind shook the supposed ghost so much, that the Jew thought he was springing forward to commence seizing upon his prey. Whereupon the son of Israel threw himself upon his knees, and in accents of the greatest terror implored the imaginary apparition to spare him for yet a short time longer.

"And what will thou promise to d if I grant thy request?" demanded the mysterious voice.

"I will do an act of justice towards one who I have long kept in poverty through withholding from him his rights," answered the Jew, trembling in every limb.

"What is the name of the man thou hast wronged?"

"Moses Lazarus, most excellent ghost."

"'Tis well," answered the imaginary apparition; "do justice to the poor man thou hast mentioned and I will never trouble thee any more; but if thou still hardenest thy heart against Moses Lazarus, I will visit thee in thy chamber, and carry thee off to—"

"Don't mention it!" interrupted the Hebrew in the greatest trepidation; "it is an evil place, and rather than pay a visit to it I will pay my neighbour the sum of seven pounds, sixteen shillings and eleven pence three farthings which I have owed to him for the last twelve years."

"And which thou would'st have owed him for twelve years to come if thy conscience had not been pricked to-night by my presence," exclaimed the hollow voice of the ventriloquist. "But the eyes of Beelzebub are upon thee, old man; he is looking out for all such sinners as thyself, and unless the money is paid without delay, thou wilt have another visit from thy foe."

"All shall be as I have said," replied the trembling Jew. "I will hie me home and pay Moses Lazarus the seven pounds——"

"Sixteen shillings and eleven pence three farthings," interposed Valentine though scarcely able to restrain the laughter with which he was ready to burst. "Remember, thou vile old man—the contract must be fulfilled, or we meet again sooner than thou may'st wish to see me."

"It shall—it shall," cried the terrified Israelite.

"On that condition then thou may'st depart," exclaimed our hero, and at the same moment a sudden gust of wind carried the bag from the branches on which it had been suspended, and laid it at the feet of the Jew. This seemed to add to the miracle, but the old man waited for no second bidding, and cramming his scattered garments into the sack, he hastily took his departure amidst the loud shouts of laughter from both our hero and his companion, which, in his terror, he mistook for the triumphant mockery of a whole legion of fiends.

"Poor devil, how he runs!" exclaimed Arnold as soon as he could recover himself sufficiently to speak. "You have frightened him almost out of his wits, and I'll answer for it, Valentine, it would take some trouble to convince him that he has not had the honour of a conversation with one of the powers of darkness."

"At all events it is to be hoped the results of our meeting will be beneficial to the man he has tried to cheat out of his money," answered our hero. "Under the firm conviction that he has seen the enemy of mankind, he will for once in his life do an act of justice, and I shall feel some consolation for the trick I have played him in the certainty of having produced a good effect by it. However, it is

now time that we leave this place, for if your Uncle Septimus should have happened to go to your house, he will leave under the idea that I shall be anxiously expecting him to return home."

"Then onward be the cry," exclaimed Arnold taking the arm of his friend and leading him in the direction which led towards that part of the suburbs of London to which they wanted to go. Luckily they had not much farther to trudge through the lane, and within ten minutes afterwards they once more found themselves in a place where gas-lights and policemen showed that they had again reached a civilized portion of her Majesty's dominions. The Jew and his terrors afforded them a subject for mirth, and laughing heartily at a scene in which they had both played a part, they arrived at the house of Mr. Harry Bramstone. Here, however, they learnt from the servant that nothing had been seen of Septimus, and that her master had been absent ever since the morning without acquainting any body with where he was going. This, as he had company at home, seemed very odd to Valentine, and in an instant the thought struck him that he was in some way or other concerned in the mysterious disappearance of his brother. This notion, however, he kept to himself and following Arnold, he entered the breakfast parlour, where he was requested to wait till his friend had changed his clothes which had been soiled by his recent tumble in the mud. This was a task which occupied some time, but at length Arnold returned, and together they proceeded towards the drawing room.

CHAPTER XIV.

A FAMILY PARTY, AND THE AMUSE-MENT IN WHICH OUR HERO FINDS THEM OCCUPIED—THE MYSTERY OF MR. SEPTIMUS BRAMSTONE'S REMARKABLE DISAPPEARANCE IS STILL UNEXPLAINED—A PRIVATE CON-

FERENCE, IN WHICH VALENTINE
EXHIBITS SOME MORE VENTRI-
LOQUISM.

ON entering the drawing room Valentine found a large party assembled, the generality of whom being engaged at cards, took no notice of his arrival, but went on with their game as if nothing had occurred that required them to leave off their favourite pastime. This was so far fortunate for Valentine, who at all times hated formality, and following Arnold as a guide, he soon found himself seated near Mrs. Harry Bramstone, who, being reminded by her son that a stranger had arrived among them, condescended to look over her spectacles at our hero, smile, and then resume the game as if nothing had occurred which required any further demonstration of civility.

To Valentine, who had been brought up in the quiet seclusion of country life, it was amusing enough to watch the various countenances of the players. He observed the inward satisfaction of those who were winning, and contrasting it with the evident chagrin and mortification of those who were losing, could not help pitying those who through making a business of pleasure so often produced for themselves moments of unnecessary pain. The elderly folks were engaged in all the perplexing mystery of whist—a game which few seemed to understand, though all chose to rate and scold their partners' whenever they could discover what they imagined to be some instance of bad play. This produced endless confusion, the result of which was that every body grew ill-tempered, and growling was heard on every side instead of that good temper that should reign predominant in every case of social intercourse.

At another and a larger table sat a number of younger folks of both sexes enjoying a round game, in which all could talk as much as they liked without interfering with, or marring the amusement in which they were engaged. As is very usual on such oc-

casions, the young ladies chose to enter into partnership with the young gentlemen, whilst the latter—as is also usual—made various sly observations, at which the aforesaid young ladies blushed, and simpered, and hid their faces in their pocket handkerchiefs as if they were really very much shocked at the idea of a temporary partnership, like that leading to one which was to last for life. There was one thing, which it affords us great pleasure to record—the males would not on any account suffer the females to lose—hoping, no doubt, by that means to win their hearts, and perhaps their love—a stake that many others, besides themselves, would be very happy to secure. At any rate there was nothing but good nature to be seen among them, and Valentine looked with delight at the contrast thus presented between the elderlies and the juveniles who were now assembled before him.

From this contemplation his attention was directed towards Arnold Bramstone, who taking the advantage afforded by the termination of a game, was speaking in whisper to his mother, whose eyes were frequently directed towards himself, as if he happened just then to be the subject of their conversation. At last her son approached, and taking a chair seated himself by the side of our hero.

"Well, my boy," he said, "I've been asking the old woman whether she knows any thing about uncle Sep. but it seems he has not been here to-day, and as my worthy dad wondered what the devil had become of him he has gone out too, by way of looking after the lost sheep I suppose."

"This is really very odd," exclaimed Valentine, "and I may add very alarming too. My friend left me but for a few minutes, for the purpose of calling upon some one on business, and from that moment to the present I have not been able either to see or hear any thing of him."

"Well, it certainly is rather singular," observed Arnold after a pause.

"Singular!" exclaimed Valentine, "I call it very alarming. Your uncle is remarkable for the regularity and extreme punctuality of his habits. With him a promise is too sacred ever to be broken, and I therefore cannot but express my surprise that you seem to treat the matter as if it was not really alarming in the highest degree."

"Psha!" cried Arnold, "why my dear fellow, you talk as if you thought I knew where the old gentleman is and would not tell you. The fact is I am stronger in the nerves than yourself, and can wait with all the calmness of a philosopher till time unriddles the mystery."

"But perhaps he has fallen into the hands of some wretch who has a motive for keeping him out of the way," observed Valentine pointedly, and looking hard at the young man to see whether his words had any effect upon him. But Arnold retained his composure, and cramming a huge pinch of snuff up his nose, he merely replied:

"Why, as to uncle Sep. having any enemies, I believe it to be quite impossible, because he happens to be so much respected by every body, that I am sure there it not a soul in the world who would harm him."

"But perhaps there are some, who, for interested motives, might wish to be rid of him," answered Valentine, in a manner as pointed as he could well make it.

"And who do you think is likely to do so?" asked Arnold, endeavouring to conceal his discomfiture as well as he could. "For my own part, I know of no person who would wish to injure uncle Sep. either by word or deed."

"And yet," returned Valentine, looking very hard at his interrogator, "I have one person in my eye who I believe would not stand very nice about trifles when his own interest happened to be concerned."

"Indeed!" replied the other somewhat abashed at the earnestness of our hero; "and who, may I ask, is unfortunate enough to fall under your suspicion?"

"That, at present, is a question that I would rather not answer," exclaimed Valentine, willing to evade the subject as much as possible. "I may be wrong perhaps, after all, in my conjecture, and it would hardly be fair to make a direct charge until I have more certain ground to go upon. There is one thing, however, that I am resolved upon, and that is to commence instant inquiries upon the subject, so that I may as soon as possible clear up a mystery that at present fills me with apprehension."

"What is the young gentleman talking about, my dear?" cried Mrs. Harry Bramstone, rising from her seat and advancing towards her son.

"Nothing that it concerns you to hear," muttered her undutiful offspring; "Valentine Vaux, the gentleman who has this evening honoured us with a visit, has, it seems, lost sight of uncle Septimus, and is a little bit uneasy at not finding him here."

"Oh, is that all?" exclaimed Mrs. Harry Bramstone;—"and pray where did he miss him, my dear?"

"Why, it's a long story to enter into just now," replied her son, "but the fact is they both started this afternoon for a trip to Richmond and back. It seems, however, that they parted company somewhere about Hungerford Market, and as the old gentleman has not been seen since, the young one has taken it into his head that something very dreadful must have happened to him."

"Ridiculous!" exclaimed Mrs. Harry Bramstone;—"your uncle, I dare say, has gone some where or other on some business that he has forgotten, and I'll be bound he has got home again before this."

"Or else he has gone up to Richmond expecting to find his young friend there," observed Arnold. "I dare say when he got to the starting-place and missed his intended companion he naturally enough supposed the vessel had gone, conveying Mr. Vaux with it contrary to his expectation. Upon this he no doubt made up his mind to follow, and perhaps on finding himself in snug quarters at Richmond, he may choose to remain there for a few days."

"Why that certainly appears to be

the best explanation I have heard of the matter," replied Valentine, musing upon the latter suggestion. " Mr. Bramstone may certainly have gone in the expectation of meeting me there, and no doubt his uneasiness will be great when he finds that I am not gone. By jove! I almost feel inclined to take a post-chaise in order to follow him as soon as possible, that I may relieve him of any anxiety he may happen to feel on my account."

" If I were you I should do nothing of the sort," exclaimed Arnold ;— " excuse me, Valentine, but I have more experience than yourself, and something strikes me that it is not very unlikely but what you may find him snug in bed at home when you arrive there. At all events it will be worth satisfying yourself about, and then, even if he should not be there, why it would be easy enough for you to go to Richmond to-morrow morning by the first boat."

" I hardly know what to think about it," replied Valentine, and yet it certainly will be worth while to satisfy myself before I go hunting about on this wildgoose-chase. So I'll e'en take your advice, and, if you will excuse my abrupt departure, I will return home without any further delay."

Now neither Mrs. Harry Bramstone nor her son were very anxious to detain Valentine after the suspicions he had somewhat plainly expressed, and they were just suffering him quietly to depart when the door of the drawing room was suddenly thrown open, and who should enter but Mr. Harry Bramstone, whose outward garments showed that he had gone forth prepared to undertake a journey of some distance. His better-half expressed her surprise at the dirty, filthy state in which he had made his appearance among her company, and she gave him a pretty broad hint that it would be but decorous if he was to go and make himsslf a little bit more decent before he exhibited himself among so many of his friends. But not a bit did Mr. Harry Bramstone heed what she had been saying, for taking her

arm he led her a little on one side, and then placing his mouth to her ear he whispered—" It's all right !" so audibly that Valentine could not help overhearing it.

" Is the old gentleman safe then ?", asked Mrs. Bramstone with extreme earnestness.

" Quite," replied her spouse, " but we had hard work to do it though, I can tell you. The old fool didn't seem to fancy it much, but we managed to do the trick, and by this time he is safely housed in ——"

Valentine could not hear the latter part of this speech, but he now felt quite convinced that what he did hear of it related to his friend Mr. Septimus Bramstone. He was now certain in his own mind that his brother had, for some reason or other, which he had yet to learn, been anxious to separate Septimus from his young friend, and the only thing that now remained for him to do was to discover by whatever means he could, the place to which he had been taken. But this he knew was not to be done without considerable caution, and after thinking the matter over for some time, he asked the old gentleman and his son to oblige him with a few minutes' private conversation.

This request was evidently not very palatable to either of them, but as they could not very well make any excuse, they led him into another room where they had no sooner got him alone than they demanded what it was he wanted with them.

" Why the fact is," replied Valentine, " that Mr. Septimus Bramstone has somehow or other most mysteriously disappeared to day, and having reason to believe you know where he is to be found, I have taken the liberty of seizing the present opportunity of enquiring, in order that my apprehensions for his safety may be satisfied."

" Indeed !" exclaimed the elder of the two gentlemen, " and pray. sir, who gave you permission to take so great an interest in my brother's concern as to make enquiries which I cannot deem otherwise than impertinent ?"

"My own suspicions are a sufficient warrant," replied Valentine haughtily," and your own confusion at once confirms me in the views I have taken of it. I have heard from Mr. Septimus Bramstone that you were jealous of the kind attentions he has been pleased to bestow upon me, and his sudden disappearance was quite enough to convince me that some foul play has been practised against him."

"Really, sir, you are the most impertinent puppy I ever met with," exclaimed Mr. Harry Bramstone;—" not content with coming to my house without invitation, but you must accuse me of committing an action which I should shudder at, and which you have no ground whatever for laying to my charge."

"The fact is, I think there must be some unaccountable mistake, or this gentleman would never have so far forgotten himself as to make so grave a charge without good foundation," interposed Arnold. "As a stranger we should treat him with courtesy, and as for his being in our house, I must excuse him there, since he would not have been here but for my express invitation."

"And if necessary I am quite ready to leave it whenever you may think proper to command me," added Valentine proudly. If I am here it is to look for a friend in whose welfare I take the greatest interest, and for whose safety I would cheerfully lay down my own life."

"Once for all, sir, I tell you we know nothing about my brother Septimus," replied the old man. "He can go out or come home I suppose without my knowing any thing about it, and surely my word ought to be sufficient when I tell you that I know no more about him than yourself, and perhaps not half so much."

"But the words I overheard when you returned home just now must certainly have referred to him," returned Valentine. "I am no paltry listener to private conversation, Mr. Bramstone, but I could not help hearing what you said, and I feel convinced that your business to-day has been to remove him somewhere or other in order that he may not be seen again."

"Upon my word, sir, you appear to have formed a very pretty opinion of me," exclaimed the old man in a towering passion. "You have thought proper to express yourself pretty plainly upon the subject, and now perhaps you will oblige me by saying what you suppose I have done with my brother?"

"Nay, this is a question which is best answered by your own conscience," replied Valentine. "There are, however, various ways to get rid of those we wish to be removed without taking away their life. For instance, I have heard of persons being arrested for fictitious debts and thrown into prison, whilst others prefer sending a relative into a madhouse—particularly if he happens to be a rich old bachelor as is the case with Mr. Septimus Bramstone."

"Is it possible that you can suspect me of doing such an act?" exclaimed the old man with well-feigned indignation; "by heavens, sir, your insolence grows almost insupportable, and therefore you must not wonder if I presently order some of my servants to show you to the door!"

"There shall be no occasion for that," replied Valentine proudly, "for when I have finished the business that brought me here, I shall leave your house without the necessity of any violence being used against me."

"Stay!" exclaimed Arnold interposing;—" you have said that it is not improbable but what Mr. Septimus Bramstone has been conveyed to a mad-house;—perhaps you will have the goodness to say whether you have any sufficient ground for such a cruel surmise."

"The visit of the two mad doctors this morning first served to excite my suspicion," replied our hero. "Their conduct assured me that their presence betokened any thing but a friendly disposition on the part of those who had sent them, and the treatment they received at my hands

VALENTINE VAUX,

OR THE

TRICKS OF A VENTRILOQUIST.

BY TIMOTHY PORTWINE.

was sufficient to engender hatred in the hearts of men who seemed to be actuated in what they did by no other feeling than that of avarice. These men were employed to do extreme dirty work, and they would have done it then had I not thrown one of them from the window, while the other thought himself fortunate in being allowed to escape with his life from the house."

"And pray what right have you to charge me with having sent them to my brother's place?" demanded Mr. Harry Bramstone with pompous consequence.

"Every man, I believe, has a right

to enjoy freedom of thought," answered Valentine. "Circumstances gave me good reason for conjecturing what you are already acquainted with, and now that my friend has disappeared so mysteriously I have thought it nothing more than my duty to use the best means I can for his restoration."

"Nonsense!—why I dare say Sep. is at home, if the truth were known, before this time," answered the elder Mr. Bramstone, willing in any way he could to shirk the question. "For my own part I have no doubt he has been detained somewhere or other by business, and as soon as that is over he will return home in spite of the evil thoughts you have imagined against those who are nearest and dearest to him."

"This is only done to evade me," exclaimed our hero, who saw clearly enough the paltry shiftings by which the person he had accused was trying to divert his attention from the proper channel. "You wish to deceive me for the present, in order that you may afterwards find an opportunity to carry your designs more securely into effect."

"You wrong me, indeed you do," cried the elder Mr. Bramstone, in a milder tone than he had yet used; "my dear brother is quite safe I have no doubt; as you will discover if you have but the patience to wait till you return home."

"Yes, yes," exclaimed Arnold, "you will find that the whole affair is nothing but a mistake; "Uncle Sep. is safe enough I'll answer for it, and I am sure he will bear us out in declaring that no one could have behaved to him with more affection than both my father and myself have always done."

"I hope it may turn out as you have said," answered Valentine, "for if I afterwards discover any unfair dealing towards him you may be assured I will resent it in a manner least expected."

But though Valentine appeared to believe what the father and son had said, he was more convinced than ever in his own mind that some unfair trick had been played off upon his friend. He therefore resolved to try the effects of a little more ventriloquism, and managing his voice so that it seemed to proceed from the kitchen, he exclaimed in a tone of much apparent agony:—

"Help!—help!—for mercy sake get me down!—I'm smothering in this close place, and shall die unless some one will lend me a hand!—help! —help!—help!"

Now this voice sounded so much like that of Mr. Septimus Bramstone, that both father and son started when they heard it, and looking at each other with the utmost consternation, they seemed to ask each other for an explanation of that which appeared to be so alarmingly mysterious. Neither of them, however, spoke, and presently afterwards the same voice was again heard imploring assistance.

"Mercy!—mercy!"—it exclaimed in piercing accents; "save me from these people—they want to drag me to a madhouse, but I have escaped from them, and now I am left to perish miserably by those who ought to be my friends!"

"That's uncle Sep's voice to a dead certainty!" whispered Arnold to his father; "the old 'un has managed to cut his wood and has come here to split upon us."

"I tell you, it can't be," growled the other in his son's ear. "I saw the porters take him away in a coach, and he's safe enough by this time, I'll warrant him."

"Do you mean to say that was not his voice?" demanded Arnold nervously of the old man.

"I mean to say that it was like it," replied Mr. Harry Bramstone, "but then, as I happen to know that it can't be him, why what's the use of saying anything more about it? I tell you he's safe, and that ought to be enough, I think."

"Will nobody help me?" cried a voice up the chimney; but this time the sound was much fainter, and it was pretty evident that the supposed fugitive was either growing much more faint, or else he had struggled to a greater height in his uneasy place of confinement.

"I'll tell you what it is," exclaimed Arnold, desperately seizing hold of a pair of tongs; "the old gentleman has gone mad and has bolted up the chimney. I know his voice, and if we suffer him to perish there, we shall render ourselves liable to be tried for—"

"Nonsense!" interrupted his father impatiently; "the thing is impossible I tell you. Your uncle has not been here I tell you, so how can he have got into the chimney? Besides, even if he should be there, we could not he expected to climb up in pursuit of him."

"No, but I can try whether these tongs will reach him," exclaimed Arnold, snapping the instrument sharply together. "We'll see what's to be done, old 'un, and if we can't bring him down that way, why it will be no fault of ours if he should happen to be suffocated in the chimney."

Saying this, Arnold made a desperate rush towards the fire-place for the purpose of putting his notable design into execution; but for some reason or other his father was determined to prevent him, and seizing his son by the skirts of his coat, he pulled and tugged with so much vehemence, that Arnold was at last obliged to give up his object in despair.

At that moment a yell of triumph was heard from the top of the chimney, and as it appeared that the fugitive, whoe he was, had found means to escape both the father and son seemed to breathe more freely. They then laughed the matter off as well as they could, and never were men better pleased than they were, when they heard our hero express his determination to take his immediate departure.

On the other hand, Valentine was more convinced than ever, that his friend had been unfairly dealt with, by his avaricious relative, but as he was determined not to throw away any chance of finding him, he resolved to pay a visit to Richmond on the following morning, in order that he might satisfy himself whether Septimus had gone there without him or not.

CHAPTER XV.

AN EXCURSION TO RICHMOND IN SEARCH OF A LOST FRIEND—THE ALARM—A MAN OVERBOARD—THE CAPTAIN IN A QUANDARY—VALENTINE MEETS WITH A DANDY, AND PLAYS HIM A TRICK THAT PROVES HIGHLY DIVERTING TO HIS FELLOW PASSENGERS.

After a restless night, Valentine rose on the following morning, and having partaken of a hasty breakfast, he set out for the place from whence the Richmond steam-boats took their departure. As he stepped on board, however, some of his uneasiness was dispelled by the changing scene in which he found himself, and throwing care to the winds for the present, he busily occupied himself in watching the arrival of numerous parties, all of whom were in pursuit of pleasure. Elderly gentlemen with their spouses, young ditto with their sweethearts, squalling brats and scolding nursemaids made up the motley company with whom he was to associate during the voyage from London to Richmond.

At last, by the time the vessel was pretty well filled, a bell rung, and preparations were made for starting. But Valentine, who was always upon the look out for fun, was determined to have some at the captain's expense, and directing his voice towards the stem of the vessel, he shouted out for help, in a tone that made every body declare a man had fallen overboard.

"Boat a-hoy!" cried the captain; "look out sharp there a-head—throw out a rope directly, d'ye hear, or we shall lose one of our passengers before he has paid his fare."

All was now bustle and confusion on board, and at the same time three or four boats put off from shore, and flew with the speed of lightning towards the place from whence the sound came. On arriving there, however, all appeared to be perfectly quiet, and the disappointed watermen were venting their anger at the fool's errand they had come on, when Valentine, shifting his voice to the stern of the vessel, again bawled out lustily for help.

"For Heaven's sake come this way, or I shall perish," he exclaimed; "make haste—make haste, I implore you, or I shall sink from exhaustion!"

Again the watermen exerted themselves to the utmost, and directing their light boats towards the spot indicated they began to look about in every direction, naturally enough expecting a handsome reward if they happened to be fortunate enough to save the life of a fellow-creature. But of course, all their well intended efforts were in vain, and after rowing about from place to place, till they grew heartily tired of useless labour, they all declared " there wasn't no gen'l'man drowning at all," and left the place amidst the jeers of those who had been watching from the shore, and who were consequently aware from the first that it was all a hoax from beginning to end.

The vessel was now making her way up the river in gallant style, but by the time she had passed Vauxhall bridge, our hero began to feel rather dull for the want of a companion to speak to. This trouble, however, he resolved soon to obviate, and having fixed upon the captain as the object of his next joke, he began to turn it over in his mind how he might best carry his intentions into effect. At last, having observed the manner in which he gave his directions to the boy by whom they were transmitted to the engineer, he determined to imitate him and thus occasion all the confusion he could on board. For this purpose, Valentine waited till they had got to a part of the river that was particularly clear of boats and barges, and just when there was the least occasion for giving such an order, he sung out in the well-known voice of the captain.

" Ease her—stop her !"

" Ease her—stop her !" squeaked the boy, and in a minute the vessel was brought to a dead pause.

" What the devil did you do that for, you young villain ?" exclaimed the captain in a towering passion.

" Please, sir, you told me," answered the lad in a whine, that told how surely he reckoned upon a sound threshing on the first opportunity that offered.

" Why, you lying young vagabond, how dare you tell me such a thing ?" roared the captain ; but never mind, my nice boy, we shall get to Richmond by and by, and then see what sort of a quilting I'll give you for daring to say I told you to stop the vessel."

The boy scratched his head and looked unutterable things, for he knew very well that his master always kept his word when he promised him a good hiding, and as the remembrance of the last affair of the kind was still fresh in his mind, he began to think how he might best avoid it on the present occasion. In the midst of his cogitation the order was given to go on, and once more to the gratification of all the passengers, the vessel was again cutting through the waters. Still, however, Valentine was on the look out for more fun, and as a wherry, with a couple of fat old gentlemen, was seen putting off from Barnes, he determined in his own mind to amuse himself and the company, at their expense. On the signal being given by the waterman that he had a brace of passengers to put on board, the captain issued his orders in the customary manner :—

" Ease her—stop her !"

" Ease her—stop her !" echoed the boy, and accordingly in less than a minute afterwards the steamer was lying as still in the waters as a sleeping whale. Upon this all the passengers crowded to one side of the vessel to see who it was that was going to join their company, and while they were thus occupied, and just as the new comers were within a short distance off, Valentine—imitating the voice of the captain, gave the well-known order to " go on."

" Go on !" shouted the boy, and in an instant round went the wheels in the paddle-box, and away went the steamer as if in mockery of the two would-be passengers.

" Why, you confounded young rascal, what do you mean by that ?" exclaimed the exasperated captain, snatching up a rope's end and making towards the lad as if he meant to swallow him up alive. But the boy wisely enough bolted, and dodging amongst the passengers, sought protection in the fore part of the vessel. The other, however, was not to be disappointed when he had made up his mind to trim the jacket of the youth, and rushing after him he would no doubt have carried his intention into effect had he not by some mischance or other kicked against a coil of rope, by which means he was precipitated at full length upon the deck. To describe the scene of confusion that now ensued would be impossible—for whilst the captain roared with anger, the boy blubbered with terror, and the whole of the boat's passengers lifted up their voices with one accord, some taking part with one, and some with the other.

Fortunately, however, order was at last restored, and even the captain, though somewhat injured by his fall, promised to forgive the lad all his past transgressions on condition that he promised never to do so any more. Of course the pledge was willingly enough given, and the lad again resumed his place, though not without certain misgivings that the devil or some of his imps must have got on board the vessel for the purpose of getting him into disgrace with his master. But Valentine pitying his case, resolved not to play him any more tricks—the orders were given with more precision and effect than they had previously been, and as the two stout old gentlemen were at length safely put on board, matters went on smoothly enough for some time afterwards.

Among the passengers to Richmond there happened to be an exquisite of the first water, whose conduct had been so ridiculous—especially towards the female portion of the company—as to call down the reprobation of everybody who had thought it worth while to notice his proceeding. Upon all he thrust his society alike, and in spite of the many warnings he had received from various gentlemen, he continued to annoy the fair sex with so much of his namby-pamby impertinence that several of the younger men had consulted among themselves how they might best punish him for his insolent presumption. Valentine, however, earnestly entreated them to leave the matter in his hands, promising if they did so, that they might afterwards assist him in any way they thought. proper. Upon this understanding our hero placed himself near the dandy, and entering into conversation with a person next to him—and who understood the motive of his question—enquired whether he had heard of the dreadful explosion that had taken place on board one of the Richmond steamboats on the previous day, in which all the passengers and crew lost their lives. This bait took exactly as had been desired, for no sooner did the exquisite overhear what he had said, than, without waiting for the reply of the person to whom it had been addressed, he hastened up to Valentine, and in a drawling manner enquired whether the story he had just been relating was indeed true."

" True !" exclaimed Valentine with astonishment—" is it possible any one can doubt it when all the morning papers are full of the horrible catastrophe ?"

" Dear me, how excruciatingly shocking!" cried the terrified dandy, growing pale with affright.

" Very shocking indeed !" exclaimed our hero, well pleased to see that his plan was likely to take so successfully. " The vessel, my dear sir, was blown to atoms, and as for the crew and passengers, not one of them has been found yet except a black boy, who swam ashore by means of a hen coop."

" Dreadful !" exclaimed the exquisite; "and prad, friend, what account does he give of the melancholy transaction ?"

" No account whatever," replied Valentine, " and no wonder either, seeing that he died as soon as they got him to the nearest public-house. Besides, it is supposed that he could not speak a word of English, so that even if he had lived there would not have been much chance of his telling how the thing happened."

" How demmed shocking to be sure !" stammered forth the terrified dandy; "but I've heard that all steam-boats are very dangerous things to travel in."

" Especially these Richmond boats," returned Valentine, who began to enjoy the increasing alarm of the other.

" Eh !—let me understand you rightly, sir," exclaimed the dandy;

" why are the Richmond steamers worse than any others?"

" For a very good reason," answered Valentine; " they buy up all the crazy old vessels they can for this trip, and now that one of them has taken it into it's head to blow up, I should not wonder if the whole lot of them follow it's example without much delay."

Valentine thought there could be no great harm in uttering this libel because he was well aware that every body about him would understand that what he said was only meant as a joke to frighten the exquisite. Nor was he mistaken in his calculations, for no sooner did the simpleton hear the very probable suggestion that all the Richmond steamers would most likely blow up one after the other, than his countenance became deadly pale, his teeth chattered, and he appeared to be ready to faint. Still, however, Valentine was determined to have his joke out, and seeming to address himself to those about him, he said :—

" For my own part gentlemen, I shall be heartily glad when we get to our place of destination, for I was once blown up in a steamboat, and that once, as you may suppose, was quite enough for me."

" And yet you are now alive to tell us so !" exclaimed the astonished dandy.

" Aye, but I had a squeak for my life though,' answered Valentine, with as much gravity as he could assume ; " I was blown up to an immense height I remember, but how I came down again I quite forget."

" I'm demmed but you must have a good memory then," exclaimed the dandy, to whom this exaggeration was a little too much.

" Nay, if you doubt my words, sir, I have done," cried our hero ; " what I have told you is a melancholy fact, and the man who dares doubt it, must be prepared to settle the affair in another way."

" Pon honour I meant nothing by it," returned the other, to whom the idea of a hostile meeting was any-thing but pleasant. " I was merely observing that you must have a surprising memory to recollect being blown up into the air,"

" And yet that is not more surprising than the fact of my recollecting the circumstances immediately preceding the explosion."

" Was there any sort of warning given, then ?" asked the exquisite with increasing curiosity.

" Aye, and one that was not very well to be mistaken," answered Valentine with all due solemnity ; " first of all we heard a low rumbling beneath the deck—then there was a spitting and whizzing as if a whole legion of devils had been let loose upon us—and then, all of a sudden, came a crash that sent us flying through the air as if we had been so many witches on their broomsticks."

The dandy was all amazement at this description of the catastrophe, and while he was heartily wishing himself safe on shore, Valentine, by his peculiar art, imitated the various sounds he had just been describing. Upon this the persons by whom he was surrounded, and who very well understood his drift, set up a loud shout of terror, while the ladies, who really supposed there was some danger that they were not exactly aware of —chimed in with a scream that put a finishing stroke on the dandy's terrors. In a moment he slipped off the stool upon which he had been sitting, and resting his head upon it as on a pillar, he groaned aloud in expectation of the awful explosion that was to carry him through the air. This was the very climax to which Valentine wished to bring matters, and no sooner did he see the plight he was reduced to, than hurrying away in search of the steward he quickly returned with a bucket of water, the whole contents of which he, without ceremony, threw into the face of the unfortunate exquisite. Nor did his punishment end here, for several of the passengers who also owed him a grudge, took advantage of paying him off now, and within a minute about a dozen buckets of water had been thrown over the simple fellow, whose own conduct had pooduced so disagreeable a retaliation.

This done, he was carried into the cabin, where the steward with praiseworthy zeal, set himself the task of recovering the dandy from the plight to which he had been reduced. This done, he—on a promise of an ample reward—lent him some dry linen and a suit of clothes about big enough for three of his size, and which had not, like his own, the advantage of having been cut by one of the fashionable London snips. In fact the transformation was as ridiculous as can well be imagined, and no sooner therefore did he once more exhibit himself on deck, than a loud peal of laughter saluted him from every side. This was more than the unfortunate devil could stand, and starting back abashed, he again retreated to the cabin, from which he did not again emerge until his own clothes were sufficiently dry to effect another change in his person.

The punishment to which this puppy had been subjected was highly approved of by the generality of the company on board, though candour compels us to admit that there were three or four who thought our hero had gone a great deal further than he ought. But it must be remembered that the exquisite had rendered himself particularly obnoxious to the females on board, and since he was too contemptible for any other punishment, it must be allowed that he met with no more than he deserved for his insolent conduct.

In a short time after the completion of this adventure the vessel arrived at Richmond, where Valentine landed, and immediately commenced making inquiries in different parts of the town in order to learn whether any person whose description answered to that of Mr. Septimus Bramstone, had lately arrived there.

CHAPTER XVI.

HOW VALENTINE PROCEEDED WHEN HE ARRIVED AT RICHMOND, AND THE AGREEABLE FRIENDS HE THERE MET WITH—MR. BARNABY BUBBLE AND HIS ESTEEMED ACQUAINTANCE TIMOTHY TWIGHT—A STROLL, AND THE PLEASANT ADVENTURE THAT FOLLOWS—THE MIDNIGHT VISITATION, IN WHICH VALENTINE EXHIBITS HIS POWERS AT THE EXPENSE OF HIS NEWLY FOUND FRIENDS.

THAT Richmond is a very delightful and romantic place everybody must allow, but we much question whether Valentine was particularly enchanted with its scenery, seeing that he was too much occupied in searching for his friend to take any notice of prospects that seldom fail to fill the mind of the spectator with admiration. But, as we have said, his inquiries proved fruitless, and when every other chance of finding Mr. Septimus Bramstone had failed, he bethought himself of calling upon one Mr. Barnaby Bubble, of whom he had heard the old gentleman make honourable mention, and from whom our hero thought he might at least obtain advice as to the best means of prosecuting his search.

By dint of inquiry Valentine soon found out the residence of the person he was so anxious to see, and having knocked at the door, he learnt to his no small satisfaction that Mr. Bubble was at home—a piece of intelligence that was no sooner ascertained than a polite invitation was sent, declaring that the person he had come to visit would be happy to see him immediately in the drawing room.

Nor was Valentine long in obeying a mandate so agreeable to his own wishes, and following the servant across the hall, he soon found himself in the presence of a remarkably good-tempered looking old gentleman who rose to welcome him with much cordiality, and immediately afterwards introduced him to his friend, Mr. Timothy Twight, an equally good-tempered, middle-aged man, who just at that moment happened to be busily occupied in looking over his fishing tackle, which was lying strewed about him in a state of the "most admired disorder." This ceremony over, Barnaby inquired after his friend Septimus, whose mysterious disappearance caused him to entertain rather alarming notions, more particularly when our hero mentioned the suspicions he had formed that the old gentleman had fallen into a trap that had been laid for him by his relatives.

"Gadzooks! but I am more than half inclined to be of your way of thinking," exclaimed Bubble, thrusting his spectacles up to his forehead, and throwing himself back in his chair in a meditative posture. "His brother, Harry, is a rum sort of customer to deal with I know, and if he has been playing off any of his deep laid schemes, it would be all up to a certainty."

"Pish! what the devil are you talking of Barnaby?" cried the good-natured Mr. Twight; "can't a man make himself scarce for a day or two, but what we must conjure up a thousand queer notions at once?"

"Aye, aye," retorted the other, "but you don't know those mischief-working Bramstones as I do. There's Harry himself that would be a match for the devil — nor is his son, Arnold, much better, and as for their two wives, I believe there are not such brimstone tartars to be found anywhere else throughout her Majesty's dominions."

"Nonsense, man!" exclaimed Timothy—"I know something of them as well as yourself, but, though it must be confessed they are rum 'uns, it would be hard to condemn them without some stronger ground for doing so. Who knows but what our friend Septimus has met with some accident, or, which is equally likely, that he has taken a sudden notion into his head, and gone off somewhere or other into the country."

"Why, London is a strange place to be sure," observed Bubble, and it must be admitted there is no accounting for the accidents a man may meet with in the course of a day's walk. For my own part I don't very often trust myself there, or there's no knowing how soon a hue and cry might be raised for my discovery."

"I should not think so much of Mr. Bramstone's absence," replied Valentine, "if it was not for the antipathy I know his friends happen just now to entertain against him. In fact, their spite would lead them to any lengths, and, though my opinion may appear an ill-natured one, I feel certain that some unfair trick has been played upon my generous benefactor."

"And pray, young gentleman, what opinion may you have formed upon the subject?" asked Mr. Barnaby Bubble, with an expression of curiosity that he could not conceal.

"My opinion is one that is likely enough to turn out correct," answered Valentine;—"during the short time I have had the honour of receiving the kindness of Mr. Septimus Bramstone, I have seen sufficient to convince me that I am an object of especial hatred to his brother; he is envious of the kindness that has been showered upon me, and in fact there is but little doubt but what he believes it possible I may come in for some share of that property which he is so eagerly looking for."

"Humph!" grunted Mr. Bubble, placing his thumbs in the arm-holes of his waistcoat and looking as big as bull beef.

"You seem to have a different opinion to that which I have formed," cried Valentine with the evident disappointment which men exhibit when they find that their own favourite theories are likely to be shaken down.

"Why, I must say it does appear to me that you have formed rather a hasty conclusion," returned the other. "Harry Bramstone is not a man after my own heart, but, as the old saying goes—give a dog an ill name and hang him; now for my own part, I like to weigh these matters fairly: so, before we go any further in this matter, perhaps you will have the goodness to answer one or two questions?"

To this very reasonable request Valentine could of course have no objection, and bowing his head slightly, he waited with what patience he could

VALENTINE VAUX,

OR, THE

TRICKS OF A VENTRILOQUIST.

BY TIMOTHY PORTWINE.

for the examination he was about to undergo.

"In the first place," began the old gentleman, "you have said that your presence has occasioned some jealousy among the relatives of my friend— perhaps you will have the goodness to state what grounds you have for the assertion ?"

"From the lips of Mr. Septimus Bramstone himself," replied our hero; "he has made no secret of his suspicions in the matter, and if that were not enough I have myself witnessed their strange conduct on more occasions than one."

"I say, Barney," interposed Timo-

thy Twight — "that's coming to the point, I think, so if you have done with your examination, let us give up this dry subject, and take the walk we were proposing just before this gentleman's arrival."

"When I have done," replied Mr. Bubble, with all the dignity of a justice of the peace, and then once more addressing himself to our hero, he continued:—"Well, Mr. Vaux, you have stated your grounds of suspicion, and now I should like to know what you imagine has been done with your friend ? We have no bravos to hire in England you know, as they have in some foreign places, so that poor

Septimus is probably in the land of the living."

"If we have no bravos," replied Valentine, "we have at least people enough who would not be very nice to a shade or two, when a reward is held out for their acceptance. Besides, we have such places as private mad-houses, and within a very short time from the present, we have seen that men are sometimes conveyed to them through the artifices of their relatives, whom self-interest has induced to the perpetration of a crime that ought to be visited with the severest punishment."

"Dear me!" exclaimed Mr. Timothy Twight," you don't mean to say that our friend Septimus has been taken to a mad-house?"

"I am afraid there is but too much reason to believe it."

"Explain yourself, my dear sir,—have the goodness to explain yourself," cried Bubble anxiously.

"Well then, sir, yesterday morning Mr. Septimus Bramstone was visited by a couple of persons, who we afterwards discovered to be mad-doctors——"

"Mad doctors!" shouted Timothy with alarm.

"Aye," answered Valentine, "or perhaps I should rather have said doctors who make it their profession to cure madness."

"Oh! then the fellows were not actually mad themselves?"

"Certainly not," replied Valentine smiling at the simplicity of the other, "but their conduct was so insolent that I was obliged to interfere in order to protect my friend. In fact —after fair warning had been given —I was compelled to pitch one of them out of the window, whilst the other was very glad to effect his escape by scampering down stairs *minus* his hat, and one of the tails of his coat."

"Ha! ha! ha! shouted both the old gentlemen, and one peal of laughter succeeded another, till Valentine was obliged to join in it himself by way of keeping them company. At last, on order being once more restored,

Mr. Bubble was forced to admit that his visitor had some cause for the suspicion he had entertained, but at the same time he gave it as his own opinion that the whole affair would turn out less serious than had been anticipated, and that the speedy return of Septimus would put an end to all doubts, and clear up the mystery. Even Valentine began to be convinced that he might be labouring under an error, and yielding to the earnest solicitations of his host, he at last consented to pass the remainder of the day with him, and to sleep that night at his house under a promise that he would return to London early on the following morning in case of Mr. Septimus Bramstone should not make his appearance at Richmond in the mean time. This arrangement being made, a lunch was brought in, and the three gentlemen having made a meal that would well have served for a dinner, rose from their seats with the determination of taking a walk, by way of producing an appetite for the good things that would be ready against they returned home.

Of course their steps were directed towards the far-famed Richmond Hill, when Valentine discovered a number of cockneys, many of whom he recognized as his late fellow-travellers. These were scattered in various groups —but all of them were seated upon the grass, and before each party was displayed, the goodly fare which they had providently brought with them by way of adding to their creature comforts. Presently a loud shout of laughter was heard from one of the parties, and on looking towards the spot, Valentine discovered an interesting looking young man in white duck, who had been tripped up in a lark, by one of his companions, and who had stumbled most unfortunately for himself and his friends into a huge currant and raspberry pie that had been ranged upon the ground along with a charming variety of other delicious viands. The unfortunate devil sat, unable to help himself out, and unaided by his friends whom excessive laughter had deprived of all power to rush to his assistance. Valentine, however, pitying his case, was just hastening forward, but at that juncture, the particularly interesting-looking young man overbalanced himself, and away he rolled down the hill, followed by the aforesaid pie, which latter, after bounding and rebounding several times to the great delight of the by-standers, at length plunged into a ditch at the bottom, at the very same moment that the interesting-looking gentleman was deposited in the mud with which it was half-filled.

As may naturally be supposed this little event caused no small amusement to the spectators; but not so was it with the principal actor in the scene, who, after extricating himself from his very unpleasant predicament, rushed down a bye-lane, and, like Monsieur Tonson—" ne'er was heard of more."

Having witnessed the termination of this little episode our party proceeded onwards, but scarcely had they gone a hundred yards when Valentine perceived approaching an old gentleman and his daughter, who he had particularly observed that morning on board the steamer. As they passed our hero bowed respectfully to them, a salutation that was returned with even more courtesy than, as a stranger, he had expected. Now, Valentine had particularly observed the young lady in the course of their short trip and being greatly struck with her beauty and modesty, he had more than once thought what a happy fellow he should be with such a woman for a wife. His adventure with the exquisite had, however, for a time put these notions out of his head, but the sight of her again revived them, and turning round, he stood gazing upon her sylph-like form as it gradually receded from his view.

"Aha!" exclaimed Timothy Twight, "are your thoughts that way young gentleman?—are you already smitten by the bright eyes of the little divinity that has just passed us?"

"By Jove! you are right, sir," ejaculated Valentine; "she is indeed a divinity, and one that I could almost find it in my heart to worship. But, perhaps, you are acquainted with her and can inform me whether she is a resident in this place or not?"

"Psha!" exclaimed Bubble, "why you don't mean to say you have fallen in love at first sight?"

"And if I have," cried Valentine, "is it very much to be wondered at? Did you ever see so beautiful a countenance, so——"

"Stay, stay, stay," interrupted Bubble, "I am an old bachelor, thank heaven, Mr. Vaux, and never professed to be a judge of beauty in my life. Not but what she is a nice young creature, I dare say—only to my notion, matrimony is a sort of purgatory, and therefore I would advise all my friends to look well before they make the fatal leap. I never fell in love, Mr. Vaux—never so far forgot myself I assure you, and yet between ourselves, there's not a jollier nor a happier old dog than I am, from Land's End to John O'Groat's house."

"Perhaps so, sir," answered Valentine impatiently, "but perhaps you never had an opportunity of obtaining the hand of such a girl as that we have just now passed?"

"Ah! that's always the way with you young fellows," exclaimed Barnaby Bubble; "everything must be done upon the spur of the moment, and because you happen to have seen this young creature once, you must fall head over ears in love with her. But it won't do, Mr. Vaux—it won't do, I tell you—her father watches over her like an old dragon, and woe be unto any foolish fellow that tries to be making love without first of all obtaining his consent. D'ye hear, Mr. Vaux—without first obtaining his consent."

"You know the young lady and her father then?"

"Only through having seen them down here very frequently," replied Mr. Bubble. "This seems to be a favourite resort of their's, and people about here do say the old man is pretty rich—so that I suppose he wants to keep her out of the way of the numerous fortune-hunters that are no doubt looking for so fair a prize."

"Do you know their name?" asked Valentine eagerly.

"I do," replied Barnaby, "and so I suppose you do; but have a care my friend, or you may love your heart without any probability of gaining the young lady's hand."

"Really, sir, you mistake me," cried Valentine, endeavouring to laugh away the notion. "The young lady is certainly very pretty, but it does not follow that I have fallen so desperately in love as you seem to imagine. The fact is, I fancy her father and I have met before, and I merely wished to know his name."

"Oh! if that is all, I can enlighten you," replied Mr. Bubble; "the old gentleman's name is Stanley—a retired merchant whose fortune is said to exceed a plum."

"And what is more," interposed Timothy Twight, "his daughter, Miss Angelina, is his only child; she will inherit every farthing—and, of course, will marry no one under the rank of a nobleman."

Valentine was romantic enough to wish she had been the daughter of a beggar, but as he saw which way the opinions of his two companions went, he wisely resolved not to say anything more upon the subject at present. He, therefore, very dexterously changed the conversation to another current, and shortly afterwards they returned to the house of Mr. Barnaby Bubble, where dinner was already waiting their arrival.

As for Valentine, he was never more lost in thought in his life, than during the meal that followed, nor would he have been easily roused from the visions in which he indulged, had it not been for the jokes passed upon him by the two elderly gentlemen, who of course attributed his reserve to the sight he had obtained of Angelina Stanley. On this account he constrained himself to be gay, and resolving to seek another opportunity to see her, he soon entered with zest into the conversation that ensued over a few bottles of Mr. Bubble's wine. In this manner the remainder of the day passed away, and when night came, according to a previously understood arrangement, Valentine retired with Mr. Timothy Twight, whose chamber being furnished with a couple of beds, would, of course, afford accommodation to both gentlemen.

And now having snugly popped himself between the sheets, Valentine began wickedly enough to ponder over in his own mind how he might best amuse himself, at the expense of the worthy Mr. Twight. Nor was he very long in arranging a little practical joke, which he only delayed until the other had taken possession of the opposite bed. This done, Mr. Timothy Twight expressed his certain conviction ___ should enjoy a delightful ni___ ___ then snuggling himself ___ ___es, he prepared to ___ ___ ___ the arms of Mo___ ___ Valentine had determ___ ___ ___ould bring no balm to ___ Timothy, a___ ___ s___ ___ begin to d___ ___ his nasal organ, ___ ___ ___ being just off, than our ___ ___ raising himself in bed, ___ ___ crowing of a cock with so much success, that the sleeper starting up, began to "hish!" and clap his hands with all his might, in order to frighten the supposed source of his annoyance away.

"Bless my soul, Mr. Vaux, did you hear that?" exclaimed Timothy, with evident chagrin;—"did you hear that infernal cock, Mr. Vaux?" he repeated, as our hero gave a tremenduous snore; and then finding that no notice whatever was taken of his question, he grasped a pillow, and threw it with all his strength at the head of Valentine. But the other continued to snore on, until all was quiet again, and then imitating the cackling of a hen, he soon drew forth once more the hearty maledictions of his irritable companion.

"What the devil have we got in the place now?" he exclaimed waspishly.

" Tuck—tuck—tuck—tuck—tuck-a-roo !" repeated Valentine, in the sharp tones of a hunted fowl, whereupon the anger of Mr. Timothy Twight waxed warmer and warmer, and at last, leaping out of bed, he threw open the window and began hunting about the room for the purpose of driving the noisy creatures from his presence. But the more he bustled about the place the more clamarous became the supposed intruders, and at last, seizing hold of the first thing which come to hand—which happened to be his breeches—he commenced battling about right and left with such vigour, that Valentine was forced to throw himself under the clothes to avoid the awkward hits that otherwise would have fallen thickly upon him. This caused a temporary cessation of our hero's mischief, and as all seemed tolerably quiet, the unfortunate Timothy began to think he had succeeded in getting rid of them. At this moment, however, Valentine threw his voice toward the window, and imitating the shrill clarion of a cock, he raised such a clatter that poor Twight started back in dismay, as if some horrible apparition had at the moment appeared to fright him with its presence.

" Mr. Vaux !—for heaven's sake, wake up, sir !" he exclaimed ; " don't you hear that we have got the whole farm-yard in the room, and unless you help to drive them out, there'll not be a bit of sleep for neither one nor the other of us."

No answer, however, was returned to this affecting appeal, and again was Timothy Twight compelled to throw the first thing he could lay hold of, at the head of his companion.

" Are you deaf or dead, Mr. Vaux ?" he exclaimed pettishly.

" Y-a-a-w !—neither the one nor the other," pretending to wake from a sound sleep ; " but what the deuce are you about, sir ?" he continued, with affected surprise —" for what has the window been thrown open, and why, in the name of fortune, do I see you walking about in your night shirt like a madman ?"

" A madman !" exclaimed Timothy ; " and if I am a madman, I've suffered enough this night to make me so. We've got a cock and his whole seraglio in our bed-room, and if you don't give me your assistance to drive them out, we shall neither of us be able to get a wink of sleep to-night."

" Nonsense ! you are dreaming, my good sir," replied Valentine.

" I tell you, I have not so much as closed my eyes !"

" Psha ! you only fancy so," answered our hero—" it's nothing but the night mare, I tell you, so shut the window and go to bed, for all is quiet enough now, as you must be convinced."

" Well, this certainly is the rummest start I ever heard of !" cried Timothy, as he slammed to the window, and then gliding across the room, he was just going to step into bed again, when his ears were once more assailed with the most discordant noises.

" Ough !—ough !—ough !—week ! week !—week !—grunted and squalled what appeared to be two or three hogs under the bed into which he was just stepping. Upon this, Timothy made a desperate effort, and leaping upon his couch, he lean't over and threw his boots, and whatever other articles he could find, after the imaginary authors of his broken rest. Every now and then as he did this, the missiles seemed to hit those they were intended for—for a louder grunt was given, and immediately afterwards their most sweet voices were heard in quite a different part of the room."

" D——n them ! they shall not have much rest here to night, any how !" exclaimed Timothy, with a grin of malicious pleasure as he thought of the retaliation it was in his power to bestow for his own disturbed slumbers. " The vagabonds have tormented me enough, and now I'll wait patiently till day break, and then let 'em look out for pepper, that's all !"

Valentine could hardly forbear laughing outright at the vehemence with which this was uttered, but his game was not yet over, and waiting till his companion was a little quiet, he once more threw his voice underneath Timothy's bed, and gave utterance to a loud—"Quack !—quack !—quack !"

"Oh, you pretty dears; I'll *duck* you by-and-bye, for all this, depend on it !" exclaimed poor Twight between his clenched teeth, and then jumping upon the floor, he crawled on his hands and knees under the bed in search of the objects of his wrath. But, of course, his heroism was exerted in vain, and coming forth once more, he threw himself again between the sheets in a fit of despair, wondering what uproar would next rouse him to renewed exertion. Over and over again did he curse his own restlessness, and envy our friend Valentine for the perfect unconsciousness with which he seemed to pass the night, and every now and then he tried to wake him up, merely because he happened to think it was rather too bad that one should have all the sleep to himself, while the other was tossing about like a ship in a storm.

Fortunately for him, however, matters now passed off a great deal more quietly, for though an occasional grunt was now and then heard, it seemed pretty evident that the imaginary pigs, like himself, were trying to court repose, and being heartily tired of his exertions, he wisely resolved to say nothing more about it at present, but to wait quietly till the morning when he could take such terrible vengeance on the disturbers of his peace, as the magnitude of their offences deserved. With this amiable resolve, he at length fell into a profound slumber, from which he did not wake till the beams of the morning sun were shining full upon him.

Now Valentine, who had been some time awake, was resolved the matter should not end here, and no sooner had Timothy leaped out of bed to examine every corner of the room in search of the noisy brutes who had kept him so long awake, than pretending to have just opened his eyes he enquired, in a tone of the most perfect innocence, what he was doing.

"What am I doing?" retorted the other in no very good humour, "why looking for those infernal devils, to be sure, that kicked up such a clatter here all night."

"What clatter do you mean?" asked Valentine with affected surprise.

"Why you don't mean to say you didn't hear it as well as myself?" cried the other turning round and regarding him with astonishment. "This room has been a scene of perfect confusion all night long;—the whole poultry yard has been here on purpose to deprive me of my natural rest;—first of all came a cock with about a dozen hens, crowing and cackling like so many born devils as they are; then followed I know not how many pigs, and by way of finishing the concert, a tribe of ducks joined in with their quack, quack, quack, till I was nearly driven to madness."

"My dear sir there must be some mistake in this," observed Valentine with as much gravity as he could assume; "you must have been troubled with dreams, or I, of course, should have heard something of it."

"Am I awake now?" demanded Timothy pettishly.

"I should most decidedly say you are," replied Valentine, "but it does not follow you have been so all night; besides, the room is quite clear now, as you may perceive, and as the door and windows are all closed, it is not possible that anything can have got in or out of the place."

"By Jupiter! it must have been a dream then I suppose," answered Timothy, scratching his head and looking as if he was not above half convinced;"—"and yet if it was a dream I never saw anything so natural in all my life. However, as every thing seems to be against me, I shall knock under for ever, so let us say no more about it, my boy; and, above all things, don't let Bubble know any thing what has passed, or I shall never hear the last of it as long as I live.

Valentine promised that not a word should drop from him upon the subject, and having dressed themselves they went down stairs, where they found their friend waiting their arrival to begin breakfast. The conversation then turned once more to the mysterious disappearance of Mr. Bramstone, and as our hero began to grow more and more uneasy, he shortly afterwards took leave of his friends, and hurrying on board the steamer, was once more on his way back to London.

CHAPTER XVII.

THE MYSTERY OF MR. SEPTIMUS BRAM-
STONE'S DISAPPEARANCE IS UN-
RAVELLED.—A SCENE IN A HACK-
NEY COACH AND THE STARTLING
DISCOVERY THAT TAKES PLACE.—
ARRIVAL AT THE LUNATIC ASYLUM,
AND THE DESPERATE RESISTANCE
OFFERED BY SEPTIMUS TO HIS PER-
SECUTORS.

But we must now leave our hero for the present, and return again to Mr. Septimus Bramstone, who we saw so unceremoniously handled by a couple of keepers, and hurried into a coach against his will. Terrified as he was at first, he seemed to loose all power of speech, but at last exerting himself as well as he could, he enquired of the man who sat next to him the reason of the violence that had been used against him, and whither he was going to be taken.

" Wot's that to you?" growled the ruffian;—" we've got hold on you, and that's enough, so make yourself easy and go quietly, or I'm blessed if I don't make you."

" Villains! you shall both suffer for this depend on it," exclaimed Mr. Bramstone fiercely. " You have deprived me of my liberty, and if there's law to be had in the country I'll follow you up, even though it be to the gallows !"

' What'll you give us if we tell where you're going to?" asked the man who had not previously spoken.

" Nothing," replied Septimus, " because I can pretty well guess what you are about to do with me. This is some vile plan to throw me into a mad-house, but who can have been the instigator to so infamous an act I have at present no means of ascertaining."

" And wot's more, old fellow, you never will," exclaimed the principal keeper, laughing at what he conceived to be a capital joke; " we always does these here things upon the sly, and when we grabs a chap like you, depend on it the game's up as safe as bricks."

" Why am I taken to such a place as that?" demanded Septimus.

" Come you're mad, to be sure," replied the other, "and it aint proper that mad people should be at large."

" 'Tis false !" exclaimed Mr. Bramstone : " I am not mad, and my persecutors, whoever they are, knows that I am not."

" Ah!" retorted the man, "that's always the case; mad folks never allow that they are so, and of course it aint likely you'd own to it old boy."

" This conduct of my enemies is enough to make me so," replied Septimus passionately; " but I will yet find out who they are, and then let them beware, for they shall find me a foe not easily to be appeased."

And as he said so he seized one of the keepers by the throat with the intention of endeavouring to effect his escape, but the effort was a vain one, for the other ruffian immediately threw himself forward to the assistance of his comrade, and by their united efforts their unfortunate victim was soon compelled to relax his hold.

" Now I'll tell you what it is, old gentleman," exclaimed the man who had been attacked; " you're not doing yourself no good whatsomdever, 'cause you see we're two to one, and moreover than that we've got a pair of bracelets here that, when once they are fastened round your wrists, will make you as tame as a lamb. Not as we wishes to be rough, you know, only we've got a duty to perform, and it must be done, so that's all about it."

"For the love of heaven, release me!" exclaimed Septimus in accents of despair; "remember the horrible fate that will be mine if ever the doors of a mad-house are closed upon me, and give me that liberty of which no one has any right to deprive me."

"Oh, I dare say you think yourself very hardly used," returned the man, "but there's them that as think it'll do you good, so go you must, and the less row you make about it the better."

"Besides," continued the other fellow, "a mad-house aint sich a wery bad place arter all's said and done. People go there to be cured, and if they only behave themselves pretty decently, why they're sure to come out again some time or other."

"That such will not be my case I feel assured," exclaimed Mr. Bramstone. "This is the trick of an enemy whose design is to get me out of the way, and never shall I know the blessings of liberty again unless some friend should chance to discover my retreat and snatch me from the fate to which I have been doomed."

"Why they does it all for your own good," returned the man, "and yet you're ungrateful enough to grumble about it. For my own part, I think that it'll do you a deal of good, and if you only behave pretty quiet, I shouldn't wonder if our gov'-nor turns you out cured in the course of a few months."

"Months!" exclaimed Septimus; "and is it possible that any human being can endure the torments of a place like that for months?"

"Why lor' bless your silly heart, it's nothing at all when your used to it," replied the fellow;—"there's some on 'em in our place at this time that are as happy as the days are long, and I'll bet a crown there aint one that ever so much as wishes to leave sich comfortable quarters."

"But they, perhaps, are really mad," returned Septimus.

"Why, of course they is,—and so's all on 'em."

"Not all," exclaimed Mr. Bramstone, "for there are, I dare say, many others who have an interest in keeping them out of the way. However, it is useless to talk thus with men hardened and obdurate as you are; I will therefore appeal at once to your sordid feelings by offering a reward for any services you may think fit to do me.

"Why, as for the matter o' that," answered the principal keeper, "we aint above accepting a reward, so, perhaps, you'll have the goodness to say how far you mean to go?"

"Accompany me home, and you shall have fifty pounds for the service," replied Septimus.

"Indeed!" exclaimed the ruffian doggedly, "but as it so happens that we shall have double the money for taking you to our gov'nors house, why of course we can't accept your offer."

"Wretch!" cried Mr. Bramstone, "then for the sake of a bribe you would torture a fellow creature by thrusting him into a place from whence he may never be suffered to depart. However, money shall be no object with me, and if you will return with me to my house, I will give you any sum that your avarice may demand."

"It won't do, Bob," exclaimed the fellow who had hitherto taken but little part in the foregoing conversation;—"the gen'l'man as employed us won't stand no nonsense you know, and as for reward, why I dare say he'll give us as much as this 'un would, when he knows that we refused to take what he's just offered."

"You're quite right, my tulip," answered the other; "we can't do no sich thing not whatsomdever. The old gen'l'man must go with us, and if he can persuade the gov'nor to let him off why that's quite another sort of thing."

"Your governor, as you call him, is, I suppose, as hard-hearted as yourselves," cried Septimus in despair.

"He's a riglar good 'un, he is," retorted the fellow; "and as for

VALENTINE VAUX,

OR THE

TRICKS OF A VENTRILOQUIST.

BY TIMOTHY PORTWINE.

being hard-hearted, I don't think you'll have much to find fault with about that, seeing as how he always treats people according to their means of paying him for civility."

"Well, well," exclaimed the old gentleman, "I suppose my best course will be to take what follows as quietly as possible. I would, however, gladly know to whom I am indebted for this evil turn, and if you think fit to inform me, I have five or six sovereigns in my pocket which shall be at your service."

"Tip 'em up, old boy, and I'll see about it," answered the brute, holding forth his hand, and winking to his companion as much as to say what a flat they had got hold of.

"But do you promise to serve me as I have said?"

"Why in course I will," was the reply.

"Then there is the money,—and now tell me who it is that has set you to the performance of this vile errand.'

"Why your own brother, to be sure.

"Merciful heaven! my brother!" exclaimed Mr. Bramstone, sinking back in the coach and clasping his hands in agony.

"The self same individual," answered the other, pocketting the money with perfect unconcern. "He it was that set us on, and a prime fellow he is, I can tell you, for he rewarded us all handsomely, and we're to have nobody knows how much more when you're safely housed."

"It is false!" exclaimed Septimus vehemently;—"my brother is grasping and avaricious I am aware, but, bad as he is, he would pause ere he committed a crime so foul and unnatural as the one you have basely laid to his charge."

"Well, you ought to know best about it, of course,"returned the man, "but I happen to know that he's the chap what's going to lock you up in a mad-house for life, and if you don't choose to believe it, why it's no fault of mine, that's all I know or care about it."

"It is a lie invented to shield the real perpetrator from the punishment he so richly deserves," cried Mr. Bramstone, unwilling to believe a story so revoltiug.

"Well, it don't matter to me whether you believe it or not," returned the man, "only one don't like to be called a liar when there ar'nt no reason for it."

"I tell you it is impossible," again exclaimed Septimus, "for my brother and I have always been good friends, and nothing I am certain, would ever induce him to so cruel, so unjust an act as that you have accused him of.

"Humph!" retorted the other, "I always thought you mad, but now I fancy we must put you among the incurables in our establishment! Aint your brother,—Harry Bramstone as they call him,—aint he, I say, looking out for your property when you kick the bucket?"

"Very likely he may be," answered the old gentleman, "but he would hardly commit such an act as this when there is every probability of being found out."

"Ah! that shows you don't know much of human natur," returned the fellow. "People don't like to be choused out o' their rights, and when they see a chance of it nobody can blame 'em for trying to take care of themselves."

"But my brother has no reason for supposing he will be choused out of what I possess," replied Mr. Bramstone.

"That I can't know nothing at all about," exclaimed the keeper, "only there's one thing I've hear'd on as is certainly wery prowoking;—it seems you've lately taken a young fellow into your house, and the old gen'l'man, your brother, has taken a fancy into his head that you mean to do more for a stranger than you will for him as is your own flesh and blood, like. So with that ere, he trumps up a story about your being mad, and arter getting a couple o' doctors to sign a certificate, he sends us to pick you up whereever we could find you, and then bolt as fast as ever we could master's lunatic asylum."

"Great heaven! can this be true?" exclaimed Septimus, who was now more than half convinced by the circumstantial manner in which the story had been related.

"True!" retorted the other, "why you don't think I'd condescend to tell a lie about it, do you? Your brother is at the bottom of it all I tell you, and it 'll all appear as plain as the nose on your face before we've had you many days at our place."

"How far off is your house situated?" asked Septimus, trying to get a glimpse from the window in order to discover, if possible, whither it was they were forcing him. But the keeper perceiving his design, held him down upon the seat with all his strength, exclaiming :--

"Come, come, old gen'l'man, this won't do at 'no price, whatsomdever. You must go along quietly, you know, or we shall fall out, and then if I'm forced to put these handcuffs on it 'll be all the worse for you."

"How far are we far from the place you are going to take me to?" asked Septimus shuddering as he thought of the utter hopelessness to which he was now reduced.

"Oh, it aint far off now," answered the ruffian; "it's not above five minutes ride from where we are, so make yourself comfortable, and it 'll all be as right as a trivet by-and-bye."

"I'll not be taken there without an effort to release myself," exclaimed Septimus resolutely.

"You'd better not be rumbustical, old chap, or we'll find a way to take it out of you," retorted the other. "When people won't go quietly you know, there's always ways to bring 'em to book in less than no time."

"Help! help! for heaven's sake help me!" exclaimed Mr. Bramstone, shouting out as loudly as he could, perceiving a number of persons passing along the road. But the keepers were too quick for him, and ere he could make anybody hear, one of them had placed his hand on his victim's mouth, whilst the other in an incredibly short time slipped on him a pair of hand-cuffs to prevent the possibility of any desperate attack being made upon them. This done, one of them struck him a blow in the mouth that made the blood spurt out, and then holding him firmly on the seat, he exclaimed

"What! you thought to bring some one to your assistance, did you?—but it's no go, old fellow. so don't try it on again, that's all, or I may give you another wipe in the frontispiece that you won't get over in a hurry."

"Don't hurt the gen'l'man," interposed the other keeper;—"I dare say it aint very pleasant to be taken off to a mad-house, and if he does try to make his escape, it's nothing more than nat'ral-like, arter all."

"Perhaps you'll hold your tongue, Jim, and only interfere when you're asked," exclaimed his comrade fiercely, "The old man shouldn't have given tongue as he did just now, and then he would not have napped it. Howsomdever, it's all over now, for here we are at home, and jumping out of the coach, and lug him into the house before he has time to make much of a bobbery at the door."

"Why, if he does it wouldn't matter much," answered the other, "for people about here are used to hear all sorts of queer noises, and if this gen'l'man should make a rumpus nobody would think it worth while to come out of their way to see what it all means."

At this moment the coach passed through a gateway, and presently afterwards drew up to the door of a handsome-looking old-fashioned mansion, where the proprietor and three or four ruffian-looking fellows were waiting to receive them. In an instant, the coach steps were let down, and before Mr. Bramstone could defend himself he was dragged out of the vehicle by main force, and carried to the place where the governor was standing. Here he was held by his two tormentors, whilst their master stared impudently in his face, as if to be quite certain that no mistake had been made in the person who was thus brought before him.

"I believe I have the honour of speaking to Mr. Septimus Bramstone?" he said, having with mock formality, and smiling as if the misery of a fellow-creature afforded him the greatest satisfaction.

"You are perfectly correct in your conjectures, sir," answered the old gentleman, "and therefore, as you are now convinced who I am, I demand that liberty of which I have been most unjustly deprived."

"Aye, aye, all in good time,—all in good time," replied the other with pretended kindness;—"you have been rather ill of late I believe, and on that account your medical gentlemen have advised a change of air and scenery. You will find this a very comfortable place, sir, I assure you, and as for kind treatment, I flatter myself we shall afford every satisfaction in that particular."

"I know nothing about who or what you are, sir," exclaimed Mr. Bramstone, "except that you are the keeper of a private madhouse, and therefore you and I have nothing at all to do with each other. I have been violently forced from my own house, and I now give you fair notice that unless I am instantly set at liberty, you will hereafter have to answer for it in a manner not very agreeable."

"Poor fellow! hear how he begins to rave!" exclaimed the governor his myrmedons with the most provoking coolness.

"On the contrary, I am perfectly calm," replied Septimus, as calm, sir, that I once more warn you to let me depart from this place before worse comes of it."

"He begins to threaten us!" cried the master of the house, addressing himself to the men. "A paroxysm is coming on I am afraid, and unless instant means are taken, there is no saying what mischief may be the result. You will not be too harsh to him unless there should be occasion for it, but if he should prove very violent, let a straight waistcoat be put upon him without delay, and as a further precaution strap him down to the bed so as to prevent the possibility of his moving hand or foot."

"Hear me, sir!" exclaimed Mr. Bramstone, vehemently, "I am not mad, and demand the instant attendance of a doctor, in order to prove my perfect sanity. You smile, sir, at my request, but you know not the agony that now tortures my heart, or you would pity rather than deride my sufferings."

. "Oh! it's a clear case of raving madness," cried Mr. Grabfast to his attendants; "however, I always like to act mercifully in these matters, so order the attendance of Doctor Dundizzy and Slop."

"Dundizzy and Slop!" exclaimed Septimus; "I'll not see them—they are villains who have been hired to effect my eternal imprisonment in this place, and the very sight of them would blast me like the lightning's flash!"

"You hear how dreadfully he raves," observed Mr. Grabfast, with affected commisseration; "but it is always the way with people in his melancholy situation, when they hear the names of their best friends mentioned. Dundizzy and Slop have been most kind and attentive to him, yet you observe what a rancorous hatred he seems to have formed against them both."

"Hadn't we better take him to his room?" asked one of the ruffians who had accompanied him in the coach. And, advancing hastily, he laid his hands on the shoulders of Mr. Bramstone, so as to be in readiness whenever the word should be given. But the old gentleman shrank from his touch as he would from that of a fiend —and placing his back against the wall, seemed to await any attack that might be made upon him, with a determination to defend himself to the last.

"Approach me not!" he exclaimed furiously—"advance not another step, or by heavens the first man that offers to lay hands upon me, shall have bitter cause to rue his temerity."

"He raves!" exclaimed Grabfast; you see what a violent customer we have got to deal with, and it now behoves us to take instant measures for securing him. Let every one rush upon him at once, and when once we have bound him he shall find that we have more ways than one to tame a madman."

"Let them beware how they approach me!" cried Septimus, who was now wound up to a state of desperation. "I am weaponless it is true, and my arms are bound with these accursed manacles, but my oppressors shall find that I am not powerless though they have sought to make me so. In my own defence I can yet exert myself, and the number of my adversaries will only serve to add vigour to my arm."

"To hear him rave one would suppose he was going to perform nightly exploits," exclaimed Grabfast. "But his boasted prowess will avail him but little—so at him, my lads, and see that he is conveyed to his cell before he forces us to do him a mischief that he may afterwards be sorry for."

With these words the two keepers made a sudden rush upon their victim, but violent as their assault was, Septimus stood prepared for them, and dashing his manacled hands full in their faces, he compelled them both to retreat a good deal faster than they had advanced. This, however, only served to increase their rage, and determined as they were to secure him, they once more repeated the charge, and with more success than on the former occasion. This time Septimus was seized in the powerful grasp of both his adversaries, but so determined was he to resist to the last, that, seizing one of the keepers by the throat, he held him with so vigorous a grasp, that the fellow's face began to grow black, as with convulsive efforts, he strove to release himself from the power of his anta. gonist. At this moment, Grabfast and three or four others rushed to the assistance of their comrade, and, laying hold of Septimus, they, by main force, compelled him to relax his hold, and then hurling him with ▓▓dful violence to the ground, slip-▓▓ over: him a straight waistcoat which e▓▓▓▓ prevented his offering any ▓▓▓▓▓ resistance to their scandal▓▓▓ ▓▓eedings.

This do▓▓ ▓e ▓▓s lifted like a helpless child ▓▓om the ground and carried into the ▓▓u▓ ▓at was henceforth to bec▓me ▓▓ pr▓▓▓. Here he was waited ▓▓ by Doctors Dundizzy and Slop, who, after feeling his pulse and pretending to consult together, order-ed him to be put to bed immediately, where he was to be strapped down securely whilst they profusely bled him, in order—as they pretended— to allay the irritation of his brain, and reduce the system to a better tone.

Deprived as he was of the use of his limbs, the poor old gentleman was now compelled to submit quietly to whatever torments they chose to inflict, and being lifted in the arms of his two keepers, he was carried to the miserable and comfortless cell where he was in all probability to pass the remainder of his days. On arriving there, he was thrown like a dog upon his comfortless pallet, and having been securely bound down with straps, his tormentors left him to all the agonies which reflection brought to his almost maddened brain.

———

CHAPTER XVIII.

VALENTINE RETURNS TO THE HOUSE OF MR. SEPTIMUS BRAMSTONE, AND IS STILL MORE PUZZLED AT THE CONTINUED ABSENCE OF HIS FRIEND. —A VISIT TO THE TOWER OF LONDON PROPOSED.—THE RIDE IN AN OMNIBUS, AND WHAT OUR HERO DID TO AMUSE HIMSELF AT THE EXPENSE OF HIS FELLOW-PASSENGERS.

As soon as Valentine had landed from the steam-boat that had brought him from Richmond, he made the best of his way through the densely crowded streets of London, and having at last elbowed his way to the house of Mr. Septimus Bramstone, he knocked at the door, and with trembling anxiety awaited the arrival of the servant, who was to solve the query as to whether anything had yet been heard of the old gentleman.

" Well, Susan, has your master returned home yet ?" was the first, and very natural question he put to the faithful abigail.

" Returned home !—lor' bless you, no, sir," replied Susan, dropping a respectful curtsey.

" Why, dear me, that is very singular," observed Valentine, with some perplexity ; " he has now been about nearly two days and a night, and yet not a word has been heard of him."

" Oh ! yes, he's been heard on I b'lieve, sir," returned the female ; " least ways, his brother, Mr. Harry Bramstone, as they calls him, has been here to say we needn't make ourselves at all uneasy on master's account, cause as how he's had a letter from him to say all about where he's gone to."

" Well, there's some consolation in that, at any rate," cried Valentine. " So that my friend is safe I am quite satisfied ; but you didn't happen to hear where he is gone to, I suppose, Susan ?"

" No, his brother didn't tell me that," answered the domestic ; " but he seemed quite happy about some.

thing or other, so I suppose there's nothing partic'lar the matter."

"Do you happen to know how long he is likely to be absent?" demanded our hero."

"In course not," answered Susan, "and I dare say if the truth was told he don't know that himself."

"How very strange!" exclaimed Valentine, half aside.

"Ah! you're right enough there, any how," interposed the domestic, "but, as I says, this is a queer world, and the longer we lives the more reason we has to say so; master was never given to leave his home in this sort of way, and if something queer don't come of it, say my name is not Susan Gabble, that's all."

"I have also my own fears upon that subject," replied Valentine, and then, after a few moments had been passed in painful cogitation, he inquired whether Mr. Harry Bramstone had said when it was likely her master would return.

"Yes," replied Susan, "he said something about its being a week, or perhaps a month, or may be even more than that, because, says he, my brother has gone some distance into the country on some very important business, and in course, says he, he won't come back till that's all finished comfortably."

"Well, it is not a very likely story at any rate," exclaimed the young man; "and what makes it look worse than all, is, that Mr. Septimus Bramstone should have gone away without sending a message home to explain his intention. Besides, if he had really been going to leave town for so long, he surely would have come here for a change of wearing apparel."

"That's just what I was thinking of myself, sir," cried Susan; "'cause master aint like a giddy young boy, you know, that could cut off on a journey at a moment's notice, driving people almost out of their wits with wondering what's become of him."

"Be that as it may," exclaimed Valentine, "something must be done to ascertain the truth or falsehood of this story. For my own part I can

scarcely credit it, and it shall be no fault of mine if this mystery is not cleared up before long."

"Do you think old Harry,—as I always call him,—has been telling us a pack of lies then?" asked the simple heart domestic.

"At present it would hardly be right to charge him with it," returned our hero. "In the absence of proof, it would be unwise to say all that I think about it, but take my word for it that not a stone shall be left unturned until I have sifted the affair to the bottom."

"You think something unfair has been done with him then?"

"That is exactly my opinion, Susan."

"Well, I declare if it aint m also," cried the female;—"I had strange dream last night about poor old master, and do will nothing will drive it out of my head ever since. I suppose it was along of those plaguy doctor that came here the other day somehow, or other I dreamt ill-looking fellows hurried in at the street door and laying hold of master, dragged him out of the house in spite of all his cries for help. Poor creature, he seemeed to be terribly frightened to be sure, and called upon me for assistance, but the moment I ran towards them, one of the villains knocked me to the ground, and then they disappeared, carrying master along with them. I shrieked out lustily as you may suppose, which soon woke me, and there I found myself lying upon the ground by the bedside, where, I suppose, I had tumbled in my fright. Now this was a strange dream, sir, wasn't it;—and don't you think it may very likely have something to do in finding out what has become of master?"

"Upon my word, Susan, I can give you very little hopes of finding your master by means of a dream," replied Valentine, half disposed to laugh at the woman's simplicity.

"My goodness, sir!—dont you believe in dreams then?"

"Certainly not," replied the other, —"however, we will not enter into the philosophy of those matters just at present; so forget the subject for a time, and leave to me the task of finding out what has become of your master."

"But suppose he should really have gone into the country for a little while as the old gentleman has told us?"

"Why, if he should have done so, it is so much the better," answered Valentine, "to be sure we shall have wronged his brother by our suspicions, but as there is no occasion to tell any body what we think there will be no great harm done after all."

"Well, I aint very rich, to be sure," exclaimed the faithful domestic, "but, as true as my name's what it is, I'd ~~e my next half~~ years wages only to ~~master walk~~ once more into his ~~house as~~ ~~~~ to do."

" ~~An~~ ~~~~ but what you may Susa~~~~ Valentine, who, for ~~~~ thought it bet- ~~~~rs than increase ~~~~ave wronged his ~~~~him to be capable ~~~~s, and therefore we ~~~~ drop until we have ~~~~tion for any charge we may ha~~~~against him."

It must not be imagined, however, that Valentine has, in any respect, altered his opinion as to Mr. Harry Bramstone's baseness, but, like a good general, he resolved to watch a favorable opportunity in order to expose the treachery which he had so much reason to believe had been practiced. He therefore changed the conversation, and, having having given Susan some necessary directions in case she should receive any intelligence of her master, prepared to set out once more for the purpose of calling upon Mr. Harry Bramstone, from whom he hoped by perseverance to draw out an acknowledgement of what had become of his brother.

"Why you aint going out without your dinner surely, sir!" cried the female, in a tone of remonstrance. "Master would never forgive me if I was to suffer that, and so perhaps you'll have the goodness to say what you'll like to have."

"The truth is, Susan, that I have several things to attend to, and, therefore, must get a snack just how or where I can," replied Valentine.

"And what must I tell master, supposing he should return home?"

"Say I shall be back here in the evening," answered our hero, taking up his hat and cane; "but in the event of your seeing him, do not let a hint be dropped of the suspicions we harboured with respect to the cause of his long absence. He would be indignant at the bare idea of my having thought his brother guilty of so vile an act, and, indeed, I should myself be ashamed of it, if, after all, he has really been in the country upon any business of his own."

Like a worthy, discreet woman as she was, Susan promised to observe the injunctions of her master's young visitor, and having again and again urged the propriety of his taking a steak or a chop before he went out, she was at last obliged to suffer him to depart, though not without still further remonstrance for what she conceived to be a very wilful and foolish act.

But the truth is, Valentine felt too restless to remain at home by himself; for his thoughts were constantly directed towards one painful subject, and he was really glad to get out into the busy streets of London, where so many objects constantly met his view, and drove away reflections that were any thing but pleasant. Taking, therefore, a less circuitous route than had been chosen a night or two before by Arnold, he arrived in the course of about half an hour at the house of Mr. Harry Bramstone. Here he knocked with trembling anxiety, and on the door being opened, he inquired of the servant whether her master was at home. At this moment the girl stared as if uncertain what answer she was to give; but Valentine's doubts upon the subject were quickly removed by the voice of her master, who bawled out at the top of the stairs that he was "*not at home!*"

"Not at home!" exclaimed our hero, with surprise; "by Jove, it is rather a strange thing for a man to say of himself! Tell him Mr. Valentine Vaux wishes to speak with him for a few minutes, and that if he happens to be particularly engaged, I'll wait till he is more at leisure."

"Can't do that, sir," replied the girl in a whisper; "master's so dreadfully passionate, and if I was to go up to him with such a message, he'd turn me out of the house at a moment's notice."

"Upon my life, this is most extraordinary!" exclaimed Valentine; "I am told Mr. Bramstone is not at home, and who should be the person to tell me so but himself!"

"Well, I suppose master knows best whether he is at home or not," answered the girl, looking round with alarm to see whether he was any where near. It's a way he's got when he don't want to see any body, and it would be more than my place is worth to contradict him."

Valentine found that it would be useless to say any more upon the subject, and merely telling the girl to say that he had called, he took his departure, without having formed any notion as to which way he should next direct his footstep. It mattered not to him, however, which direction he took, and after pondering over various plans, he at length resolved to pay a visit to the Tower of London, where he had heard many curiosities were deposited, which would be well worth his seeing. Having made up his mind to this, he proceeded in the direction which he knew would conduct him towards the quarter of the town he wished to go to; but as the distance was greater than he had anticipated, he hailed the first omnibus that was passing, and taking his seat among the other passengers, fell into a train of thought, suggested by the events which had so recently passed.

But our hero was of too vivacious a disposition to remain long in a state of quietness, and having taken a rapid survey of his companions, he soon hit upon an expedient that he thought would afford him some little amusement. Next to him sat an old gentleman, whose ill-natured disposition frequently manifested itself in growls and broken imprecations whenever the least thing happened to put him in the least out of the way. First of all, the vehicle was too full to please him; then it went at too slow a pace, and then, as if in the spirit of perversity, it travelled at a rate that put him in fear of his life. In this way he continued to grumble on, to the great annoyance of all those who, with more contented dispositions, were contented to take things as they might happen to fall out. Now, exactly facing this elderly grumbler, sat a stiff, starch-looking old lady, whose vinegar aspect declared as plainly as face could do that she was a disappointed old maid. These two persons, Valentine observed, seemed to regard each other with the most sovereign contempt: for, though neither of th[...] exchanged a word with the other, it [was] very evident that the m[...] trifling cir cumstance would serve t[...] them by the ears.

Nor was it long [...] found a way to p[...] operation; for tak[...] moment of profoun[...] the voice of a child ju[...] sleep with to much ex[...] the eyes of every body were [...] turned towards the old maid, from whose muff, as it laid upon her lap, the sound appeared to come. In an instant the most injurious suspicions began to take possession of each mind, and whilst all her fellow-travellers were staring at her with astonishment, the old gentleman who sat opposite broke forth with :—

"Well, I don't know what some people think about the matter, but, for my own part, I can't help saying, that if ladies choose to carry their squalling brats with them, a muff seems to be a very dangerous place to cram the pretty dears into."

Upon this the old maid first looked very red and then very white, and having bit her lips till they almost bled, she directed a withering look of contempt towards the old gentlemen, as much as to say she considered him as nothing better than a brute. But her venerable tormentor was proof against the rebuke, and fixing his small grey eyes upon her, he exclaimed :—

VALENTINE VAUX,

OR THE

TRICKS OF A VENTRILOQUIST.

BY TIMOTHY PORTWINE.

"Pray, ma'am, is that squalling little brat yours?"

"S-i-r!" ejaculated the lady, prolonging the monosyllable as much as possible, in order to convey an idea of the extreme displeasure his question had given her.

"I was merely remarking ma'am," returned her unabashed opponent, "that if the child is yours, the company, generally, would be extremely glad to have it kept as quiet as possible. And perhaps you will also permit me to observe, that a muff is an extremely improper place to carry an infant in."

"What do you mean by insulting me in this way, sir!" said the elderly spinster angrily,—"I would have you know, sir, that I am a respectable female, and—"

"Well," interrupted the old gentleman," and pray don't respectable females have squalling brats then?"

"But I am a single woman, sir," retorted the other with increased fury."

"And if you are, that don't alter what I have said in the least," answered the old man with perfect composure. "Single women are not always immaculate, and, though I don't wish to affront you by saying so, yet the fact of your having a child concealed as that is, affords ample grounds for my suspicion."

"Good heavens! what do you mean, sir!" cried the lady with the utmost indignation;—"I have no child here, and what is more I hope never to be troubled with such disagreeable little creatures."

At this moment Valentine renewed the squalling, and again the old gentleman gave way to his ill-natured observations.

"It's very likely ma'am you may have good reasons for endeavouring to conceal the fact, but I believe there is no one in this company who will be easily inclined to give credit to it. That a child is concealed somewhere is but too evident, and any body that has ears to hear with may be convinced that the poor little creature is crammed into that muff of yours.

"Ah!—monster!—barbarian!"— shrieked the ancient vestal, "did any body ever hear anything so infamous; —but I'll not stay any longer to be insulted;—here, coachman!—conductor!—let me out, I say, or I shall die!—I shall — indeed — indeed I shall!—

And the venerable lady gave loose to her tears and lamentations, appealing first to one and then to another of the passengers to ascertain whether they thought her to be as guilty as the disagreeable old gentleman had asserted. Nay, more, she even turned the muff inside out in order to convince the good folks of her innocence, but no sooner had she done this than Valentine again imitated the crying of a child, only taking care this time to change the place from whence the sound seemed to come to the back part of the seat which she occupied. This appeared to strengthen her former determination,—again she screamed out loudly to be put down, upon which the omnibus was suddenly brought to a stand still, and after floundering about between two rows of knees, she at last reached the steps, and precipitately leaped to the ground. But even then Valentine's love of mischief predominated over all other feelings, and just as the conductor was about to

close the door, another baby-squall was uttered that was most decisive in its effects. As the sound met the old lady's ears she made a desperate rush to the pavement, and then turning down the first street that presented itself, she was fortunately, for herself, soon beyond the reach of the laughter and jeers with which she was assailed by a swarm of boys who had just broke out of school.

For some time Valentine rode on in perfect quietness, smiling now and then at the tricks he had played upon the travellers, and listening with no little pleasure to the sage remarks that were uttered by those who thought fit to give an opinion as to the old lady's very extraordinary con There were none, however, who se inclined to give her any quarter. the first and foremost of those w seemed anxious to throw discredit on her character was the elderly gentleman to whom she was indebted for the commencement of hostilities. Upon him, therefore, Valentine resolved t practice a little of his ingenuity, an again imitating the feeble cry of a infant, he so contrived it that the sound should appear to proceed from close by the surly old fellow's side, who upon this, immediately bawle out to the conductor desiring him to stop the carriage immediately.

"Send somebody after that old hag," he exclaimed;—"bring her back, I say, directly, for like an artful hussey as she is, she has slipped away and left the infernal squalling brat behind."

"Who do you suppose is going to stop an omnibus every minute for such nonsense as that?" demanded the man gruffly. No one brought a child into the carriage, I know, and whats' more, I'm very certain nobody's likely to take one out.

Upon this the old gentleman grew very outrageous and threatened every body with heavy pains and penalties if they dared to laugh at him under such circumstances. As his violence grew to a greater pitch several of the passengers thought fit to leave the vehicle, and among them was Valentine who, having had his joke out, left the omnibus for the purpose of walking the remainder of the way to the tavern.

CHAPTER XIX.

A VISIT TO THE HORSE ARMOURY, AND AN INTRODUCTION TO A CITIZEN AND HIS FAMILY. — VALENTINE LEARNS SEVERAL MATTERS ON ENGLISH HISTORY THAT HE NEVER HEARD OF BEFORE. — CONFUSION GROWS WORSE CONFOUNDED.— AN INTERVIEW WITH KING HENRY THE EIGHTH, IN WHICH THE BLUFF MARCH EXHIBITS SOME OF HIS OVERBEARING TEMPER.

SHORT walk brought Valentine to Tower Hill, when the fortress he was about to visit stood frowning before him as if rather repelling his advances than tempting him to proceed any further. After gazing at it a minute or two, however, he moved towards a gateway at the western end where a sentinel was passing up and down with solemn steps, from whom he received some necessary directions as to the route he was to take; this done, he crossed a stone bridge built over the ditch, which brought him to another gate much stronger than the other he had passed, having a portcullis hanging above which looked very much as if neither persuasion nor force would ever induce it to come down and perform the service it was originally intended for. Having made his way thus far, he was met by several singular looking fellows, who he afterwards understood to be the warders, and whose extraordinary uniform struck our young novice with amazement. Their coats were of a very singular form, being made with large sleeves and flowing skirts of fine scarlet cloth; these were ornamented round the edges and seams with several rows of gold lace, and the whole was confined round their wastes with a broad laced girdle. On their breasts and backs they wore the Queen's silver badge, representing the rose, thistle, and shamrock, together with the initials V. R. As for their headgear they were the queerest looking things Valentine had ever seen, being fashioned, as he supposed, to make them look as much like animated Guys as possible.

Having engaged the services of one of these singular looking beings, Valentine marched onwards with the intention of seeing the horse armoury of which he had heard so much talk, and which had consequently raised his curiosity to the highest pitch. On reaching the spacious room in which this is situated, he found several other persons who were on the same errand as himself, and as they seemed to be a family party he drew near them expecting to derive some amusement from their observations on what was presented to their view.

"Well, this is wonderful!" exclaimed a remarkably fat, podgy little man who appeared to be the head of the family ;—" and so this is all real armour, and the 'dentical things as was worn by the great chaps nobody knows how long ago?" Then addressing himself to his son, a gauky youth who stood at his side, he continued : " Now Bob, I expect you to tell me all about what we've come to see; I've edicated you at a boarding school, you dog, and its cost a mint o'money to make a man of you, so of course your old father has a right to expect summat of you at last."

" Well, what do you want to know, pa?" squeaked the young gentleman; " I've learnt all about history you know, and master used to say I was the best boy in the school for remembering what I'd been reading about."

" That's right," exclaimed the delighted father, and then nudging the warder, he enquired who the gentleman was that he saw in a cast-iron coat at the left hand corner.

" That," replied the attendant is Edward the First; the armour, as you see, consists of the hawberk and its sleeves of mail, the hood and chausses of the same material. He is in the act of sheathing his sword, and is said to have been one of the bravest of our ancient kings."

"And pray who was this Edward First?" asked the old gentleman of his highly talented son.

"Ah! who was he, Bob?" demanded the mother and her two daughters in a breath.

"Oh, I can tell you all about him," replied the youth:—"Edward the First was the father of George the Third, and was chiefly celebrated for his battles with Julius Cæsar the Grecian hero. He was the inventor of steam guns and was surnamed the Great, though history describes him as a very little man."

"Good boy!" exclaimed the old man in a tone of exultation; but bless me what a delightful study history must be when a person has such a clear head and excellent memory as you have.

"Bob's a wonderful boy, that's certain," whispered his mother, glancing proudly towards her darling son.

"And pray who is that other rum looking chap?" asked the old man pointing to the figure he alluded to.

"That," replied the man, with technical precision," is King Henry the Sixth. His plate armour is of the most beautiful form, particularly the back plate. The battle-axe of the period, the long pointed toes of the sollerets, and the great spurs are particularly worthy of attention. The horse is caparisoned with the arms of France and England; and the king wears on his head the salade, on which is the knight's cap, surmounted by the crest."

"It's all very curious, no doubt," observed the elderly gentleman, "but it certainly does surprise me that a king like him should appear among so many of his friends in a night cap."

"Excuse me, sir," interrupted Valentine, "but the guide described the head dress as a knight's cap which is a very different article to the one you have mentioned.

"Very likely,—very likely," returned the old gentleman, "but my son Bob knows all about that. He can tell the history of every one of these chaps, and if you only wait with patience he'll give us the story as pat as possible."

"Who was Henry the Sixth?" asked Bob's mother with the very laudable intention of drawing him out a bit in order to exhibit his remarkable talents to the stranger.

"Henry the Sixth," answered the youth, "was one of the most wonderful men of modern times;—he commanded a division of the allied army in the battle of Waterloo, and afterwards joined in the crusade against Mahomet the impostor. His son was the celebrated Henry the Fifth, whose night adventures are supposed to have inspired the present Marquis of Waterford wi noble emulation of ating helpl women, and wr the kn and bells off d . In fact, as Byron says, in is poem of "Par Lost,"—"Take im for in all, e ne'er shall look his ike again."

"Did you eve ar th a clever fellow as my son ke Mr. Jones Jenkins, " n't st onishin youth, sir?"

"Remarka so? re ied V entine, ready to burst out into fit of laughter, "his knowledge of history is wonderful, and I can safely say that he has now told me of many curious facts that I never heard before."

"There," cried Jenkins to his wife, "didn't I tell you Bob would be an honour to his family some day or other? you hear what this gentleman says, my dear—he's thunderstruck at the boy's knowledge, and no wonder either, seeing what a genius he is."

In this way they passed on from figure to figure, till their attention was irresistibly attracted by an equestrian representation of King Henry the Eighth. Here our party stopped, while the warder informed them that the highly curious suit of armour in which this monarch was habited was a present from the European Maximilian the First to the King of England, on his marriage in 1509 with Catharine of Aragon. He also informed them of the fact of the armour being covered with engravings representing the legends of saints, interspersed with the king's badges; and moreover informed them that it was washed over with silver. Valentine was particularly struck with the attitudes both of the horse and the rider, which are exceedingly spirited, the animal rearing up on his hind legs, whilst the king leans forward in the act of elevating a drawn sword. All present seemed to be particularly struck with this figure, and, as usual, the old gentleman called upon his son for a brief history of the monarch's reign.

"Henry the Eighth," began the sensible youth, "was the husband of Queen Elizabeth, but previous to entering further into the events of his reign, it may be necessary to inform you that I'm ——"

Fool!" exclaimed Valentine, so ——— that it appeared to ——— from the mouth of Henry the Eighth. Thereupon the old gentleman ——— amazement; the ladies screamed ——— whilst Bob and the warder ——— figure, as if wondering ——— would come next.

"Is that ———?" at length asked Mr. Jonas Jenkins, in a tone of mingled ——— and amazement,

"Alas! God bless you, not as I knows on," answered the horror-struck warder. "It's only an effigy, sir, and though I've been here for the last ten years I never heard him speak a word before, as I'm an honest man."

"He called me a fool, at any rate," exclaimed Bob, indignantly, "and king or no king, I'm blest if I'm going to stand that sort of caper."

"Ha, ha, ha!" laughed the monarch in a sepulchral voice, that made them all stare at one another, as if expecting to see the effigy dismount and try the temper of his sword upon their hapless bodies. Luckily for them, however, the bluff old monarch kept to his saddle, while the visitors were arguing within their own minds the propriety of making a hasty retreat.

"Jonas, my dear, hadn't we better leave this horrible place?" asked Mrs. Jenkins, seizing the arm of her husband, and pulling vigorously to move him from the spot. But Jonas could

be obstinate on occasions, and he now took it into his head to stay where he was as long as he thought fit. Whether this was done to prove his own courage, or to contradict his better half, we know not, but the lady seemed to think the latter, and plunging her dexter arms into his ribs, she declared that she knew she should faint unless he took her immediately from that nasty haunted place.

"Nonsense, my love," he exclaimed, "there can't be any danger, you know, while so many people are about, and as for this King What-d'ye-call-him, why if he begins playing any of his pranks, we'll soon show him that kings are not now as they used to be when he had the management of the people."

"Excuse me, sir," interrupted Valentine, heartily enjoying the joke, "but the king you are speaking of was never used to contradiction, and if we may credit the assertions of those who lived in his days, he thought no more of chopping people's heads off than you or I would think of walking from one end of this room to the other."

"And I've heard it said—though I don't know how true it is," whispered the warder, "that he was like a Turk among his wives, when he got tired of 'em he made 'em a head shorter, and then married another just to serve her in the same way."

"What a horrible wretch," groaned Mrs. Jenkins.

"Who dares call me a wretch?" exclaimed Valentine, again directing his voice so that it appeared to proceed from the inanimate figure before them.

"Gracious me! did you hear that?" cried the lady, addressing herself to those about her. "The monster is getting in a passion, I declare, and the place will soon be too hot to hold us."

And so saying, she once more tried to move her husband, but he like all other obstinate people, refused to stir a peg till the affair had been explained to his entire satisfaction. Upon this the young ladies joined the old one in her entreaties, and when it appeared to be quite certain that he would not be persuaded by their united prayers, then did Master Bob put in a word expressing his opinion that they had better leave the angry monarch to regain his good temper.

Sharn't do no such thing, Bob," replied the old gentleman, striking his stick very hard upon the ground, a little bit of pantomime that he was often subject to, and which always showed that his mind was completely made up. "Sharn't do no such thing, Bob, because you see there's something curious about the matter, and I don't mean to stir from this place till I've found it all out."

"Now Jonas, do go, there's a dear," entreated his plump rib.

"Tell you I shant," replied the citizen:—"I've made up my mind to see the matter out, and here I mean to stay till I've got to the bottom of it."

"Rash man forbear!" exclaimed the same sepulchral voice, "and meddle not with things you have no business with."

"Who do you call a rash man?" demanded Mr. Jonas Jenkins rather fiercely.

"For goodness sake don't go quarreling with his majesty!" exclaimed the lady. ' You hear what a passion he's getting into, and I expect every moment to see him jump off his horse to punish us for daring to speak against him."

"Oh, he knows better than that," returned the old gentleman, and then addressing himself to the warder, he enquired whether the figure was often gifted with the power of speech.

"Lor' bless you I never heard him open his lips before," replied the man. "To be sure I have always thought he looked uncommonly cross, but I never expected to hear him talk to us for all the world as if he was a Christian like ourselves.

"It'll be a fortune to you," exclaimed Jenkins; "the news will spread abroad like wildfire, and then every body will want to come to the Tower for the sake of talking with his Majesty, Henry the Eighth."

"Then they will be d—nably mistaken," cried the voice, "for after this day I shall not condescend to speak again."

"My conscience how he swears!" ejaculated Mrs. Jenkins.

"History tells us he was always very much given to the use of bad language," observed Bob.

"Then history tells an infernal lie!" roared the voice.

"Well, well, there's no occasion to get in a passion about it," was the mild rebuke of the little fat citizen. "If people have told lies about you it's no more than has been done with other folks besides yourself."

"Hold your tongue, sir!" exclaimed the supposed king; "I am one that will never be talked down by a little ignorant shop-keeper, who has no more sense in his brains than born with, and unless you leave directly I may be tempted you hence at the point of m

"Then here goes for one!" Bob, preparing for a father was resolved him upon such easy ing the retreat you waist, he held with so firm grasp that all his e release himself were made in vain. At last, however, they both stumbled, and falling upon the floor they rolled over and over with so much rapidity, that every body present burst into a roar of laughter, in which they were joined by the supposed ghost of Henry the Eighth, whose hollow " ha! ha! ha!" served to bring the two wrestlers once more on their feet.

"Now I'll tell you what it is, Bob," exclaimed the old man; "fair play's a jewel, and I don't mean to stand any nonsense, my boy, so make yourself comfortable here till I choose to give the word."

"But who wants to stay here talking to a king that's been dead, I don't know how long?" demanded Bob.

"Nonsense! there's some gammon in all this depend upon it," returned his father. "I don't believe in ghosts and goblins, not I, and if this is any thing more than a trick that's been played us by some one or other, why then say my name's not Jonas Jenkins, that's all. What do you think about it, young gentleman, eh?"

This latter question was put to Valentine, who finding himself thus compelled to give an answer, said :—

"Why, really, sir, I would rather you had appealed to any body else than myself. That the affair is a very singular one it must be admitted, but when we have the evidence of our own senses to bear us out, why then I think we can do nothing else than believe whatever we may hear or see."

"Then you believe that the figure before us spoke?"

"Have we any proof to the contrary?" demanded Valentine; "was it not very evident that the voice proceeded from his lips, or is there any ⟨…⟩ present that can con⟨…⟩ the sound came from ⟨…⟩

⟨…⟩ng that spoke!"

⟨…⟩

"And th⟨…⟩ speaks again!" ex⟨…⟩om the lips of the ⟨…⟩rns you to be less ⟨…⟩nture, and to take ⟨…⟩ his place with as little ⟨…⟩ as possible!"

"⟨…⟩hang me if I give you the troub⟨…⟩" exclaimed Jenkins, and taking his wife's arm within his own, he commenced a hasty retreat follow-ed by his son and daughter. Valentine could not help laughing to see the speed with which they took their departure, and giving a tremendous groan as they reached the door, he heard them scrambling away with all their might, each one seeming anxious to take care of themselves, and caring very little who was left behind so that they got clear off.

This done, Valentine explained to the warder the means by which he had succeeded in frightening them out of the place, and then, having liberally rewarded the man for the trouble he had given, he took his departure, intending to call once more upon Mr. Harry Bramstone, in order to see whether he had yet returned. At Grace-church-street he found an omnibus that was going to the part of town he wished to visit, and having taken his seat therein, he was soon put down within a few hundred yards from the house he was going to.

On the door being opened, he learnt from the servant, that Mr. Bramstone had returned, and following her across the hall, he soon found himself in the room where the father and son, with their wives, were assembled in earnest conversation. At first, he could perceive that his presence was by no means agreeable to the quartette, but they were all too cunning to betray themselves through any want of caution, and, taking the cue from the old man they welcomed their visitor with an appearance of the greatest cordiality.

"I am very glad to see you, Mr. Vaux, very glad indeed," exclaimed the old man rising and shaking hands with our hero, as if his presence really afforded him the greatest pleasure.

"I am afraid you will think me rather troublesome," returned Valentine, "but I feel so exceeding uneasy about my friend, Mr. Septimus Bramstone, that I could not resist the desire to walk here, in order to enquire whether any thing has yet been heard of him."

"Oh, yes, the old boy's been heard of," replied Arnold—"we have had a letter from him, and would you believe it, he talks of being absent from town for some time to come?"

"How very singular!" ejaculated Valentine.

"Very!" cried both the ladies in a breath.

"But does he give no reason for his absence?" asked our hero.

"None, whatever," replied the elder gentleman, "and therein lies the principal part of the mystery;—he tells us indeed, that very particular business has compelled him to leave London for a time, and in one part of his letter he even hints that it is possible he may never return to town.

"Bless me!" exclaimed Valentine, "I hope nothing very serious has happened to him."

"Oh dear no, there's no fear of that," answered Harry;—"my brother was always an eccentric character, and two or three times before he has almost frightened us out of our lives, by going away nobody ever knew where."

" But you have received a letter from him ?"

" We have."

" Then of course the post mark will explain the place he has gone to," observed Valentine.

" Unfortunately it does not," replied the elder Mr. Bramstone, " my brother seems to have been aware of that, and the letter has been sent up by private hands to be put into the twopenny-post office. So you see he has taken every precaution to keep us in the dark, and I am afraid we must wait with patience till he chooses to enlighten us."

" But what motive can he possibly have for alarming his friends in this way ?" asked Valentine.

" It's done out of a mere whim I suppose," returned Harry ;—" he perhaps wants to see what effect it will have upon us, or possibly wishes to withdraw himself altogether from those relatives who love him so dearly."

" Well," observed our hero, " one thing seems pretty certain, and that is that I must immediately look out for other lodgings, since I do not choose to encroach any longer upon the hospitality of a man who is not present at his own house."

" That is the very point I wished to speak to you upon," cried Harry Bramstone, " but as it was a very delicate subject, I hardly knew how to bring it about. In fact, to deal plainly with you, my brother has, in his letter, requested me to say that he will be glad if you can make it convenient to find temporary apartments somewhere else, as he rather thinks of selling off the whole of his furniture by auction. It's a strange whim of his to be sure, a very strange whim, but as it is no fault of mine, I hope you will not take this notification amiss."

" I have no reason to do so," replied Valentine, " since my friend, Mr. Septimus Bramstone, has a perfect right to do as he pleases in his own house. One thing, however, strikes me as being peculiarly odd; I allude to his determination of selling his furniture, because

it is not many days since he declared that nothing would hurt him so much as to be compelled to part with his furniture, as the greater part of it had formerly belonged to his father.

" Aye, aye," replied the other, " but what Septimus says one day he generally unsays on another. His mind is as fickle as the winds, and that will easily account to you for his sudden determination of selling his household furniture even after he has expressed so much veneration for it."

" At present, I shall not hazard any opinion upon the subject," answered Valentine; that the affair is involved in a good deal of mystery, is however, very certain, and I shall never satisfied until I have searched to very bottom."

" And very kind it is of you to take so much trouble," returned Mr. Harry Bramstone, and then for Valentine preparing to depart became pressing for him to der of the evening refused to do, and night he took his departure, meditating intently upon numerous suspicions that began to float through his mind.

" That same night he took a lodging as near as possible to the house of Septimus Bramstone, and having removed his trunks there he made up his mind to watch all that went forward with a careful and vigilant eye.

———

CHAPTER XX.

THE SINGULAR CONDUCT OF THE BRAMSTONE FAMILY GIVES RISE TO VERY PAINFUL SUSPICIONS.—VALENTINE LIES IN WAIT AND DISCOVERS THAT WHICH CONFIRMS HIS DOUBTS.—AN INTERVIEW WITH THE SUSPECTED PARTIES.—THE QUARREL AND THE REMARKABLE MANNER IN WHICH OUR HERO ESCAPES BEING ENGAGED IN A PUGILISTIC ENCOUNTER.

THE first thing Valentine did on the following day was to take a stroll out for the purpose of observing the motions of the Bramstone family, now that they

VALENTINE VAUX,

OR THE

TRICKS OF A VENTRILOQUIST.

BY TIMOTHY PORTWINE.

were not aware of any body being engaged in observing them. Of course, he commenced by directing his steps towards the house of his absent friend, and perceiving Arnold and his father approaching from an opposite direction he stepped into a public house, from the window of which he could see what was going on among those whose intentions he had so much reason to suspect. First of all, he saw the old man and his son enter the house, having previously, looked cautiously about to see whether any one was observing them; shortly afterwards, two queer-looking fellows with carpet caps upon their heads and having the appearance of belonging to that class of bipeds called auctioneers' porters followed them, and their commenced a vast deal of bustle, such as removing cumbrous articles of furniture from one room to another. In the midst of this, the auctioneer himself, accompanied by a clerk, arrived at the place, and no sooner had Susan admitted them, than she came out crying fit to break her heart, and carrying under her arms the boxes which contained all the goods and chattels she was worth in the world. This made Valentine wonder more and more as to the cause of this unwonted stir, and he was just preparing to follow the girl, when he perceived that she was making her way across the road with the evident intention of seeking a temporary refuge in the place where he was now an unsuspected oberver of all that was going on. Having ascertained this fact, he waited till she had entered the house, and then ringing the bell, desired the waiter to ask the young woman into the parlour. This message rather puzzled the faithful abigail, but, if her astonishment was great before, how much was it increased, when, on entering the room, she saw it occupied by her master's esteemed young friend. For a moment or two she was completely abashed, but at last dropping a low curtsey, she asked why she had been sent for, and whether anything had yet been heard of the old gentleman.

"I sent for you, Susan," he replied, "to give me whatever information you can relative to the proceedings that are now going on over the way. Every moment serves to increase my uneasiness as to the fate of Mr. Septimus Bramstone, and I am resolved by some means or other to get at the truth."

"Ah, sir!" cried the woman shaking her head, "this is a bad world, and I'm afraid there aint much worse people in it than those I've just left opposite. They tell me master will return some day or other, and yet, would you believe it, they've brought a chap with 'em that they call an auctioneer, and they're now talking with him as to the best way of selling off the furniture just for all the world as if it was their own."

"Nonsense! this must be some mistake of yours," exclaimed Valentine, startled at the villainy she had disclosed.

"Oh, bless your heart, there's no mistake sir," she replied; "I overheard all that was said, and Mr. Harry Bramstone told the auctioneer that whatever was done must be set about quickly; and then it was agreed between 'em to sell every thing off by auction."

"And by whose authority I should like to know?" cried our hero, starting up with the intention of rushing over the way to remonstrate against so foul a proceeding. But a moment's reflection served to convince him that his interference at this moment would be of very little avail, and addressing himself once more to the girl, he enquired whether she had been dismissed from the service of her late master.

"Ah, sir! you have just guessed it," she replied; "the old villain seemed to think I was in the way, and after asking what wages were due to me, he paid me the money and then ordered me to clear away with bag and baggage in less than no time at all. It was heart breaking work, sir, to leave a place where I had been so comfortable, but what could a helpless woman like me do, when such a bashaw of a fellow as that says I must go?"

"And you have been driven forth, then, by those who have no business whatever to take so much upon themselves."

"Yes sir," she replied; "here I am as you see me, and I only wish my poor old master knew the goings on at his house now he's away. And yet," she continued, "it would be cruel to wish that, too, for if he only guessed half the shameful doings he'd go stark staring mad;—I'm sure he would!"

"At all events, something must be done in the matter," observed Valentine, after a pause;—"that these people are acting most iniquitously I am but too well convinced, and it shall now be my task to frustrate them. You say they are going to sell off all the furniture by auction?—let that only be confirmed, and I will immediately take measures to prevent the sale, until I have good reason to suppose that they are acting under proper authority."

"And that they'd have a hard matter to prove," returned Susan, "seeing that, even according to their own account, master is still living, and of course they can have no right to make away with his things just as they please."

"Nor shall they do so," exclaimed Valentine resolutely;—"in all this I can perceive a system of deep laid rascality which my vigilance shall some day or other turn towards their own destruction."

"But are you quite certain it's all their doing?" asked Susan, who, bad as she knew the principal perpetrators to be, could scarcely bring herself to credit that they were so far sunk in crime as to practice against the peace and happiness of their relative,

"I fear there is not the slightest ground for believing them innocent of it," answered Valentine. "From the little I have seen of them, I can learn that extravagance has made them poor, and immersed as they are in difficulties, this perhaps is the only method that offers to relieve themselves. They have by some means or other got your master out of the way, and interested as they are in his absence, I very much fear they will take care to prevent his ever returning home again."

"Lor', sir! you frighten me out of my wits," cried Susan with alarm.

"Alas! I fear there is but too much cause for your terror," added Valentine, he is in bad hands I can assure you, and, in my opinion, his worthless relatives will take care to prevent a discovery, for at least some time to come."

"Why what in the name of wonder can they have done with him then?"

"That," replied our hero, "is the mystery that remains to be cleared up. His enemies have been working with secrecy and care so, that at present I can do nothing more than surmise the means they adopted for carrying their foul designs into execution. Circumstances, however, favour the notion I have formed, and it now only remains for me to keep my own counsel for a time and I dare say they will be unmarked at a moment, when perhaps they consider themselves most secure from discovery."

"Heaven send it may be so," cried Susan fervently.

At this moment the attention of Valentine was directed toward the house opposite, before the door of which a coach had just drawn up, and into which a vast number of parcels and packages were being crammed with all haste, by those who were engaged in this cruel act of spoilation and robbery. As he perceived this it was with extreme difficulty that he could restrain himself from rushing over to the marauders, but recollecting that his interference would do more harm than good just at present, he at last succeeded in conquering the inclination under a determination to use his utmost exertions towards defeating the villany that was now being carried on. He therefore dismissed Susan, after taking her address in case her assistance should be required, and then stationing himself once more at the window, he saw two or three more coaches loaded with the lighter goods belonging to his friend, which were driven away he knew not whither.

At length he observed Arnold Bramstone coming from the house with a costly oil painting under his arm, which Valentine had often heard his friend speak of as being extremely valuable, from the fact of its being a master-piece of one of the old painters. This sight impelled him to leave the place where he had concealed himself, and hurrying across the road he overtook the young man just as he was about to turn down a by-street, where his motions would be less likely to be watched. In his eagerness to escape notice, Arnold did not hear the rapid footsteps that were now in pursuit of him, and when at last Valentine touched him on the arm, he turned round with a countenance deadly pale to see who it was that had followed him at such an unfortunate moment.

"Good morning," said our hero, with as much composure as he could assume; "I thought I could not be mistaken in your person, Arnold, though it must be confessed when I saw you gliding down this out of the way street, I almost began to think my eyes had for once deceived me."

"Y-e-e-s," stammered Arnold, "it

must be confessed this is really an out of the way place as you say, but the fact is, my dear boy, I had this infernal great picture under my arm, and one don't like to be met, you know, lugging these things about like a confounded porter."

"Why," announced Valentine slyly, "it is rather awkward to be sure, because if any one met you that you knew they might imagine that you were carrying the picture *to your uncle's* instead of *from* him."

Arnold was too much confounded just at the moment to make an immediate reply to this home thrust, but presently recovering himself he said with his usual composure:—

"You knew this picture then?"

"To be sure I do,—it belongs to your uncle Septimus."

"Right," exclaimed Arnold, who finding that any paltry evasion would not do now, made a virtue of necessity, and at once confessed the fact.

"Oh, I was perfectly well aware of that," answered Valentine, "because the old gentleman has often shewn it to me as a splendid specimen of art. Indeed he prized it exceedingly, and I have heard him say its value was very considerable."

"That is the very reason why I am going to take care of it," replied Arnold with his usual cunning. "I know it was a favourite with the old gentleman, and as his absence is likely to last some time longer I thought it better to carry it home, where it will be better protected against injury."

"Indeed!" exclaimed our hero in a tone that showed pretty plainly the degree of credence with which he heard this explanation."

"Yes, that's a fact, 'pon honour," answered the other with unblushing impudence. "Uncle Septimus, you know, is a particular old bachelor in his way, and as Susan is such an abominable careless huzzy I thought it much better to carry it to a place where there is less danger of its being injured."

"And yet, Susan's carelessness can have very little to do with the matter," exclaimed Valentine with an ill-suppressed sneer, "seeing that she has

been paid her wages and abruptly dismissed from service at a moment's notice."

Arnold was evidently confused at this, but again recovering his former self-possession, he said with affected surprise:—

"Why, who in the name of fortune has been telling you so monstrous a falsehood?—Susan been dismissed from her service! Why the thing bears a lie upon the very face of it, seeing that she was a great favourite of my uncle Septimus, and nothing could offend him so much when he returns home as to find that she had been sent away without his leave."

"And yet," answered Valentine, "the girl told me so herself not half an hour since."

"Then she must have been imposing upon you most cruelly."

"How could that be," asked our hero, "when I saw the girl, with all her bag and baggage, crying along the streets as if her heart would break. Curious to know the cause, I enquired it of her, and from her own mouth I heard that your father paid the wages that were due and had told her her services were no longer required."

"Well, if it is so I know nothing about it," answered Arnold indifferently. "The old man naturally feels a great interest in his brother's affairs, and if he —as is not unlikely,—has found the girl out in pilfering from her master, it is likely enough that he may have given her the sack."

"Nay, this is most ungerous!" exclaimed Valentine indignantly, "the girl has always borne an irreproachable character for honesty, and I have heard your uncle say repeatedly that he would never part with her if it was only on that account."

"Damn it, man, you needn't be so warm in her behalf," returned the other, "Susan, for some cause or other, might have been a great favourite of yours, but if my dad saw reason to think less favourable of her, he has done wisely,— in my opinion,—in sending her off abour her business. Besides, there's a vast quantity of valuable property in the house, which,—being at her mercy, would be very unsafe if she should not happen to be quite so honest as you and uncle Septimus appear to have imagined."

"And yet," observed our hero sarcastically, "there could not be much fear of her taking away the property since a great portion has been already removed, and the remainder, I have no doubt, is doomed to follow it before long."

"Upon my life I don't understand you, sir."

"Then I must speak more plainly I suppose," answered Valentine, "the fact is, sir, I have seen a great deal of your uncle's property removed in hackney coaches, and the natural inference is, that the whole of it is to be removed in a similar manner at your father's earliest opportunity."

"Upon my soul, your prying curiosity is very impertinent," exclaimed Arnold, sorely perplexed at these direct charges, but perceiving the approach of his father he continued;—but let that be sir, here comes the old man, and I dare say he can best explain his reason for acting as he has."

"What's all this about?" demanded Mr. Henry Bramstone, who at that moment came up to the place where they were standing, "who is it that disputes my right to act in any way I please?"

"This young man does," replied his son, pointing contemptuously towards Valentine,—"it seems he don't approve of your taking care of my uncle's property, and, as if that was not enough, he actually finds fault with your having discharged a servant of the old gentleman's."

"Humph!" growled his father; "it would be a great deal better if people were to mind their own affairs better and interfere less with those of other people."

"Nay, if your intentions are correct you will readily excuse me," answered our hero; "that I have,—as your son says,—expressed my surprise at certain things that have taken place during the mysterious absence of my friend, is very true. It certainly does appear very strange, and, for your own sake, I should say a thorough explana-

tion of the whole affair would be much better for all parties."

"Perhaps Mr. Vaux will reserve his advice for those that need it," exclaimed the old man sullenly.

"At any rate he cannot expect it to have any effect upon us," chimed in Arnold. "We are acting,—as we consider,—in the best way to serve uncle Septimus's interest, and all that know us will speak a good word in our favour in spite of the malicious misrepresentations of a stranger, who having being kindly received by our family would now turn round and stab our credit.

"I have already told you," replied Mr. Henry Bramstone, "that my brother has left town for a time, but where he has gone to, or what the nature of the business is that has taken him away, is, I must confess, as great a mystery to me as it appears to be to yourself. Yet you see I make no fuss about it, as you have done, and I dare say, by-and-bye, he will return in spite of all your gloomy prognostications to the contrary."

"I should rejoice if it were so," answered Valentine, "but I cannot help saying that at present I see no chance of it. That there has been foul play I am very certain, and equally positive am I that he has been injured by those from whom he had least reason to expect such conduct."

"Upon my word, young man," exclaimed Henry Bramstone, "your words are enough to provoke a saint! I have repeatedly denied knowing anything about my brother's present place of abode, and yet you pertinaciously persist in accusing me of having practised some foul device or other against him."

"Perhaps Mr. Vaux will state broadly what he means," cried Arnold, who by this time began to think it would be as well to act the part of a bully.

"If you wish it I will certainly do so," answered our hero with perfect composure.

"Well, then, I wish it for one," exclaimed Harry Bramstone.

"And I, for another," continued his son,

"Then I will certainly no longer hesitate," replied Valentine. "The fact is, I believe that for some guilty purpose of your own he has been placed in a lunatic asylum, where it is intended he shall pass the remainder of his days, unless I am fortunate enough to discover the wretched dungeon to which he has been consigned."

"Incredible audacity!" exclaimed the elder Mr. Bramstone; "and pray, sir, if I may be as bold as to ask, what reason may you have for fixing so foul a stigma on our characters?"

"Aye, aye, explain that, sir, if you please," exclaimed Arnold.

"Oh, I have pretty good ground for the supposition, I can assure you," answered our hero firmly, "You remember the visit that was paid your brother not many days since, by a couple of persons calling themselves doctors?"

"We have only your asssertion in proof of it," replied Harry.

"Nay," resumed our hero, "you forget that the servant girl you have just now thought fit to dismiss from her master's house is a witness who can and will confirm what I have said. I have taken care to procure her address, and whenever her evidence may be required, she will be ready to come forward."

"You don't mean to say that you intend to carry this foolish affair before a police magistrate?" exclaimed the old man with alarm.

"But I do mean it, though," answered Valentine cooly.

"Then in my opinion, young man," resumed the other, "you had better employ yourself in a more creditable way. Was it for this my brother brought you into his house? was it for this he treated a perfect stranger as if he had been his own son?"

"To you I owe no kindness," returned Valentine, "whilst to your brother I owe a heavy debt of gratitude that never can be cancelled. For that reason I am resolved to use all exertions for his discovery, and if your own character should suffer by it, let it be remembered that t e fault was none of my own."

"Upon my soul, I feel half inclined to thrash you for your d——d impertinence!" exclaimed Arnold, unable any longer to restrain the passion that had been for some time working within him."

"In a good cause I can defend myself, I dare say," replied Valentine, unmoved by the threats of the other.

"Then take that!" exclaimed Arnold fiercely, and at the same time aiming a heavy blow at the object of his wrath. Fortunately, however, his father interposed and himself received the blow which had been intended for our hero.

"Don't be such an infernal fool, Arnold!" he exclaimed; "if this quarrel goes on, we shall attract the notice of the passengers, who will, no doubt, believe the version of the affair given by this young man."

"And what care I if they do?" demanded Arnold fiercely; "they may think as they please, but fortunately in England they must do something more than think before they can convict a man."

"Well, then, don't be such a fool as to go quarrelling in the streets," exclaimed the old man, giving him back the picture which he had put into his hands when he made his attack upon Valentine. But the other was too much excited now to be easily pacified, and thrusting it back he threw off his coat, whilst a crowd of people thronged round, having been attracted to the spot by the loud tones in which the latter part of the conversation had been carried on.

"Five to one upon Shirt-sleeve!" exclaimed a dirty-looking butcher's-boy, who with his tray on his shoulder was standing by to see the fun. But Arnold was in no humour to put up with any nonsense, and feeling deeply offended at the term by which he had been addressed, he let fly a tremendous blow at the youth, which sent him, tray, meat, and all into the kennel. Upon this a tremendous outcry was raised by the mob. and before Arnold had time to secure his safety by flight, he was seized in the arms of a sturdy coal-porter, who, lifting him up with about as much ease as a cat would a mouse, carried him to a place where there happened to be a large collection of mud, and there deposited his burden, amidst the laughter and applause of the bystanders.

All this was scarcely the work of an instant, so that had Valentine been able there would not have been sufficient time to prevent the perpetration of the punishment he had thus been made to endure. As soon, however, as the mob dispersed—which it did immediately upon a cry being raised that the police were coming—he rushed towards the place where Arnold had been laid, and assisting him out of his present very aukward situation, he did what he could towards his comfort—an act of kindness which the other was by no means inclined to refuse, though only a minute before he had been vowing vengeance against him. Even Henry Bramstone could not help thanking our hero for his generous conduct in not leaving them to their fate, and no sooner had they entered a coach which had been called to convey them home, than offering their hands to him, they invited him to pay them a visit as soon as he could divest himself of the opinion he entertained with respect to their supposed conduct towards Septimus. This our hero promised to do, and as soon as they drove off he returned to his lodgings there to ruminate upon the past, and to form plans by which to discover the place in which Mr. Septimus Bramstone might be discovered. But it was not easy to satisfy himself in the latter respect, and abandoning one scheme after another as fast as they were formed, he at last determined to wait until he could obtain some satisfactory clue, and then prosecute his enquiries with untiring energy.

CHAPTER XXI.

VALENTINE EXHIBITS SOME OF HIS GENERALSHIP.—SCENE AT AN AUCTION, IN WHICH A COUPLE OF RIVAL ISRAELITES FIGURE RATHER PROMINENTLY. — VALENTINE SHOWS HOW CONSCIENCE MAY BE AWAKENED IN THE GUILTY BY THE MOST TRIVIAL CIRCUMSTANCE. — ANOTHER ROW.

THERE is nothing so harrassing and vexatious as uncertainty, when the happiness of those we regard is at stake. Valentine endured tortures when he reflected upon the probable misery to which his friend was subjected, and each hour that passed away served but to increase his alarm, and confirm him more and more in the opinion he had formed with respect to the rascally part which had been played by Harry Bramstone and his son. Once or twice he thought of applying to a magistrate for a warrant against the supposed delinquent, but then he had no absolute proof to support the charge he wished to make, and if he failed in his evidence against them, he knew it would only encourage them to proceed in the villainous affair with more determination than ever. Thus restrained, he determined to remain quiet for the present, and by apparent carelessness as to the fate of his friend, to throw his enemies off their guard, and then pounce upon them when least prepared to deny whatever he might bring against them.

On the two days immediately following that on which his last interview with Arnold and his father took place, he observed with wonder and alarm, that the goods were removed from the residence of Septimus, and conveyed to an auction room in the neighbourhood. This pretty well explained the business that was going on, but if further proof was needed, it was afforded within a day or two afterwards by some large placards, with which the walls were ornamented, announcing the sale by auction of the furniture belonging to a gentleman retiring into the country. This excited his indignation, but swallowing his wrath as well as he could he determined to attend the sale, and if possible, frustrate by his presence the villainous project which had been set on foot.

At last when the morning arrived, Valentine left his new lodgings with an aching heart, and having made his way through the crowded streets, arrived at the place where the sale was announced to take place. As he entered the room he took a rapid survey of the motley group there assembled, and observing among the company the well-known features of Harry Bramstone and his son, he slipped into a place where he was least likely to be recognised, and waited with anxious impatience until the business of the day should commence. Here he had time to look about him and ascertain the various, and in many respects, eccentric characters by whom he was surrounded. Among the most prominent of this singular assemblage, were numerous brokers who make it a rule to attend all sales, and either by their insolence or their jeers, to prevent any lots of importance being purchased by those who do not happen to belong to their cheating fraternity. These fellows were easily to be distinguished by the low cunning expressed in their countenance, and the blackguard attempts at wit, that every now and then broke from them. There, too, they elbowed their way to the best places in the room, and when any ladies happened to be in their way, they commenced a filthy conversation among themselves, which, from past experience, they well knew would be sure to drive them away to another and less advantageous post. On several occasions Valentine could scarcely refrain from punishing these vermin as they deserved —but their numbers deterred him, and with indignation he was compelled to hear their blackguardism poured forth in the presence of those whose sex should have been their protection.

In addition to those, were a number of Jews, all of whom were anxious to " puy a pargain," and whose long beards wagged again, as they thought of the profits they should make out of their day's work. They were a villanous looking set of rascals, and perhaps were awake of the little estimation in which they were held, for they associated with none except those who belonged to their own fraternity, and even the brokers, bad as they were, stood aloof from men whose grasping avarice if possible, exceeded their own. These our hero watched with particular interest, and in his own mind he determined they should have no bargain if he could help it.

" After waiting an hour and a half over the time announced for the commencement of the sale, the auctioneer, a dapper looking fellow, stepped into the rostrum, and having ran over the condition with a rapidity that rendered them perfectly untelligible, he commenced by offering the first lot to the attention of his customers. This and the few lots that followed offered but little temptation for competition, but at length, when a portrait of Mr. Bramstone was put up, Valentine resolved to save it from the fate to which it had been doomed. At first the biddings went on very languidly in spite of the high-flown eulogiums passed upon it by the crafty auctioneer, but no sooner had the knight of the hammer passed his word as an honest man that it was the work of an eminent artist than the price rapidly increased from a small sum to what appeared to be a very evtravagant price.

" Gentlemen," said Mr. Doublebid, the auctioneer, " here is a painting offered to your notice for which no less than three hundred guineas could be anything like its real value. You are already aware that it is the work of that eminent painter Mr. Daubphiz, and I need not tell you the large sums his pictures always fetched in the market. Observe the colouring—the tone—the keeping,—are they not exquisite, and do they not tempt you to possess a treasure that of itself would be a fortune to your children? I have told you it is worth three or four hundred guineas, and yet the biddings have only reached the paltry sum of nine pounds ten shillings ;—going for nine pounds ten; —for nine pounds ten shillings if there is no further advance ;—for nine pounds ten—

" Ten pounds," squeaked a little old man who had been examining it for the last few minutes through his eye glass."

"Ten pounds is offered," exclaimed the auctioneer, " this truly magnificent picture is going for ten pounds. Really, gentlemen, you cannot be aware of the prize you are thus suffering to escape through your fingers :—the work of Daubphiz are immortalized, and after the death of that truly eminent man his pictures will fetch the prices that will put the works of other men to the blush.

VALENTINE VAUX,

OR THE

TRICKS OF A VENTRILOQUIST.

BY TIMOTHY PORTWINE.

"Eleven pounds," again squeaked the aforesaid little gentleman.

"Five and twenty guineas," exclaimed Valentine in a tone so much like that of Mr. Septimus Bramstone that both Harry and Arnold looked round them with terror.

"Thank you for that bidding," said the auctioneer, chuckling at the rapid advance he was making.

"Where's the gen'l'man as gave that ere last bidding?" enquired one of the brokers, glancing round to have a look at what he imagined to be a regular flat.

"I don't see the gentleman," replied the knight of the hammer, "but he is somewhere at the bottom of the room, and will, of course, come forward if the picture should happen to be knocked down to him."

"I say, Moses," whispered one of the Jews to another who was standing next to him, "this here picture seems to be a good 'un, and we mustn't let a stranger have it. Go halves with me, and while you bid I'll remain silent."

"It's a pargain, Mishter Lazarus," returned the other in an under tone, "we'll have it between us,—but no gammon, you know, ma tear,—we'll divide the profit, and no mistake."

"Will you!" thought Valentine

who happened to have overheard them. "we shall see them presently."

"Now, gentlemen," resumed the auctioneer, "you have heard the last bidding for this valuable picture,—five and twenty guineas only have been offered for it, and unless some more spirited person advances upon that small sum it must be knocked down at a price that is really melancholy to think of."

"Thirty pounds for de rubbish," cried Moses, endeavouring as much as possible to depreciate the article he wanted to purchase.

"Forty," exclaimed Valentine, imitating the voice of Lazarus, and directing it exactly towards the spot where the crafty Israelite was standing.

"Going for forty pounds," exclaimed the auctioneer,—for forty pounds if there's no further advance."

"Vot a blessed fool you are, Lazarus," muttered the other Jew between his teeth, "didn't you promise not to bid agen' me, and there you've gone and advanced the price when it was just going to be knocked down to me for thirty."

"S'elp me bob I never did nothing of the sort," answered Lazarus.

"You didn't! vot hinfernal liars some people are!" exclaimed his antagonist. "But others heard it as well as myself, I dare say, so I just axes the gem'men about it if they didn't hear you as well as I did."

"In coorse we did," responded twenty voices at once; for whenever a bit of mischief is afoot there are always plenty who are willing to take part against the weaker side.

"There!" exclaimed Moses with triumph, "others heer'd yer as well as myself, and I mean to say yer ought to be ashamed o' yerself for trying to cheat an old pal in this here sort of a way."

"Really, gentlemen, this disturbance must not take place here," interposed the auctioneer, "business must not be interrupted like this, and I can only say that, if any body feels inclined for a fight, there is a spacious yard at the back of these premises, where you may amuse yourself to your heart's content.

"He knows better," exclaimed Valentine, directing his voice so that it should appear to proceed from the lips of Lazarus.

Hereupon Moses felt that his courage had been called in question, and eyeing his antagonist with the fury of an enraged tiger, he struck him a blow in the mouth that sent the unfortunate Israelite reeling half across the room. But the other recovered himself in an instant, and darting forward upon the aggressor he seized upon his long flowing beard, which he pulled and tugged at with so much violence that the other was fain to roar out lustily through the torture he was thus made to endure. Presently, however, the spirit of retaliation fired his soul, and grasping his adversary by the same grizzly appendage, he gave the hapless Lazarus such a vigourous shaking that in his turn he also was obliged to cry out for quarter. But this was not granted by the incensed Jew, and as it was absolutely imperative that they should try for the mastery, a struggle ensued, which it would baffle any description of ours properly to describe. It is sufficient to say that the greatest confusion prevailed, some portion of the company taking part with one side and the remaining portion with the other. At last a messenger was despatched for a couple of policemen, upon the arrival of whom, the belligerents were taken into custody and conveyed to the station-house, there to remain until a magistrate should decide upon the punishment to be inflicted upon the uproarious Jews.

Order having been restored, the auctioneer once more commenced the business of the day, and taking up the bidding at thirty pounds, was about to knock it down at that sum, when Valentine imitating the voice of Septimus Bramstone, advanced the price to fifty. The effect of this was instantaneous upon Harry and his son, who gazed upon each other with guilty astonishment, and then turning their eyes to the end of the room from where the voice seemed to have come, they looked as if expecting to be at once confronted by the relative, whom their infamous arts had incarcerated in a madhouse. To their surprise, however, the old gentleman was not to be seen anywhere about the place, and whilst they were yet wondering what all this could mean, the picture was knocked down at the price last mentioned.

"What name shall I say for the purchaser?" asked the knight of the hammer, looking round him with the complacency of a man who had just done something highly satisfactory.

"Septimus Bramstone," replied Valentine in the voice of his kind old friend.

"It's false!" exclaimed Harry vehemently, "Septimus Bramstone is not at this time in London, and this is only some hoax to interrupt the sale."

"I should like to catch somebody trying to hoax *me!*" cried the auctioneer pompously.

"Then, I can only tell you that somebody is trying to do it now," observed Arnold, glancing uneasily about him.

Upon this a shout of laughter was raised among the company, which served considerably to increase the discomfiture of the auctioneer. But he was not a man to be trifled with in this sort of way, and after swallowing his indignation, he, in an authoritative tone, desired the purchaser to come forward and complete the purchase he had made.

"I can't," replied the supposed buyer,—"some villains have got hold of me, and there are those in the room who will take care to have me carried back to the horrible place I have just escaped from."

"Dear me, this is very odd!" cried the auctioneer, looking very grave; "a very singular circumstance, indeed; but, perhaps, the gentleman will be good enough to come forward in order that we may ascertain the truth of what he says."

"Not on any account," cried the elder Mr. Bramstone, shuddering at the suggestion. "There is some mystery in this; but in my opinion, it will turn out to be the raving of a madman, and if so, who knows what mischief he may do us all."

"Very true," returned the auctioneer, and then addressing himself to those at the further end of the room, he entreated them on no account to suffer the unfortunate man to approach. On this, every body hurried forward as far as they could, leaving thereby a large space where, a short time ago, a dense crowd had been assembled. As for Valentine, he took advantage of the opportunity then afforded, and still speaking in the voice of Septimus Bramstone, he enquired by whose authority the sale had been ordered to take place?"

"By that of your brother," answered he of the rostrum.

"Then he is a villain!" cried the voice.

"Who says my father is a villain?" demanded Arnold, jumping up from his seat, and looking as fierce as possible.

"I say no," replied the imaginary Septimus; "your uncle charges him with having foully plotted against the peace and happiness of his own brother, and if any body doubt me, I am here to substantiate the charge. I have found means to escape from my keepers, and never will I rest satisfied until justice has been done upon my cruel foes."

"Upon my life this is a very extraordinary affair," exclaimed the auctioneer. "The business begins to wear a very black aspect, and I begin to wish I never had any thing to do with it."

"You will have reason to wish so still more before long," replied the mysterious voice. "There is law in the land to protect people against the villany of rogues, and every one that has been engaged in this plot against me, shall find to his cost that I am not to be thrust into a lunatic asylum without an effort being made to punish my persecutors."

"But, my good sir——"

"Don't good sir me!" interrupted the imaginary Septimus.

"I am an ill-used man, and no blarney in the world shall prevent the infliction of speedy vengeance upon every rascal that has injured me. I have been locked in a madhouse without cause, and having by good luck made my escape, there shall soon be such a breeze stirring, that my enemies shall quail before the storm they have themselves raised."

"And pray," demanded Harry Bramstone, "who do you charge with having practised against your peace and happiness?"

"Yourself for one!" answered the voice.

"And who else?" asked Arnold tremblingly.

"Yourself for another!" continued the mysterious personage.

"Good heavens!" exclaimed both father and son, "how could you ever think us so base and unnatural?"

"Oh, I have proof against you," replied the supposed Septimus; "your actions are pretty well known to me, and now my turn for triumph is come. You shall both suffer for this, depend on it, and even if the gallows were to claim you for its victim, I would not raise my voice to save either the one or the other from a well-merited doom."

"I hope you don't think I have any thing to do with the business," cried the auctioneer.

"How can I think otherwise, when I find you in the very act of selling my property?" demanded the voice.

"And yet that was no fault of mine," answered he of the hammer. "I have only acted in the way of my business, and who is there that would refuse a job when it is brought, I should like to know?"

"Very good! very good!" cried a dozen or two of Jews, who fully concurred in the tradesmanlike view taken of the affair by the auctioneer.

"He will find it very bad, I'm thinking," replied the same mysterious and unseen person. "He is engaged in a conspiracy to injure me, and unless he consent immediately to stop this sale, I will let him know that people are not to be wronged by those who are hungering after property that is not theirs to dispose of."

"Am I to understand then that it is your wish the sale should be stopped?" asked the man of business.

"Most assuredly you are!"

"And do you consent that I should do so?" asked the auctioneer of Mr. Harry Bramstone.

"Why, between ourselves," whispered the party addressed, "it may perhaps be as well to comply for the present. There seems to be some mistake here, and as I do not wish to do any thing unfair, it may be better to postpone the sale till we have ascertained whether there really exists any impediment to its completion."

"Gentlemen," said the auctioneer, addressing himself to the company, "it appears that there is some objection to the sale being completed to-day, and therefore I must beg of you to give me your attendance at some future time, when, I have no doubt, the obstacle will have been removed."

"Ish deré to be no more lots put up den?" cried a disappointed Jew, with evident vexation.

"No more to-day," replied the auctioneer.

"Den all I can say ish that it ish a damned shame," exclaimed another of the Israelites. "Ve vas brought all dish vay to puy pargains, and den you stop de sale and tell us to valk home again like so many fools."

"It can't be helped, gentlemen," answered the other; "you have heard what has passed, and of course I cannot run the risk of an action being brought against me after a formal protest has been given in by the person who declares himself to be the owner of the property."

"Ve harn't nuffin at all to do vith that," cried a greedy broker, who had been amusing himself by pinning a couple of his neighbours to each other. "If so be as you advertizes a sale to take place, ve expects as how you'll keep yer vord, and not gammon us arter ve're all met together, jist as if ve varn't nobody nor nuffin."

At this moment the two men that had been pinned together by the skirts of their coats, began to give certain indications that they were not altogether satisfied with their situation. First of all they began by gently pulling to disengage themselves; but as this had not the desired effect, they forthwith commenced dragging, and bawling, and swearing away with all their might, as if blaming each other for that of which they were perfectly innocent. But even this was not sufficient to release them from their awkward situation, and at last, rendered desperate by rage, they both made a rush in opposite directions. The effect of this movement may be readily imagined;—the skirts of their coats were both torn off by the violence, and when this impediment was got rid of, they flew reeling forward till each lay sprawling on the floor. Curses "both loud and deep" now succeeded, and the probability is, that a desperate battle would have taken place between them, had not some of the spectators interfered to prevent the collision. Neither, however, seemed resolved not to be disappointed in this John Bull mode of seeking satisfaction, and retiring to the yard which had been previously mentioned by the auctioneer, they then set to in gallant style until both had received a drubbing that they were not likely to forget in a hurry.

As for Valentine, he succeeded, through imitating the voice of Septimus Bramstone, in procuring the postponement of the sale, and not wishing to be seen by either Harry or his son, he left the place as soon as possible, resolving in his own mind not to leave a stone unturned till he had discovered the place where his friend had been secre'ed, and restored him to that happiness which the villany of his relatives had deprived him of."

———

CHAPTER XXII.

SHOWS HOW VALENTINE RESOLVED TO PASS AWAY AN HOUR OR TWO. — A GREAT MEETING OF THE SOVEREIGN PEOPLE. — A SPECIMEN OF POPULAR ORATORY, AND HOW THE BUSINESS OF THE DAY WAS INTERRUPTED IN A MOST DISGRACEFUL MANNER. —A FIGHT BETWEEN MR. BOWBELL AND THE GENTLEMAN IN THE WHITE WAISTCOAT, AND THE WAY IN WHICH MATTERS WERE BROUGHT TO A CLOSE.

WHEN our hero left the auction, he proceeded at a pretty brisk pace, scarcely knowing and certainly not caring much which way he was going. He thought deeply upon the subject of his poor friend Septimus, and the events of each day only served more and more to confirm the opinion he had formed as to the melancholy fate to which he had been reduced by his artful relations. At length, however, these cogitations were disturbed by the distant humming of many voices, and looking in the direction from whence the sound came, he perceived a long procession of low looking fellows marching along with banners, the mottos and devices upon which were of anything but a peaceful character. Wondering what all this could mean, he ventured to enquire the cause of the demonstration of the first person he could speak to, and, from him, he learnt that a great meeting was to beheld of the "Sovereign People," on Kennington Common, and that this was only a small portion of the mass expected to meet on the present occasion. This piece of information was enough for Valentine, who was as all times ready to rush into scenes where information and amusement were to be gathered, and having nothing to do, he determined to visit the place of meeting, and observe the conduct of men whose intentions he felt satisfied were anything but peaceable. No sooner was this intention formed, than he jumped into a cab, and ordering the driver to take him to the place described, he fell into a train of thought, the principal subject of which was the folly of men who endeavoured by physical force to overpower a government which possesses so many and such ample means to defeat the plans of their enemies.

Arrived at the spot he discharged the vehicle, and then elbowing his way towards a waggon which had been placed there to serve the purpose of a platform for the speakers. Here he found himself closely jammed in by the "unwashed and unshaved," who having waited a couple of hours beyond the time appointed for the commencement of business, were vociferous in the demands that some one should be placed in the chair, and that the important affairs for which they were assembled, should be instantly proceeded with.

But they might as well have blustered to the winds as give vent to their fury on the present occasion, for it so happened that no influential person happened to be present, and the consequence was that the tempest of fury kept on increasing till fears begun to be entertained that a serious outbreak would take place and that their object would be defeated by giving their opponents an excuse for interfering to put an end to the meeting. Just at that period, however, a shout was raised that the procession was in sight, and a passage having been opened through the crowd, about a dozen of the leaders marched pompously through to take their places on the temporary stage or platform. This matter being arranged, and sundry terrific cheers having been given by the multitude, a little man enveloped in a huge cloak, stepped forward to propose that Mr. Bowbell should take the chair on the present momentous occasion. This was seconded by a remarkably tall personage, with a very thin, wiry voice, and as no one ventured to hold up a hand against it, the aforesaid Mr. Bowbell advanced, bowed around him with great complacency, and thus addressed his auditors :—

"Men and brothers,—we are as-sembled here to demonstrate to England and the whole world, that we will no longer consent to be trampled on like slaves. The respectable assemblage I see before me will by their numbers strike terror into the hearts of our foes, and at our mighty voice the tyrants shall tremble and yield up those rights which have been so long and so shamefully withheld from us."

"Put your head in a bag old un !" exclaimed Valentine, throwing his voice so that it seemed to proceed from one of the persons standing behind him on the platform.

"Who was it that made use of that ungentlemanly allusion ?" demanded the incensed Bowbell. "Who was it, I say, that desired me to put my head in a bag ?"

"The gemman in a vhite vaistcoat at the back of the waggon," replied one of the crowd.

"Then I'll thank the gemman in a white waistcoat to hold his tongue," exclaimed the indignant Bowbell ;— "he is interrupting the business for which we—the sovereign people— have assembled, and his conduct convinces me that we have spies among us, and that the sooner we get rid of them the better."

"He ought to be ducked in a horsepond," exclaimed Valentine, directing his voice to another part of the crowd.

And so the multitude seemed to think, for a desperate rush was made towards the hustings, and there is little doubt but that the gentleman and his white waistcoat would have made acquaintance with the nearest muddy ditch, had not the little man with the huge cloak advanced and claimed a hearing from his dearly beloved multitude. Being a mighty favourite he was allowed to proceed, and assuring his friends that discord among themselves at this moment, would ruin all their prospects, he succeeded in postponing the ducking to a future opportunity. This done, Mr. Bowbell once more advanced to the front of the husting ;—

"It ain't," he continued, "that I mind what any body says, but the respectability of this meeting must be upheld, and how can that be done if speakers are to be interrupted by those who are sent among us as spies and informers?" [Bravo Bowbell.] I say, fellow countrymen, that we are an ill-used, despised, trodden-upon, oppressed, and tax-devoured people. Our rulers have no pity for the productive classes,—of which I am proud to call myself a member. [Hear! hear!] Yes, gentlemen, I am proud to call myself one of you, and I only wish to convince you that no man can be happy till every one of us, rich as well as poor, are brought to a level with each other."

At this period a huge hard-hearted cabbage was thrown by some unseen hand with such fatal precision, that taking the unfortunate Mr. Bowbell in the paunch, it laid him sprawling among the select few who had been admitted to a place on the platform. This was a levelling system that was very unpalatable to the leaders, and no sooner had Bowbell been picked up and placed once more upon his legs, than the busy little gentleman in the huge cloak, advanced to the front of the platform where he stood thumping a roll of papers which he held in his hand till he seemed to have worked himself into a perfect frenzy of passion.

"Gentlemen," he at last exclaimed, "that cabbage could have been thrown by no other hands than those of some scoundrel sent among us by government to interrupt and disturb the harmony of our meeting. But we will disappoint our oppressors, and they shall find that we can throw cabbages quite as well as themselves."

As he said this, he spurned the vegetable missile with his foot, and sent it rushing through the air amidst the laughter and jeers of the motley assemblage. Unfortunately, however, the cabbage happened to alight upon the head of a patriotic tailor, who, thinking some insult was intended to be conveyed thereby, hurled back the hard-hearted symbol of his profession with such admirable precision and effect, that the little man in the cloak would have been violently dashed upon the platform had not a stout gentleman behind caught him in his arms. This incident served to excite the wrath of the small gentleman, who, looking daggers at the populace, turned away, and was immediately lost amongst his bigger associates. Upon this the chairman thought it necessary to read the crowd a lecture on the impropriety of their conduct, in a manner not quite so mild as it might have been.

"Really, my friends," he exclaimed, "this conduct is the most extraordinary I ever witnessed in my life, and I cannot designate it under any other terms than as being ruffianly, blackguardly, and disgusting to a degree—"

"Sit down, you old fool," cried Valentine, so managing his voice that it appeared to proceed from a gigantic coal-heaver, who had taken his place on the nave of the wheel, at no great distance from the speaker's right hand.

"Countrymen and brothers!" roared Bowbell, "will you suffer me to be insulted by a rascally, black-visaged ruffian like that?—Is there no one present that will tear him to pieces for me, or must I be insulted whilst performing a great public service for the good of my country? Pull him down, I say, and let him feel from your hands that a man who comes forward in defence of your liberties is not to be called a fool with impunity!"

"Hear, hear, hear!" shouted the mob, but not a man among them attempted to interfere with the coal-heaver, whose colossal proportions were enough to obtain for him that respect which he otherwise would not have experienced at the hands of the "sovereign people." Bowbell saw that his auditors were not likely to punish the offender as he desired, and throwing himself upon his seat, he made room for the next gentleman who wished to deliver himself of speech. This personage was no other than Mr. Kagmag, a respectable butcher, from Clare Market, who, being one of the million, was of course an ill-used individual.

"Gen'l'men," he exclaimed, "I ain't altogether used to public speaking, but that don't sinnify when a man's going to unbussom himself. I see some ladies on my right hand casting sheep's-eyes towards me, but I'd advise 'em to keep their hearts for some other customer, 'cause you see I've got a rib of my own at home, and she'd make no bones about giving a little more tongue than perhaps they'd like to put up with —so you see——"

"Question! question!" shouted the mob.

"This is not the place nor the time for a man to be alluding to family jars," exclaimed Mr. Delph, the chinaman.

"Chair, chair!" vociferated a lusty little fellow, who it afterwards appeared was an itinerant repairer of the article he had named.

"I'll tell you what it is, my friends," interposed Bowbell, "it appears to me that you all wish to be talking instead of setting about the business that has called us together. We ought to be speaking in thunder to our tyrants, and yet you are fretting away the time in useless talk, whilst our enemies are laughing in their sleeves at our want of unity. Let us show a bold front to our rulers, and take my word for it they will shake in their shoes before another week is over their heads."

"And who is to be our leader," demanded Valentine, who really enjoyed the fun.

"I will," replied Mr. Bowbell with heroism,—let the people only follow my example and they shall be free!"

"The police are marching down upon us in a body!" cried Valentine lustily.

"The devil they are!" exclaimed Mr. Bowbell;—then here goes to look out for number one!"

And jumping hastily from the chair he was preparing to leap from the platform among the crowd, when some one seizing him by the shoulders, dragged him once more back to his seat.

"What do you mean, Mr. Chairman?" he asked,—" would you desert your friends because a few policemen are coming here to intimidate us?"

"Wh-a-a-at do you mean?" stam-mered the alarmed Mr. Bowbell,— "would you have me to stay here to be slaughtered by the blue devil rascals?"

"It's all a hoax!" shouted a voice from the crowd, "there's no police coming, and if there was, ain't we strong enough to send 'em all to the right about?"

"Are you sure it's a hoax?" asked Mr. Bowbell, somewhat reviving under this assurance.

"Quite certain," answered the same voice from the crowd.

"Then all I can say is," resumed the chairman, "that it's an infamous thing to be frightening people out of their lives when there's no occasion for it. For my own part I'm as bold and courageous a man as you'll meet with, but one can't help being nervous when fools raise a cry of danger."

"You are an infernal coward!" exclaimed Valentine, again throwing his voice that it seemed to proceed from the before mentioned man in the white waistcoat. Upon this, Mr. Bowbell looked unutterable things, and darting a look of sovereign contempt upon the person he supposed had insulted him, he said:—

"This is the second time, sir, you have dared to speak to me that no Englishman with any blood in his veins can put up with. You have called me a coward, sir;—a coward—"

"So you are!" retorted our hero in the same tone as before.

"There! you hear him, gentlemen!" exclaimed Bowbell, "you hear what he says, and if that ain't actionable I don't know what is. I'll go to law with the scoundrel, and bring him to his senses that way,—that's what I will."

"Damn the law!" shouted the little man in the cloak, "pitch into him, old boy, and let him find that a true-born Briton like you ain't to be called a coward for nothing."

"Let him call me so again, and see if I don't give him what he won't like," replied Bowbell, shrinking as if afraid lest his challenge should be accepted.

"You are an infernal coward!"

VALENTINE VAUX,

OR THE

TRICKS OF A VENTRILOQUIST.

BY TIMOTHY PORTWINE.

again shouted Valentine, and so successfully did he perform this feat of ventriloquism that everybody could have sworn the words were uttered by the gentleman in the white waistcoat. Indeed, poor Bowbell was so convinced of it, that clenching his fist in a mortal passion, he made a rush at the supposed delinquent, and dealt him such a facer that the other reeled and would have fallen had not some one or other been civil enough to save him. Upon this, he began to think that it was high time to retaliate upon his aggressor, and seizing him round the waist, raised him up by main force, and would have dropped

him over the side of the waggon if the people underneath had not resisted, a feat that would have been by no means a pleasant one for themselves. In fac't they would not allow the worthy chairman to be got rid of in this way, so that the gentleman in the white waistcoat was obliged to desist and content himself with dropping his load upon the platform, and then administering a kick to that part of the body which is usually called the seat of honour. This seemed to arouse all the energies of the insulted party, who, jumping up from his recumbent position, darted upon his antagonist, and closing in upon him

No. 16.

commenced operating upon his ribs with such violence that the other began to roar aloud for quarter. It was, indeed, an interesting sight to watch the motions of the combatants as they writhed to and from, administering and receiving thumps with a rapidity that would have excited the admiration, if not the laughter, of our scientific pugilists.

At last it became evident that both the parties were exhausting themselves, and equally certain was it that they were striving with all their might and main to obtain some advantage by which the struggle might be brought to a speedy termination. For this purpose they were gradually approaching the edge of the platform, each of them being in hope that he might be able to hurl his antagonist over, and then terminate an affray which both of them found had been protracted for too long already. But in this they were both doomed to suffer alike, for in the midst of the tussle they kicked against a piece of projecting wood, and over they both went amidst the laughter and jeers of the spectators.

At this moment, too, a shout was again raised that a strong body of the police was coming, and as the report was on this occasion perfectly correct, every body began to look out for his own safety with surprising agility. In fact, so effectual was the report, and so greatly did it operate upon the crowd, that in a few minutes the place was nearly deserted by the thousands who had, but a short time before, covered the common with a dense mass of human beings.

As for Valentine, he, wisely enough, thought that discretion the better part of valour, and having no wish to be taken up on a charge of riot and disorder, he turned from the spot, and taking the first bye-street he came to, passed onward until he once more found himself in one of the main streets, at some distance from the scene he had just been visiting. By this it was growing dark, and enquiring his way to Drury Lane Theatre, he entered its portals, resolving to spend the evening there with more rationality than had marked the previous part of the day.

CHAPTER XXIII.

Septimus Bramstone and his persecutors.—The art of torturing made easy; or, how to convince the commissioner of a man's madness.—The old gentleman entertains serious thoughts of effecting his escape.—An attempt is made, and the result which follows it.

It is now time that we return to Mr. Septimus Bramstone, who, unfortunately for himself, was still an inmate of the lunatic asylum to which he had been sent through the treachery and avarice of his nearest relatives. On first arriving at the place, he continually raised against his cruel oppressors, and threatened to hurl upon them his heaviest vengeance whenever he had an opportunity of so doing; but this, after all, he found did him more harm than good, for it gave his enemies an advantage over him, as it thus was easy for them to attribute his violence to the disorder with which he was said to be afflicted, and thus it became pretty certain that the remainder of his days would be spent in the madhouse unless he could find means to lull their suspicions, and then effect his escape when such an attempt might be least expected. With this determination he became suddenly mild in his conduct, but at the same time he was anxiously watching every opportunity, and framing, in his own mind, certain projects which he fondly hoped would ultimately lead to his release.

Among other things that had brought him to this way of thinking, was the conversation he frequently had with a fellow-sufferer, named Lawson, who had been a prisoner in this place for upwards of two years, through the rascality of his next heir, who thus hoped to hasten the death of his relative; and consequently possess himself of his property some years before he other-wise might. From this person, Mr. Bramstone learnt many of the infamous practices carried on in these receptacles for the insane, and it was through his advice that he adopted another course for the furtherance of his own release.

One day when they were conversing together in the small yard where they were allowed to exercise themselves for a few hours in the day, our old gentle-man resolved upon making a confidant of his newly found friend, and suddenly changing the conversation in which they were engaged, he inquired whe-ther, in his opinion, it would not be practicable to effect their escape by violent means from the asylum. At this question, Mr. Lainson looked very grave, and shaking his head doubt-fully, he replied :—

" You know not my friend, the dif-ficulties that would beset us on every hand, if such an attempt should be made. Grabfast, the keeper of this place, is ever upon the watch to prevent the escape of any of his unfortunate prisoners, and the keepers that has to guard us know that their situations depend upon the vigilance with which they execute their abominable tasks. They are men without one particle of humanity in their bosoms, and, were we detected in effecting our escape, the result would be to aggravate the mise-ries we have already been made to endure."

" Let them do as they please," ex-claimed Septimus earnestly, for even if they should a'terwards kill me it would be a fortunate escape from the power of wretches whose only purpose seems to be to torture and afflict us."

" Alas! you know them not as I do." exclaimed his companion with a sigh. " The master of this den of misery is paid well for the fiend-like employment he is engaged in, and his object is to keep his victims alive as long as he possibly can. When they die he loses a considerably sum annually, and there-fore, have we little fear of being wor-ried to death, since his own interest is so deeply concerned."

" The scoundrel!" exclaimed Septi-mus, fiercely; " but he shall yet find that he has in me a more difficult cus-tomer to deal with than he expects. I am resolved to make one bold effort for my release, and if you think fit to join me in it, why our chance of success will be all the greater."

" Nay," cried Lawson, " I feel as-sured that it is impracticable,"

" Well," returned the other, " and even supposing it should turn out so, we are not in a worse situation than we were before. They can but keep us here for the remainder of our lives, and that I can see they are determined to do, whether the attempt is made or not."

" But you forget," interposed his friend, " that our condition may be made the worse for it. They have chambers in this place, where the most cruel and unheard-of sufferings are en-dured by those who attempt to regain their liberty. In every case, the poor wretches have been re-captured, and from that moment their sufferings are increased ten fold. They are placed in cells like so many wild beasts; their food is of the worst possible description, and such tortures are inflicted upon them that they, in almost every in-stance, become confirmed maniacs; though before, they had been as little affected with madness as either you or myself."

" All that is very horrible," exclaim-ed Septimus, " yet still am I resolved to make one bold effort rather than remain all my life caged like a wild beast in this horrible 'place. I have fallen into their snares, it is true, but it shall be no fault of mine if I do not give them the slip now when they least expect it. So now tell me—will you join me in making one bold and decided attempt for freedom ?"

" I will," answered Lawson, after a brief pause."

" Good !" exclaimed the other with glee; " your acquiescence has inspired me with renewed hope, and already do I promise myself the success I so much desire. We will leave this place to-gether, and if once I regain my liberty, the first use I will make of it shall be to apply to a magistrate, through whose assistance the rest of our fellow captives shall be released from this loathsome den of iniquity."

"You are ardent in your expectations," replied Lawson, shaking his head, doubtfully, "but I much fear the task is not quite so easy a one as you seem to anticipate. We are closely watched by Grabfast and his vile myrmidons; the gates leading from hence are strongly secured and guarded, and every precaution is used to prevent the possibility of an escape, when once an unfortunate wretch has been brought into the place. The villain knows the certain consequences that would follow an exposure of his infamous conduct, and, for that reason, he takes good care to avoid the possibility of an event which would surely terminate in his own utter ruin and disgrace."

"That may be all very true," answered Septimus, "but even the most cunning are sometimes overreached in spite of all their arts to avoid it. Villany seldom triumphs for ever, nor shall it in this case if I only once contrive to get beyond the walls that at present confine us. The artful machinations of our enemies must be defended, and how is that to be done unless a strenuous effort is made to burst the bonds that confine us?"

"I have already said that you may depend upon my exertions in the cause," replied Lawson, "and it therefore now only remains to arrange the plans we mean to adopt. Do you intend to try violent means, or shall we rather wait till an opportunity occurs to elude the vigilance of our keeper?"

"Nay, we may stay here long enough, if we wait for that," replied Septimus, "so my advice is, that we boldly make an attack upon those who have the charge of us. They will not be prepared for a sudden attack, and in the confusion which will be sure to follow, we may fight our way through every difficulty, and thus regain that liberty of which we have been so unjustly deprived."

"It shall be tried, at all events," exclaimed Lawson, "though, to confess the truth, I must acknowledge that my own expectations of success are not so sanguine as yours. If we fail, our enemies will be more severe than ever, but on the other hand, if the attempt is not made, the probability is that we shall pass the remainder of our lives in this wretched abode of misery and despair."

"Then let the attempt be made immediately," said Mr. Bramston, for it is only by striking a decisive blow that our success depends, and upon that I rely entirely for our release from the captivity to which we are now subjected."

"Be not too sanguine, my good friend," exclaimed the other, "for between ourselves, the chances we have to combat against are greatly to our disadvantage. These men know that every thing will depend upon preventing our escape, and they will not suffer us to slip through their fingers without making an effort that will be more vigourous than you perhaps expect."

"To tell you the truth," answered the old gentleman, "I think very little about the matter, because I know when the time arrives, we must be bold and resolute, so that it would be folly to reflect upon any difficulties we may have to encounter when the moment for action comes. I am not so young as you, Mr. Lawson, but I think, should a struggle take place, these fellows will find that I am a rougher customer than they expected to meet with. This evening, then, we will make the attempt, and may heaven aid us in our effort to overcome the malice of our foes."

"But you have not yet told me your plan," exclaimed Lawson, as the other was about to turn away, for fear of being observed by those who might afterwards frustrate their design."

"Oh, that is simple enough," answered Septimus, stepping back a pace or two, and whispering so as not to be heard, if any listeners should happen to be near. "This afternoon we shall be suffered again to walk about the yard for a short time, and then we must take an opportunity to knock down the keeper whose turn it is to look after us, and who we may then drag into the scullery, and there lock up safely, whilst we rush through the house and force our way through the gates that have been put up to prevent the escape of those whose misfortune it is to enter them. This done, we must run for our lives, for depend on it there will be a desperate effort made to get us once more in their power."

"Hush!" cried Lawson, "one of the keepers is now coming this way ; keep your own counsel, or we shall be suspected, and then all will be lost."

"Well, you fellows, what the devil do you want to be talking to one another for ?" exclaimed the surly ruffian, advancing and giving Septimus a shove that sent him reeling half across the yard ; "what mischief are you up to now, eh? Some mischief, I'll warrant, or you wouldn't be talking in such a low voice, that people mayn't hear what you say."

"I suppose we are not to be debarred the pleasure of speaking to each other," said Lawson meekly. "It is the only indulgence allowed in this place, and surely we may be suffered to enjoy it without incurring all this ill-treatment."

"Don't give us none o' your cheek, or it will be all the worser for yer," retorted the ruffian fiercely, at the same time holding up a stout cudgel, by way of enforcing what he sai d.

"You are a scoundrel for your pains," exclaimed Septimus, who had by this time reached the place from whence he had been so violently thrust ; "you have dared to lay hands upon me, and be assured that it shall not be long before I make you suffer for it. There is law to be had, sirrah, and when once I get out of this accursed den, I'll—"

"Ha! ha! ha!" shouted the fellow, scornfully, "you said *when* you get out, I believe ; but, between you and I, old chap, that 'll be a precious long time first."

"Not so long, perhaps, as you think for," replied Septimus.

"Ah! well, we shall see all about that, I s'pose," retorted the other, with a sneer. "It's all werry well to be bounceable, you know, but I can tell yer, that when once a fellow gets inside these here four stone walls, we always takes precious good care that he sha'n't see the outside on 'em again. So make yerself quite easy, my buffer, and jist take my adwise for the futur', and that is, to be civil to them as has the care on yer, 'cause yer know, they've got yer in their hands, and can make yer jist as uncomfortable as ever they like."

"Aye, aye," you may chuckle as much as you please over your own villanies ; but, remember, the wicked do not always triumph, though circumstances may for a time give them an advantage over those whom they delight in torturing. I have endured insult and ill-usage from you long enough, and hitherto have borne it with tolerable patience, but it will not always be thus, and I warn you that the hour is not far distant when you, and all others who have been concerned in this dastardly plot against me shall be made to suffer for the foul wrongs I have been made to endure."

"Vell, I'm blest if you ain't a going it nicely, old fellow," exclaimed the keeper instantly ; "you're a talking as if you was going to do mighty fine things ; but I can tell you, my tulip, that is won't do here ; and if you're at all rumbustical, there's a strong room for queer customers, like yerself, and yer shall have a taste of it too, in about no time at all, if yer ain't precious quiet about it."

"Scoundrel! do you dare talk to me in this way?" cried Septimus in a towering passion.

"For heaven's sake, my friend, don't irritate the man by saying anything more to him," interposed Lawson, endeavouring to assuage the anger of the old gentleman ; "remember we are both of us in his power; and he can carry his threats into execution at any time he pleases."

"I b'lieve yer, my buffer," exclaimed the keeper with an impudent lear. "We has wonderful persuading ways to deal with obstropolous people in this here place; and I'm blest if I don't put yer up to a move or two in a brace o'shakes, if yer don't be civil. I'm as good and tender-hearted a cove as any in this house, when I has it all my own way, but if people will put me out o' temper, why people must take the consequences; that's all I can say about the matter."

"Well, well, you must make some allowances for this gentleman's infirmity of temper," said Lawrence, endeavouring to soothe the ruffian as well as he could. "People, you know, can't always help their passions getting a-head a little, and I'm sure Mr. Bramstone had no meaning for what he just now said."

"Oh, you're a talking uncommon sensible for a madman, ain't yer?" muttered the keeper; "you want to make yerself out sensible, but it's no go, my fine fellow; I'm a wide awake un, and not to be done; so jist make yerself scarce, that I may settle the difference with this old chap."

"If you think to drive me to the commission of any act of violence, you are mistaken," answered Septimus, calmly. "I was, perhaps, foolish to shew so much warmth as I did just now, but that has passed away, and now all I require is, that we may part before any fresh cause for anger may arise."

"Oh, it's astonishing what a way I've got of bringing people down a peg or two," cried the keeper in a tone of self-satisfaction. "Just now you was a going to do I don't know what, but see what a little bit o' good management will do; it's shewed you that I ain't to be frightened by any o' your big words, and now I can do what I like with you, as if you was a mere child in my hands."

"I would have you beware how you lay hands upon me, though, as you did just now," retorted Septimus; "I was struck without cause, but, much as I might suffer for it afterwards, such another blow would be resented in a manner that would cost one or both of us our lives!"

"Oh, the gen'lman's as mad as a March hare!" exclaimed the fellow, grinning like a fiend at the torture he inflicted. "He wants the straight wes-kit, I'm a thinking; and blow me if he won't have have it too to-morrow, if he ain't a precious sight better than he is now. It's a capital cure for our customers when they grow rumbustical; and many's the one I've put into it for about half what you've said to me jist now, old boy."

"This insolence is not to be borne," exclaimed Mr. Bramstone, furiously.

"Nay, bear with it yet a little while longer," whispered Lawson; "be more composed; it will throw the fellow off his guard, and our chance of escape will be all the better."

"What's that you're a whispering together?" demanded the keeper; "tell me what it was you were a saying, or I'm blessed if I don't—"

"Be more civil my friend," interposed Lawson, with forced calmness, "and, remember, that it is your duty to soothe rather than aggravate the misery of those whose misfortune bring them to this place. I was merely persuading this gentleman to be more composed, and I believe my efforts have not been thrown away upon him."

"Oh, you're a nice man, I don't think" exclaimed the fellow, shaking a huge bunch of keys that he held in his hand. "But come, its time that you should go to dinner now, so stir you, will you? or else I shall give you a gentle rap that you won't forget in a hurry."

Thus admonished, the two friends followed the keeper to the dining room, where between fifty and sixty others were already seated at the table. The two new-comers silently took their places,—swallowed the coarse fare that was placed before them, and when the meal was over, they both repaired once more to the yard, there to await the opportunity to escape, which they so anxiously desired. Nor was it long before the same keeper once more sauntered up to them, and having struck Lawson a smart blow across the shoulders with his stick, he was about to administer a similar dose to Septimus, when the latter, clenching his fist, struck him so sharply and severely that the fellow rolled heavily to the earth, and at the same time raised a shout for assistance.

This noise, however, was quickly stopped by Lawson placing his hand over the ruffian's mouth, and having succeeded in preventing any instant alarm being given, they dragged him to the scullery, where he was left to rent his rage until somebody should go to his assistance. This done, the two friends rushed into the house, broke down the first barrier that interposed itself in their way, and then darting towards the principal gate they soon found themselves engaged with three or four fellows who were placed there to prevent any possibility of escape. But desperate men will dare anything for self-preservation, and battling bravely with their antagonists, they would soon have succeeded in overpowering them had not a fresh gang rushed forward to the assistance of the gate-keepers. In this conflict Lawson was struck down, and once more secured, but Septimus was not to be so easily captured by his enemies, and snatching a bludgeon from one of the men, he dealt two or three of them such severe blows that they started back, yelping like so many curs, and thus gave him an opportunity of springing from the door towards the fields with which the place was surrounded.

Septimus ran with all his might, followed by the whole pack of ruffians by whom he had just been surrounded. Each step, however, served but to convince him that they were gaining upon him, and that, exhausted as he already was, he must again fall into the hands of his enemies. But he knew the fate that awaited him, and resolving to give them as much trouble as possible, he made towards a tree, and placing his back against the trunk, he determined to give his assailants a reception for which they were little prepared.

By this time all his pursuers, but two, had paused from utter exhaustion, but the remaining fellows made fiercely towards him, and in a threatening tone demanded him instantly to surrender. To this command, however,

Septimus Bramstone paid little attention, and as the foremost of the men advanced to seize him by the collar, he dealt him such a tremendous blow under the left ear that the fellow, uttering a dismal howl of agony, sank fainting to the earth. Upon seeing this, the other keeper approached for the purpose of securing his victim, but so resolute was Septimus that it was not until after the man had received several severe blows that he was enabled to close in upon his adversary, and then, once more, make him his prisoner. This done, Septimus was deprived of the weapon he had made such good use of, and being strongly bound with cords he was lead back to the lunatic asylum, from whence two or three people were immediately afterwards despatched to bring in their disabled comrades.

Poor Septimus knew that his fate would now be worse than ever, but resigning himself to whatever might follow, he slowly accompanied one of the keepers to the room where he was henceforth to be confined.

CHAPTER XXIV.

VALENTINE PURSUES A LOVE ADVENTURE, AND WITH WHAT SUCCESS THE READER WILL NOW DISCOVER.—AN APPEARANCE AND A DISAPPEARANCE.—MISS LINWOOD'S EXHIBITION, AND CERTAIN MARVELLOUS EVENTS THAT TOOK PLACE THERE.—HAPPY MEETING, AND MATTERS TAKE A MORE FAVOURABLE TURN.

THE reader, we dare say, has not forgotten Valentine's trip to Richmond, and the young lady he met with on board the steam boat, whose beauty had made so deep an impression upon his very susceptible heart. Her father, it is true, had given him his card but this had unfortunately been lost by Valentine, amidst the confusion attendant upon the mysterous disappearance of his friend Septimus, and the consequence was that all he could recollect was, that the young lady's name was Angelina Stanley, and that she lived with her father in one of the fashionable streets at the west end of the town. With no clearer guide than this, it was of course very unlikely that he would ever succeed in tracing out her residence, and as his thoughts were each day more and more directed towards that particular interesting subject, he resolved to keep a sharp look out whenever he was walking in the streets, and thus endeavour to trace out the fair object of his rapidly increasing admiration.

One day, as he was strolling through Leicester Square, his attention was suddenly attracted by a sylph-like figure before him, and at once he became convinced that she was no other than the beauteous female he was in search of. In this opinion he was confirmed, by closely examining the countenance of the old gentleman on whose arm she leant, and who he immediately recognised as the same person who had accompanied her in the trip to Richmond by water. Unfortunately, however, for our hero the young lady wore her veil down so as to conceal her face, and he was just planning to himself how he should still further satisfy himself of her identity, when a crowd of persons interposed themselves between him and the lady of his love, and by the time he had found his way through the mob, the maiden and her father had disappeared, he knew not whither. This was vexing enough to our hero, who paced madly, backwards and forwards, upsetting sundry old apple women, and blind beggars in his way, and directing towards himself the attention of numerous curious people, who began to argue among themselves whether it would be most proper to convey him to the police station house, or to the County Lunatic Asylum, at Hanwell. Happily, for Valentine, he was not aware of what was going on among those meddling folks, and as chance had by this time taken him to the door of Miss Linwood's exhibition, he stepped in, thinking to pass away an hour there, as well as any where else.

On entering the rooms, Valentine was surprised at the really beautiful pictures with which the walls were covered. It is true he was no judge of the peculiar art by which they had been produced, but the effect was exceedingly good, and he, perhaps, felt quite as much amused as if he had been looking upon any thing that he really understood. Still, however, his thoughts were bent upon the young lady who had so provokingly disappeared just as he had made up his mind to accost her; and he was in his own mind arguing the propriety of once more sallying forth in search of her, when a remarkably fat old gentleman, and a remarkably lean young lady—his daughter of course —stationed themselves opposite a picture which had just before rivetted the attention of our hero.

" Well, I declare, if the figure don't seem to be alive," papa, " said the young lady." Did you ever see such a thing in your life—look at the eyes, and the hands, and the mouth—why bless me, one could almost declare that the lips move ! "

" Bah !—nonsense !—fiddlesticks ! " growled her sire—" whoever heard of such foolery !—The lips move, eh ? ha ! ha ! ha ! ha !—we shall hear it speak presently, I suppose ! "

This was overheard by Valentine, and taking the hint, he threw his voice so dexteriously, that it appeared to proceed from the mouth of the inaminate object they were gazing on.

" Unbelieving old gentleman ! " he exclaimed, " know that your words have filled me with anger and indignation. I can speak, as you shall find to your cost, and unless you instantly quit this room, I may, perhaps, be tempted to tell things of you that will not be very pleasant"

" Gracious me !—did you ever ! " cried the trembling young lady.

" Psha ! there is some trickery in this " exclaimed her somewhat obstinate papa ;—" it is all humbug I tell you, and if I hear any more of this

VALENTINE VAUX,

OR, THE

TRICKS OF A VENTRILOQUIST.

BY TIMOTHY PORTWINE.

nonsense, I'll send the point of my cane through the canvas, and convince you that what I say is true."

"Profane old man, beware!" muttered Valentine in a low sepulchral tone.

"Upon my life this is very astonishing!" observed a remarkably diminutive individual, stepping back a pace or two, in order to be on the safe side, in case anything very serious should happen; "I have been a visitor at this place for twenty years, and though I have seen that picture over and over again, I can't charge my memory with ever having heard it speak till this moment."

"That is because I have never had

No. 17.

such cause to do so till now, answered Valentine, still managing his voice so that it should appear to proceed from the lips of the picture; "I have hitherto been treated with proper respect; and till this moment never have I met with one who has dared to insult me like yonder crazy old gentleman."

"This is really most extraordinary !" exclaimed an exquisite with green spectacles.

"Very !" chimed in a chorus of every body present.

"Extraordinary or not, I'll sift the matter to the bottom!" cried the old gentleman; and raising his cane he was about to apply it to the right eye of the picture, when one of the attendants rushed forward and seized the desperate man in his arms.

"Hollo ! old feller !" he exclaimed : this won't do at no price, whatsomdever ! what the devil are you going to do with that picture, eh ?"

"I'm going to find out the deception, sirrah," answered the elderly gentleman, struggling with all his might to release himself from the grasp of his assailant ; "you are practising some rascally imposture, and if I don't find it out, say my name's not Timothy Thimblerig, that's all."

"Police ! police ! *will* somebody have the kindness to run and fetch a policeman or two ?" cried the attendant in his alarm, lest his prisoner should escape.

"Hands off, rascal !" bellowed old Thimblerig ; "take your hands off me, I say, or I'll serve you exactly as I mean to serve that confounded picture, when I get loose."

"Ha ! ha ! ha !" laughed Valentine derisively, and at the same time giving his voice the proper direction towards the portrait ; "let the old fool have his way ; and if he does me any injury, see how soon I'll commence an action against him for heavy damages ; I'll trounce him for his insolence ; and if that is not enough, I have got a pair of fists that he will feel the weight of in a way that he will not like."

Incensed by these threats the old gentleman struggled more violently than ever ; and no doubt he would soon have succeeded in releasing himself from the attendant, had not a couple of policemen, at that moment, entered the room, and taken him into their own especial keeping. Hereupon Mr. Timothy Thimblerig waxed more wrathful than ever ; and after spluttering and vowing vengeance upon all about him, he concluded by pathetically calling upon the officers to take his two adversaries into custody as well as himself.

"Point them out," said one of the policemen ; and we'll take them as well as yourself before a magistrate."

"That's one of them," exclaimed the old gentleman, pointing to the attendant who had so roughly handled him, "that

fellow assaulted me in the presence of all this company, and if he is not made to smart severely for it, why then I say there is neither law nor justice in the land."

"Well, sir," said the policeman as soon as he had taken the attendant by the collar ; "we've got one of the people you charge with this outrage, and if you point out the other man, he shall be served after the same fashion."

"That's him," said Timothy, pointing towards the portrait that was suspended against the wall—"that's the rascal who has led to all this row."

"Which ?" exclaimed the policeman, looking very hard in the direction indicated by the old gentleman, and then glancing round the room for an explanation of what appeared to him to be perfectly unintelligible.

"Which !" reiterated the testy old gentleman, again pointing towards the the inanimate object against the wall. "Haven't I told you that the scoundrel is there ; and oughtn't that to be enough for a man that calls himself an officer of justice ?"

"Well, I'm blessed if I know what you mean," said the man, scratching his head, and looking round upon the bystanders "I see nothing but a picture in a frame, and——"

"Why that's it you fool !" exclaimed Timothy ; that's the very chap that has insulted me ; and if you don't take him up this instant, I shall be obligated to do it myself, and then see what sort of a complaint I'll lay against you before the magistrates. I'll teach you what it is to refuse to take a charge in this sort of way."

"Poor fellow ! he's touched here, I suppose," said the policeman, pointing significantly towards his own forehead. "He's mad, escaped, I dare say, from some madhouse ; so the best thing I can do will be to take him to the station house, where he will be properly secured till we can find out who his friends are."

Upon this, the attendant was released from custody, and both the policemen laid hold of Mr. Timothy Thimblerig, with the very laudable intention of carrying him by main force to the place that had been proposed.

At the intercession of his daughter, however, who begged to assure the company that her papa was perfectly sane he was allowed to depart, though not without a promise that he would return immediately, and never again attempt to lay violent hands upon a poor harmless picture. This, after some persuasion, Timothy promised to do; and he was just turning away to depart, when Valentine once more speaking from the portrait, exclaimed:—

"Well, good bye, old boy,—glad you're going though,—but take my advice, and never go out again as long as ever you live."

Mr. Thimblerig looked unutterable things at the supposed offender, and there is no doubt that his anger would have been vented in no very mild manner, had not the police, who saw the dangers of delay, dragged him out of the place, and put him and his daughter into a hackney coach, with a strict injunction to the driver not to stop to put down his fare until they had reached home.

Upon the departure of Timothy and his daughter, order was once more restored among the visitors to the exhibition, and Valentine, who had enjoyed the scene amazingly, was just about to take his leave of the place, when his attention was attracted to the further end of the room, where, to his inexpressible delight he beheld Angelina Stanley and her father, who had, at that moment, mingled among the throng that surrounded one of the principle pictures in the place. Overjoyed at this, his first impulse was to dart forward and claim acquaintance with the old gentleman, whose kindness and genuine warmth of heart he had experienced on a former occasion. Nor was he disappointed in the reception he met with; Mr. Stanley was delighted to renew the acquaintance, and as for Angelina, it was quite easy enough to see by the blush that tinged her cheek, how much gratified she was at a meeting which afforded her so much pleasure.

"Mr. Vaux," exclaimed the old gentleman, "you know not how much pleased I am to see you. I have often thought of you, though, since our last meeting, and so has Angelina too, in spite of all her seeming don't-carishness about the matter. We have neither of us forgotten you, my dear boy, now that we have met again, egad, you must promise to be a frequent visitor at our house."

"My dear sir, your kindness quite overpowers me," cried Valentine, "to be remembered by you with kindness is indeed the height of happiness, more particularly since Miss Angelina is kind enough to bestow a thought upon one who scarcely ventured to believe he deserved it."

Angelina made no reply to this, but it was evident by the tuned glance she directed towards Valentine, that the pleasure of this unexpected meeting was equally shared by both. Mr. Stanley saw that the young folks had formed a mutual liking for each other, and having himself already entertained a strong partiality in favour of our hero, he resolved that the intimacy which had been thus happily commenced, should not be damped by any coldness on his part. Addressing himself, therefore, to Valentine, he said:—

"Excuse me, Mr. Vaux, but I am rather a positive old man in my way, and having once made up my mind to a thing, it is rather hazardous for any one to attempt to thwart me. Now Angelina and myself are going to be alone to day, and as I want a cheerful companion to take a glass or two of wine with, why I must insist, provided no other engagement stands in the way, that you go home and dine with us. Nay, no hesitation, sir, so take my daughter's other arm, and oblige me in the only favour I have ever asked of you."

There was so much heartiness and warmth in all this, that Valentine could not refuse an invitation that promised him so much happiness. He, therefore, readily accepted it, and taking the disengaged arm of Angelina within his own, he began to believe himself one of the happies dogs under the sun. By this time too, the young lady had got over the agitation, caused by their unexpected meeting, and joining in the conversation that followed, she charmed Valentine more and more by the modesty and good sense that seemed to guide her through life. Shortly after this, they left the exhibition, and directing their footsteps towards the west, proceeded towards one of the fashionable streets near Belgrave-square, where Mr. Stanley lived. Here our hero soon felt himself quite at home, and after an elegant dinner had been served up, he was left alone with Mr. Stanley to enjoy an hour's conversation over a bottle oi wine. In the course of this it came out that Mr. Stanley and the father of Valentine had been school-fellows and companions, during tho first years of their lives, and had been separated only when the former had left England for India, where he had amassed an immense fortune, which he was now spending in the land of his birth. It also appeared that he had made every inquiry he could to ascertain what had become of his much loved friend, but that all his efforts had proved unavailing, and that the utmost he could learn was, that Mr. Vaux having proved unfortunate in business had retired into the country with the remnant of a once ample fortune, and that there he had died, leaving a widow and one son. This was all Mr. Stanley could learn of the fate of his friend —no one knew whither he had gone to, and, at last, finding all his efforts useless, he had given up all further search in despair.

It would be impossible to describe the joy of the good old gentleman at this discovery; he was in extacies at it, and having convinced himself that there was a natural regard already existing between his daughter and our hero, he resolved to seat their happiness by bestowing her upon one, who, notwithstanding their short intimacy, he was convinced, in every respect, deserved her. Valentine learnt this resolution with a feeling of rapture that he could not restrain, and seizing the hand of the old gentleman, he fer-vently poured forth the gratitude that filled his heart almost to bursting.

"Come, come," exclaimed Mr. Stanley, good humouredly—"this is not exactly the time for thanking me, Valentine; at present you know we are working in the dark; Angelina has not yet been consulted in the affair, and it is not impossible, though perhaps rather improbable, that she might happen to put her veto against all our fine schemes."

"You surely do not mean to imply that her affections are already engaged?" cried Valentine anxiously.

"I mean to imply nothing, my dear boy," answered the elder gentleman smiling at the fears he had thus excited. "Angelina, I believe, is entirely free, unless, indeed, you happen to have taken her heart by storm— which, by-the-bye, though I wish it to go no further—I think is highly probable."

"Then am I indeed most happy," exclaimed Valentine. "From the period of our first meeting, I felt assured that my affections could never be bestowed upon another, though I almost feared my presumption was doomed to be disappointed. From that time, however, I have never ceased to dwell upon the lovely vision that once blessed my sight, and it was only an imperative duty that I owed to a dear valued friend, which prevented my earlier seeking. her whose destiny I felt assured was closely linked with my own."

"And may I ask who that friend is?" inquired Mr. Stanley.

"Mr. Septimus Bramstone," answered Valentine,—"a gentleman of sterling worth, who I should be most happy on some future occasion to introduce to your acquaintance."

"I have seen him some years ago," answered the old gentleman, "and principally remember as having been a friend of your father's. He is one who I should be much pleased to know intimately, and therefore you must promise to bring him with you the next time we are favoured with a visit."

"Alas!" exclaimed Valentine, "I much fear whether that will be possible. Mr. Bramstone has fallen into the hands of bad men, who have an interest in keeping him out of the way. In fact, I have good reason to believe that he has been trepanned into a private madhouse by his own brother, and I am now anxiously waiting for a conformation of that suspicion to hurl a just retribution upon his foes, whilst, at the same time, I release him from the hands of those who have sought his ruin.

"But have you any clue that may lead you to his discovery?" asked Mr. Stanley, with deep anxiety.

"I have," answered Valentine, "and yet, it must be confessed, that at present it is extremely uncertain. I have learnt that he has been taken to a private madhouse, but in what quarter of the town the place is situated, I know not. In a few hours, however, I hope to be in possession of evidence that will lead to the liberation of my friend, and the just punishment of those who have thus basely sought to build their fortune upon his utter ruin."

"Of course," observed the old gentleman, "you are quite sure that the intelligence you have received is correct."

"It is impossible to be otherwise," answered our hero, "since it is founded chiefly on my own careful observation. I have discovered that since he has been missing, his brother has removed his property and put it up to public auction. In that, however, I fortunately succeeded in frustrating them; but I much fear, unless Mr. Bramstone is shortly discovered, that means will be found to keep him in his present place of confinement, in order that his avaricious relations may fatten upon his own hard earned savings."

"Tell me how I can be useful, and command my services," exclaimed Mr. Stanley. There is nothing in life I so much enjoy as to defeat villany, and if you will only make me your confidante in this affair, I can safely promise you the assistance of a zealous friend, to help the poor old gentleman against the arts of his enemies."

"Thanks, a thousand thanks for your generous feeling in behalf of my poor friend," cried Valentine, gratefully; "the person for whom you feel thus interested is in every respect worthy your esteem, and I hope, ere long, to introduce you to one who, I feel convinced, will never forfeit the good opinion I have thus given you of him."

Here the conversation was broken off by a message from Angelina, informing the gentlemen that tea was ready for them, a summons that was obeyed with equal alacrity by both. In the course of the evening, Mr. Stanley, was called out of the room on urgent business, and during his absence, Valentine took an opportunity to declare his passion to Miss Stanley, a declaration which, we need scarcely say, was not rejected, and from that period our hero was received as the accepted lover of one of the richest heiresses in England.

CHAPTER XXV.

VALENTINE VAUX ALMOST DESPAIRS OF FINDING HIS FRIEND, BUT IS AGREEABLY SURPRISED AT LEARNING SOME NEWS OF SEPTIMUS, WHEN LEAST EXPECTED.—A VERY UNWELCOME VISITOR; THE CONFERENCE; THE EJECTMENT; AND THE ULTIMATE TRIUMPH OF OUR HERO.

HAPPY in the thought of having obtained one of the chief objects of his hopes, Valentine now set himself seriously about the task of finding out the place to which his friend Bramstone had been conveyed by his unprincipled relatives. But this, as he had already experienced, was by no means an easy undertaking, and day after day passed by without obtaining the smallest clue by which to arrive at a satisfactory conclusion. Disguising his own feelings as well as he could, he frequently visited at the house of Harry Bramston, in hopes of picking up something or other that should afford him a prospect of ultimate success, but the old villain and his son were too cunning to be easily caught in this way, and his visits always ended without yielding any of that information which he was so anxious to obtain.

At last, Valentine began boldly to ask them whether they could give him any information relative to the whereabouts of his friend, a question that they at first treated with more civility than he expected, but when he grew more importunate, and began to express an opinion that they knew more about the affair than they chose to acknowledge, both father and son flew in a violent passion, and our hero was glad to make his exit from the street-door, rather than run the risk of being ejected from the window.

All this, however, only served to convince Valentine more and more, that his suspicions were but too correct, and returning home to his lodging, he was just resolving in his mind certain projects that he meant to put in operation for the recovery of his friend, when the servant entered the room and presented him with a dirty piece of paper folded up in the form of a note, addressed to him, in a hand which he at once recognised as that of Mr. Septimus Bramstone. Delighted at this, he instantly tore it open, and read as follows :—

"DEAR VAL.,—I am confined in a madhouse at Bethnal green; come to me instantly on the receipt of this, or I shall be murdered. By good luck I found this paper and a piece of pencil, and at the first opportunity, I will throw the note over the wall, to be brought to you by the person who happens to pick it up. Come to me directly, for they talk of taking me to some other place, and in that case we shall never see each other again.
SEPTIMUS BRAMSTONE."

"Who brought this letter?" asked Valentine of the girl, as she was preparing to leave the room.

"A boy, sir."

"You have not let him go, I hope?"

"Oh, dear no, sir," answered the wench; "he's waiting down stairs in the hall, and says he should like to see you, because he expects to get some money for bringing it."

"Excellent! send him up stairs to me directly."

The girl obeyed the command, and in a minute or two the lad entered the room.

"How came you possessed of this note, my man?" asked Valentine eagerly.

"Please sir, I picked it up," replied the boy. I sometimes goes to the mad'us walls, to hear the poor creaturs shriek and holler, and while I was there this morning, what should I see but that piece of paper directed to you."

"But the direction is to the house where I used to live with the person who wrote the letter," said Valentine. "How was it my man, that you contrived to find me?"

"Why you see, sir," replied the lad, "I'm a 'cutish chap in these matters, so, when I picks up the letter, "Ho! ho!" thinks I, "there'll be something for my trouble any how," so with that I takes it according to the direction, and there I finds you had gone away, and there was only an old woman left to take care of it. Howsomdever, I heered from her that you had come to live here, so I jist runs over with it, thinking as how that your honour would make it worth my while coming a little out of my way."

"Aye, aye, here is a sovereign for you, my lad," exclaimed Valentine, delighted at the prospect that had thus opened upon him. "You have done well, and if things only turn out as I expect, you shall afterwards be rewarded in a more substantial manner."

"Thankee, sir,—good morning to your honour.

"Stay!" cried Valentine, as the youngster was going to leave the room, "you have not, yet, told me where I shall find the house from where' you brought this note."

"Do you know Bethnal green, sir?" asked the messenger.

"I do,—I believe it is not far from Mile end, and an omnibus will take me directly to the spot."

"Well, then, when you get there" returned the boy, "you must ask your way to Prospect Villa—"

"Prospect Villa!" exclaimed our hero, "what a fine name is that to give an abode of misery and despair."

"Ah! you may well say that," answered the boy, "It's a horrible place sure enough, and many's the time I've stood listening to the poor creatures confined in it, for you can't think how they howl and groan when the keepers flog 'em for anything they do wrong!"

"Are there many unfortunate wretches confined in it?" asked Valentine.

"I believe you, sir," answered the other, shaking his head with concern. "There's a great many on 'em in the place, and folks do say that not one half on 'em's mad."

"Not mad!—why are they taken there then?"

"'Cause they've got greedy relations that wants to get hold of their money, to be sure." replied the boy. "Grabfast, the man as keeps the place, ain't very particular about trifles, and if anybody wants to get rid of a friend, all he's got to do is to send him there, and pay so much a year for his keep as long as he lives."

"Horrible!" exclaimed Valentine, shuddering at the bare thought of such villainy, and then, recollecting himself, he resolved to dismiss the boy at once, and immediately set about the pleasureable task of releasing his friend from the evil hands into which he had fallen.

"You can, now, leave me, my man," he said, "and if you call upon me again in the course of a few days, I dare say I shall have thought of some means or other to reward you in a more substantial manner for the service you have performed."

Upon this, the boy's countenance brightened up, and making his very best bow, he retired, leaving our hero to complete those plans which he had already resolved to put into immediate operation.

His first act was to apply to the nearest magistrate for advice under existing circumstances, and fortunately for himself, he happened to meet with a gentleman who was willing to afford him every assistance in his power to bring the guilty parties to justice. By this person's order four policemen were desired to accompany Valentine to Prospect Villa, with instructions to remain close by, so as to be in readiness should their assistance be required. With this re-inforcement, Valentine felt convinced he should be able to succeed in his efforts, and appointing the place to meet the officers he set out to execute the task he had thus undertaken.

It was nearly dusk when our hero reached his place of destination, and having seen that his men were all in readiness to assist him at a moment's notice, he rang the bell, which was almost immediately answered by a surly porter, by whom he sent a message to Mr. Grabfast, stating that he wished for an immediate interview upon very pressing and emergent business. To Valentine it appeared that the man was gone a long time, but at last he returned, to say that his master was particularly engaged, but that he had, graciously, condescended to see the stranger in his little back parlour. Hereupon our hero followed the aforesaid surly porter, and after passing through two or three well guarded portals, he was conducted to the room in which the master of the house was waiting to receive his visitor. Grabfast rose, and bowed stiffly as Valentine approached, and even held out his hand to welcome him, but this honour our hero rejected proudly, and taking a seat that had been pointed out to him, he commenced the business which had occasioned his present visit.

"I have called, sir," he said, "in consequence of information I have received that a Mr. Septimus Bramstone is confined in this house against his will. You, of course, know the gentleman I allude to; and, it's therefore my request, that you allow me to see him immediately,"

"Bramstone! Bramstone!" exclaimed the fellow, appearing as if he was trying to recollect whether he had ever known such a person. "Let me see—Bramstone!—Bramstone!—no,—we have no such person here, sir, never knew such a person in all my life."

"Liar!" exclaimed Valentine, unable to control his rage.

"Sir," retorted the other independently; "do you happen to recollect who you have the honour to be speaking to?"

"I know perfectly well," replied our hero, "that I am talking to a person utterly devoid of both honour and honesty. Aye, sir, you may frown and storm as much as you please, but it so happens, Mr. Grabfast, that you have now to deal with one who cares not for the authority you think fit to exercise over the unfortunate creatures committed to your charge. Your character, sir, is not unknown to me, and I therefore warn you once more to deliver up Mr. Septimus Bramstone into my hands lest I take other measures that may prove not over pleasant to yourself."

"Upon my life this is not to be borne!" exclaimed Grabfast; "is a respectable man to be treated in this sort of way merely because you happen to have taken it into your head that a a friend—of whom I never heard till this moment—is in my establishment!"

"It's false!" cried Valentine; "the person I speak of is only this very moment beneath your accursed roof, and unless you consent to deliver him up at once I will raise such a storm over your head that shall make you bitterly repent the moment when you undertook the dirty work of which I have so much reason to complain."

"Hush! don't talk so loud," exclaimed Grabfast, who now began to feel rather afraid that the affair would not end quite so pleasantly as he would have wished. "Let us speak calmly upon this matter, sir, and I dare say I shall presently be able to convince you of your mistake."

"Let it be done quickly, then," answered our hero, "for I am impatient to see my friends, and I do not mean to give you time to put him into some place of concealment where he may possibly escape the search, I may presently be compelled to institute under proper authority."

"And pray what authority do you possess to search my house?" demanded the other in a bullying tone. "Who, I should like to know can have authorised you or any body else to go over my premises without permission?"

"No less a personage than Mr. Clause, the magistrate."

"Come, come, that won't do for me," answered the ruffian; "Mr. Clause has no reason for suspecting me of doing wrong, and I'm very certain he would never authorise a visit like this unless he was well assured that there was something wrong going on."

"He is well assured of it, sir," exclaimed Valentine; "and if you wish to know from whom he has heard it, you now see that person before your eyes, sir; you may look as angry as you please, but I have certain strong confirmations for what I say, and, if need be, my witness can be produced in the course of a very short time."

"This is some vile plan to ruin me," cried Grabfast, trembling with rage; "you have entered into a conspiracy against me; you would destroy me; but your infamous projects shall be frustrated, and I will yet teach you that the character of an honest man is not to be attacked with impunity. You shall smart, for this, sir,—you shall suffer for it, I say, or my name's not Grabfast."

"Then prove your innocence by letting me go over the premises," returned Valentine. "I shall thus convince of the truth or falsehood of my charges; and, if I should be wrong, you will find me quite as willing to retract all I have said, as I can possibly wish."

Grabfast made no answer to this, but pulling the bell violently, he was presently attended by one of the keepers, who bounced into the room as if he knew for what sort of duty he was summoned.

"Locksly," exclaimed his master; "you see this person here, and I desire that you instantly turn him out of the house. He has insulted me, and he shall learn to his coat whether a

VALENTINE VAUX,

OR THE

TRICKS OF A VENTRILOQUIST.

BY TIMOTHY PORTWINE.

respectable man is to be treated in this sort of way with impunity."

"Werry good, sir," replied the keeper, "but do you wish me to show him to the door and bow him out, or shall I take the gemman in my arms and chuck him out of the window?"

"If you value your own bones, you will do neither," exclaimed Valentine, stepping back a pace or two, and raising his stick so as to guard himself against an attack. "I have come here on an errand, and will execute my task fearlessly, even though the odds may be against me."

"Locksly, you have heard my com-

mands and I expect them to be obeyed," cried the master fiercely. "You must either rid me of this scoundrel, or prepare to quit my service at a moment's notice."

"Come, young chap, are you going?" said Locksly, addressing himself to Valentine; "you've heard what the guv'nor says, and I aint going to lose a good sitivation for want of doing my duty. March, will you, or I must set about making you in less than no time at all—that's the way to say it."

"When I have done all that brought me here, I shall go, and not one moment before," answered our hero, resolutely. "I came here to release Mr. Septimus Bramstone from the hands of villany, and, until that is accomplished, I certainly shall not remove without the application of superior force."

"I don't know nothin' about no Mr. Bramstone," answered the keeper taking the cue from his master. "There's no such a gemman here, and even if there was, I should not be fool enough to let him out without orders from his friends."

"You don't know him, eh?" cried Valentine, "then perhaps your memory may be refreshed from that letter which I happen to have received from him this morning, and through which I have at last succeded in tracing him to this place."

"A letter!" groaned both master and man."

"Aye, you are both confounded now, I see," exclaimed Valentine, "you are conscience-stricken at the evidence against you; and now, if you take my advice, you will suffer my friend to depart with me, lest any further mischief should happen to yourselves."

"Grabfast and his assistant now consulted with each other in whispers, and at the end of the brief conference the former left the room, though not without directing a grim look of defiance at his unwelcome visitor. Valentine felt assured from all this that some treachery was hatching against him, but he resolved not to be intimidated from carrying his purpose into execution, and he was just preparing himself for any emergency when two other keepers rushed into the room and secured him before he was able to offer any effectual resistance. Thus situated he was rendered perfectly unable to defend himself, and ere he could recover from the surprise into which he was thrown, he was hurled with some violence into the streets, and the door of the asylum was thrust to, in order to prevent his readmission. At this moment the policemen who had been lying in wait close by, came to his assistance, who, hearing the way in which he had been treated, resolved among themselves to gain an entrance to the place by some other means than the door.

For this purpose an examination was made of the premises, and a ladder having been procured from one of the neighbours, it was determined to scale the walls, and thus to pounce upon the inmates before they had an opportunity to thwart them in their places. With the aid of a strong piece of rope this was easily accomplished, and Valentine with his allies found themselves in the yard of the asylum, where about a dozen of the unfortunate inmates were exercising themselves just before being locked up in their cells for the night. From Lawson, who happened to be one of them, our hero ascertained that Mr. Bramstone had just been taken away by a couple of keepers who had beaten him most unmercifully, and that in all probability he was now secured in some part of the premises, where there was the least chance of his being discovered. With this intelligence the police were about to break open the gates that communicated with the house, but just as they were going to commence operations, a party of the keepers, headed by Grabfast, rushed out upon them and commenced an assault that at one time seemed likely to terminate in their favour. At that juncture, however, the poor fellows who had been so long confined there, joined the deliverers, and ere many minutes had elapsed, the keepers and their infamous employers were prisoners in the hands of the police. Upon this a loud shout of triumph was raised by the poor creatures, and it was with no little difficulty that they could be prevented inflicting summary vengeance upon those who had so long and so barbarously tormented them.

This done, one of the keepers was ordered to conduct Valentine, and a policeman to the cell which contained Mr. Bramstone,—a task which he executed with evident unwillingness,—but which, under circumstances, he could not of course refuse without evident peril to himself. In a few minutes, therefore, Valentine was led towards the place, but before they reached it he could plainly distinguish the groans of his friend, who had been doomed to experience more ill-treatment than ever, on account of the attempt that had been made to liberate him from confinement.

When they entered the cell, they found the old gentleman fastened down to an iron bedstead, his arms being secured with cords at one end, and his legs at the other, whilst round his throat was fixed an iron collar, by means of which his head was kept in a most painful and irksome position. In an instant, however, these bonds were removed, and a little water having been poured down his throat, he presently recovered sufficiently to recognise the hands by whom he had been delivered from the horrors he had so long endured. On being thus far restored, he began to narrate the cruelties by which he had almost been tortured to madness, but Valentine found the excitement was too much for him, and stopping him in the midst of his narrative he begged of him to postpone the remainder until he was better able to bear the remembrance of the horors he had been made to endure. To this the old gentleman consented, and as he was excessively weak from what he had undergone, a coach was sent for to convey him home. In the meantime, those of the inmates, among whom was poor Lawson,—who it was evident were not insane, were released from confinement, whilst the others were left in the asylum under the care of their former keepers, over whom, however, the policeman was left in charge until the further pleasure of the magistrates should be known.

When their arrangements were completeted, Valentine and his friend Septimus entered the coach, and immediately afterwards they took their departure from ther place whee they had witnessed so much misery and sorrow.

———

CHAPTER XXVI.

VALENTINE AND SEPTIMUS ONCE MORE SPEND A HAPPY EVENING TOGETHER.—A VISIT IS PAID THAT PRODUCES SOME REMORSE, AND A GREAT DEAL OF HAPPINESS.—SEPTIMUS EXHIBITS HIS OWN MAGNANIMITY, AND FORGIVES HIS ENEMIES.—ARRIVAL OF TWO IMPORTANT PERSONAGES IN LONDON.

IT was too late in the day to commence operations according to the plans proposed, and as Valentine did not wish Arnold and his father to know how far he had succeeded in tracing out the object of their cruel persecution, he took the old gentleman home to his own lodgings, intending to carry out his designs in the following morning.

Never did two people sit down with more pleasure to enjoy each other's society than did our hero and his friend on this joyful occasion. In fact, Septimus dwelt as little as possible on the sufferings he had endured whilst under the roof of Grabfast, and looking forward to the happiness he hoped to enjoy, he listened to Valentine's narrative of the meeting with Angelina Stanley, and the subsequent events that had so greatly tended to ensure him a life of uninterrupted joy. Indeed, upon this subject, Valentine was most eloquent, and the young lady's beauty and accomplishments lost nothing in the vivid description with which he treated his listening and attentive friend. That night they retired early to bed, and on the following morning, after an early breakfast, they prepared to put their designs into execution. Accordingly, a coach was ordered, in which they comfortably ensconced themselves, and anticipating nothing but success for the design they had in view, they set forward to the place of destination. But know, as they did, the cunning of those they were about to visit, they ordered the vehicle to stop at the end of the street, from whence, after discharging the driver, they proceeded to the place where they expected to meet Harry Bramstone and his equally scheming son. On the door being opened, it was evident that the servant was alarmed at the unexpected appearance of Septimus, and stammering out the best excuse she could, she declared that neither her master nor his son were at home. But Valentine could see plainly enough that this was a mere trumped-up story, and taking his friend by the arm, he led him into the room where Harry Bramstone and Arnold were busily engaged in looking over a heap of papers connected with the infamous transaction they then had in hand.

Never were men more utterly confounded than were these two when they beheld the unexpected apparition of Septimus Bramstone and his young friend. They both of them started from their seats—a deadly paleness came over their countenances, and starting back to the further end of the room, they stood trembling, as if in expectation that some terrible punishment was about to fall upon them for the villainy they had been guilty of towards their unsuspecting relative. In an agony of suspense they awaited the judgment they had good reason to suppose was going to be awarded to their baseness, and looking alternately upon the two unwelcome guests, they seemed to implore that mercy which they had so little reason to claim.

"Nay. Harry," exclaimed Septimus, "never fear, man, that I am going to revenge myself for the cruel wrongs I have endured. It is sufficient if you only repent the course you have adopted towards me, and from this day forward we will never again meet together, except as perfect strangers to each other."

"Hang it all, uncle, don't be unforgiving," cried Arnold, venturing to put in a word. "Dad and I have been infernal rogues, and that's the truth; but we both of us heartily repent what we have done, and I hope Valentine will not refuse to say a kind word or two in our favour, just by way of making it all right between us."

"My friend will do just as he pleases," answered our hero; "he alone has been the sufferer through your conduct, and, of course, his own feelings are to be consulted in such a case before my own."

"In that case I certainly shall not be very vindictive," exclaimed Septimus, "though, to speak the truth, I do feely highly indignant at the infamous measures that have been adopted to get me out of the way. I have suffered much both in mind and body, but as I have happily escaped from the hands of my enemies why perhaps, after all, forgiveness would be my best course."

"Huzza! we are pardoned then!" cried Arnold giving a turn round the room somewhat after the fashion of Jim Crow—"Uncle Sep. has forgot all about it, and it shan't be any fault of mine if he gets into a madhouse again! He is a trump after my own heart, and from this moment down goes the first man that says a word against him in my presence."

"Well, well, I thank you for your zeal though it comes somewhat at the latest," exclaimed the old gentleman smiling benovolently at the extacies of his nephew. "You have behaved scurvily to me, Arnold, but when a man acknowledges his faults, why it becomes the injured party to look over the offence and sign articles of immediate peace."

"And am I to be included in the amnesty? asked Harry Bramstone, advancing, though not without some trepidation. Can you indeed forgive one who has injured you almost beyond the power of reparation?"

"Aye, even if your offences were a thousand times greater than they are," answered Septimus evasively.

"Ah, brother! brother!" cried Harry in a tone of remorse;—"I always felt that you were better than myself, and now am I convinced in a way that I never could have expected."

"Pho!—don't talk in that way Harry, interrupted the old gentleman; if my heart is not as hard as a piece of marble I have to thank heaven for it, and now that I find myself once more on the outside of that cursed lunatic asylum, I feel that it is not very difficult to forgive even those who were the cause of the sufferings I endured there."

"I was fool as well as villain for pursuing the course I did," exclaimed Harry bitterly. "You must have endured much, brother, but nothing in comparison with the pangs of conscience that have been gnawing out my heart ever since the fatal moment that I first saw you dragged away by those two ruffians. My name has been constantly harrassed, and had it not been for fear of encountering your just reproaches I should some days ago have procured your release from the hands of that scoundrel Grabfast."

"Had you done that it would at least have shown the sincerity of your repentance," observed Valentine, who had no great opinion of the old man's sudden remorse. "It would, in fact, have proved that you were worthy of a brother's forgiveness, and that your own feeling of shame was stronger than the motive that induced you to do him so foul an injury."

"Tut, tut! let us say as little about part of the business as possible," interposed Septimus. "I must be owned that I did feel hurt at what has been done, and so, indeed, did my friend Valentine, particularly when he saw my house stript from attics to kitchen, and the furniture dragged out to be disposed of as if I had been really dead."

"I can offer no excuse for my conduct," exclaimed Harry, "but of one thing I am heartily glad, and that is that the sale was somehow or other most unaccountably stopped almost at the beginning, and the consequence is that nearly the whole of your property is now lying in the auctioneer's warehouse."

"And that it is so we have to thank the humble talent I happen to be possessed of," said Valentine smiling at the prospect of harmony which now appeared. "I take to myself the credit of stopping the sale and thus preventing the distribution of much valuable property which I know my friend Bramstone sets the greatest store by."

"You! exclaimed both father and son at the same moment.

"Aye, even so," answered our hero; "there was not much time to think about the means which it was to be done, you know, and I was perfectly well aware that it would be in vain were I to attempt to stop the sale by declaring that it was not authorised by the real owner of the property. Those who had commanded it to take place, would, of course, have argued stoutly in their own favour, and most likely I should have been scouted from the room as an impertinent meddler who had no business there. With that idea I determined to be there as a spectator and with what success I carried my project to an end you are of course quite aware."

"Explain yourself, sir," cried Harry Bramstone.

"Aye do, there's a good fellow," chimed in Arnold. "That you were there I perfectly well remember, but that you stopped the sale exceeds my comprehension, seeing that that event was entirely brought about by—"

"Ha! ha! ha! by myself, of course," interrupted Valentine, "you know that I possess the gift of ventriloquism, and by imitating the voice of your uncle and creating a bit of confusion in the room, I ultimately succeeded in bringing about a postponement of the sale. That done, I set myself diligently about the task of finding the place where my friend had been taken to, and no sooner had I succeeded in effecting my object so far than I applied to a magistrate for assistance, and the consequence is, that he has been set at liberty at a moment when you thought him most completely in your power."

"Give us your hand, my boy," cried Arnold, delighted at the explanation. "You have done both dad and I a great service, and as uncle Sep. seems inclined to look over the past, why we'll see if we can't make amends for it in our future conduct."

"Well then, let us say no more about it," exclaimed the old gentleman. "I am not unforgiving you know, so keep your own council, and you shall never hear a word of reproach from my lips."

" Bravo !" shouted Arnold, "then we shall all of us get off a great deal better than we deserve."

" Not all," replied Valentine, "for there is one whose conduct has been so brutal and infamous that I should say it would be impossible to forgive him the heinous offences he has been guilty of."

" Indeed !" said Septimus, " well really I am not aware that there is a person in the world who at this moment I am not ready to forgive."

" Aye, aye, who is he?" demanded Arnold.

" Grabfast, the keeper of the mad-house."

" Well," exclaimed the old gentle-man, " he certainly, did all he could to make me absolutely mad, but as he failed in his base design, why I suppose we must pardon him as well as the rest."

" Of course, sir, you have a right to do as you please," replied Valentine, " but in common justice to the rest of mankind, I think he ought not to be let off without some punishment for the dreadful cruelties he has been guilty of towards yourself and others. At any rate, he must be stopped in his career of infamy, and the only way to do it effec-tually is to make his character known, and thus exclude him from all society."

" Oh, if that is all, depend on it his character will very soon be spread abroad, now that so many of his vic-tims have been suffered to escape," an-swered Mr. Septimus Bramstone. " The fellow will hardly dare show his face in the neighbourhood again, and even if he should do so, it will only be to be scowled by all those who hate and despise cruelty. However, we are only prolonging a subject that is painful to us all, and as I am anxious to get back once more to my own home, we will now take our departure, with a further assurance of good will and unity be-tween these gentlemen and myself."

With this, Septimus shook hands once more with his brother, as if there had never been any rupture between them, and, followed by Valentine, he left the house in order to make arrange-ments for his own immediate return to the home from which he had been so violently torn. To do the auctioneer justice, he was perfectly ready to afford facility to the accomplishment of this design, and whilst we are paying this tribute to the honesty of one man, we must not forget that Arnold Bram-stone exerted himself almost to the utmost to bring matters to as speedy a close as possible. In fact, both his uncle and Valentine found him a most useful ally, and it was principally to his aid that Septimus at the end of three days found himself once more established in his old quarters, and in the enjoyment of as much happiness as if it had never been disturbed by the events we have related.

As for Valentine he was absolutely compelled to accept the hospitality of his friends, who would not hear of his continuing in the lodgings he had taken when so suddenly ejected by the pro-ceeding that followed the mysterious disappearance of his generous protec-tor. He, therefore, again became an inmate beneath the same roof until the period should arrive when he was to claim the hand of Angelina Stanley, an event, by-the-bye, which was expected to take place almost immediately.

In a few days after this, a letter was received from uncle Sam., announcing that it was the intention of his mother and himself to be in town in time to be present at the nuptials, and within a week from that period Valentine had the pleasure, once more, of meeting those who he had never seen since the morning when he left home for his visit to London.

CHAPTER XXVII.

IN WHICH MATTERS BEGIN TO RESUME THEIR FORMER APPEARANCE OF COMFORT.—VALENTINE GROWS REST-LESS, AND LOOKS OUT FOR A NEW SOURCE OF AMUSEMENT.—THE READER IS ONCE MORE INTRODUCED TO DOCTORS SLOP AND DUNDIZZY, WHO GET INTO RATHER AN AUKWARD SCRAPE.—SCENE IN A POLICE COURT.

On the morning of the day when it was expected that Mrs. Vaux and uncle

Sam. would arrive by coach from the country. Valentine and his kind friend were seated at the breakfast-table, talking over past events, and anticipating the pleasure they should both experience in the expected addition to their society. The newspaper which the former had been reading was thrown down and taken up half a dozen times in the course of as many minutes; and at last, taking himself to the window, he watched the numerous pedestrians, who, at that hour of the morning, were hurrying along in all the bustle of business. But even this ever-changing scene was insufficient to arrest his attention for any long time from other thoughts, and as he was just going to return to his seat at the table, when his attention was drawn towards a crowd of persons who had collected round a fat podgy little man and a tall cadaverous looking one who were addressing the mob, and at the same time using the most violent gesticulatios. In these Valentine quickly recognised the two mad-doctor's, Dundizzy and Slop, and as he had long wished for an opportunity to retaliate upon them for their conduct towards his friend, he resolved not to let the present chance slip without carrying his intentions into effect. A little observation served to show him that the two worthies were engaged in a controversy with a hackney coachman, who, having made what appeared to be an exorbitant charge for a short ride, was now insisting upon having his full charge under pain of sending them both to the station-house. Valentine enjoyed their dilemma, and throwing his voice among the crowd, he called lustily for the police.

"Ah!—police!—police!—" shouted the mob vociferously;—"take the two swells off to a beak. Scoundrels! who ever heard of such a thing as trying to cheat a poor jarvey out of his money!"

"What's the row here?" exclaimed a sergeant bustling up with all his might, and shouldering his way through the crowd, and dealing his blows right and left with surprising activity. "Now then, my tulips, who am I to take into custody, eh?"

"Why them two shickery coves, to be sure," said a knife grinder who was rather prominent in the fray;—"they've had a ride in the man's rattler, and then wont pay him for it."

"They're swell mobsmen," cried Valentine, managing his voice so that it appeared to proceed from the mouth of a little costermonger that stood just behind the sergeant;—"I knows 'em vell enough, seeing as how they vas pals o'mine not long ago on the Brixton mill."

"Oh ho! that's it, is it my fine fellers!" said the policeman politely collaring the two doctor's. You're swell's, are yer? and may be wants to get a crowd round about whilst some o' yer companions are picking the pockets of the people."

"It's false!" exclaimed the enraged Dundizzy; "we are respectable gentlemen, I tell you, and if you doubt my word there is my card and address to convince you."

"Don't believe him," shouted Valentine with all his might.

"It's all very well to give this here card," said the policeman, after turning it over and over again without being able to make out the name inscribed on it; "It's all mighty fine, I dare say to give this thing as a proof of your respectability, but who the devil's to know whether the card is yours or not."

"He's a humbugging on you, Mister Pollissman," said a rosy gilled little barber, who now thrust himself forward that he might be seen as well as heard. "These fellows is downright bad 'uns, else they wouldn't be trying to cheat a poor honest man out of his browns."

"Who dares say we want to cheat the man?" exclaimed Dr. Dundizzy, looking around as if he intended to eat up the last speaker at a mouthful. "Who, I repeat, dares make such an insinuation as that we wish to wrong the man out of a farthing?"

"We all say so," replied the mob with one accord."

"And you know that you deserve it," vociferated Valentine from his place at the window.

"Come, we can't have the streets blocked up for you," said the policeman, "so either dubb up the browns, or just make up your minds to take a gentle walk along with me to the station house."

"I would sooner die than put up with such a rascally imposition," exclaimed Doctor Dundizzy.

"And so would I," chimed in Doctor Slap, with equal resolution; the fellow is a cheat, and if a magistrate only heard our version of the story we should have justice done us."

"Ho! wery well," cried the policeman, "if so be as how you want to go before his worship, I can accommodate you both in less than no time at all. So come along my fine fellows, and if you don't like it after all's over don't go for to lay the blame on me, that's all about it."

"Take them away!—take them away!" shouted Valentine with all the strength of his lungs.

"Who's that ordering me?" exclaimed the police officer, looking round very sharp to detect the daring intermeddler,—"who was it, I say, that had the imperance to tell me my duty?"

"I aint quite certain mind ye," said the rosy-faced barber, "but if I was to be ax'd for an opinion, I should say it was that coal-heaver yonder;—him as is smoking his pipe as if nuffin at all was the matter.

The policeman looked at the aforesaid coal-heaver, and having taken a good survey of his gigantic proportions, said nothing more just then upon the subject. The fact is, he liked not the look of his customer, who, if put to it, was a match for twenty such fellows as himself any day in the week.

"Now, I'll just tell you what it is, little un," said the knight of the black diamonds, advancing and very quietly depositing his hugh carcase close beside that of the barber; " you've told a d——d lie this time, old chap, any how, and if you says it was me again I'll just lay your dirty little body in the kennel in about half a minute."

The barber shrank back aghast at this threat, and presently hid himself among some of his taller neighbours for shelter and protection. On this the people indulged themselves with a hearty laugh, and the coal-heaver was about to demonstrate how easily he could put his threat into execution, when Valentine from his lofty position exclaimed with a groan and a hoot.

"A-a-ah! coward! why don't you hit a man of your own size?"

Enraged at this, the coal heaver began to show fight in earnest, and there is no knowing where the mischief might have ended had not the policeman sprang his rattle furiously, upon which he was quickly joined by three or four of his comrades, who making to the spot shortly cleared away the mob, who ran to take care of themselves, with about as much celerity as if they had been charged by half a dozen mad bullocks.

As for Doctors Slop and Dundizzy, they would very gladly have followed so sensible an example, but the police took care to prevent their escape, and hurrying their prisoners into the backney coach, they were driven by the incensed jarvey to the nearest seat of justice, where the merits of the case might be fully entered into.

Valentine perceived this movement and at once demanded whither they were going. He therefore left his friend to arrange some business, which he knew he had to transact, and promising to return in an hour or two, took his departure in order to witness the scene that was to take place before the magistrate. It was with no little difficulty however, that he managed to gain admittance into the crowded office, but being once let in, he ensconced himself in a corner by himself, from where he could observe all that was going on without being seen. By this time the magistrate had taken his seat, and when he had amused himself for about a quarter of an hour over the morning's journal, he deigned to enquire into the nature of the first charge.

VALENTINE VAUX,

OR THE

TRICKS OF A VENTRILOQUIST.

BY TIMOTHY PORTWINE.

"Please your worship," said the policeman, "I was called off my beat about half-past nine o'clock this morning to take these two men into custody for refusing to pay their coach fare. When I gets to the place I found a great crowd round the prisoners at the bar and the driver of the vehicle, and as they was a-kicking up the devil's delight I thought as how the best way would be to take 'em into custody to see what yer vusship would like to say to 'em."

"Very proper, indeed," exclaimed the magistrate pompously, "this is a very serious case, and the author of the disturbance must be taught that the queen's peace is not to be broken with impunity."

"They deserved to be heavily fined," cried Valentine, throwing his voice into the midst of the throng.

"Who was it that dared to speak in this august assembly?" demanded Mr. Muddle, looking round him as if he would have eaten the culprit could he but have found him. "Who was it? I say; point out the rascal, and I'll find out how he likes to be fined for his impertinence."

"Please your vusship, I don't know who it was," said the gaoler, to whom this question had been particularly addressed, "but I shouldn't at all wonder if it was one of the prisoners as said it."

"That's a very likely story, very likely indeed that a man should propose a fine for himself," said the magistrate, becoming more and more fidgetty, and then recollecting that he had a great public duty to perform, he enquired whether any body present could take it upon himself to say that either of the prisoners had ever been in custody before.

"Can't say for certain, your vusship," answered the policeman, "but somehow I fancy I've seen 'em here before to day."

"By the powers I've seed 'em both in trouble for worse things than this," said Valentine, assuming an Hibernian accent, and so managing his voice that it seemed to proceed from the lips of a poor Irishman who was standing quietly among the spectators.

"Let the witness stand forward," said the magistrate.

A couple of policemen now advanced, and taking the person alluded to by the shoulders, pushed him unwillingly forward. In truth, the Irishman was bothered at the unexpected situation in which he was placed, and scratching his head he stood wondering what the devil was coming next.

"What's your name, friend?" asked the magistrate.

"Sure, and isn't Dennis O'Sullivan, I am?"

"And what do you know about the prisoners at the bar?"

"Just nothing at all, at all, your honour."

"How!" cried the magistrate frowning as black as thunder, didn't you tell us but a minute or two ago that you could prove them to have been committed as thieves?"

"That's a lie, your wurtship!" exclaimed Valentine, imitating the voice of the Irishman so accurately, that a murmur of astonishment ran through the crowd at Paddy's supposed presumption.

Hereupon the magistrate's face grew very red with passion, the chief clerk's hair stood an end with wonder and indignation, and half a dozen police-

men stood ready to rush upon the imaginary delinquent, to carry him off to the strong room on the least hint to that effect being given.

"Fellow!" rored Mr. Muddle with the fiercest indignation, "you are an insolent rascal, and I have not yet made up my mind whether or not to commit you for a high contempt of this court. Do you know who you are standing before."

"Divil a bit," replied Pat sorely puzzled to know how he had offended: "and what's more, your worship, I don't care."

"Then listen to me, fellow," resumed Mr. Muddle. "I sit here as the representative of her Majesty the Queen."

"Then her Majesty the Queen has a fool for her representative any how," exclaimed Valentine, again imitating the voice and peculiar accent of the Irishman. Hereupon the dispenser of justice grew exceedingly wrathful, and jumping up from his seat, he ordered Mr. Dennis O'Sullivan to be placed in the dock by the side of the other prisoners.

"What's that for, you spalpeens?" exclaimed the Irishman indignantly, and at the same time hitting the man, who had been most forward in placing him there, a blow that sent him sprawling into the middle of the court.

"If he is not quiet put a pair of handcuffs on him," said the magistrate almost bursting with passion! we'll teach him to call the representative of her most gracious Majesty a fool!"

"By the powers I never said nothin' o' the sort."

"Ho! ho!—I see you begin to repent your conduct already," said Mr. Muddle chuckling at the supposed efficacy of his discipline." You see the folly and wickedness of calling one of the instruments of the law a fool, and I am half disposed to deal leniently with you if you state fairly what you know against these men."

"By St Patrick that's nothing then, for by the holy Virgin I never seed either of 'em before in all my born days."

"This is most extraordinary," exclaimed Mr. Muddle, throwing himself back in his seat, and twiddling his thumbs in a manner that showed he was really very much perplexed. Then ensued a whispering conversation between himself and his chief clerk, which being ended, the Irishman was ordered to be set at liberty, and turned out of the office. Upon this the examination of the two prisoners was resumed, and though nothing was elicited against them, a determination was expressed to remand them for a few days, in order to see whether a charge could not in the mean time be brought against them."

"And what's to become of me, your worship?" asked the jarvey, who now began to find that he was likely to be a loser of his whole fare by the course pursued.

"Don't talk to me about such nonsense, man," answered the administrator of the law." It's the duty of every man to put up with a loss, if the good of his country demands it; and supposing we are able to bring a direct charge against these two prisoners, you must console yourself with the reflection that your loss has not been greater."

"Pardon me, your worship," exclaimed Dr. Dundizzy, who began to feel uneasy at the turn matters were beginning to take against him;" but really it appears to me that you have no grounds for detaining in custody my lawyer."

"Don't talk to me, sir, I desire!" cried Muddle indignantly.

"What charge have you against either me or my friend?"

"None at present, sir," answered the magistrate complacently; "but it is my will that you shall be remanded, in hopes that we may be able to find something that will either hang or transport you both. Ah! you may smile, but such indecencies will not be allowed in Botany Bay, when you get there."

"Really sir," interposed Doctor Slop, "it seems to me that you are greatly exceeding your duty in thus seeking to deprive two respectable persons of their liberty."

"Respectable!" shouted Muddle, "and pray sir, how do you mean to prove your respectability?"

"There is my card, sir," said Dundizzy, giving one to the turnkey, and requesting him to hand it to the magistrate.

"Dr. Dundizzy," said the functionary, reading the superscription, and then throwing it back scornfully,— "aye, aye, I see,—you have some how or other possessed yourself of the card of a respectable man, and would now impose yourself upon me as that person;—but it won't do, sir,—I must have more satisfactory evidence in your favour, before I give liberty to men who are declared to be reputed thieves."

"And pray how long are we to be remanded for?" asked the alarmed doctor.

"For a week, sir," answered the magistrate, "and during that time we shall institute the most rigid enquiries we can, so as to secure the punishment your crimes so justly merit."

"And let me tell you, sir, that I shall not fail to make you suffer for this conduct," exclaimed Dundizzy in a towering passion;—"I ll bring an action against you for false imprisonment, and then we'll see ——"

"Take them away, gaoler, take them away!" roared Mr. Muddle, at the extent of his voice, and in obedience to the magisterial commands, the two doctors were dragged out of the office, and shortly afterwards conveyed to the prison where they were to await the expiration of the period for which they had been remanded.

Valentine felt half sorry at first for the punishment to which they were subjected, but when he came to reflect upon their conduct towards his friend Bramstone, he could not help acknowledging that they richly deserved the restraint they would have to put up with. In this mood he returned home to inform Septimus of the fate which had befallen Doctors Slop and Dundizzy.

CHAPTER XXVIII.

A VISIT TO THE GEORGE AND BLUE
BOAR. —WAITING FOR THE COACH.
—VALENTINE PLAYS SOME MORE OF
HIS PRANKS, AND PRODUCES A
GLORIOUS QUARREL.—EDGED TOOLS
PROVE TO BE VERY DANGEROUS TO
THOSE WHO PROVOKE THEIR USE.—
ARRIVAL OF UNCLE SAM. AND MRS.
VAUX.

DINNER being despe tched and a
bottle of wine emptied by way of wash-
ing down the substantial fare that
had been provided, the two gentlemen
began to think it was nearly time to
go to the coach office, for the purpose
of receiving the travellers on their
arrival, and conducting them from
thence to the hospitable mansion of
Mr. Septimus Bramstone.   The old
gentleman, however, as is the case with
many others besides him, felt rather
sleepy after the indulgence of the
table, and as he seemed rather inclined
for an afternoon's nap, it was agreed
that Valentine should go alone to the
George and Blue Boar, where it was
expected his mother and Uncle Sam
would arrive about seven o'clock.

This being so far arranged, the
worthy Septimus threw a silk handkerchief over his head, threw himself
back in the chair, and in an inconceivable short space of time, gave
audible tokens through his nasal
organs, that he and sleep had found
sweet companionship together. Upon
this hint our hero acted, and softly
leaving the room for fear of disturbing
the slumbers of his exce llent friend
he soon emerged into the street, and
betook himself towards the far-famed
tavern to and from which, so many
coaches to all parts of England arrive
and depart.

Valentine felt quite in spirits at the
near prospect he had of once more
seeing those he loved, and hurrying
on with what speed he could, through
the crowded streets of London, he at
last found himself in the inn yard of
the George and Blue Boar. As he
turned the corner he perceived a coach,

which had just arrived at its place of
destination, standing near the office
door, and from which the passengers
were just alighting. Hastening up
to it, however, he was disappointed
at finding that the vehicle was not the
one he wanted, and on further enquiry
he learnt that the one he expected,
would not arrive for at least half-an-
hour.   This was an age in the opinion
of Valentine, and looking round for
some object upon whom he might exercise his peculiar talent. he observed
a remarkably bilious looking old gentleman who was haggling with the
coachman touching the propriety of
certain charges which the latter in-
sisted upon making for sundry large
trunks and packages which had just
been taken from various parts of the
coach.

"I'll tell you what it is, sir," said
the watchman finding at last that all
remonstrance was utterly useless
"you've made yourself wery disagreeable all the way up, and I'm blessed
if I see any use in a feller being civil
to such a rum sort a customer as you're
likely to be."

"Here's insolence!" exclaimed the
passenger in a quarrelous tone, "here's
pretty treatment for a gentleman to
receive after he has patronised you
with his favour."

"*Gentlemen!*" cried the driver
scornfully,—" beg your pardon, sir,
but you don't call yourself a gentleman. do you?"

"He's a nasty villain, that he is,"
said Valentine in a feminine voice,
and so contriving it that the sound
should appear to proceed from a prim
looking old maid, who, having been
an inside passenger with the bilious
looking gentleman, was now transfer
ing her antiquated person to the interior
of a hackney coach which had been
engaged for her especial use and
accommodation. Her late fellow traveller looked unutterable things at the
venerable spinster, and it was evident
that rage had completely overmastered
his gallantry when the coachman
bursting out into a horse laugh exclaimed with a sneer :—

"There ! you see other people have

found out your disagreeable ways as well as myself. The lady calls you a nasty villain, and I dare say she could prove her words, if you want any further explanation."

"I defy her to prove her words," shouted the other, in a desperate passion, "she has uttered an abominable falsehood, and—

"Me utter a falsehood!" cried Valentine in the same sharp shrill tone he had used on the former occasion;—"did anybody ever hear such impudence. Gentlemen he tried to kiss me in the coach, and I don't know what might have been the consequence if I had not threatened to call out for assistance."

Hereupon a loud laugh was raised by the bystanders, and the old gentlemen raising his umbrella with a menacing air, was about to rush furiously towards his supposed accuser, when the driver, lashing his horse, drove off, to the great amusement of the crowd which by this time had gathered around. The irritable passenger became more than ever incensed and there is no doubt he would have followed the old maid for the ungallant purpose of inflicting summary vengeance had he not been restrained by those who thought the joke had gone quite far enough.

"Let me go," he exclaimed vociferously, "my character has been infamously attacked by that liar in petticoats, and I shall never rest satisfied till I have made her confess that she has scandalously endeavoured to destroy the character of a respectable man."

"Respectable be d——d!" cried Valentine, suddenly changing his tone and managing so that it appeared to have proceeded from a sturdy looking fellow who was just at that moment busily engaged in rubbing down a horse

"Scoundrel! how dare you insult me?" roared the angry passenger, rushing forward and dealing a blow with his umbrella upon the unconscious ostler, which sent him rolling into an odoriferous heap of dung, that was lying piled up behind the stable door; "you must join in the outcry that has

been raised against me, must you? but I'll be revenged!—I'll punish the whole gang of tormentors, and, if no other redress can be obtained, I'll indict you all for a conspiracy—that's what I will!"

"I say, mister!" exclaimed the ostler, picking himself up as soon as he could, "was that meant in earnest or did you go for to do it on purpose?"

"I did it purposely, to be sure," replied the enraged traveller, shaking his fist threateningly in the face of the poor fellow he had so unceremoniously treated, "and what's more, you rascal, if you dare say another word, I'll repeat the dose, only taking care to give it a little stronger than I did last time."

"You'd better not try it on any how," said the man, not at all moved by the threats of the other.

Hereupon the passenger grew more and more outrageous, and grasping his umbrella tightly, he was about to administer a second blow, when he was stopped in a way as unpleasant as it was unexpected. In fact, the ostler naturally thought he ought to take the best care of himself that he could, and raising the curry-comb he held in his hand, he gave his opponent a scrape with it down one cheek that set the blood flowing from about a score of wounds in an instant. Enraged at this, the other began to belabour about him with his umbrella, to the infinite amusement of the lookers-on, and there is no knowing where the affair would have ended, had not the before-mentioned coachman stepped in between the combatants, and fairly carried his late passenger from the scene of action.

"What the devil are you at now?" he exclaimed, as he dropped his burden at the further end of the inn-yard; "do you want to get your precious countenance marked worse than it is, or are you for a reg'lar stand-up fight and no mistake, where one man has as good of it as the other?"

"Do you suppose I would demean myself by fighting with the low fellow?" exclaimed the other indignantly. "No, he has lacerated my flesh with that barbarous instrument of his, and he shall smart for it in a way he won't like, he shall be taken before a magistrate, and if he has three months upon the treadmill it will be no more than he deserves for tearing my face as he has."

"Really, sir," said Valentine, approaching and speaking in his own natural voice, "it appears to me that you are far more to blame than the man you complain of."

"And pray who asked you for an opinion?" demanded the traveller very testily,

"I have ventured to give one without being asked for it;" answered our hero with constrained civility; "in fact, sir, I have been an eye witness of your furious attack upon the man, and, if the truth must told, I must say, you richly deserve all you have got."

"Indeed" said the other, furiously gnashing his teeth, and looking as if he would like to let fly at Valentine as he had previously done at the ostler.

"Aye, you have heard what I think of your conduct," answered our hero, "and now I would advise you to go home before your unfortunate temper involves you in an unpleasant dilemma. There are witnesses present who saw your savage attack upon the man, and no one, I believe, will venture to say that you were justified in knocking him down as you did."

"The scoundrel was insolent to me."

"On the contrary, I, for one, am ready to swear that he did not open his lips till after you struck him.

"Did ever any body hear such an assertion!" cried the angry traveller looking round to see whether he could reckon on having any friends among the crowd. A single glance, however, was sufficient to convince him that he stood there unfriended, and therefore, dropping the high tone in which he had been hitherto speaking, he said with forced resignation :—

"Well, well, I see I have no chance among so many enemies, but depend upon it, I will not let the matter rest where it is; I will immediately take out a warrant against the fellow, and to-morrow he shall suffer for treating me in the scandalous manner he has."

"And if so," replied Valentine, "I, and I dare say others, will be present also to give our testimony in favour of the man you would crush for this imaginary insult. Shame on you, sir, to betray so much malevolence about such trifles."

"Trifles do you you call them?" shouted the other passionately ;—" is it a trifle, think you, to be accused of keeping a rusty, fusty old maid in a stage coach?"

Fortunately at this moment the sound of a horse was heard, then came the rolling of wheels and the clattering of horses feet, and presently afterwards the vehicle for which Valentine was impatiently waiting was seen turning down the entrance that led to the inn-yard. Full of expectations he sprang forward to catch a sight of his friends, and there seated by the side of the coachman, he saw Uncle Sam waiving his hat and looking as rosy and happy as ever.

"Ah, Val. my dear boy," he exclaimed," there you are, I see ;—come to meet us, eh?—well, well, that's right; very dutiful and proper to come and see after your friends on their arrival."

Valentine clambered up the forewheel of the coach to grasp the offered hand of his worthy relative, and then looking round he said with some appearance of disappointment.

"How is this, sir? my mother was to have come up with you, but it seems you have travelled without her."

"Bah! you should make good use of your eyes, man!" exclaimed Uncle Sam, chuckling at his nephew's chagrin!—"The old woman's not far off I can tell you, only perhaps the journey has had the effect of sending her into a sound sleep."

"Where is she then?" demanded Valentine, looking round once more in the expectation that he had somehow or other overlooked the object of his search.

"Why inside, to be sure," replied the old gentleman, "she took it into her foolish head to grow very nervous all on a sudden as we came along, and so the coachman, civilly enough, put her among the insiders, where, I dare she's asleep and dreaming of her long intended visit to her son."

Valentine heard only the first part of this speech, for no sooner did he hear where his mother was, than jumping down from the wheel he opened the coach door, and was at once greeting in the well remembered voice of Mrs. Vaux.

"Ah, dear Valentine!" she cried eagerly pressing his hand, " this is indeed a pleasure, after the long absence I have been doomed to endure. But bless me, how thin and pale you look child !—Ah! that's the effect of living in London, I suppose, late hours and other indulgences are sad things to make havoc on the constitution."

Our hero felt vexed at these ill-timed remarks, notwithstanding the pleasure he experienced in once more meeting with his mother, and, taking her hand, he assisted her in alighting from the coach, at the same time taking care to whisper in her ear that there were people about who it would be as well to keep in the dark, in respect to matters that they had no business with. By this time they were joined by Uncle Sam. who had contrived, with some trouble, to place himself on *terra firma* by the side of his relations.

The next thing to be considered, was to see to the careful collection of the luggage, and when all this had been disposed of in a corner by itself, a coach was called from the stand to convey the newly arrived travellers and Valentine to the house of their mutual friend Septimus Bramstone. Never before did any of them feel so truly as upon this particular occasion ; Mrs. Vaux, over and over again wept and laughed in turns, as if she had taken leave of her senses. Uncle Sam. was boisterous and hearty as usual, and as for Valentine he felt so happy, that it seemed as if nothing in the world was wanting to complete the pleasure he now enjoyed.

At last, after a good deal of jolting and lumbering over the roughly paved streets of London, they arrived at the house of their generous friend by whom they were greeted with a welcome as

hearty as it was sincere. But we will leave them to the full enjoyment of each other's society, merely observing that the hospitality of the host produced an evening of calm rational enjoyment such as true friendship only can yield.

CHAPTER XXIX.

VALENTINE GETS JOKED ABOUT HIS LOVE AFFAIR ;—AND MR. SEPTIMUS BRAMSTONE AMUSES HIS COMPANY WITH A STORY OF HIS OWN AMOURS.— A VISIT TO SMITHFIELD ILLUSTRATES THE DANGERS LIKELY TO ARISE FROM TRUSTING YOURSELF AMONG HORNED CATTLE.—THE PICKPOCKETS AND THEIR FATE.

IT was not till rather a late hour on the following morning that Mr. Bramstone and his friend met again in the breakfast parlour, but when they did assemble, Mrs. Vaux could not help again expressing her uneasiness at what she was inclined to term Valentine's altered and pale appearance. At this, Uncle Sam. wickedly laughed and winked at Septimus, who, laughed and winked in return, while poor Valentine sat upon thorns, wondering what in the name of fortune could be the cause of all this extraordinary pantomime business. As for Mrs. Vaux, she could not help thinking it was extremely unkind to make a joke of what, to her, appeared so serious an affair, and she was more than half inclined to be a little pettish upon the matter, when Septimus, leaning across the table, whispered mysteriously in her ear.

"The fact is, my dear madam," he said, " love plays the very devil with one's good looks. Val., poor fellow, has lost his heart, and I suppose, like all other persons in the same predicament, he has sighed himself into the interesting condition that has called forth your maternal commisseration."

"Valentine in love !" cried the mother, startled, and yet not a little pleased at the announcement.

"Aye, as surely as that you are now sitting in that easy chair."

"Is it possible!" exclaimed the lady, hardly knowing whether to take the affair in joke or earnest.

"Aye, aye," said Uncle Sam., "it's all true enough, I believe. My friend Bramstone told me the whole secret last night after you had retired to your bed-chamber, and, between ourselves, sister, it seems the lad has not made such a very bad choice."

"And yet he has not consulted me in the affair," cried Mrs. Vaux reproachfully.

"That, perhaps," said Mr. Bramstone, "is because he wished to give you an agreeable surprise on your arrival in town. But all I have said is true enough I can assure you, and if I have stated a word of falsehood, there sits your son to contradict me."

"Oh, it's all true enough," said Uncle Sam., after indulging himself with a hearty laugh, "and if anything was wanting to confirm it Valentine's confusion would be quite sufficient for the purpose."

"Well then, I confess it, and throw myself upon your mercy," exclaimed our hero, mustering what resolution he could. "The fact is, I have been caught, as has been the fate of many a one before me, and all I ask is that you will suspend any further opinion upon the subject till you have had an opportunity of seeing the lady in question."

"Why, that's nothing more than fair," observed Uncle Sam., "so here let the matter end for the present, though I must needs confess I should like to know how my friend Septimus comes to be so conversant in matters of this kind. I'faith, I should have thought an old batchelor like him would have been as ignorant upon the subject as I am myself."

"Aye, aye," answered the old gentleman, laughing, but, perhaps, you are not aware that I have been over head and ears in love, and that not so long ago that I have a vivid recollection of all the circumstances attending it. Like Valentine, I grew pale and thin, and if the matter had not come to a

termination when it did, I dare say I should have been worn down to the state of a perfect living skeleton."

"Ha! ha! ha!" shouted uncle Sam., "and so you confess to having made a fool of yourself for once in your life?"

"Oh!" exclaimed Septimus, "you would not call it making a fool of myself if you had once set eyes on the charming widow Maxwell. She was a fine stately-looking creature, with eyes like a hawk and a tongue——"

"Like the clapper of a bell, I suppose," interrupted Uncle Sam., nudging Valentine, and scarcely suppressing a titter at his friend's unexpected confession,

"Aye, aye," said Septimus, "it's all very well to laugh at a man's weakness, but if you had ever known the widow Maxwell it's a hundred to one but you had fallen as desperately in love as I did."

"And pray how was it the affair was broken off?" asked Mrs. Vaux, with true woman's curiosity.

"Why, the fact is, madam," answered Septimus, "the fault was entirely my own, my passion was too ardent for her delicate susceptibility, and in a moment of thoughtlessness I offended her beyond all forgiveness."

"Indeed!—your offence must have been of a highly aggravated character," observed Mrs. Vaux.

"The fact is, madam," answered Septimus, "that as the lady one afternoon indulged in a sleep, I ventured to approach and kiss her delicate cheek. The widow woke up in a perfect frenzy, and I was dismissed with an imperative command never to show my face in her house again."

"And a very proper punishment too," observed Mrs. Vaux.

"Proper, but rather severe though," quoth Uncle Sam.

"And yet, after all," exclaimed Valentine, "it was nothing more than you might have expected from a spirited woman such as you have described the widow Maxwell."

"Humph!" ejaculated Septimus, "I see there is not much commisseration for me here, so, if you please, we will change the subject as soon as possible,—perhaps you two gentlemen

VALENTINE VAUX,

OR THE

TRICKS OF A VENTRILOQUIST.

BY TIMOTHY PORTWINE.

will have the kindness to say how you think of amusing yourself till dinner time?"

"For my own part, I have to meet an Essex farmer in Smithfield this morning, and if Valentine has no objection he can accompany me thither. Mrs. Vaux, will, of course, rather decline making one of our party seeing that the place is not adapted for the ladies."

"Why, I dare say she will," said Mr. Bramstone, "and so, if she has no objection to trusting herself to my guardianship we'll take a quiet stroll together in the parks, dropping in, perhaps, at one or two of the exhibitions."

This arrangement seemed perfectly satisfactory to all parties, and breakfast being by this time finished, Uncle Sam and Valentine took their departure, leaving Septimus and his remaining visitor to take their proposed stroll together.

On reaching Smithfield they found the place thronged with men and cattle, for it happened to be one of the market mornings, and as there had been a little rain in the night, of course, the place was ankle-deep in mud and filth. Through this, however, they were obliged to wade, to the infinite amuse' ment of numerous drovers and butchers boys, who enjoyed exceedingly the sight of a pair of swells, as they called them, making their way through an ocean of mud, and every now and then rushing and splashing away as they saw, or fancied they saw, some enfuriated animal making towards them. At last, however, they managed to reach the pavement, and then taking their stand beneath the entrance to St. Bartholomew's Hospital, they waited with what patience they could the arrival of Uncle Sam's friend, the Essex grazier.

Now, of all the annoyances in life there is none greater than that of having to loiter in a crowded thoroughfare for some person or other who chooses to be half an hour beyond his appointment. Yet to such an infliction were Valentine and Uncle Sam obliged to submit,—the former fidgetting about and continually changing his place, and the latter whistling the ghost of a tune for want of some better employment. Every now and then, by way of a change, he broke forth into violent invectives against all people who could not be punctual to an appointment, whilst Valentine, who was equally impatient, chimed in with a hint that all such persons' were only deserving of being sent to a place not to be mentioned to ears polite.

Presently, however, the attention of our hero was attracted towards a couple of young men, dressed in the very extreme of fashion, who seemed to have fixed their especial attention on a couple of jolly looking farmers who were engaged in conversation with a third person who appeared as if he had been endeavouring to prevail upon them to purchase a watch which he affirmed to be gold, but which anybody could see with half an eye, was made up of the basest sort of materials. All this struck Valentine as being very suspicious, and whilst Uncle Sam was still occupied with the tune that had so long haunted him, the nephew resolved to keep a close look out upon the motions of the parties before him. He had at once set it down in his own mind that the three men were confederates in villany, and that they were scheming to ease the pockets of the two farmers by transferring their contents to their own. Satisfied in this respect our hero was just to step up to the farmers, in order to put them on their guard against the thieves, but at the very moment he was about to do so the two well-dressed rogues stepped up close to their intended victims, and with an action almost too quick for sight, their hands were plunged into the pockets of the yokels, who were just then engaged in earnest conversation with the confederate. Not a moment was now to be lost, and invoking the aid of ventriloquism, he exclaimed, so as to throw his voice among the party :—

"Hollo, you rascals, what the devil business have your hands in my pockets?"

In an instant the two exquisites turned away a few paces, but finding that the farmers were still engaged in conversation with their confederate, and that consequently their danger was not so great as had been imagined, they once more returned to their former positions, and after a hasty glance round to see whether they were observed, their hands were again in readiness for another plunge. This time, however, Valentine would not give them as good a chance as on the former occasion, and directing his voice towards them in a whisper he said :—

"Be cautious !—you are observed !"

Again their hands were dropped, and staring timidly at each other, they seemed to be considering between themselves whether it would be most prudent to run away, or make one other attempt upon the pockets of their unwary victims. But the latter seemed to be the course they meant to adopt, and at that moment a crowd gathered round; they for the third time prepared to carry their necessary project into execution. Still, however, Valentine kept his eye upon them, and judging the time when they were about to make their final attempt at the robbery, he raised a tremendous shout of "Mad Bull !—Mad Bull !" that sent all the people scampering from the place in search of safety. In the scramble the two pretended exquisites got rolled in the mud, and no sooner had they managed to regain their feet for the purpose of making their escape from the place, than Valentine gave them both in custody of a policeman for attempting to pick pockets. Thereupon the swells began to bluster and threaten what they would do to them who dared bring such a charge against two persons of their respectability; but the policeman was not to be prevented doing his duty by all this swaggering, and grabbing each of the fellows by their collars, he enquired whether he had not before had the honour of having them in his custody.

"What do you mean, fellow?" said the taller of the two thieves.—"Do you mean to say that I,—Horatio Julius Crackit, would ever so far forget my high birth as to condescend to the low occupation of a common pickpocket."

"I knows nothing about your high birth and all that sort a' stuff," exclaimed the police officer; "but I remember your phisog very well, and if I ain't mistaken, it ain't so very long since you served five years in the Penitentiary for robbing a watchmaker over the water."

"What horrid insolence!" drawled out the other thief; "but thank goodness we are among men of honour here, and I'm sure there is not a gentleman present that would believe either myself or my friend would be guilty of so vulgar a propensity as that of picking pockets."

"At any rate, you have a strange fancy for putting your hands into the breeches pockets of other people," said Valentine, stepping forward:— "I have been watching you for some time past, and I distinctly saw three several attempts made to rob two farmers, who have just disappeared from the place."

"Gracious powers! did ever any body hear the like of that?" exclaimed Horatio Julius Crackit, in a tone of assumed indignation. "The fellows actually accuses us of trying to commit a robbery, as if we were any more

likely to do such a thing than he is himself."

"Oh, this here gammon won't suit at all!" cried the policeman.

"You thieves is always very innocent till you've found out; but I ain't to be done with all this flummary about your respectability, and all that nonsense. I'm used to it, I am; and if you want any body to believe the story, you must pitch the gammon to a magistrate, and then you'll see how much of it he'll swallow."

"A magistrate!" exclaimed the indignant Horatio;—"why you don't mean to say that you are going to disgrace my friend and me by carrying us like felons before a man that would as soon commit as look at us."

"And sarve you right too," said a countryman, who at that moment forced his way through the crowd, "for if I'm not mistaken you two's the very chaps that robbed me of a fifty pound note about three months ago, and left me only a bit of flimsy paper drawn upon the Bank of Elegance, or some such swindling concern that nobody can ever find out."

"Never saw you before in all my life," said Mr. Horatio Julius Crackit.

"Indeed! then it was some one uncommonly like you."

"That may be;" returned the prig, "for it unfortunately happens that my face is remarkably like half a dozen fellows that the world call rogues. Twice or three times before now I have been taken up on charges of felony, and each time the magistrates have been unjust enough to commit me, though I gave them my word and honour as a gentleman that I never was a thief in all my life."

"But perhaps you forget to call any witnesses to confirm the good character you gave yourself," said Valentine, who was now more than ever convinced that they were two notorious thieves.

"There you are most decidedly wrong," answered Horatio, "for on one occasion I called a very particular acquaintance to speak to my character, and though he spoke most favourable of me the judge would not believe a word he said, and the consequence was that I was sentenced to imprisonment with hard labour, whilst my friend, poor fellow, was sent to the House of Correction on an infamous charge of perjury. So you see how ill-used I have been, and therefore it is not to be much wondered at if I dread being taken before a magistrate."

"Can't stop here preaching all day," said the policeman; "so, come along, my fine fellows, and if you don't get three months in Bridwell for this, say I knows nothing at all about the law, that's all."

"We won't stir a peg without a coach, so don't expect, it old fellow," exclaimed Horatio, forgetting his former high flown manner.

"Not an inch," added his companion, looking round him to see if there was any chance of bolting through the dense crowd by which they were surrounded.

"Then I must put a pair of bracelets on each of you, so that's all about it," said the policemen, producing a couple of pair of handcuffs, which he slipped on the wrist of his prisoners with amazing rapidity. "That's the way we serve our obstreperous customers when a little gentle persuasion is of no use; so, now move on, will you? or I shall call upon these people here to lend a helping hand towards taking you off."

"I shall not stir from this place," said Horatio.

"Nor I," chimed in his friend and companion.

"Well then, here goes to make you," exclaimed the officer, giving them a tug in the direction he wanted them to go; but the two fellows were resolute in their determination, and regardless of mud they threw themselves on the pavement and used their legs with so much force and agility that it was sometime before any one could approach to carry them off to the station-house. At last, however, on the arrival of two or three more officers, the culprits were secured and carried off amidst the laughter and jeers of the by-standers.

When this excitement was over, Uncle Sam, who had highly enjoyed the scene, begun to recollect the business that had brought him there,

and once more he cursed in his heart all those people who could not, or rather, would not, keep an appointment.

It was in vain that Valentine tried to restore him to his customary good humour, he was too much vexed just then to listen to him, and he was just going to relieve himself by another volley of abuse against all loiterers when the very person for whom he had been so long waiting made his appearance. Fortunately, Uncle Sam was not of an unforgiving temper; the apology was accepted, and as our two worthies were tired of standing so long it was agreed that they should adjourn to a neighbouring Burton ale-house, where they might enjoy a glass in comfort, and, at the same time, arrange the business that had brought them together. Upon this, they proceeded down a very narrow and very dark passage which presently conducted them to one of the best and snuggest coffee-room in the metropolis.

———

CHAPTER XXX.

SNUG QUARTERS INVADED.—THE INCONVENIENCE OF A CROWD, AND AN EXCELLENT METHOD OF CLEARING A ROOM.—VALENTINE CONTRIVES TO STIR UP A DESPERATE FRAY, BUT IS GLAD TO EFFECT AN HASTY ESCAPE FROM THE UPROAR HE HAS GIVEN BIRTH TO.

SEATED in a comfortable box near the fire—for they were both cold and wet, through their long exposure in the market—Valentine and his friends gave themselves up to the free enjoyment of the present hour. When a man has had his temper tried, there is nothing like a glass of good ale for restoring him to good humour; over this he soon forgets his troubles, the past—for a period at least—is buried in oblivion, and if he looks forward to coming events, they are divested of all the grim horrors which an over nervousness of body may have given rise to. Uncle Sam seemed to feel the cheering influence of the potation, his friend was not far behind him in good spirits, and as for our hero, he had no sooner swallowed a glass or two of the stingo than he began to look about him to see if there was nobody present upon whom he could practice some of his facetious jokes. As he glanced round the room he perceived that it was completely thronged with a crowd of persons who had been compelled to take refuge there from a heavy shower of rain that had just fallen, and as most of these were larkishly inclined, and consequently very troublesome, he began to ponder over in his mind whether some device could not be thought of to clear the room of some portion of this superabundant population.

"This is what I call a confounded nuisance," said Uncle Sam, glancing at the new comers who were amusing themselves in sundry ways to the great annoyance of those who preferred quiet to disorder. "A man comes into a house of this kind to enjoy himself in the company of his friends, and then a parcel of noisy fellows are to break in upon the harmony, as if they were so many of the brute beasts we just left behind us in the market."

"Dang 'em I should like to have a shy at some of 'em," said Uncle Sam's friend, clenching his fist, and preparing to let fly at the very next that trod upon his gouty toe; then, addressing himself to a roughish looking fellow who had been amusing himself with bonnetting his companion, he exclaimed; "I say, my fine fellow, just stow that larking will you, or confound my carcase if I don't give you a dig in the ribs that shall send you and your companions out of the room in less than no time at all."

But the man paid no attention at all to this gentle hint of the enraged farmer, and merely removing himself a little farther off, he continued his boisterous amusement with even more violence than before.

"Well, I'm blowed if this is to be borne any how," cried the stout yeoman with increased fury. "These fellows ain't got any manners, except what's very bad 'uns, so the best way will be for us to walk our chalks before any further mischief comes of it."

"And why should we be driven away by such a pack of low ragamuffins as these?" demanded Uncle Sam, whose courage had been excited by the ale he had drunk; "if anybody ought to leave the room it's these fellows that's kicking up the row, so, for one, I shall remain where I am, and if they annoy us much more, we'll give them in charge, and then, perhaps, the aldermen at Guildhall, will give them a lesson to learn that they will not forget in a hurry."

"Bless your soul, that'll be no good," said the farmer, with a knowing shake of the head; "these fellows would cut as soon as they saw any danger, and then all we should get would be to be laughed at for our pains."

"I have a thought," exclaimed Valentine, slapping the back of the Essex yeoman with a vehemence that made him wince again—"I have a thought, old gentleman—a glorious thought."

"Well, you needn't hit a fellow quite so hard," cried the other, in no very good humour at the force with which our hero had made this announcement. "It's all very well, sir, to have a glorious thought, as you call it, but dang my buttons if there's any occasion to be so hard upon a fellow for all that."

"Oh, you mustn't mind, Val." interposed Uncle Sam; "he's a rum dog you must know, and if he has some queer ways with him you should laugh at them as I do."

"But he touched my feelings, sir," returned the farmer, to whom the gout had given rather a sour temper; "and moreover than that, I don't choose for young 'uns like him to be taking liberties with a man that's old enough to be his grandfather."

"Upon my word I beg your pardon for being so rude," cried Valentine, who began to find that an apology had become necessary;—"the fact is, sir, I was thinking how to rid you of all this annoyance, and when the idea struck me I could not help—"

"Stricking me at the same time," interrupted the farmer, and so delighted was he at the little bit of wit he had given utterance to, that seizing the hand of Valentine he gave it a bear's squeeze that made our hero, in turn, cry out with pain. Hereupon the good humour of the farmer was restored, and then slapping his young companion a similar blow upon the back he continued :—"There now, my friend, we are quits, so out with your glorious thought, and if it only turns out well, dang my old shoes if I don't stand a rump and dozen."

"Agreed," exclaimed Valentine, "so now listen to me, and if my project seems a little far fetched, wait with patience and you shall see that I will not be worse than my word."

"What's the rogue driving out now ?" cried Uncle Sam, chuckling at the idea of winning a rump and a dozen from his rustic friend ;—what the deuce new trick is the fellow up to now I should like to know ?"

"If I do not succeed in completely clearing the room I'll at least thin it of a great part of its present company," answered Valentine ;—"the Smith's as you know, form a pretty large portion of her Majesty's liege subjects, and, as I dare say there's a fair sprinkling of them among us, I have thought of a way of getting rid of them by one stroke of policy."

"Excellent," exclaimed Uncle Sam rubbing his hands with delight ;—" I begin to see what you mean now, my boy, and by Jupiter if you only succeed in your plan, I'll willingly add another half a dozen of wine on condition that three or four friends shall be invited to assist in drinking it."

This was agreed to by Valentine and the farmer, and as the coffee room door happened to be just then thrown wide open, our hero thought he could not have a better opportunity than was at present offered him. Taking advantage therefore of a brief pause in the hubbub that had taken place, he directed his voice towards the passage,

and assuming the voice of a person out of breath with running, exclaimed :—

"Mr. Smith !—Mr. Smith !"

"Well, here I am," exclaimed a dozen different voices, and at the same moment as many different persons made a rush towards the door, upsetting, in their progress, sundry chairs and tables, and creating a scene of confusion highly amusing to Valentine and his two friends, who knew the cause of the mistake and therefore could thoroughly enjoy it. Meanwhile the noise of strife and discord grew louder and louder, curses and oaths were mingled together in singular contrast, and three or four of the Mr. Smith's threw off their coats, and prepared for a set-to by way of a chastisement on those who, in their hurry to reach the door, had been guilty of various acts of violence. Indeed, there is no saying how far they would have gone in this noisy warfare had not Valentine again changed the course of events by his extraordinary powers of ventriloquism.

"Is Mr. Smith coming ?" once more shouted the same voice that had already occasioned so much confusion.

"I am," answered the same deep chorus that had replied to the former question ;—and again a grand rush was made towards the door with the same effect that had marked the former attempt. This time, however, the twelve Smiths were better prepared for action, and when at last they were all jammed together in one corner of the room they commenced swearing and kicking away at each other in a manner that would have done credit to as many savage Indians. But the more they pushed and kicked and swore the more completely did they frustrate their own views, and after about five minutes had been passed in this edifying struggle they were once more startled by the same voice that had created all this confusion.

"Mr. Smith is wanted at home directly," shouted Valentine.

"Let me out, let me out," roared out all the twelve gentlemen at once; and at it they went again pell mell, dealing out blows and execrations with an activity and force that was truly astonishing. Some lay rolling on the floor whilst others were pummelling them with all their might, in one part of the room two or three were engaged at fisticuffs; and, in another, one of the Mr. Smiths was just revenging himself by dashing the best part of a pot of beer in the face of another Mr. Smith, who, having armed himself with a poker, was seeking retaliation for injuries received by aiming the deadly instrument against the *os frontis* of all who stood in his way. It was in vain that the landlord had rushed among the thickest of the throng in order to allay the fury of the antagonists; he was alike disregarded by all, and the consequences were beginning to assume a serious aspect, when the landlady, at the head of half a dozen waiters, bounced into the room and commenced an indiscriminate attack upon all who refused to cease from the uproar in which they were engaged.

The scene was now of an animated though somewhat of a noisy description; pewter pots and even glasses flew about the room to the great danger of all who were not sharp-sighted enough to avoid the missiles, and two or three times Valentine narrowly escaped the dangers which his own natural love of mischief had occasioned. As for Uncle Sam and his friend from Essex, they began to think that any place would be better for them than where they were, and nudging their younger companion, they threw out sundry insignificant hints, that it would be better to be off whilst their shoes were good. But this was easier to be done in imagination than in practice, as they soon found out, for two or three times, by dint of hard pushing and driving, they succeeded in nearly reaching the door, yet no sooner had they done so, than a counter-stream met them full butt and back they were forced to their former *locus standi*, much to the annoyance of the two elder gentlemen, who began to be heartily tired of the aukward situation in which they were placed. At last, however, a more favourable opportunity occured; an opening was made towards the door, and then bidding his friends follow him with what speed they could, Valentine made a bolt to the passage, and in less than half a minute, he found himself on the outside of the house. A single glance served to satisfy him that Uncle Sam and the farmer were close at his elbow, and then calling a hackney coach, they all three jumped in, glad enough to escape from a scene that would most likely terminate in an appeal to magisterial interference.

CHAPTER XXXI.

FRESH PLOTS AGAINST SEPTIMUS BRAMSTONE, AND MATTERS BEGIN TO WEAR A SERIOUS ASPECT.—THE CONSULTATION IN WHICH CERTAIN PARTIES SHOW THEMSELVES IN NO VERY FAVOURABLE LIGHT.—A NEW PROJECT OF VILLANY IS PROPOSED AND ACCEEDED TO BY THE CONSPIRATORS.

OUR readers will not have failed to observe the deep contrition expressed by Mr. Harry Bramstone and his son Arnold, for the infamous treachery they had been guilty of towards their kind relative, Septimus, but we have now to record a further act of perfidy committed by, and which their previous cunningly expressed sorrow had completely disarmed him against.

In truth, they were determined to possess themselves of his property by hook or by crook, and, in spite of their plans having been once thwarted by Valentine, they determined not to relax in their endeavours, but rather to strike out some new project which would be more certain in its effects, than the one that had been so signally defeated. From the period that Septimus had been released from the private mad-house, the sire and son were in frequent conference together; nor were the ladies kept in the dark as to the manœuvres of their liege lords and masters; they were consulted as admirable councillor's in so difficult an affair, and to do them justice, they admirably seconded the views of those who they had sworn to "obey." Indeed, both father and son discovered that they had resolute allies in their spouses; and it was now resolved to go the whole hog in any design that might be considered necessary for the safe keeping of their unsuspecting relative, and securing his money to their own use.

It was on the afternoon of the same day, that Valentine and his friends had visited Smithfield, that Harry Bramstone and Arnold, with their two wives, sat down to a little after-dinner chit chat, that was to conclude the arrangements by which poor Septimus was once more to become the victim of there shameless perfidy. It had been already agreed that whatever was done must be done effectually, and quickly, lest their plot should be discovered, and it now only remained to settle some minor points in order to set in motion the infamous work in which they were engaged.

"For my own part," said Arnold, who had been for some time engaged in cracking nuts, with as much in-difference as if no treachery was in contemplation,--"for my own part, dad, I see no use in delaying matters so long as we have; the old fellow has once contrived to defeat us, when we thought him safe, and if we don't take care we shall lose all our trouble and the blunt into the bargain."

"And whose fault will it be if we do?" demanded the other;--"I'm sure for my own part, I have over and over again expressed my willingness to do the business at once, and if any one is to be blamed for the delay it's your mother, whose heart is always so plaguy tender whenever we come to the point."

"I tender-hearted!" cried the elder Mrs. Bramstone indignant at such an unjust insinuation; "I'd have you to know, sir, that if my advice had been taken before, Septimus would not at this time be giving us all this trouble."

"And, as for myself," continued her daughter-in-law, "I'll defy any body to say that any of the fault rests upon my shoulders. I always said it would have been better to have sent him a great deal further off, and if you had condescended to listen to my suggestions for once, we should have been very differently situated to what we are now."

"My love, how you do talk to be sure!" exclaimed Arnold, who began to think there would be very little business done if the women were suffered to go on with too loose a rein. His better half, however, was indignant at this rebuke, and tossing her head with offended dignity, she said:

"Talk, indeed, why of course I do, sir, and what's more I shall perhaps say a great deal more before I have done. Talk, forsooth! and pray, sir, what should we poor helpless women do against the tyranny of the men if it was not for having the free use of our tongues? They were given us to use, sir, as you ought by this time to know, and it's not you, nor any of your false-hearted, cruel sex that's going to stop me when once I've made up my mind to speak."

"Drat the woman, will you be quiet a moment?" exclaimed Mr. Harry Bramstone fairly worn out of patience by the volubility of the younger lady; "haven't we met together for the purpose of discussing very important business, and shall we defeat our own objects by starting such trifling subjects as these to become stumbling blocks in the very outset of the affair?"

"Mr. Bramstone, I'm surprised at you!" cried the senior lady with indignant emphasis; "*you* call yourself a man, you, indeed! but I can't give utterance to half my feelings, and I shall therefore conclude by insisting that you will be a little more respectful for the future when you happen to be addressing a lady, and that lady your daughter-in-law!"

Harry Bramstone was struck all of a heap by this imperative speech of his overbearing dame, but he knew from bitter experience that submission was his wisest course, and after

VALENTINE VAUX,

OR THE

TRICKS OF A VENTRILOQUIST.

BY TIMOTHY PORTWINE.

coughing away sundry angry expressions that had well nigh escaped his lips, he said with forced composure :—

"Well, my dear Mrs. B. I'm dumb upon that subject; but you must allow——"

"I' make no allowances at all, sir," answered the lady, "so you needn't expect to wax me with any of your ridiculous folly. No, Mr. Bramstone, it's high time that something should be done about that troublesome old fool of a brother of yours, and as they seem determined to put him once more into a mad-house, why the sooner the thing is done the

better, and then his property will be ours instead of going to enrich that needy beggar that he has lately taken so much notice of."

"Meaning Valentine, of course," said Arnold at last venturing to put in a word or two,

"I do mean him."

"Well then, have patience, and I dare say we shall be a match for any designs he may entertain of wronging us out of property that he can have no right to," answered the elder Mr. Bramstone. "A little management will shortly set all these matters to rights, and this young adventurer will have rather more difficulty in tracing out the old gentleman than he had on the former occasion."

"That is if you can keep your own counsel," interrupted Mrs. Harry Bramstone sharply.

"And pray, my love, why should I not do so?"

"Because you are such an easy fool," retorted the lady; "Valentine and his friends know how to pump you, and I'll answer for it they somehow or other contrive to draw the secret and release the old gentleman as they did before."

"Aye, aye," replied Harry Bramstone, "but I shall take care on this occasion that he is conveyed to a place where he will not be so readily discovered. I have seen an empty cottage in a lonely place on the borders of Hainault Forest, and there we may keep him snug enough till death thinks fit to release us from any further care on his account."

"A very sensible suggestion, considering from whom it emanates," exclaimed the elder lady, "and yet, when I come to think of it, you have not yet told us how he is to be taken care of, the old fool, when we have got him."

"Oh, all that has been well arranged beforehand," replied her husband;—"the stake we are playing for is a desperate one, and I know very well that it will require all our running to avoid an exposure that would end in utter ruin;—beware of this; I have opened my plans to Grabfast—the man who had the care of him before, and he has undertaken to manage the affair so as to avoid any of those dangers which we have so much reason to apprehend.'

"That's just what I thought!" exclaimed Mrs. Harry Bramstone, "I was sure you would go blabbing the thing to some one or other, and now we shall be foiled in our plans by the very person you have trusted with the secret."

"Excuse me, ma'am," interposed Arnold, "but something strikes me that you are making a confounded fool of yourself. It seems that the old fellow must have somebody to take care of him, and, for my own part, I don't know any body so fit for the office as Grabfast. His prisoner, it is true, once managed to escape from him, but that is the very reason why he should never be able to do so again. Besides, I've heard him say no longer ago than this morning, that nothing would give him greater pleasure than to have Uncle Bramstone in his clutches again, because he would take good care to pay off old scores for serving him the last slippery trick. Dad has therefore done right for once, and I hold up my hand in favour of his proposition."

"And so do I," said the younger Mrs. Bramstone, who for once in her life thought fit to agree with her husband.

"Well, I don't care a farthing how you manage it among you, so that the thing is properly done this time," exclaimed the other lady. "For my own part, I like to live in peace and harmony, so follow your own inclinations, and all I shall say about it is, if any harm comes off it don't lay the blame on my shoulders."

"Damn it, madam!" shouted Mr. Bramstone, senior, "how can any harm come of it I should like to know?"

"Oh! that's right, sir!—that's right!" cried his spouse with affected calmness;—"you can bluster out and bully against your poor suffering, uncomplaining wife, as much as you please; but remember, if you talk so loudly the servants may chance to hear you, and then away goes the secret at once, and no sooner will the old gentleman be missing than folks will point out to us as the cause of his sudden disappearance."

"They will be pretty sure to do that whether or not," observed Arnold. "It is perfectly well known that he was confined on the last occasion by our orders, and as a matter of course, people will give us the credit on the present occasion."

"Then we must brazen it out the best way we can, that's all I know about it," returned Harry Bramstone, who did not feel very comfortable at this suggestion of his son's;—"to be sure they will have a hard matter to fix the affair upon us, and if we boldly assert our own innocence, I dare say the world will be as ready to believe our assertions as those of our accusers."

"But I do not half like that Valentine Vaux," observed the younger of the two ladies:" he's a great deal too inquisitive for me, and depend on it if once his suspicions are directed towards us, he will never give up his inquiries till he has brought the matter fairly home."

"Poh, poh! who cares for such a paltry young jackanapes as that?" cried her mother-in-law contemptuously. "We have too long submitted to his impertinence as it is, and if my husband had but the spirit of a mouse, he would turn him out of the house the very next time he dares thrust himself within our doors."

"It shall be done Mrs. B." returned her husband with all due deference;—"your advice is excellent, my dear, and as I am rather too old for those things myself, I'll delegate the duty to our son Arnold, who, I dare say, will effect his ejectment in a manner to please all parties except the one principally concerned."

"I'll do it," said Arnold, who thought it as well to appear particularly brave when danger was not very near at hand. "The impertinent fellow shall be showed the outside of the door in less than no time, and if he chooses to ride rusty, why the only way will be to give him in charge for coming to create a disturbance in the house of respectable people."

"For my own part," exclaimed the junior lady, with a laudable regard for her husband's safety, "I think it would be quite as well if we had a policeman or two in constant attedance upon us. Poor Arnold may chance to get hurt, and I'm sure husband's are not so plentiful that one can afford to lose him, merely because *some people* don't choose to run their own persons into danger."

The elder Mrs. Bramstone's eyes flashed fire at this insinuation, and there is little doubt a serious affray between the ladies would have been the consequence had not their husbands interposed to allay the rising storm. Mrs. Harry Bramstone declared loudly that she scorned the paltry action that had been laid to her charge, and Mrs. Arnold vociferated with equal vehemence, that she always did, and always would, speak her mind, whoever it might offend; and the altercation would, no doubt, have proceeded to a very serious height had it not been for the earnest entreaties of their liege lords and masters.

Finally, an apology was unwillingly wrung from each for any inadvertent expressions that might have fallen; and the ladies, after much prevailing upon, kissed each other with a declaration that they had not meant a single word which had been said, and that in reality they loved each other so much, that the only wonder was how they could ever have been so foolish as to quarrel about such a simple affair as their own husbands. This was a compliment which the two gentlemen could not very well agree with; yet, for the present, they said nothing about it, preferring to take a more favourable opportunity when their remonstrances might not be so likely to give rise to another quarrel.

It was now arranged that two men should be sent to Septimus Bramstone's house the following morning—that he should be dragged by violence if any resistance should be offered, and that a gag should be applied to his mouth in case he should persist in calling for assistance. This was a cruel plot against the poor old gentleman; yet, cruel as it was, the two females cordially agreed in their voices in its favour; and shortly afterwards Harry Bramstone and his hopeful son left home in order to visit Grabfast, and make the necessary arrangements for conveying Septimus on the morrow, to the lonely cottage near Hainault Forest.

CHAPTER XXXII.

A SNUG PARTY.—ARRIVAL OF A COUPLE OF SUSPICIOUS VISITORS.—MR. SEPTIMUS BRAMSTONE ONCE MORE FINDS HIMSELF IN THE HANDS OF HIS ENEMIES. — HIS JOURNEY AND ARRIVAL AT THE LONE COTTAGE.—BRUTAL TREATMENT BY GRABFAST AND HIS ASSOCIATES.

LITTLE did poor Septimus think, when he rose on this eventful morning of the vile plot that was in agitation to tear him once more from the peaceful home to which he had been so lately restored. In fact, he was remarked to be in better spirits than usual at breakfast, and many were the jokes that passed between him and his guests, and various the plans for parties of pleasure that were to take place at the approaching nuptials of Valentine and Angelina Stanley. Mrs. Vaux, too, was particularly cheerful on this occasion; and as to Uncle Sam, who was always in high good humour, he cracked his jokes with a rapidity truly exhilirating, keeping his friends in so happy a cue, that, perhaps, never in their lives did they think less of approaching danger than at this moment.

Breakfast ended; it was next proposed that all the party, except the host, should visit some of the exhibitions at the west end of the town, and as this would necessarily occupy some time, it was further agreed that they should dine at the house of a friend, who lived in the neighbourhood of one of the places they intended to visit. As for Septimus, he had to wait at home to see a person whom he had appointed to meet on particular business; and having some other affairs to attend to after that, he resolved to devote the whole of that day to these matters, in order that the remainder of his time might be more at the service of his friends.

He had not, however, been alone very long when a loud knocking was heard at the door; and, presently afterwards, his servant, Susan Gabble, came running into the room to announce that a couple of gentlemen were in the hall, who wished to see her master immediately, on an affair of pressing emergence.

"Indeed!" exclaimed Septimus throwing down his pen, " and pray, Susan, who are these gentlemen?— Did they send in a card, or have you enquired their names?"

"Neither one nor t'other, sir," replied the girl; "they bounced in at the door as soon as ever I'd opened it, and as they looked like such outlandish queer chaps, I ran off as quick as ever my legs would carry me to let you know about 'em, for fear they should be what they oughtn't."

"Poh! for what reason did you run away from them?" demanded her master. "You know I expected a gentleman here this morning on business, and I dare say one of them is the person I was looking for."

"If you're looking for a *gentleman*, sir, I'm sure it ain't one of them," answered the girl. "They're rum looking chaps as ever you see, and summut or other tells me they arn't arter no good, and so now that's just my mind on the subject."

"Really, Susan, this is quite ridiculous," exclaimed her master, half angry at the girl's freedom; "who do you suppose would come here upon any business that was otherwise than good,'

"That's a question that a poor girl like me can't answer in a hurry," replied Susan, "but if the truth must be told, I should say they look a deal more like bum-baillies than anything else in the 'varsall world."

"Preposterous!—and pray what should such people have to do at my house I should like to know?"

"That's just what I thought to myself," answered the wench; "but then I don't pretend to know nothing at all about your affairs, sir, and so I thought I'd make haste here to let you know who was in the house in case you should like to bolt out of the windows before they come."

Septimus Bramstone could hardly help laughing at the girl's simplicity, but suppressing the merriment she had caused, he said with what gravity he could assume :—

"Well Susan, I am under no apprehension of meeting any of the class of gentry you have named, so pray return to these *gentlemen*, as you have called them, and say I will see them."

Susan Gabble would have ventured to remonstrate with her master, but she knew it would be in vain to do so, and uttering three or four audible expressions of pity for those who would not take care of themselves while they could, she slowly departed from the room to convey the message with which she had been charged.

Being thus left alone, Septimus began to consider whether he had acted wisely in giving an audience to men of whose objects and intentions he was perfectly ignorant. He thought of the trick that had once been played him by his brother and nephew, but then they had since expressed so much sorrow for the wicked part they had played in that transaction, that the notion had no sooner entered his mind than he sought to banish it by directing his attention to other objects less injurious to those he had so generously forgiven. Yet who it could be or what the motive of the visit could consist of, he was utterly at a loss to divine, and having turned the matter two or three times, he was about to adopt Susan's advice by leaving the room, when two rough looking fellows, each armed with a stout stick, made their appearance at the door he was about to pass through.

"Stop a bit, old gentlemen!" said the foremost of the two men putting out his arm to prevent the retreat of Septimus, "you and I've a little conversation to have together, we have, and I'm blessed if we part till the thing's made all right, yer see.

"What do you, friend?" said Septimus, with alarm; "surely you and your friend have made some mistake? My name is Septimus Bramstone, and very certain am I that you have nothing to say to me or any body in the house,"

"Ah, ain't I though, old boy!" exclaimed the other with insolent familiarity. "It's all wery well for you to pitch your gammon about it being all a mistake, but I happen to know my business, and that there's this here,—that's to say you're out of your mind—mad as a March hare, old cock, and I've got to take care of of yer till sich times as yer gets better able to manage yerself a bit."

"Ah! I see it all!" exclaimed Septimus sinking back into a chair,— "this is some more villany of those infamous scoundrels who have before done to —"

"Hush, old gentl'man will you :" interrupted the ruffian;—" ve ain't the sort o'chaps you takes us for, I can tell yer—ve is gemmen all over, ve is, ain't ve, Bill?"

"That ve is, and no mistake," answered Bill, in a grating tone that sounded more like a coffee mill in work than anything human. "Ve is gemman, every hinch of us, and him as says ve haint, says a damn'd lie, and so that's all about it."

"Again I tell you there is some mistake in this," cried Septimus. "I am not mad, as you may judge for yourselves, and even if I were so, you have no right to drag me from my home without a proper certificate signed by medical men!"

"Oh, ve knows all about that ere as vell as you can tell us," answered the principal of the two ruffians ;—" ve knows all about such certificates and such like stuff and nonsense, but then they don't happen to be wanted in your case, 'cause yer see, yer've lately 'scaped from a 'sylum, and all as we've got to do is to take yer safe back agin."

"That's about the ticket," chimed in Bill, who thought a word or two might not be thrown away now and then ; "we've got our horders to take yer back, old chap, and I'm blessed if ve don't do it to, and no mistake."

"Villains!" shouted the alarmed Septimus, "leave me instantly, or my cries shall alarm the whole neighbourhood!"

"No they von't, old 'un, and I'll tell yer for vy," exclaimed Bill, producing a gag from his pocket; "yer sees this here thing, don't you? Vell, I shall clap that over yer mouth in about a minute if yer comes any of yer nonsense; and then I'm blow'd if you'll be able to make much noise, and so that's all about it."

"Stop, Bill," cried the other fellow interposing, "we don't want to hurt him if he'll only be civil; so, now, I'll just tell yer what it is, old boy, come quietly along with us and it shall be all right, but if you kick up any row on goes the gag, and may be a straight waistcoat as well just by way of bringing you to your senses a bit."

"Scoundrels!—I am not to be terrified by your threats," cried Septimus, trying the effect of firmness upon his foes. "I am here in my own house, and I warn ye both that worst may come of this than ye expect unless ye choose to take warning and instantly depart before I call for assistance to eject you both from the window."

So saying the old gentleman was rushing towards the balcony in order to be ready to raise an alarm unless they instantly quitted the place, but the two keepers were aware of his intentions, and rushing forward at the same moment they brought him back once more struggling to the room.

"Vot a damn'd fool you are to make all this bobbary about nothing," exclaimed Bill, giving his victim a shake that threatened to drive all the breath out of his body. "Can't you be quiet when people comes for yer good, 'cause if yer can't ve'll just try if there ain't not no wertue in the gag."

"I'll resist even if I die while doing so," cried Septimus, struggling with all his might to release himself.

"Come Bill," vociferated the principal ruffian, "this won't do not no how; the old 'uns cantankerous like, so just slip the handkercher over his head, and then give me a helping hand to carry him to the coach outside."

"No, but you don't though!" exclaimed a female voice at this moment, and before either of the keepers were aware of her intention, Susan Gabble, armed with a long broom, rushed into the room, and flourishing her formidable weapon, she fetched Bill a rap over the head that laid him sprawling upon the floor. This done, she was about to administer a similar dose to his companion, but the other was upon his guard, and rushing upon her with all his force, he at once avoided the blow, and then slipping the gag over her mouth, he effectually prevented any alarm being given from that quarter. To secure her arms behind her with a piece of cord which he took out of his pocket was the work of a single instant; and having thus got rid of one enemy he hastened with Bill—who by this time had recovered the effect of the blow—to secure Septimus in a similar manner, and then bear him to a coach which was waiting for them at the door. Unfortunately, no persons were passing at the time, so that the deed was accomplished without interruption, and immediately afterwards, the vehicle was driven off from the door at a rapid pace.

It was in vain that Mr. Bramstone,—as soon as he had in some degrees recovered his senses,—looked around him to discover which way the fellows were taking him, they had foreseen that such would be the case, and as the driver was but too well accustomed to affairs of this description he took a circuitous direction which it would be almost impossible to remember, if at any future time it should be rendered necessary to restore the captive to his home. In addition to this, the blinds were now drawn down, so that no part of the route should be discovered, and, in this manner, they travelled for nearly three hours, sometimes going over cross roads that threatened every now and then to overturn the vehicle.

At first, Mr. Bramstone endeavoured to prevail upon the two men to let him return home but all his entreaties were in vain, and he had the mortification of finding that no hopes whatever, remained for him in that quarter. Then he tried what virtue there was in bribes; offering to give them any sum of money in his power, and further, promising never to make any complaint for the part they had taken in thus dragging him from his happy home.

But in this case, they were as deaf as in the former, and to his utter despair, he found that neither tears, prayers, nor promises, were of any avail with the brutal fellows in whose clutches he had thus unhappily fallen.

Thus situated he gave way to reflection, revolving in his mind the events that had befallen him, and endeavouring to fix upon the party who had been guilty of so gross an outrage. Of, course, his brother's name rose first in his mind as the origin of the base act, but then when he considered the deep repentance with which he seemed to regard his former villany he discarded the idea as altogether unworhty of him and too horrible to be encouraged. Nay, he had made up his mind to believe that this was the act of some one else, when the name of " Harry Bramstone " was whispered by one of the keepers who had been for some time passed engaged with his companion in a suppressed conversation. In an agony of horror, Septimus was about to enquire whether it was, indeed, to his brother that he owed his present misery, when the vehicle stopped before a low cottage which stood entirely by itself at the skirt of a wood, and ere he could ask where he was, the two men seized him in their arms and hurried him into the house.

All this had been affected with so much rapidity that the old man had not been able to cry out for assistance during the short interval that elapsed between his leaving the carriage and entering the place which, he had no doubt, was intended for his future prison. On looking round him he saw that the window was secured with strong iron bars, and the door fastened with immense locks, besides being strongly bound with huge pieces of iron-work that might defy any attempts that might be made to escape. In despair at the helpless situation in which he found himself, Septimus was about to demand once more the reason of his being thus detained, when a trap door was suddenly thrown open in the centre of the room, and Grabfast made his appearance from it, carrying a lantern in his hand which it seemed was rendered necessary through the extreme darkness of the vault he had just quilted. Septimus, at once, recognized the harsh, disagreeable features of his former gaoler, and sinking back upon a seat, he exclaimed faintly :—

" All—all is lost !—again am I in the power of my worst enemies, and never more am I doomed to enjoy the blessed liberty of which I have been so unjustly deprived."

" Aye, aye, you are right enough there, my man," replied Grabfast, with a grin of satisfaction; " we've had trouble enough since you last bolted from us, but I'll be hanged if ever you have a chance of serving us such a slippery trick again."

" Have you no feeling of compassion for an unfortunate man who has been betrayed into this snare by a villain ?" cried Septimus in despair.

" Why, as for feeling," replied Grabfast, " it ain't to be expected that a chap belonging to my profession can possess any great share of that sort of article. When people pay me well for doing a job, why, of course, I execute it as well as I can, and as I've had a good round sum for this affair, it stands to reason that my only feeling is to take the best care of you."

" Hear me," exclaimed Septimus ; " I have been foully wronged by those who wish to keep me out of the way for their own vile purposes, and I appeal to your humanity whether you would not be doing a duty by letting me go free and unharmed from this place. Nay, more, I will double the reward that has tempted you to the perpetration of this act, and my future life shall be devoted to furthering your interests by every means in my power."

" It's no go, old'un, I can tell yer !" interposed Bill, " we're all mix'd up together in this ere job, and I'm blowed if you're a going to go out of this place upon any of these promises. No, we've got yer safe enough, my tulip, and so the best thing yer can do is to make up yer mind to be comfortable where you are for the rest of your days."

" Hah ! is there no hope for me then ?"

"Not the least, that I know of," answered Grabfast; "it's true you did once manage to give us the slip, but I'll suffer my right hand to be cut off if ever you do it again.

"Who is it that has employed you to perform this cruel task?" demanded Septimus,

"Oh, I dare say we're going to tell you that," exclaimed Grabfast;—"it's a very likely thing indeed, that we should be such fools, as well as rogues, after taking our employers money! No, no, old chap, make yourself easy about that, and be as resigned as you can to your fate, because you see violence will do no good, and I'm so tender hearted, that I shouldn't like to be obliged to put you under any further restraint."

"I warn you that this act of yours must be answered for, in a way that will make you bitterly repent the share you have had in the transaction," cried the old gentleman, trying the effect of threats now that entreaties had failed.

"Oh, as for that," replied the other, "we must take the rough as well as the smooth in these matters. If I get into a scrape, I can't help it, but at any rate I shall take precious good care to prevent you getting out of my reach.

"And so shall I, for the matter o' that," exclaimed Bill. "I've been promised something handsome if I take good care of you, and so for the future I never means to go to sleep with both eyes at once."

"Aye, aye, I'll forgive him if ever he contrives to get away from us again," cried the other man;—"it may be all very well for a chap to play a slippery trick once, but it will be our fault if we let him do it again."

"Alas! alas!" cried Septimus, "is there no inducement I can hold out that will prevail upon you to restore me oncce more to my home."

"Lor, bless you, we couldn't do it not on no account whatsomdever," answered Bill. "It's no use your trying to bribe us, because we're honest chaps that mean to do our duty to the chap wots employed us. We've taken the man's money, and as he's promised to give us—"

"What the devil are you talking about you fool!" roared Grabfast. "Is there any occasion to blab every thing just to put him up to our moves?"

"Well then put an end to it at once," said Bill peevishly, "by sending him to the hole where he's to pass the rest of his days; that'll finish the business, and then we can enjoy ourselves over a bottle of rum, till the gen'l'man wot employed us comes as he promised he would.

Before Septimus was aware of what they were going to do, the two men who had brought him to this place, forced him into a straight waistcoat, and then carrying him down the trap door, by which Grabfast had made his appearance, they threw him down on a heap of straw in a dark room, or vault, beneath the small apartment they had just quitted. Upon a promise, however, from Septimus, that he would remain perfectly quiet, they released his limbs from bondage, and then placing a lamp against the wall, and some food and water by his side, they disappeared from the gloomy chamber, to enjoy themselves with Grabfast.

CHAPTER XXXIII.

THE SURPRISE THAT AWAITS VALENTINE AND UNCLE SAM ON THEIR RETURN HOME.—SUSAN GABBLE'S ACCOUNT OF THE AFFAIR.—A COUNCIL OF WAR IS HELD, AT WHICH SUNDRY IMPORTANT PLANS ARE PROPOSED.—MAGISTERIAL INTERFERENCE IS ASKED FOR AND GRANTED.

WHEN Valentine and Uncle Sam returned, which they did at a later hour than usual, having left Mrs. Vaux at the house of a friend, who had not seen her for so long a time, that she was resolved not to part with her until she had remained several days on a visit. On arriving at the house of Septimus, our hero and his worthy relative were somewhat surprised and alarmed at observing that the street door had been left a-jar, and from the disordered state of the

VALENTINE VAUX,

OR THE
TRICKS OF A VENTRILOQUIST.

BY TIMOTHY PORTWINE.

floor cloth in the hall it was pretty evident that all things were not quite right. Uncle Sam was the first to observe this, he nudged his nephew, exclaiming :—

"I say, Valentine, my lad, what the devil's the meaning of all this? The place seems to be in confusion, and between ourselves, it looks very much as if the house had been entered and robbed in our absence,"

"It does, indeed," replied Valentine, looking round him with a searching glance:—"something wrong seems to have taken place in our absence, and yet, when I come to recollect myself, Susan, the housemaid, is an industrious

wench, and, I dare say, these are only some of her preparations for a general clearing up."

"Then, in my opinion, she has made more litter than a tidy servant would have thought necessary," observed Uncle Sam; "look at the chairs, how they have been knocked about and overturned, and here, too, is the skirt of a man's coat lying on the floor betokening that a desperate struggle must have taken place among those who, no doubt, have entered the place for no good purpose."

"By heavens, that is a part of Mr. Bramstone's dressing gown," exclaimed Valentine, starting with alarm as his eye fell upon the fragment which his uncle had picked up. "Hah! I begin to see it all now!—villany has been again at work, and my poor friend has once more fell into the hands of his former persecutors."

"So saying, he rushed into the first room he came to, followed by his equally alarmed relative, and upon looking round upon the scene of disorder which there presented itself, they became more and more convinced that Septimus had indeed been again dragged by his merciless enemies from his own peaceful and happy home. Everything was in confusion; in one part of the room a table was upset, and near it lay a desk and papers, the latter of which were strewed about the apartment in a manner that plainly indicated a very desperate struggle must have taken place.

"Horror-struck at these confirmations of his worst fears, Valentine was about to rush forth in order to make further enquiries into this mysterious affair, when a low stifled groan fell upon his ear, and directing his search towards the part from whence the sound came, he was still further horrified at beholding Susan lying in one corner of the room where she had been left by the ruffians after they had gagged and bound her.

"To release the girl from this situation was scarce the work of a moment; but Susan was for some time unconscious of the presence of friends, and it was not until she had received every attention that could be bestowed that she at last sufficiently recovered the use of her faculties to recognize those who were about her, and to afford that explanation which was so eagerly demanded.

"Speak, girl!" exclaimed Uncle Sam, almost bursting with impatience; "what is the meaning of all this that has met our sight on returning home?"

"Oh, sir!" cried Susan nearly going off into hysterics, "there's been such a dreadful to do since you have been out;—they've been here and—oh dear! oh dear!—I am undone, girl, for all the rest of my life!"

"Who has been here?" demanded Valentine unable to command his patience;—"speak, Susan, and tell me the worst, lest I go mad with the uncertainty that involves the fate of my friend."

"Ah! Mr. Valentine, there's been such a kettle of fish!" cried Susan; "them fellows have been here again, and as for poor master, where they've taken him to it's quite unpossible for me to say."

"The rascals have laid hold of him again, that seems pretty plain," exclaimed Uncle Sam; "they have taken advantage of our absence and now the chances are that we shall never see him again as long as we live."

"Nay, the scoundrels shall not make so easy a prey of him as they expect," cried Valentine with resolution. "I know perfectly well who we have to thank for all this; his worthless brother and nephew are at the bottom of this infamous affair, and they shall find, through me, that the hour of retribution is near at hand. But we waste time in idle threats when we should rather be collecting evinence by which to crush those villains who have not paused at the most infamous acts by which to carry their foul designs into execution."

Then addressing himself to Susan, he entreated her to relate what had taken place as briefly and clearly as possible. But this was asking the housemaid more than she could undertake to do, for her tongue was naturally rather of the longest, and when once she had an opportunity of giving a free rein to it, she seldom failed to pour forth a torrent of eloquence that was perfectly electrifying.

In the first place, gentlemen," she commenced, "I was sitting down before the kitchen fire, thinking of nothing at all, when all of a sudden, I hears a coach stop just opposite our door, and then I thought to myself, thought I, that's a very queer thing any how, because you see, gentlemen, master has but few visitors, and I couldn't for the life of me guess who could have come to see us—well, with that—"

"For heaven's sake Susan, cut this

long story short," interrupted Valentine impatiently. "Who was it that came in the coach you speak of?"

"Goodness gracious only knows," answered Susan, "but they were two as great ruffians as ever you chanced to clap your eyes on. They both on 'em carried great sticks in their hands, and they bounced into the room where master was sitting, just for all the world as if they had a right to be there. "Oh, how I did tremble to be sure, when I seed 'em, for I know'd something was the matter by their queer looks, and then when they came to talk to master you'd ha' supposed that they took him for a madman."

"Hah!" exclaimed Valentine, "then my fears are confirmed;—these fellows were employed by Harry Bramstone and his son, and this time, I dare say they will have managed matters so secretly, that our utmost efforts to trace out our friend will prove in vain."

"At any rate, we'll stick to them like wax," returned Uncle, "and one thing I can tell them,—they will be cunning indeed, if they manage to get over us after we know so much of their former dirty tricks, and so I would have them beware, for this time they'll find that they have got to deal with a couple of chaps that are not to be put off the scent while there is a chance of bringing the affair to a successful termination."

"Oh, how I should like to see them two villains that took poor master away hanging in front of the Old Bailey, one of these here fine mornings," exclaimed Susan warmly; "it would do my heart good, and it would serve 'em both right too, for stopping a poor girl's mouth with that nasty gag of theirs,— that's what it would."

"Why that," observed Valentine, "was a very grave offence, indeed, and deserves a severe punishment."

"I suppose," said Uncle Sam, "if the truth was known, you made a rare noise while they were here, and that they were obliged, in self-defence, to take that course in order to prevent any interruption in this scandalous outrage."

"Ah! you may well say I kicked up a bit of a bobbery," exclaimed the housemaid; "I rather fancy did scream out above a bit, and then the nasty villains stopped my mouth and bound my limbs while they dragged master out of the room and shoved him into the coach which I heard drive off as hard as it could go as soon as ever they had got him safe. I tried to shriek out and alarm the neighbours, but they had taken good care to prevent me doing that, and as to getting my arms and legs free, I might as well have tried to move the house as to stir away from the corner the brutes had thrown me into."

"The infernal villains shall suffer for all this they may depend," exclaimed Valentine; "they have undertaken a dirty job from those who were more infamous than themselves; and the whole party implicated in this vile transaction shall find that they have, for once, overreached themselves."

"Not if we stand here all day talking about it instead of acting vigourously," observed Uncle Sam. Every moment is of the utmost consequence, and whilst we are debating about trifles, the poor old gentleman is perhaps suffering tortures that may drive him to that state of madness they wish to produce."

"How would you advise me to act then?" asked Valentine.

"Why, in the first place," answered the old gentleman, "I should propose going immediately to a magistrate, to whom we can relate the affair as it has taken place, and who will, I dare say, render all the assistance in his power. At any rate, we shall have the benefit of his advice, and that, under circumstances, is exceedingly desireable."

"Your suggestion is worth trying, at all events," exclaimed Valentine, "and if our visit to his worship should prove of little use, we can then proceed according to our own notions, which I'll be bound to say in the end, will not prove altogether useless."

"Perhaps, gentleman," interposed Susan Gabble, "you won't be offended if a poor girl gives her advice in this here affair?"

"Certainly not," replied Valentine,

"so pray give us the benefit of it with as little delay as possible."

"Well then, I was only going to say," returned Susan, that old Harry Bramstone and his son, Arnold, are just as cunning as a couple of born devils, and if they think you suspect either of 'em of having a hand in the business they'll take precious good care to move master about from place to place so as to prevent your ever finding out where he is."

"Why, in some respects," answered Valentine, "your counsel is good enough, but then it does not happen to be altogether practicable. They are artful enough to know that I shall at once suspect them, and if I appear to be too friendly they will know that I am secretly at work to bring a charge fairly against them. For that reason I think the better way will be to accuse them point blank with their villany, and then afterwards to take measures for compelling them to restore Mr. Septimus Bramstone to that liberty which they have unjustly deprived him of."

"Good!" exclamed Uncle Sam; "all that is excellent enough, but I think we should first of all solicit the advice of a magistrate who may greatly aid us in our search."

To this Valentine readily assented, and after having cautioned Susan as to how she should proceed during their absence, the two gentlemen set out on the important business which at present engaged their attention, and having hired a coach, they were soon carried to the police office, where the object of their visit was briefly and at the same time clearly explained. The magistrate, who happened to be a man of sound judgment and discretion, listened with the greatest attention to their statement, and having seriously considered over the matter, he declared it to be his opinion that much caution would be necessary in the steps that it might be necessary to adopt.

"I can see," he said, "that you have artful men to deal with in this affair, and any undue precipitation would assuredly defeat the object you have in view. For my own part, I am willing to give all the assistance in my power;

I will immediately put the affair into the hands of one of our most trustworthy officers, who, by diligent enquiry, will, I dare say, be enabled to discover the place to which your friend has been so violently conveyed."

"Your worship has fulfilled the hopes I ventured to entertain," answered Valentine, bowing to the worthy magistrate, "and I am most willing to leave every thing in your hands;—but, at the same time, I would humbly suggest that the brother and nephew of the party who has thus been torn from his home, are strongly suspected of being the cause of all the mischief, and that therefore active measures should be instantly adopted to force them into a confession of the share they have had in the business."

"Have you any evidence to prove that they have hired these men to commit this abominable outrage?" asked the magistrate.

"Nothing further than that they were engaged in a similar transaction a short time ago," replied Valentine.

"And that, of course, will not be be sufficient to fix them with the crime on the present occasion," returned the other. "The case, I grant you, is fraught with very strong suspicion, but till we have some more decisive evidence, the guilty parties, whoever they may be, must be suffered to exult in the success of their nefarious designs. I have, however, already told you that a person belonging to this office shall be ordered to make every enquiry, and I need hardly add, that anything which lies in my power shall be cheerfully granted towards effecting the recovery of your friend."

Valentine and Uncle Sam was obliged to rest with this arrangement as far as it went, and thanking the worthy magistrate for the attention he had bestowed upon the case, they departed from the office, with a determination to prosecute the enquiry with unremitting diligence, till they had succeeded in restoring Septimus Bramstone to the home from which he had been so violently forced away.

"If ever I give up hunting out the infernal scamps that have been guilty of this piece of rascality, say I'm no true man," exclaimed Uncle Sam, as soon as they had gained the exterior of the police office. "I'll follow them to the very ends of the earth, and they shall never have any peace till justice has been done to their poor victim."

"Nay," cried Valentine, smiling at his friends earnestness, "there will be no occasion for us, I hope, to go quite so far as the ends of the earth to obtain justice; yet we will both of us hunt together, and unless fortune should be against us, it shall not, be many hours before the matter is brought to a satisfactory conclusion."

"No conclusion will be satisfactory to me," exclaimed Uncle Sam, "that falls short of bringing all the parties concerned against poor old Sep. to the gallows. They must be hung, Valentine, if the law will go so far, and though I never saw an execution in my life, I'll get up early that morning on purpose to see the scoundrels swing."

"Well, really," cried Valentine, "I have the advantage of having a thick and thin supporter in this affair, and something strikes me it will be no fault of ours if our plans should unfortunately happen to miscarry. At any rate we both of us enter heart and soul into the business, and if resolution will do any good, we shall have the old gentleman back with us again before any of us are much older."

It was then arranged between them that they should return back to the house of Septimus, where an hour or two should be passed in perfecting the measures before they put them in progress. This was done accordingly, and while they were discussing the merits of the tea and toast which had been provided on the occasion, by the ever careful Susan, they talked over the means that should be adopted for carrying forward the design in hand. The housemaid was then called in and examined, touching all that had taken place during the time the two men were in the house, and a number of questions were put to her in order to see whether any clue might be obtained that would lead to the forma-tion of an opinion respecting the place to which Septimus had been taken. But either Susan had been too much alarmed or the men had been to conceal every thing that might in any way serve to bring them to justice; for, after all manner of questions had been asked, Valentine and his uncle were forced to come to the conclusion that they had a difficult task to execute, and that whatever was done, must be performed with the greatest caution and secrecy. It was, however, arranged that they should visit the house of Harry Bramstone that evening, to see whether anything could be gathered in that way, and thus to put matters in a state of immediate activity.

CHAPTER XXXIV.

OPERATIONS AGREED UPON BETWEEN VALENTINE AND UNCLE SAM.— THEY SALLY FORTH ON A VOYAGE OF DISCOVERY, AND THE INCIDENTS THAT BEFEL THEM THEREIN.—THE AMBUSCADE, AND THE MYSTERIOUS MAN IN THE CLOAK.—VALENTINE PROVES RATHER UNRULY, BUT IS CHECKED BY HIS MENTOR.— AN INTERVIEW WITH A COUPLE OF ROGUES.

IT was dark by the time Valentine and his uncle set out on the way to the house of Harry Bramstone, but as that was a more likely time to find him at home, they consoled themselves with the certainty of bringing matters to a conclusion at the earliest possible moment. Wishing to take the parties they were about to visit as much by surprise as possible, they preferred walking to riding, and upon reaching the neighbourhood of the place, they stationed themselves at the corner of a street nearly opposite, where they could watch all that was going on, without themselves being observed. Nor was this precaution without its use, for they had not been at their post many minutes, when a man closely muffled up in a cloak knocked at the door, and was admitted by the younger Bramstone, though not till he had cast an anxious look up and down the street, to see whether any body was about who seemed to be looking after them. Having satisfied himself in this particular, the stranger was admitted, and then the door was cautiously shut to, so as to make no noise that might attract towards them the attention of their neighbours.

"I'll wager my life that's some one connected with this infamous job," exclaimed Uncle Sam, as soon as the two worthies had disappeard from sight. "The fellow in the cloak looked as if he had come on some dirty business or other, and I'll be bound, by this time, they are all in full chat about the affair that they think has been managed so nicely."

"Something strikes me that I know the fellow they have just admitted," cried Valentine; "the rascal has taken great pains to conceal himself as much as possible, yet, I think I could take it upon myself to swear that he is no other than Grabfast, the keeper of the madhouse where our friend was confined before."

"Do you think so?" exclaimed Uncle Sam with surprise.

"I am almost certain of it," answered Valentine, "there is something in the fellow's appearance that is not to be mistaken, and in order to convince myself that it is so, I'll run across the way, and knock at the door as if I had merely called on an ordinary visit."

"Don't make such a damn'd fool of yourself, Valentine," cried his Uncle Sam, seizing hold of his arm at the moment he was about to rush across the street. "Remember we have no evidence yet, and if you commit yourself in this way we shall never be able to arrive at the rights of it."

"But I'll broadly tax them with having kidnapped the old gentleman," exclaimed Valentine, "and if they dare to deny knowing anything about it, I'll threaten to take them before a magistrate, and in that way, perhaps, we may get to the truth sooner than by any other method."

"And by so doing, you will put them on their guard, and thus we shall be placed in a worse situation than we are now," answered Uncle Sam. "No, no, take my advice, my boy,—let's watch them from this place, and, by-and-bye, perhaps, we may pick up enough information to make out a good broad case against them."

"And while we are making out what you call a good broad case against them, our poor friend is suffering tortures that I cannot bear to think of," cried Valentine. "No, my advice is to bring matters to an end as speedily as possible, and, if we can't obtain justice any other way, I'll take out a warrant against both father and son, so that they shall find there is one friend of their victim who is determined to sift their villany to the bottom, let it be at what cost it may."

"Then I see you are an obstinate young fool, and I shall never be able to do any good with you," exclaimed the old gentleman with resentment. "I thought to have found some sense in my nephew, but now, when that very necessary article is most needed, I find him flying helter skelter into mischief, and the devil a word of advice will he listen to from one who has lived long enough in the world to learn prudence."

"I will listen to any thing in reason," answered Valentine; "but when I see my friend in danger of falling a victim to the rascality of others, it is high time to take desperate measures for his release."

"Hush! for heaven's sake, hold your tongue!" cried the elder gentleman, "for see the door again opens, and the same mysterious man in the cloak comes out of the house. See how heartily he shakes hands with that young imp of the devil, Arnold Bramstone; these fellows are sworn friends I'll be bound to say, and as to getting a word of truth about this matter out of either of them, why you might as well expect fair dealing with a lawyer, or honesty from Satan himself."

"See," exclaimed Valentine, "they have parted, and the man I believe to be Grabfast, comes this way. Be silent for a moment and if it should indeed prove to be that arch scoundrel I'll seize him by the throat and never leave my hold until he has confessed the whole of the villainous affair in which he has been engaged."

Uncle Sam knew that his nephew would be as good as his word if he only had a chance given him, and having certain fears of the station house before his eyes, he held Valentine with all his strength until the man in the cloak was fairly out of sight. It was in vain that our hero remonstrated against having been thus forcibly detained, for the other only met his anger with an argument against the folly of being too rash, to which was appended a little piece of advice never to do anything of importance, without twice thinking about it. By this time, Valentine had regained some of his former good humour, and acknowledging that he was wrong, he entreated the old gentleman to accompany him to Harry Bramstone's house where they might probably pick up some information that would prove useful to them in a subsequent stage of the proceedings.

" Why, as to going over the way with you," returned Uncle Sam, " I can see nothing objectionable in that, provided you choose to behave yourself prudently. But mark me, Val, there must be no flying out, no coming Captain Grand, you know, or else you and I shall be likely enough to part company and so make an end of the affair at once."

" Psha! you take this matter too cooly, my dear sir," cried the impetuous Valentine.

" And on the other hand, you take it up too warmly," retorted the old gentleman. " The job, it is true, is a very bad one, and all that are concerned in it, deserve to be well flogged at a cart's tail, but then it is not by blustering and bullying that we shall do any good; caution and prudence, my boy, are required here, so if you don't choose to promise me to be upon your guard over the way, why I shall

leave you to finish the matter in the best way you can."

Valentine now began to find that he would gain very little by remaining obstinate, promised to keep himself as cool as possible, and having thus somewhat allayed the old gentleman's indignation, they crossed the road together and knocked at the door of Harry Bramstone's house. Arnold appeared almost immediately to answer the summons, and when he saw who was there, he started back aghast, and would have shut them out had not Valentine placed his foot against the door so as to prevent it.

" Why, Arnold, my boy, it's only me," he exclaimed in a voice of friendship that his tongue almost refused to give utterance to.

" Who is it?" cried Arnold with terror.

" Why, a friend, to be sure—Valentine Vaux—

" Indeed!—but who was that I saw standing by your side?"

" Oh, only Uncle Sam,—an old friend from the country;—but you don't mean to keep us waiting at the door all night do you?"

" Why of course not," exclaimed Arnold, who was by this time convinced by Valentine's manner that it was all right, and then thinking it was necessary to make some apology for the extreme caution he had used, he continued:—" the fact is, old fellow, there's such things as duns that now and then have the impertinence to call upon me, and as I am expecting two or three of those gentry just about this time I thought it as well to be on the right side of the hedge."

" Humph," retorted Valentine, " then perhaps I have just now had the felicity of seeing one of them. A fellow in a mysterious looking cloak, just before we knocked was dodging about the place, and thinking he was a suspicious looking chap, I was going to ask him what business he had here, only that Uncle Sam would not suffer me."

" Your Uncle Sam is a very prudent old gentleman," exclaimed Arnold, bowing to the person he had named. "The fact is, my dear fellows, these are very awkward affairs, and one don't know the mischief you might have done me had you been rash enough to have accosted the fellow."

"I was thinking it would not have done you much good," answered Valentine with emphasis.

This was being rather personal, and Arnold would have replied to it sharply had they not at that moment entered the drawing room where they found the elder Mr. Bramstone, with his wife and daughter-in-law, seated at a whist table, and waiting impatiently for Arnold, who, it appeared, had been disturbed in the midst of the game.

"Glad to see you, gentlemen, glad to see you," cried Harry Bramstone, eagerly seizing the hands of his two visitors though it was easy enough to see that he wished them both at the devil.

"This is really very kind of Mr. Vaux," exclaimed the elder Mrs. Bramstone, curtseying with profound gravity,—"perhaps the gentlemen would like to join us in a rubber of whist, or suppose we make a table at loo because then we can all of us join in the amusement."

"Rather not, ma'am, I thank you," answered Uncle Sam, bowing with an elegance that was fully equal to the grace of the lady's curtsey; "cards are all very well for those that like 'em, but, for my part, I never found any amusement in shuffling and dealing out a parcel of paste-board things that have no more sense in 'em than ——."

Uncle Sam was going to add, "those that play with them," but gallantry came to his rescue, and clearing his throat with a loud "hem," he looked round to Valentine to get him out of the dilemma in the best way he could.

"The fact is, sir," said our hero, addressing himself more particularly to the elder Mr. Bramstone, I came to inform you of a misfortune that I am sure you will deeply sympathize in. Your brother, sir, has again disappeared, and I am sorry to add, under circum-stances that lead us to suspect, his removal has been effected by force."

"Dear me! you don't say so!" exclaimed Harry Bramstone in a tone that would really have induced any body to suppose that he was much shocked at the intelligence.

"Poor dear soul! who can have been so base as to treat him in such a scandalous way?" snivelled the elder lady, applying by turns a bottle of salts to her nose and a white cambric handkerchief to her eyes. "Poor dear Sep. never had any enemies that I was aware of, but it's all along of his own foolishness; we wanted him to come and live with us—didn't we Harry, love? but he was obstinate, and would have a house to himself, and now see what a pretty plight he has brought himself to!"

"Only let me find out the villain that has done this," exclaimed Arnold, pompously; "only let me find him out, I say, and confound me if I don't serve him out in such a way that he shall never kidnap any more of my uncles, I'll warrant me."

"And cannot you give a guess?" asked Valentine, "is there no one that you think of who has been guilty of this most base and cowardly act?"

"How should I be able to guess any more than yourself, sir?" asked Arnold, who felt the blow as it had been intended.

"Aye, how indeed?" chimed in his affectionate mother.

"The fact is, you must excuse Valentine," said Uncle Sam, who began to fancy that matters were going a little too far; "he is a giddy-pated youngster, and having, somehow or other, lost sight of his best friend, he is now going about to search for him every where he can think of."

"Then, you expected to find him here, I suppose?" growled Mr. Harry Bramstone, who did not half like the turn matters seemed inclined to take. "It seems that my unfortunate brother has fallen into bad hands, and as a natural consequence, you come here to look after him."

"Why, the truth is, sir" replied Valentine, "I came here because I

VALENTINE VAUX,

OR THE

TRICKS OF A VENTRILOQUIST.

BY TIMOTHY PORTWINE.

thought you were more likely to give us information of Mr. Septimus Bramstone's present abode than any body else."

"Psha!—we know nothing about him," cried Arnold snappishly.

"Indeed!—then I have been mistaken," returned our hero.

Uncle Sam trod upon Valentine's toes to make him hold his tongue, but all was of no use, he had got upon the subject, and he was resolved not to leave it till the matter was set at rest.

"Hold your tongue, you young dog, will you?" whispered the uncle of

our hero, in his zeal to stop the progress of hostilities.

"Perhaps, sir," said Mr. Harry Bramstone, who had observed this little piece of pantomime;—"perhaps you will have the kindness to let your nephew speak for himself."

"Perhaps he had better do nothing of the sort," cried the old gentleman crustily;—"these young chaps, sir, are very apt to make confounded fools of themselves, and I am not going to suffer my Valentine to become a laughing-stock to please you or any body else."

"This is not to be endured," exclaimed Valentine, impatiently ;—" I have come here to satisfy myself as to the fate of my friend Septimus Bramstone, and let the consequences be what they may, I am resolved not to leave the place until some sort of explanation has been afforded."

"Did I ever !"

"Well I never !"

These latter exclamations were uttered by the two ladies, who had been listening to the foregoing conversation, and who, as a matter of course, thought their own husbands perfectly in the right ; whilst, equally as a matter of course, they believed Uncle Sam and his nephew to be a couple of the most impudent scoundrels that ever had the audacity to walk themselves, unbidden, into another person's house.

"Now, I'll tell you what it is, young fellow," exclaimed Arnold, looking at the two visitors through his eye-glass !—" the fact of the matter, appears to me, that you fancy I'm afraid, and that I haven't the pluck to call you out for this infernal insolence. But you must understand, my boy, that I am quite a different character to that ;—I've smelt gunpowder before to-day, and if you feel inclined to settle the affair at Wormwood Scrubs, or any other place, why I'm your man."

"Ho, ho !—you are for frightening us, are you?" shouted Uncle Sam.— "Well, if you like to settle the difference in that sort of way, why you will find me agreeable to anything. Only let one thing be remembered— if there is to be any collision,, let the affair be settled with the aid of the fists—not with swords or pistols, that too often make matters worse, by leading to the death of one of the parties."

"Vulgar individual !" cried Arnold, "do you suppose I would disgrace myself by an act so like that of two costermongers when they fall out? No, I must have the satisfaction that one gentleman has the right of demanding from another, and if your nephew refuses to give it me, why I shall be obliged to post him for

an infernal coward, and thus he would be for ever excluded from all respectable society."

"That is to say from all society which *you* call respectable," observed Uncle Sam, with a sneer, which could not be very well mistaken.

"What do you mean by that, sir ?" demanded Arnold, advancing fiercely, and almost thrusting his nose into the face of the old gentleman ;—"do you mean to say, sir, that I don't know good society from bad ?"

"I mean to say, sir, that you are an impetuous fool," answered Uncle Sam very coolly ; "and that the sooner we have the good fortune to be out of your company the more lucky I shall esteem myself."

"And on the other hand," exclaimed Harry Bramstone who seemed to think it was high time to interfere, "I shall feel much gratified by your immediately leaving my house."

"Oh, you need not flurry yourself about that," answered the old gentleman, "because I mean to be off in about a brace of shakes. But don't make yourself too safe, old chap ;— you have put my spirit up, and hang me if I don't stick to you and your young fellow there, just like a piece of wax. Poor Septimus has been deluded away from his home—you, and that hopeful fellow there, have done it all, and now I'll set about the task with Valentine to circumvent your base designs, and restore my friend to his liberty."

So saying, Uncle Sam and Valentine took their departure without waiting to pass the usual compliment of a " good bye," and hardly had they got into the street when the door was shut after them with a bang that shewed the towering passion of those they had left behind. Our two friends then returned home, discussing on their way various plans for releasing Septimus from the villainous hands into which he had been unlucky enough to fall.

———

CHAPTER XXXV.

VALENTINE RECEIVES AN ANONY-
MOUS COMMUNICATION THAT
THROWS SOME LIGHT UPON THE
MYSTERY.—A VISIT TO THE COTTAGE
IN THE FOREST, AND THE SORT
OF RECEPTION OUR HERO AND HIS
UNCLE THERE MEET WITH.—THE
RETURN, AND PREPARATIONS ARE
COMMENCED FOR ANOTHER CAM-
PAIGN.

IT may be all very well for a man to brag about what he will do, but when Uncle Sam began to grow a little more cool, and at the same time a little more reflective, the thought occurred to him that it was not quite so easy to discover the whereabouts of Septimus, and the infamous conduct of his brother as he had at first imagined. This notion was quickly communicated to Valentine, who, in his turn, began to see the folly of wasting time in useless surmises, and they had just resolved to commence operations in real earnest, when that mysterious rat-tat, known as the postman's knock, was heard at the street-door, and presently afterwards Susan Gabble darted into the room, holding a particularly dirty looking letter in her hand, which she handed to Valentine, as the party to whom it was addressed.

"Who can this be from?" exclaimed our hero, hesitating for a moment before he broke the seal, and examining the post-mark, as people will sometimes provokingly do, when other folks are anxiously standing by to learn from whom the epistle has been sent. "Who *can* it be from?" he repeated more emphatically; "the hand-writing is totally different from any that I have been used to, and the bad spelling of the address proves that my correspondent belongs to the more numerous but least refined portion of society."

"Why don't you open the letter, and satisfy yourself at once?" cried Uncle Sam, impatiently. "I hate people that are so slow about things, and upon my life, if you don't break the seal in about a minute, I shall be tempted to snatch the note out of your hands, and thus ascertain who your correspondent is, and the nature of his communication."

This threat was not heard by Valentine, who, by this time, had opened and perused the letter, which having perused, he threw over to his uncle with an exclamation of chagrin and disappointment.

"Well, Valentine, who is it from?" asked the old gentleman, glancing his eye towards the dirty scrap of paper before him, "is it from any body you know?"

"That's more than I can inform you," answered Valentine, "for the letter is an anonymous one, and relates to poor Mr. Septimus Bramstone, whose present abode it pretends to point out."

"Aye, aye!" exclaimed Uncle Sam, "then the hint may be worth our while attending to, if we only strike while the iron's hot; so, tell me all about it, and off we start to set our enquiries on foot after the old gentleman."

"The letter will inform you better than I can do myself," replied Valentine, and Uncle Sam, who began to think there was some truth in the last observation, took the aforesaid scrap from the table, and after turning it over and over in his hands, read as follows:—

"DEER SUR,—

"If so be as you wants to noe any thing about your affexinate frend, S. Bramstone, go to a ouse nere the west borders of Hanold Forest, and, p'raps, you may find him as you looks for. They're a trying to drive him out o' his senses, and I'm blessed if they won't do it too, and no gammon, onless you stur your stumps like a brick.

"ONE AS IS UP TO SOMETHINK."

"Well, uncle," exclaimed Valentine, "you have now finished this precious epistle, and now, I should like to know your candid opinion of its value?"

"It's all damn'd rubbish, Val" cried

the old gentleman, in reply,—"the thing has no name to it, and is, therefore, worthy of little attention."

"And yet," observed Valentine, "the time occupied in our search might not be altogether thrown away either. A sort of clue is afforded to a cottage, said to be the place of his concealment,—and if we can only discover that, we will soon satisfy ourselves whether our friend is there or not."

"Let's see, what's the name of the place where the cottage is?" exclaimed Uncle Sam, again glancing his eye over the note. "What does the fellow say?—an old forest!—what the devil old forest does the fellow mean?"

"Hainault Forest is the place signified, no doubt," answered Valentine, "though he has spelt it 'Hanold,' either through ignorance or a wish to deceive us into a belief that the writer belongs to a different class of society to that which he really moves in."

"Well, I was thinking there might be some sort of trickery in it," exclaimed the old gentleman;—"the writing seems to have been purpose disguised, and now that I come to think of it, I shouldn't wonder if it may be a plan of old Harry Bramstone's, to get us into that confounded forest and there murder us!"

"Why, that he is bad enough for any thing is not to be denied," answered our hero, "but then, on the other hand, it must not be forgotten that he has the fear of the gallows before his eyes, and that if he was to go too far, the chances are that his own unfortunate neck would be sure to suffer for it.

"You think there's no danger then?"

"None whatever, if we proceed with proper caution," replied Valentine. "Depend on it this letter was never written either by him or with his knowledge;—in fact, the thing may be nothing more than a hoax to deceive and put us off the true scent, which would ultimately lead to the discovery of our friend."

"If that is the case we had better not pay any attention to the letter," exclaimed Uncle Sam, who was notorious for giving up a design almost as soon as it was formed.

"Nay, my good sir, then I must differ from you," answered Valentine smiling at the sudden change. "This may be a hoax, as I have said, but, on the other hand, we have no evidence to prove that it is so, and as the letter may have been written by a friend, we will run the risk of being laughed at, by proceeding to the place which has been pointed out as the scene of the old gentleman's captivity."

"Gadzooks! but I like your notion, my boy," cried Uncle Sam, whose opinion had again swerved round to the notions of his nephew. "We'll go and see whether there is such a place as the writer has mentioned, and if we find the cottage, I'll warrant it shall not be long before Septimus finds himself among his friends again."

"You will accompany me then?" said Valentine, jumping up from his seat, and ringing the bell with a violence that brought Susan into the room with the velocity of a shot just discharged from a gun.

"Goodness, gracious me, what in the name of fortune is the matter?" she exclaimed, breathless with alarm;—"is the house on fire, or have either of you two gentlemen had the misfortune to fall into a fit?"

"Neither," replied Valentine;—"the fact is, Susan, we have no time to waste; and as dinner is, in these cases, a secondary consideration, my uncle and myself have determined to have a lunch, and immediately to set out on some business that requires the earliest attention.

"And your dinner—"

"Must not be thought of to day." answered Valentine; "the fact is, we have to go a short distance out of town, and it is not impossible but what we may return with your master in our company."

"Lawks, sir! you don't say so?

"But he does say so," exclaimed Uncle Sam, "and a very foolish fellow he was to do so, seeing that you will be spreading the news all over the neighbourhood and perhaps mar whatever good we were in the hopes of doing."

"Who; I chatter about the business of other people?" cried Susan, indignant at such a notion.

"Never mind defending yourself against this charge just now," exclaimed Valentine, who plainly enough saw an hour's argument of the matter was not put a stop to at once; "the fact is, Susan, we can place the utmost reliance in your prudence and discretion, so now run away as fast as your legs will carry you, and see that we have our lunch with as much dispatch as possible."

Susan took the hint; dropped a very low curtsey, and bolting from the room, left the two gentlemen to discuss the affair between themselves. As for Uncle Sam, he appeared to be rather out of sorts, and it was only after taking repeated pinches of snuff that he got into anything like his usual good humour, Then followed a substantial lunch that was sufficient to bid defiance to hunger for at least some hours to come, and when the chops had been discussed with a fair allowance of Barclay's double stout, the old gentleman began to grow facetious, and in that happy state of mind, he sallied forth with his nephew to execute the task they had so willingly imposed upon themselves.

At the first coach stand they came to, a cab was engaged to convey them to the place which had been pointed out, and after a full description of the site of the cottage in the forest was given to the driver, and a handsome gratuity offered on condition that he exerted all his diligence, they were driven of at railway speed towards the spot where they were in some expectation of meeting with poor Septimus Bramstone. Owing, however, to the ignorance of the driver, as to the exact locality they were desirous of reaching, it was some time before they got into anything like a train for finding the cottage, but having at last met with a person who knew the lonely habitation at the skirts of the forest, they turned down a bye-road in the direction pointed out, and ultimately reached a public-house, where it was agreed by the two gentlemen that they should leave the vehicle while they proceeded to the place of destination with as much quietness as possible. Orders also were given to the man to be in readiness to start homewards at an instant's notice, should it be necessary, and whilst the man amused himself with a pipe of tobacco, the two friends set forth on their errand.

"How do you find yourself for spirits?" asked the elder gentleman, whose courage began to ooze out at his elbows, as they caught a glimpse of a white cottage at no great distance off, and which, without doubt, was the very place they had come in search of; "do you think Val. you shall have pluck enough to give them a turn if they should prove rumbustical at our arrival."

"I feel quite inclined to insist upon justice being done to my friend," answered our hero. "These fellows may probably endeavour to carry matters off with a high hand, when first they understand the object of our visit, but I am very much mistaken if they do not shrink before us like guilty villains as they are, when they find out that we know the whole of their rascalities."

"But suppose there should happen to be a dozen of them against us two?" exclaimed Uncle Sam, who always liked to look well at both sides of the question.

"Why, in that case," answered Valentine, "we must behave like men, and show those designing scoundrels that villany is never any match against those who come armed with a good cause."

"Aye, aye" returned Uncle Sam, shaking his head knowingly, "it's all very well, I dare say, to be armed as you call it, with a good cause, but give me such arms as a brace of pistols, or a small sword, and then I know what I am about."

"Hush! speak lower!" whispered Valentine; "we are now near the house, and the fierce growling of the watch dog, proves that our approach has not been unobserved by the faithful guardian. Ha! the door is at this moment shut to, and I fear the business that brought us hither is, for a time, at least, brought to an unsuccessful termination."

"Nonsense, man !" exclaimed Uncle Sam, " we won't have it said that we come all the way here for nothing, either. "Their playing at bo-peep, and bolting themselves in the cottage as soon as they catch sight of us, is a pretty good proof that something is wrong, and if you feel inclined to run any risk, why your old uncle will not desert you, and who knows but what we shall find Septimus here after all !"

"By heavens he is here," exclaimed Valentine, stooping, picking up a fragment of the old gentleman's cravat which he at once knew, by its peculiar pattern, to belong to Septimus. "This I know for a certainty to have been worn by our friend on the morning he was so treacherously dragged from his home, and with such evidence against the inmates of this cottage I will never leave the place until I have either released Mr. Bramston, or satisfactory proof is afforded that I am mistaken in supposing he was here."

"Why that piece of stuff certainly does look very much like the pattern of your friend's cravat," observed Uncle Sam, examining the fragment through the medium of an eye glass. " I should say it is decidedly like it, but then it so happens that many other people may wear a similar looking article, and it would be almost too much for us to assert positively that Septimus Bramstone is prisoner in this house merely because—"

"For heaven's sake, throw no obstacles in the way, now !" interrupted Valentine, half angry at the unbelief of his relative. " In my own mind, sir, I am quite positive that all doubt is at an end, as to the place of Mr. Bramstone's captivity, and it now only remains to be seen whether you are as ready to assist me, as you professed to be within this last half hour ?"

"Why, Val, my boy, you don't doubt me, do you ?"

"I certainly don't doubt you," answered our hero, " but I never like to see a man try to shirk off when the moment for action has arrived."

"Shirk ! you undutiful rascal, what do you mean by making use of such a word to me ?" exclaimed the old man.

"Well, well, I admit the expression was ill-chosen," answered Valentine ; " and my impatience in a friend's cause must plead my excuse. All I want to know is whether you are still inclined to back me in demanding the immediate delivery of Mr. Septimus Bramstone into our hands, or whether I must perform that task without your assistance.

"Why, of course, I mean to stick to you like wax," exclaimed Uncle Sam ; " it's my principle never to leave a friend in difficulties, and hang me if I don't go through fire and water, rather than leave an old acquaintance to become a prey to the harpies that would feed upon his vitals before the breath has left his body. So now, Val, knock away at the door as soon as you please, and if they don't open it, why we'll find a way to get into this house without much trouble, I'll warrant."

Acting upon this hint they hurried towards the cottage, and on reaching the door, Valentine rapped against it with a stick he carried, in case circumstances should arise to render it useful. The first two or three summonses were unheeded by the party within, but as our hero listened he thought he could distinguish groans, proceeding from some poor wretch in mortal agony. Aroused by this he hammered yet more loudly at the door, and on this occasion a window above was thrown open, through which the shaggy head of a man was thrust, as if to take a survey of the enemy before more decisive steps were taken.

"Who the devil are you, young fellow ?" demanded a rough voice, as Valentine looked up to see who it was that had at last made his appearance.

"Who I am you shall presently know, if you will give me admittance to the cottage," answered our hero ;— " prithee my friend, descend will you, and give half an hour's rest to a couple of cockneys, who having wandered thus far out of London, have lost their way."

" Well, that's no business of mine, is it?" growled the ruffian;—" if you've lost your way you must find it again, that's all I know about it,—so I wish you a good day, and if you ever happen to lose your way in this neighbourhood again, look out for some other place, will you, and don't give a fellow the trouble to answer, that has no wish to be disturbed by every fool that takes it into his head he wants shelter."

Having delivered himself of this brief oration the gentleman with the shaggy head of hair withdrew from sight, and thus our two friends found themselves as far off as ever from the object they had immediately in view. A short council of war was then held, and when three or four projects had been suggested and as many times withdrawn as impracticable, it was finally arranged that, with a huge stone, which stood near the gate, they should batter down the door, and thus gain admittance to the cottage by storm. Again, Valentine thought he heard groans issuing from the interior, and roused to fury by the thought of what his friend might be suffering, he seized hold of the ponderous stone, and, with the assistance of his companion bore, it to the portal he intended to break down. Here they rested for a minute or so, and then having recovered breath, the weighty missile was raised between them, and after being swung backward and forward two or three times, was sent full against the door with such force that the. whole house seemed to be shaken to its very foundation, and it became evident that it would only require one more such blow to give them immediate access to the citadel. Whilst however, they were preparing for this, the same grim looking head was seen peering forth from above, and a hoarse voice called to them to desist from their labour or expect such a resistance as would most likely lead to the death of both the assailants.

" Open your door, will you?" exclaimed Valentine, regardless of this threat; " open! I say, or we will our-selves force a way into the cottage, even against your consent."

At this moment, the report of a pistol was heard, and, at the same time, a bullet whizzed past the ear of Valentine, passing through the rim of his hat, and dashing against the pavement at his feet, where it lay flattened by the force with which it had struck against the stones. Yet even this failed to terrify Valentine, though his uncle retreated a few paces behind the angle of the house, where he stood peeping round the corner, and calling upon our hero to leave a place where so much danger was threatened them. But Valentine rightly judged that their only weapon had now been discharged, and anxious not to give the ruffian time to re-load, he entreated the old gentleman to come and afford his assistance once more in getting the door open. This, after some hesitation, Uncle Sam, at length, did ; again the huge stone was lifted between them,—once, twice, thrice, they swung it backwards and forward, and, at length, away flew the ponderous missile, forcing open the door, and leaving a free passage for the besiegers to enter. Nor was Valentine long in making up his mind upon this matter, and followed by the old gentleman, he rushed through the door, and was about to force his way up a narrow flight of stairs, when he was met by the man who had given him so rough a salutation from the window."

" Let me pass, fellow !" exclaimed Valentine, preparing to enforce his demand, if it was not at once acceded to. " Let me pass, I say, or you may be made to pay dearly for your recent attempt at assassination."

" I only wish the bullet had gone where I intended it, " growled the man, " because then there'd have been an end of the matter, and the old gen'l'man would have stopped snug in the quarters we've provided for him."

" Ha! you acknowledge, then, that Mr. Septimus Bramstone is unjustly detained beneath this roof ?"

" I acknowledge nuffin' o' the sort,"

answered the fellow angrily;—"what should I know about Mr. Sappimus Brimstone, or any other old gen'l'man you may take it into your head to look arter."

"But I have evidence to prove that my friend is in this house," replied Valentine, "and what is more, I do not intend to leave the place until I have a satisfactory answer from you, and one that will lead to the instant restoration of Mr. Septimus Bramstone to the home from which he has been unjustly dragged, through the rascality of his relatives."

"Yonder comes master if you want an answer," growled the fellow;—"he knows how to serve sich chaps as you and t'other old gen'l'man, and I'm blessed if I don't think he'll lock yer both up, and put a strait vescut upon yer, just to see how yer likes it."

Before Valentine had time to reply, Mr. Grabfast and half a dozen of his keepers—all a most ferocious set of ruffians—bustled through the door which had been so unceremoniously broken open, and strode up directly to the spot where our hero and his companion were parlying with the fellow who had opposed their entrance.

"Who is this?" exclaimed Mr. Grabfast, looking round and observing the evident tokens of a forced entrance to the house;—"what is this I see?—the cottage broken open, and two strangers beneath my roof!—Zounds! What insolence is this?—speak, Peter, —and if these two men have dared to effect a forcible entry upon my property I'll have the law of 'em—that's what I will!"

"Before you proceed to threats it may be as well to hear a little reason," returned Valentine coolly. "In the first place, Mr. Grabfast,—for I recognise you now, sir,—you will never have the temerity, to make any noise about this affair; and, secondly, if you did do so, the chances are, that you would involve yourself in such a dilemma, as to be heartily sick of the rascally part you have played towards Mr. Septimus Bramstone. I know you, sir, for a scoundrel, and unless my friend is immediately set at liberty, I

shall take such measures for his deliverance as will at once secure his release and your justly merited punishment."

"I—I—I—know no-no-nothing of the p-person you speak of," stammered Grabfast, terrified at the manaces used against him.

"Why, you infernal old scoundrel, how dare you give utterance to such a lie?" roared Uncle Sam,—"don't we know that our friend is concealed some where about your dog-hole of a place?—and what's more, if he is not given up safe and sound into our hands before another minute has passed we'll——"

What the threat of Uncle Sam would have been we know not, for ere he could finish his speech, he was seized by three of the keepers, who, raising him up in their arms, extended at full length, carried him out of the house in spite of all his kicking and the voice of terrible vengeance with which he threatened them. This done, Grabfast assumed an appearance of perfect composure, and addressing himself to Valentine, he said:—

"Now, young gentleman, you have seen how we serve those who come here for no other purpose than creating a disturbance. Your friend has been properly punished for the part he has thought proper to play, and I now warn you to leave my premises with as little delay as possible, unless you would share his fate."

"I shall remain where I am till my friend Mr. Septimus Bramstone is suffered to depart with me," answered Valentine with firmness;—"nay, sir, with the numbers I see you have at command, you can of course proceed to what violence you may think fit, but of my own free will I certainly shall not leave this place till he I come to seek has been rescued from the hands into which he has fallen."

"You are insolent, sir! exclaimed Grabfast.

"I am at least resolute, sir," answered Valentine, "and shall not shrink at forcing the duty I owe to friendship."

By this time the patience of Mr. Grabfast was completely worn out, and

VALENTINE VAUX,

OR THE

TRICKS OF A VENTRILOQUIST

BY TIMOTHY PORTWINE.

beckoning to his men, Valentine was immediately afterwards lifted from the ground, in a manner, exactly similar to that in which Uncle Sam had been served. It was in vain to offer resistance, for the numbers by whom he was attacked, precluded all hopes in that quarter, and yielding to the stern necessity of the case, he soon found himself placed side by side with Uncle Sam, who was swearing vehemently at the rascally treatment he had received, and wishing with all his heart and soul that they they had only one or two more on their side, to give their opponents a Roland for their Oliver.

Finding further resistance to be in vain, Valentine now persuaded the old gentleman to leave the place with him, and returning once more to the house where they had left the cab, they entered the vehicle, and hastened back to town with a determination of bringing the matter of Septimus Bramstone's escape to a speedy close.

No. 24.

CHAPTER XXXVI.

VALENTINE, IN WANT OF SOMETHING
BETTER TO DO, VISITS A SOCIALIST
LECTURE-ROOM. — NON-RESPONSIBI-
LITY, AND THE ANTI-MARRIAGE
PROPOSITION ARGUED. — A RIOT, IN
WHICH THE DISCIPLES OF OWEN
SHOW THEMSELVES IN A NEW
LIGHT.

BEING rather dull that evening, and
as Uncle Sam took it into his head to
retire to rest at a very early hour,
Valentine was compelled to take a
stroll by himself, though where to go,
or how to seek for amusement, were
matters that had not passed seriously
through his mind. One time he thought
of visiting Covent Garden Theatre,
but on reaching the doors he ascertained that he had seen the whole of
the same performance not very long
before, and therefore he was obliged to
look elsewhere for amusement. Directing his footsteps towards Lin-
coln's Inn Fields, his attention was
attracted towards several persons, —
the majority of whom were females, —
who were entering a place, which, on
enquiry, he ascertained belonged to
that truly vicious society the "Socialists." A placard at the door announced that admission might be obtained by any one for a few pence,
and Valentine, — though detesting the
tenets of this class of men, resolved to
enter the place, if it were only for the
purpose of convincing himself whether
men and women could be so utterly
depraved in principle as report had
stated.

Paying his money, therefore, he
followed others who seemed to know
more of the ways of the place than
he did himself, he at last entered a
room where a number of persons,
males and females, were refreshing
themselves with tea and coffee. Now,
this appeared to Valentine rational
enough, but when he overheard the
horrible blasphemies with which their
conversation was thickly interlarded,
he could not help acknowledging to
himself the humiliating fact, that of
the numerous assemblage around him,
not one was there but who came to
add his or her mite to the baneful
poison with which it was sought to
destroy that wholesome morality
which has hitherto sustained the
beautiful fabric of society. That
women should unblushing lend their
aid to such monstrous indecencies,
was pitiable; — our hero had been used
to regard the sex as the surest de-
fenders of morality and religion, and
yet here he heard females supporting
with whatever eloquence they possessed, the pernicious doctrines of the
wretched old man who had founded
the society.

The lecture for the evening was to
prove that marriage is opposed to the
happiness of mankind, and, consequently, that the sexes ought to live
together in a state of nature. This
was a horrible proposition to any person
of common decency, yet, the females
present came to support the views of
the lecturer by their presence, and it
was pretty evident from the bold appearance of many of them that their
notions of propriety were not excessively rigid. It was melancholy to reflect that so many persons were led
astray by the vicious example of a few
bad people, but, on the other hand,
Valentine consoled himself with the
certainty that there were always
enough of good people in the world to
very prevent any wide-spreading evil
resulting from such a filthy sink of
corruption.

Whilst he was ruminating upon the
scene before him, a buz was heard,
and then the door was thrown open
when in strutted the pompous lecturer,
followed by about half a score of those
who had the honour of ranking themselves among the number of his friends.
Then came thunders of applause, in
which the voices of the females were
heard far above the men, and by the
time this had somewhat subsided, the
lecturer had taken possession of the
forum, where he stood arranging his
hair, and glancing round upon the
company who had come still further
to poison with his pestiferous doctrines.
A single look served to convince our

hero that this man was worthy of the infamous task he had undertaken, and the enthusiasm with which he was received, proved but too surely how willing his auditors were to listen when a profligate was come among them to be their teacher. Presently, every tongue was mute, and the learned professor of humbug commenced:—

"Ladies and gentlemen," he said, "I have the honor of appearing once more among you, to inculcate those glorious doctrines that have been promulgated by our truly excellent founder, for the up-rooting of those evils that, in the course of time, have crept into the world. In a former lecture I explained and proved the non-responsibility of man, who, as a free agent, is not bound to obey any laws, or submit himself to the control of those whom circumstances have placed above him, (applause). You were all convinced by the overpowering arguments I brought forward to show the state of degradation into which mankind has fallen, and I shall therefore, now, take up the next important subject, and demonstrate the utter folly of those laws which relate to marriage. (Loud applause.)

Here Valentine became so disgusted with the fellow's argument, that, giving utterance to a loud hiss, he attracted the attention of the lecturer and his auditors, to a fat old gentleman who was standing at the further end of the room. Against him, therefore, murmers of disapprobation were heard, and some even proposed turning him out of the room;—a proposition that would, no doubt, have been carried into effect had not the learned professor benignantly interposed to entreat their patience.

"My friends," he exclaimed, "it is clear that we have an enemy in the room, but let us proceed with temper, and I dare say the force of the arguments I intend to bring forward will make him a convert to those admirable principles which it is our endeavour to spread abroad."

"Wretch!" muttered Valentine, throwing his voice to quite another part of the room.

"Well, really this is most extraordinary!" continued the speaker;—"we have spies among us my friends, and it is necessary to keep a vigilant eye upon all who are unknown to us, in order that those who dissent from our principles may be expelled the room. And now to resume the thread of my discourse:—I was going to ask why men and women should shackle themselves in the bonds of marriage? Is it, I would ask, a state of nature? Is it not making rational beings subject to a law whether he will or no, and shall intelligent creatures submit to bind themselves to one another for life, when the effect of that very act may be to render themselves miserable? No,—I for one disclaim against it, and I know the generality of my auditors are of the same opinion. (Vociferous cheering). Do we not know that many persons grow weary of each other in a month—that they wish to separate— and that the constraining them to live together is to render them unhappy? I myself am able to answer in the affirmative from past experience—I married,—grew weary of my wife,— quarrels ensued, and there is no knowing where the wretchedness would have ended had we not mutually agreed to separate, and each to look out for another partner more congenial to our tastes;—since that time, (now nearly two years) my late wife has had the advantage of having no less than three husbands, and for my own part, I am now looking out for a fourth partner to share with me in my domestic cares and felicities."

At these words the lecturer ogled all the ladies in the room, who, in their turn, ogled at him, in the hope that he might at once make up his mind as to which should be the next happy object of his love. As for Valentine, he grew more and more disgusted with the fellow's unblushing impudence, and whilst a buz was running round the room, he demanded in a sepulchral tone, what was to become of the children of these indiscriminate associations.

"Some gentleman," answered the lecturer, "has asked what is to become of the children;—to this I reply that it is the duty of children to take care of themselves. The young of all animals except those of man, are made to provide for themselves as soon as they can do so;—this proves clearly enough that nature warrants us in doing so, and I therefore contend that the principle I have laid down is correct."

"Then you at once level mankind with the brute creation?" cried Valentine, again disguising his voice.

"Our doctrine is nature," responded the professor pompously, "and the man who encourages a false state of society is no better than an ass."

"Not so much of an ass as the last speaker," bawled our hero, sounding his voice so as to make it proceed from some one in the crowd on the lecturer's right hand. Hereupon the worthy looked unutterable things, and glancing towards the spot from whence the insult appeared to proceed, he seemed as if he should like to deliver the delinquent over to the tender mercies of the crew by which he was surrounded. He, however, could not fix the expression upon any one in particular, and thinking probably that an expression of his indignation would do very little good, he composed himself as well as he could and thus proceeded:—

"If there is any body in this room who does not approve of the sentiments he hears, I should advise him to leave the place, before the indignation of my friends compels him to do so in a way that he does not like. I am here to lecture upon a subject upon which the happiness of mankind depends, and he who interrupts is neither more nor less than a mortal enemy to——"

"Humbug!" shouted Valentine at the top of his voice.

"Where's the rascal that said "humbug?" exclaimed the professor fiercely. "Who dares fix such a stigma upon our admirable institution as to designate any of its acts or its disciples as humbugs?"

"Hear, hear, hear!" vociferated the magnanimous Owenites, and then, after a general call to proceed, the speaker went on with his flimsy oration.

"I was speaking," he said, "upon the folly and absurdity of the institution called marriage, and having proved to your satisfaction that the happiness of mankind is not advanced, I will next proceed to show you how much more blessed people would be if they could only be prevailed upon to join our society. We are for a community of goods — every thing is to belong in common to one another, and why, therefore, I ask you, should not our women be common also? Is it not the nearest approach to nature? and if you answer me in the affirmative, then, I say, the principle of our great founder is most just and excellent. (Hear, hear.) Then, touching this said marriage, about which our adversaries say so much,—what, I ask, is the consequence of it? A man weds himself to a woman because she is beautiful; but her beauty fades, and when she no longer becomes an object for his admiration, he is, perhaps, glad to cast her off, as we throw aside a threadbare garment, and to take unto himself another whom he can better love. Or, perhaps, he marries her for the sake of her money, yet, we all know that money will not last for ever, and, therefore, my argument is, that he should be able to get rid of her as soon as her portion is gone and spent. This is the rational view of the subject, and our illustrious founder has declared that, if he was a younger man, it is the only principle he should act upon." (Cheers.)

"Horrible depravity!" exclaimed Valentine, "and pray what sort of a license do you give your women?"

"The same as we give the men," answered the professor. "Women, according to our rules, are not compelled to be what the generality of people call, faithful to their husbands. They are to enjoy perfect freedom, and may do as they like. How many women do we daily see who are ill-used by those who call themselves their lords and masters? Is it just, then, I ask, that such women should be bound for a whole life to those who treat them ill?—No,—let the women prove to the men that they are not bound to them like slaves, and then the other sex will learn to estimate them at their just value. Suppose a woman joins her destinies with a man whose circumstances in life are fair and prosperous; this is all very well while it lasts, but by-and-bye comes adversity; the poor fellow loses all the property that tempted her to become his!—he, perhaps, becomes the inmate of a prison, and then, I say, it is high time that she should look for some other protector than he whose misfortunes have crushed him to the earth."

"Curses light upon the woman who would forsake the husband who has fallen into trouble!" cried Valentine, indignant at the glaring barbarism of the lecturer's views. "In difficulties a man should be strengthened and supported by the tender care of his wife, and yet there are hollow miscreants who would deprive him of this;—perhaps his sole remaining consolation upon earth!"

"Really," exclaimed the professor, with affected surprise, "the gentleman, whoever he is, seems to be so strongly bigotted to his own old-fashioned customs that I am afraid he will find little to amuse him here."

"For once you are right," cried Valentine warmly;—"I am, indeed, bigotted, as you call it, to the cause of virtue, and it is sincerely to be wished that I could say as much for those in whose society it is my present misfortune to be cast. Shame on you, I say, for thus daring to stand up and give utterance to language that would be a disgrace even to a barbarian."

"Turn him out, turn him out!" exclaimed a number of these friends to free inquiry.

"Can any lady or gentleman inform me who it is that has had the temerity to address me in that way?" demanded the enraged lecturer.

"I can't, for one," said a cadaverous-looking wretch, who had been amusing himself with whispering soft nothings in the ear of one of the female socialists.

"Nor I," exclaimed another of the members.

"Nor I," cried a third, "and som-

how, I think there must be a lot of them chaps in the room, for I've heard ever so many voices, and they seem to come from a dozen different parts of the room."

"Keep a sharp look out and catch hold of the very next rascal that dares interrupt the business of the meeting," exclaimed the lecturer. "We allow no one here to speak against the principles of the institution, and if any scoundrel——"

"Scoundrel in your teeth!" vociferated our hero, so managing his voice that it sounded close to the ear of the professor. Upon this the last named important personage turned round very sharply, and fancying he had discovered the speaker he seized him by the collar of his coat and dragged him forward to the foot of the chair on which he was seated. But the person assaulted, who happened to be a strong muscular fellow, did not altogether relish the idea of being so roughly mauled, and clenching his fist he gave the learned lecturer upon licentiousness a blow in the face that sent him reeling from the chair among a party of friends who were just then rushing to his rescue. Hereupon the ladies set up a shriek, and the men uttered horrible imprecations upon the head of the unfortunate wight, who had unconsciously become the object of their wrath. Then followed blows, kicks, and cuffs, accompanied with curses both loud and deep, tables were overturned, lights extinguished, and only enough candles were left burning to show the scene of confusion and uproar that was taking place.

It was in vain that Valentine endeavoured to interfere for the restoration of order:—war had been declared, the Socialists were no longer social, and women as well as men took part in the fray that was now raging. In the midst of this riot a party of policemen rushed in, and seeing that the thick of the battle was raging still between the lecturer and the man he had assaulted, they made a grab at the two principals and were about to drag them both out of the room when, at the earnest entreaties of the women, who were horror-struck at beholding the hapless plight into which their dearly beloved professor had fallen, they condescended to pause for a moment before they committed the two delinquents to "durance vile." Then came a clatter of many voices that would have put even Babel itself to shame, and the policemen were just despairing of making anything out of the explanation that was offered, when Valentine stepped forward to give the best account he could of the affair that had taken place.

"The fact is," he said, "I came into this room by mere accident, and having heard a great deal of nonsense uttered that no man of common sense could listen to with patience, I ventured to express my disapprobation, and from thence has proceeded the riotous conduct which you have just now witnessed."

"That's false!" roared the discomfitted lecturer; "there were a dozen or more that came into the room on purpose to create this disturbance. I heard the scoundrels in different parts of the room, and if the police don't take them all into custody, I shall immediately proceed to lay a complaint before the commissioners."

"This is strangely against the doctrine you have been endeavouring to inculcate," exclaimed Valentine. "When you commenced what you are pleased to call your lecture, you spoke of the non-responsibility of man, and yet you would now make your enemies answer for the little inconvenience you have been put to."

"I demand the protection of the laws!" again roared the incensed promulgator of nonsense.

"And yet," answered Valentine, "how short a time it is since you were labouring to prove to these poor deluded creatures that all laws were useless, and that they were only made to fetter and degrade mankind. You spoke too of a state of nature, as being preferable to any institution that ever was formed, and now you would seek the aid of a power that you affect to despise."

The professor was rather puzzled what answer he should make to this, and looking round upon his late audience, he seemed to expect that a desperate effort would be made to release him from the hands into which he had fallen. The police, however, anticipated some such result, and resolving not to be cheated of their preys they were about to drag them off the station-house, when the clamour of the women again broke upon the ear, Valentine, too, felt bound in honour to prevent the matter going any further, as he had been the principal cause of bringing the affair to this crisis, and advancing once more towards the police, he said :—

"Under all circumstances, my friends, perhaps the better way will be to let this matter drop without taking any further notice of it. All these unfortunate deluded creatures require is notoriety, for without it, they are doomed to remain in the darkness and obscurity that will always have the effect of rendering them harmless. Once, however, raise them to importance by dragging them from this filthy den into notice, and there is no saying where the mischief will end. At present, few reputable persons have been fools enough to enlist under their banner, their own absolute wickedness will ultimately wreck the frail vessel they have launched, and by suffering them to meet in darkness, and obscurity, you will do them a far greater injury than could be inflicted upon them by any punishment the laws they affect to despise, could by any possibility oppose to them."

As the learned professor showed evident tokens of alarm at the plight to which he was reduced, the police began to give way to the arguments brought forward by Valentine, and on condition that the room was immediately cleared, all parties were allowed to return to their homes.

Matters having been thus amicably arranged, our hero returned home to consider what measures should next be adopted for the release of poor Septimus Bramstone. The night proved a restless one to him, and early on the following morning he again met Uncle Sam, with whom he was soon engaged in earnest conversation as to the object they both had so dearly at heart.

CHAPTER XXXVII.

HOW UNCLE SAM AND VALENTINE ALMOST GET TO LOGGERHEADS UPON AN ALL-ABSORBING SUBJECT.—A REPENTANT LETTER, AND THE MEASURES THAT ARE RESOLVED UPON IN CONSEQUENCE. —A VISIT TO THE PARK, IN WHICH UNCLE SAM EXHIBITS HIS SUSCEPTIBILITY TO FEMALE CHARMS.—THE ROBBERY AND PURSUIT.—THE STATUE OF KING CHARLES, AT CHARING CROSS, PLAYS SOME STRANGE TRICKS.

IT's easy enough for a man to talk about what he will do, but when he comes to the practical part of the business, matters begin to wear quite a new aspect, and then he wonders how the deuce he could have been such a simpleton as to reckon without his host. It was precisely in this dilemma that Valentine and Uncle Sam found themselves when they fairly come to sit down and propose various schemes for the liberation of their friend from the merciless clutches of the scoundrels who had succeeded in tearing him from a once happy home, for the mere purpose of dispossessing him of his property, without for a single moment considering or even caring for the dreadful tortures he would be made to suffer. The more our hero and his worthy relative talked over the matter, the more difficulties arose in their way to prevent their plans succeeding to their wishes. It was all very easy to say that Septimus Bramstone must be released from his den, but then the question was how could they best set about their task so as to make sure of the object they had in view?

It was pretty evident that in Grabfast they had an opponent to deal with, who was a match for the very devil himself in cunning, and since he had found out that the place of Septimus Bramstone's

imprisonment was discovered, it was quite certain that immediate steps would be taken to remove him to some other asylum, where he was less likely to be followed by those who had showed so much resolution to carry him off *vi et armis*. This was a poser both to Valentine and his uncle, and now that the thought had struck them, they began to devise all sorts of schemes to bring affairs to a termination as speedily as possible.

"Gadzooks, Val!" exclaimed the old gentleman, breaking forth after a long interval of silence," we shall be done after all I'm afraid. These rascals are too much for us, that is very clear, and now, when we have taken so much pains to get the old boy out of his scrape, we find ourselves just as far off from the main point as ever."

"Why surely, uncle," cried Valentine, "you are not going to give up the chase already?"

"Why, as for that matter," answered Uncle Sam, "I am one of those that never give up while a feather remains to fly with; but in this case we have to do with scoundrels, and depend upon it if we get over them, there will be only one more to cheat, and he shall be nameless.

"And what is to prevent our going to the cottage where we know our friend is, and bringing him away by main force?" demanded Valentine.

"Ah! there it is, "exclaimed his uncle, "you young fellows think every thing is to be done that you once set your minds on. Now, I happened to have picked up a little experience in my time, and the consequence is, that I see plainly enough violence would do no good in the present instance."

"You would then give the matter up for a bad job," cried Valentine, reproachfully, "and so leave our poor friend to become an easy victim to his heartless oppressors."

"Upon my soul, Valentine, you pay me a very fine compliment," exclaimed his relative a little warmly.

"Does not your present conduct warrant me in what I have said?" demanded our hero. "Half-an-hour ago you were all anxiety to set about the task of delivering poor Septimus, and now all of a sudden you seem inclined to let matters take their own course merely because some fancied difficulty or other seems to oppose itself."

"Blockhead!" exclaimed Uncle Sam, indignant at having his conduct misapprehended, "have you not lived long enough yet to discriminate between discretion and fool-hardiness? You saw what sort of a reception we met with at the cottage yesterday, and yet, like a simpleton as you are, you would go again to get what few brains you have knocked out."

"But by taking a few policemen with us, an immediate entrance could be forced, and thus our intentions could be accomplished without much trouble."

"Oh, you ninny-hammer!" cried the old gentleman, "and so you really suppose these fellows have not been taking any measures to prevent the success of such a measure as you have proposed!"

"What can they have done?" asked Valentine.

"Half-a-dozen things," answered the old gentleman. "In the first place they may have got nobody knows how many ruffians to assist in opposing admittance, and that they have fire-arms, we had very nearly found to our cost. Then it is likely enough they may take our friend Septimus to some other place, and in that case the less noise we make in the affair, till things are ripe for action, the better."

"By heavens, uncle!" exclaimed Valentine, "but this is far too cool and calculating to suit me. While we are waiting to put things in a right train, as you call it, poor Mr. Bramstone is suffering the tortures of the damned, and, for ought we know, may fall a victim to the treatment he is made to endure."

"You would advise rash and immediate measures?"

"Immediate measures must not be necessarily rash," answered our hero. "If our enemies are more than ordinarily cunning, it behoves us to be

on the alert in order to frustrate their abominable practices."

"And pray," asked the old gentleman, "how would you proceed most sapient nephew, if left entirely to yourself?"

"I would not let another hour pass away without doing something or other that should have for it's object the liberation of a kind friend," replied Valentine,—"in fact, our enemies should find out that they had at last got those to deal with who are not to be bamboozled by any of their tricks or artifices. I would have the whole party, from Henry Bramstone and his son down to the lowest of the turnkeys, before a magistrate, and if they did not give a good account of themselves, they may feel the vengeance of the law as far as ever it will go."

Uncle Sam gave a long whistle as his nephew concluded, but as the affair was too important a one to be decided upon immediately, he threw himself back in his chair, and began to reflect how far it was possible to act upon this suggestion of his nephew's. In the midst of this temporary calm, the door was suddenly opened, and Susan placing a note in Valentine's hands, departed again with as much mystery as she had made her appearance.

"What the deuce is the girl after now?" exclaimed Uncle Sam, eyeing her departure with some suspicion;—"some love-letter, I dare be sworn, and, in that case, away go all your fine plans for the deliverance of your friend."

"Nay, there you are wrong, my dear sir," answered Valentine, as he finished perusing the epistle." The intelligence this conveys is of rather a cheering character, and if I am not greatly mistaken, it promises a speedy restoration of our friend to the home to which he is now unhappily a stranger."

"Confound the boy!" cried the old gentleman, "why does he keep chattering instead of coming to the point at once? Who is the letter from, and what hope does it hold out that you are thus all high cock-a-whoop of a sudden?"

"The fact is, my dear sir," answered

VALENTINE VAUX,

OR THE

TRICKS OF A VENTRILOQUIST.

BY TIMOTHY PORTWINE.

Valentine, " the letter is from old Harry Bramstone, who it seems, is very ill, and consequently his conscience not quite so easy as it ought to be when a man fancies he is going to die. He has written to me, requesting that I will call upon him at his house, at six o'clock this evening, when he will speak to me on a subject of great importance."

" Aha! then my life on it, he means to confess all his iniquities, and restore your poor brother to the society from which he has so cruelly dragged him."

" That is certainly my impression," answered Valentine, " and, therefore, if you think proper to accompany me to his house this evening, I think I can promise you a result that will be equally gratifying to us both."

" I would go with you, my boy, if it were to the farthest extremity of the earth," cried Uncle Sam, jumping up and seizing hold of his hat and umbrella. " I'm at your service, you dog you, so now, on with your upper toggery, and off we go about our business."

" Nay," replied Valentine, laughing, " you are now altogether in as great a hurry as you were just now most provokingly apathetic. Recollect, the hour named by Harry Bramstone is six o'clock this evening, and we have not yet dined."

"Damn the dinner!" vociferated the old gentlemen,—"what the devil have we to think about dinner for, when there's such a piece of business as this in the wind?"

"Well, damn the dinner, with all my heart," responded Valentine, smiling at his uncle's earnestness. "I am not one of those that would care about gratifying his appetite, even while he knew his friend was languishing in misery and torture, for want of his assistance. Like yourself, I like to strike whilst the iron is hot, but in this instance, it appears to me that we cannot, with any propriety, visit Harry Bramstone till the hour appointed by his note."

"And that is nobody knows how long first."

"It certainly does seem a long time to wait," answered Valentine, "so, suppose, by way of passing away some of the interval, we take a stroll into St. James's Park, — there's always something to be seen, and with a sandwich or two by way of lunch, I dare say we shall be able to do very well till our minds are set at rest by the disclosures the old man is inclined to make."

To this proposition Uncle Sam heartily agreed, and sundry little arrangements having been made, they both of them set out together, resolving to take a route that would offer them as much amusement as possible. On several occasions, Valentine was very much inclined to exercise his talent in ventriloquism upon various persons, who, he thought, required a little rubbing up, but at his uncle's earnest entreaties, he forbore for the present, lest they should get into trouble, and thus bring upon themselves the interference of those blue-coated guardians of the public peace and morals, who are at all times so willing to thrust their noses in where their services are not required.

In the Park, Valentine, and even Uncle Sam himself, found great amusement in ogling the thousands of nursery-maids who were promenading there under the pretext of taking care of their mistresses' children, but, in fact, to carry on some little intrigue of their own. With one of these fair nymphs in particular, Valentine found himself getting upon very familiar terms, but just as he was wishing his venerable uncle at the devil, or, indeed, any where else than where he just then happened to be, a strapping grenadier, at least six feet high and stout in proportion, bounced over the fence, and looked such unutterable things at our hero, that he was not altogether sorry when his elder companion hauled him away from a spot that was growing rather too warm for him. Indeed, it was quite evident that the aforesaid tall grenadier was a lover of the girl's, and both Valentine and his uncle thought themselves fortunate in getting out of the reach of the gentleman in scarlet, without getting into a regular row.

This served completely to cure Valentine of his love-making propensities for the present, at the same time it afforded Uncle Sam an admirable opportunity to lecture his young protege upon the heinousness of even looking at one female, when you have another. Valentine could not for the life of him see any great crime in a man having a little innocent chat with a nurse-maid, but then his uncle's notions belonged rather to the old school of morality, and therefore he was obliged to acknowledge his own error, and promise amendment for the future. To be sure, this lecturing came with a very bad grace from the old gentleman, who had himself been as forward as Valentine in ogling these park beauties, but the other thought that "least said is soonest mended," and not wishing to prolong the subject, he very wisely dropped it, by leading his relative down to the water-side, where, seating themselves on the banks, they amused themselves by throwing crumbs of bread to the innumerable water-fowls that crowded round that particular part of the lake where they found such a good supply of food. Now this was all very well as a pastime, and it struck Uncle Sam as being a very innocent amusement for a couple of full grown children like Valentine and himself, but he soon began to grow tired of duck-feeding, and having pulled out his watch half-a-dozen times, and observed the slow progress of the time, he grew weary for want of better employment, and then starting upon his legs with a sudden effort, he asked whether they could not do something better than make a couple of fools of themselves, as it was very evident they were now doing. Now at this very period, Valentine happened to be thinking of Angelina Stanley, and the progress of his affection in that quarter, together with certain surmises that her affection for himself was growing stronger and stronger every day; he was picturing, I repeat, in his own mind, a blissful feature in the society of that beautiful girl, when he was most provokingly awoke from his dreams of happiness by a blow on the back that threatened to send all the breath out of his body.

Enraged at so unexpected an assault, he turned sharply round to see who was the aggressor, when, instead of seeing any one upon whom he could retaliate, he saw only his Uncle Sam, who was rolling his fat body about and laughing most violently, in a tone somewhat between a wild hyena and a donkey in hysterics. It was in vain, he knew, to be angry with his good-tempered relative, and having suppressed his indignation as well as he could, he enquired with a forced grin what new move the old gentleman was now up to.

"Always like to keep moving, Val," answered the elderly biped;—"never can rest quiet for five minutes together unless I happen to be asleep, so up with you my fine fellow, and let's be for jogging after something fresh."

"Any thing you please, sir," answered Valentine, still wincing from the effects of the blow he had received; "I am ready to go with you any where, only I should like to know what in the name of fortune could have put it into

your head to fetch me that blow across the back?"

"Oh, all fun, my dear boy,—all fun!" exclaimed the merry old gentleman, once more bursting out into a roar of laughter at what he was pleased to call the joke of the thing. "Always like to see people alive and merry, and as I fancied you seemed to be going to sleep I thought it as well to rouse you with.—"

"A blow fit to knock a bullock down!" interrupted Valentine whose feelings had been acutely touched.

"Nonsense man!" exclaimed Uncle Sam, "it was all done in a bit of a frolic,—sheer fun, Val, upon my life, and so shake your feathers, my boy, and let's be toddling from this precious place, as quick as our legs will carry us."

"And pray what has caused all this hurry, sir?" asked our hero, who was himself in no humour to leave the place till it was nearly time to keep the appointment they had with Harry Bramstone. "What infernal demon has put it into your head to be scampering off as if a whole herd of mad bullocks had just made their appearance?"

"I tell you this is a dangerous place for a man to trust himself in," replied the old one with affected gravity. "I am in danger every moment I stay in the place;—don't you see how those roguish, black eyed girls are ogling at us? Zounds! sirrah, I am but flesh and blood, and if you don't take me away I shall be making a fool of myself presently."

"What!" cried Valentine, his late anger disappearing, and bursting into a loud shout of laughter;—"is it possible that a quiet, staid, respectable old gentleman, like yourself, can fall into the weakness and follies of youth merely because a pair of sparkling eyes happen to be directed towards him?"

"Its a failing Valentine, and should be treated leniently," answered the old gentleman;—"I was always susceptible in the matter of love, and though I never happened to get married, I should say there is ne'er another man in all her majesty's dominions who has felt the tender passion as frequently as myself.

"And yet you have lived all these years a merry old batchelor?"

"Aye that's it," exclaimed the other; "its through loving so many at once that I could never make up my mind which girl I should marry. Then the girls too began to find out that I was growing older all the while I was making up my mind which, and when at last I screwed up my courage to the sticking place,—when in fact I asked one of the girls if she had any particular objection to becoming bone of my bone, she turned up her pretty little nose, and told me I ought to have asked that question at least a dozen years before! That was the cut direct, Valentine; I began to see it was all up with me in the matrimonial line, and from that day to the present I have made up my mind to live and die a jolly old batchelor."

"And yet it seems you were somewhat moved just now by the pretty wenches about us."

"Aye, aye, that's all true enough," replied Uncle Sam, "and that's the very reason why I want to get away before I make a fool of myself. There! yonder you see is a wench kissing her hand at me,—and—"

"Between ourselves, uncle," observed Valentine shly, "I rather think it is at me she is kissing her hand."

"That's because you are a self-sufficient booby," exclaimed the old gentleman in no very good humour at the latter remark. "Like all the rest of the young fellows, you never think a man above the age of fifty can possibly have a chance with the girls. But I would have you to know sir—"

How far the anger of Uncle Sam would have gone, we know not, but just at this moment he was run against by a rough-looking fellow, who, pretending to apologise, for nearly knocking him down, ran off again as fast as ever his legs would carry him. The old man was in no humour to put up with this very quietly, and he was just indulging in an ugly expletive or two, when Valentine, who began to think there might be some roguish design in the fellow's conduct, interrupted his worthy relative, by requesting him to look if his watch was safe.

"Safe!" cried Sam, "why of course it is," and as he said this, he pulled out a time piece, that was very nearly large enough for a warming pan.

"And your purse?" cried Valentine, "is that equally safe?"

"Safe!—yes;—no!—damn that fellow, I'll be hanged if he has not managed to pick my pocket!"

"Then let's after him, before he is out of sight," exclaimed our hero, and raising a cry of "Stop thief!" away they set off, followed by a crowd of men, women, and children, all of whom joined in the cry, whilst not a few were left sprawling on the ground, to which they had fallen in their eagerness to join in the hunt.

Valentine and his uncle, however, kept the object of their pursuit well in sight, and away they both tore with might and main to come up with the rascal who had made so free with property that was not his own. As for our hero, he was young, and well able to continue the pursuit, but with his relative the matter was very different, and after puffing and blowing a good deal, he was fairly compelled to give in, though not before he had bawled out to Valentine to meet him presently near the statue of King Charles, at Charing Cross. Being thus rid of his companion, the younger man now darted forward with more speed than ever, and making his way into Parliament-street through the Horse Guards, he there had the satisfaction of seeing the thief pounced upon by a policeman, who had just seized him as he was in the act of throwing away the purse, lest it should be brought in evidence against him. Valentine now had to promise that the old gentleman should go down to the station as soon as he could find him, and having satisfied the captor in this respect, he next directed his steps towards Charing Cross, where it had been arranged he and his uncle should meet.

Now it so happened that patience

was not one of the virtues most conspicuous in the character of our hero, and it also happened that on this particular occasion he had more need of it than usual. In fact Uncle Sam made not his appearance, though more than time enough had elapsed for him to do so, unless something or other very particular had happened to prevent him. In a state of feverish anxiety Valentine walked up and down wondering what the deuce could possibly have kept the old gentleman so long. Then he looked over at the National Gallery, in Trafalgar Square, with its pepper-box looking ornaments, and to his mind he fancied he had never seen anything quite so ugly and tasteless in the whole course of his life;—then he took a glance at Northumberland House, with the huge lion on the top, with tail projecting as if he was just lashing himself into a fury. Then he again had a look round to see whether Uncle Sam had yet made his appearance, when finding that he had not done so he stepped up to the statue of King Charles, and began examining both the rider and his steed with the eye of a critic.

But even in this quiet occupation he was doomed to be interrupted, for it so happened that first one person came to see what he was looking at, and then another, that at last Valentine saw to his great discomfiture that he was surrounded by a crowd of from fifty to a hundred gaping fools. At last one of them, a soft looking young gentleman, stepping up to our hero, enquired what such a crowd of people had collected together for.

"To hear the statue of King Charles the First talk, I believe," answered Valentine determined to have a bit of fun at the expense of the booby.

"Talk!—nonsense,—you don't mean that?" cried the dandy.

"But I do mean it though," replied Valentine,—"I have been here now more than half an hour, and I can be positive that I have heard the statue speak as plainly as you now hear me."

"Dear me!" cried the little whipper-snapper, "how very much I should like to hear it."

"Should you!" exclaimed Valentine, so managing his voice that it seemed to proceed from the lips of the statue;— "then you now have your wish gratified. and if you don't get a little further off from my horse's heels, I shall just make him rear up, and send you where I was despatched long since by Oliver Cromwell."

"And where's that?" asked the trembling exquisite.

"To kingdom come!" answered the same hollow voice from the bronze figure.

"Well, I'm blessed if the old gen'l'man aint come to life again, and no mistake," exclaimed a fine piece of humanity in the shape of a costermonger;—"he speaks almost as well as myself, so if he don't come down I'll try what a taste of my shilalah will do for his kingship, whether he likes it or no."

"Stand back thou scurvy rascal!" again exclaimed Valentine in a deep sepulchral tone;—"stand back I say, or with one leap my steed shall be among you and disperse the whole vile herd!"

"Will ye, bedad!" cried the Irishman, and raising his cudgel he would have dealt his bronze majesty a severe blow had not a policeman rushed forward and arrested his arm.

A short scuffle served to bring matters to a conclusion, and upon a promise being given on the part of the Hibernian that he would make no more attempts to assault his majesty, he was allowed to depart without any further notice being taken of his mad pranks. Hereupon the crowd quickly dispersed, and soon afterwards Valentine had the gratification of seeing Uncle Sam coming towards him. From thence they proceeded to the station-house, where a charge of robbery was entered against the fellow who had snatched the purse, and the parties were ordered to attend at a stated time and place before a magistrate.

By this time it was getting towards six o'clock, and remembering their appointment with Harry Bramstone, they took the first public vehicle they came to and drove off in the direction towards the house of the sick man.

CHAPTER XXXVIII.

THE FORCE OF CONSCIENCE EXEMPLI-
FIED IN THE INSTANCE OF HARRY
BRAMSTONE.—PARENTAL AFFECTION
AND FILIAL OBEDIENCE.—STRONG
SYMPTOMS OF MENTAL DERANGE-
MENT.—AN ALARMING INCIDENT,
WHEREIN A MANIAC MISTAKES HIS
OWN SHADOW FOR A DEMON, AND
THE STRANGE MEANS HE TAKES TO
DRIVE IT AWAY.

WHEN the two friends arrived at the domicile of Harry Bramstone, it appeared quite plain that the presence of one of them was rather considered as an intrusion, for the servant who had opened the door looked first at one and then at the other, as if uncertain how to proceed in so difficult an affair. Uncle Sam in a moment understood how matters stood; but as he did not choose to suffer Valentine to bear the whole of the brunt of the interview,— supposing any foul play was intended, he determined, right or wrong, to accompany him into the presence of the persons they had come to see.

"Master disengaged, Mary?" he said to the perplexed domestic.

"N-n-no,—y-y-yes," stammered the girl, quite undecided which way it would be most prudent to answer.

"Really this is very strange," exclaimed Valentine impatiently; "I am here by your master's own appointment, and yet, it seems, after all, that it will end in a fool's errand."

"Please sir, master's very bad," answered the wench; "very ill indeed, and I don't know about letting two gentlemen go into his room, when I know he only expects one of you."

"Nonsense, girl," cried Uncle Sam, slipping a half-crown into her hand;— "never mind who was expected, but let us both see the old gentleman, and I'll undertake that no harm comes to you for it."

"Well, ralely, you have sich insini-vating ways!" simpered the girl, pocketing the coin and the same time re-laxing amazingly in her deportment towards them. "It's a hard thing to refuse such kind, nice gentlemen as you are, and I suppose I must run the risk of catching a blowing up from old master, who, between ourselves, I ralely believe is gone stark staring mad."

"Mad!" vociferated the elder gentle-man, "why, you don't mean to say that we are to have an interview with a confirmed maniac?"

"I don't know whether he's con-firmed or no," replied the girl, "but that he's mad I'm quite certain, for it's only this morning that he dashed the sugar bason at my head, because I couldn't help laughing at the queer outlandish things he kept on talking about."

Uncle Sam now seemed to hesitate whether he should trust his precious person within arm's length of a re-puted madman, and he had pretty nearly made up his mind to retreat while his shoes were good, when Val-entine, anticipating his intention, took him by the arm and led him towards the door which communicated with the room in which Harry Bramstone usually passed his evenings.

"Stop, Val, stop, there's a good fellow," whispered the old gentleman, —"you know I would do anything to make matters square between Septi-mus and his brother; I would go through fire and water to serve them, but hang me if I half like trusting myself in the company of a madman."

"Psha! this is only the idle gossip-ing of a foolish girl," replied Valen-tine. "Her master was, perhaps, justly excited to wrath by her pro-voking misconduct, and it would be hard to set every one down as a mad-man who happens to fly into a passion."

"Oh, it ain't myself alone as says it," answered the girl; "Mr. Arnold told Missus not more than half-an-hour ago, that he was sure the old gentleman was going out of his mind, and Missus said as how she was afraid so too."

"There! you hear what the girl says!" exclaimed Uncle Sam. "She don't give it as her opinion alone, but the argument is backed by the suspi-cions of two other persons, who, one would suppose, would be the very last persons in the world to raise such a report unless there were good grounds for it."

"Well, even granting that it were so," replied Valentine, "is that any reason why we should give up the affair upon which so much depends? Remember, our friend Septimus Bramstone's very existence itself may depend upon this interview, and if we weakly endeavour to avoid it, the poor old gentleman may pass the remainder of his days in the dreary cell of a Lunatic Asylum."

"Gad, so he may !" answered Uncle Sam with sudden energy.

"And in that case, how much we should afterwards have to reproach ourselves with," continued Valentine. "We have now an opportunity of serving him, and if we suffer it to pass without making an effort to release him, the results may prove to him most disastrous."

During the latter part of this conversation the girl had entered the room, where her master was, to announce that Mr. Valentine Vaux and his uncle had waited upon him according to appointment. Having delivered this message, she returned to say that the old gentleman had desired them to be immediately showed in.

"Master seems a little bit more composed now," she said; "but he still looks uncommonly wild, and Mr. Arnold tried all that ever he could do to persuade him not to see you to day."

"Perhaps it would be as well to put off our visit till to-morrow," observed Uncle Sam.

"Nay," exclaimed Valentine impatiently, "now that we are here, I am resolved not to leave the place till I have seen him. That he has something important to communicate is very certain from the note he sent, and it would be childish to suffer our fears to prevent that which may restore my excellent friend to liberty."

At this moment the door opened, and Arnold popped out his head to see how the land lay. On perceiving Valentine and his companion he advanced towards them, and affecting much pleasure at seeing them, he said :—

"Really, gentlemen, I am very glad to see you, for old dad has taken it into his precious head to be very rumbustical, and between ourselves, I've more than half a notion that he has taken leave of the little sense he was ever possessed of."

"He wishes to unburden his mind to us, as I understand," observed Valentine, watching the effect of this upon Arnold.

"Why, I believe the old 'un wants to make a fool of himself," returned the other with a look of contempt. "He has been preaching about the horrors of dying before certain things have been accomplished, and between ourselves its likely enough he may be telling you some yarn or other about Uncle Septimus; but whatever he may say to you on that subject receive with great caution, for the old boy has gone clean mad about something or other, and now he fancies that he has behaved very unkindly to his brother."

"Which appears to be likely enough if I am not greatly mistaken," answered Valentine.

Arnold looked as red in the face as a turkey cock, and there is no doubt there would be a terrible explosion of wrath had not Uncle Sam interposed to prevent anything of that sort from taking place at such a moment. He now therefore made up his mind to face the enemy under all circumstances, and taking his nephew by the arm, dragged him away from Arnold and from thence into the sitting room where Harry was waiting to receive them.

On entering both Valentine and his uncle were struck with the alteration that a few hours had effected in the appearance of the old man. His countenance was now pale and care worn; his eyes restless and wandering, and indeed his whole manner proved that the servant girl had not exaggerated, when she discribed her master as either quite mad or very near it. He was seated in a large easy chair near the fire;—his head resting on his hand,

and his lips moving rapidly as if he was muttering to himself the uneasy reflections that passed in quick succession through his mind. For an instant he did not appear to have noticed the approach of his visitors, but when the voice of Valentine fell upon his ear, it seemed to rouse him from his mental lethargy, and half raising himself from his seat, he exclaimed wildly :—

"Who's there!—who is it I say?—speak, that I may know if ye are fiends come to drag me to my doom!"

"You see the old cock's quite up in the stirrups," whispered Arnold to our hero; "his upper works are touched, and if he goes on in this manner, we shall have to send him to old Grabfast till he gets better."

"Who named that villain Grabfast?" demanded the old man in a tone of frenzy, "who was it I say that dared pronounce the name of the demon that has made me what I am?"

"Oh stuff and nonsense! don't go to make such an infernal fool of yourself," exclaimed Arnold. "Grabfast is about as decent a chap as a fellow need claim acquaintance with, and I'll back him against any body that may dare say a word to his injury."

"Arnold!" cried his father firmly, "your presence is not required here. I told you before these gentlemen came that I wished you to leave me with them, and I now desire you instantly to leave the room."

"I shall not do anything of the sort," replied the dutiful son,—"you want to be opening your mouth to those that will take advantage of every word you utter, and as I am very likely to be mixed up in the matter, I don't see but what I have as much right to remain here as any body else."

"Aye, aye," groaned the old man; "this it is to have brought you up from infancy to manhood with too much indulgence. I have made an idol of you, Arnold, and now you would turn round upon your father, and poison the last few remaining days of his life with base ingratitude."

"Now, I'll tell you what it is, dad,"

exclaimed Arnold flippantly, "you want to make fools of both yourself and me ;—but it's no go, old chap,—I am not to be put down in this manner, so you had better not say anything to raise my monkey, or there may be the devil to pay and no pitch hot."

"Hush!" interposed Valentine ;—"be more guarded in your language to to your father, Arnold. You see he is somewhat excited by something or other, and the least irritation may bring down upon your head the maledictions of one to whom, by all the laws of nature, you owe the most entire obedience."

"Then let him reflect." exclaimed Arnold; "let him reflect, I say, before he goes to preach about matters that may get us into a hobble that it will not be a very easy matter to get extricated from."

"I have reflected," answered Harry Bramstone; "I have turned the subject over and over in my mind, till I believe my brain is almost turned with it. In my waking visions I have seen poor Septimus writhing under the tortures inflicted upon him through our means; I have heard his shrieks of of agony whilst wretched stood around to triumph in the wrongs he was made to endure, and his cries rent my heart till it seemed to bleed at his sufferings. Oh, Arnold, you know not yet what it is to feel the sharp gnawings of remorse, and I would fain retrace my steps ere you become quite hardened to those crimes which it was my duty to have warned you against."

"Hark ye, Mr. Bramstone," exclaimed Uncle Sam ;—"my nephew Valentine, and myself, came here according to your own appointment, in order to learn something about your brother, Septimus. Now it seems to me that this breeze between yourself and your son will do very little good, and, therefore, what I am going to propose is that you will postpone your lecture to Mr. Arnold to some other time, and immediately come to the point I want to arrive at."

"Patience, and you shall hear all,"

VALENTINE VAUX,

OR THE

TRICKS OF A VENTRILOQUIST.

BY TIMOTHY PORTWINE.

answered Bramstone, "you shall know me for the villain I am, and then curse me, if you please, for one of the greatest scoundrels that ever heaven suffered to live and triumph in his infamies."

"Gentlemen," interrupted Arnold, "I should be very much obliged to you not to believe a word the old tar says. You have heard him call himself a villain, and that, perhaps, I have nothing to do with; but, perhaps, presently he will take it into that precious queer old nob of his to say the same of me, and that, as you are aware, would be excessively annoying to a young fellow like me that wants to hold his head up in the world a bit."

"Ah boy!" groaned the old man, "you know not how anxious I am to shield you from any blame in this affair. I acknowledge that all the blame of this business rests with myself, that the thought which now maddens me was engendered in my own brain, and that you would never have conceived the injury against poor Septimus if I, villain as I am, had not urged it as being necessary to repair my own bankrupt fortunes. I—I alone am to blame, and let the punishment of the fault fall only where justice demands that it should."

No. 26.

"Why it's all very well for a father to try and get his son out of a scrape as well as he can," observed Uncle Sam;—"but then I should like to know whether Arnold made any objections when you first opened the business to him;—whether, in fact, he pointed out how heinous an offence it was to injure a harmless and inoffensive man, whose every thought was directed to the means by which he could confer happiness upon his fellow-creatures."

"That, my fine specimen of an old gentlemen," exclaimed Arnold insolently; "is a question that you can have no right to ask."

"Come, come," retorted Uncle Sam, "lets have none of your impertinence if you please. I came here by your father's express invitation, and as he seems inclined,—though rather late, to do an act of justice to his brother, I certainly feel myself warranted in sifting the matter to the bottom."

"Perhaps then you mean to take the law of us?"

"That will depend upon circumstances," answered Uncle Sam, who began to pluck up courage in proportion as he saw the other lose his own share of confidence. "For my own part,—and I am sure such is also the feeling of my nephew Valentine,—I only wish to see our friend Septimus Bramstone restored to the home from which he has been so unjustifiably foreed, and on that condition, I am quite willing that the affair shall rest where it is."

"Well, thank you for nothing!" exclaimed Arnold with an impudent leer;—"it's kind of you, too, not to wish to see us hanged, drawn and quartered; but, for all that, if I had my own way, you shouldn't know a word more than you do at present; and if old dad, there, persists in blabbing the secret, why I can only say he's nothing short of a madman, and his words ought not to be taken as throwing any slur on our characters."

"You seem to misunderstand the motive of our visit," strangely interposed Valentine;—"we are here to effect the ends of justice calmly and peaceably. As the relatives of Mr. Septimus Bramstone we can have no possible motive for seeking to injure either of you, and, for my own part. I pledge my word that no further proceedings shall arise out of our present conversation, provided my kind old friend is released without delay from the cruel confinement he has been compelled to endure."

"And so you expect that I am fool enough to take you word for all this?" exclaimed Arnold. "No, no, if dad likes to make an ass of himself I can't help it; but remember, I acknowledge nothing against myself, and as for any thing that he says, why, being already pretty well crazed, his words will just be valued at what they are worth, and that's nothing at all."

"Hush, Arnold!—for heaven's sake hush!" interrupted his father, who for some few minutes had been absorbed in the thoughts that rushed wildly through his mind;—"your hasty speech is calculated to injure rather than do us any good;—I tell you, boy, my mind is ill at rest—a load weighs upon my heart that I would fain get rid of, and how otherwise can I relieve myself but by freely confessing the base acts that have brought this misery upon me?"

"Well then, out with at once," exclaimed Uncle Sam;—"tell us what has become of Septimus Bramstone, and I promise you that no harm shall come of it."

"And what is there to tell?" asked Arnold; "the fact is, the old gentleman showed pretty strong symptoms of insanity, and it was our duty as his nearest relatives, to see him properly taken care of. Consequently, we called in two respectable medical gentlemen, Doctors Dundizzy and Slap, who both pronounced their patient to be most decidedly mad, and the consequence was, that we popped him into a lunatic asylum, in order to get him cured as speedily as possible."

"Or rather," observed Uncle Sam, with a sneer that he could not suppress, "in order that he might be worried into madness by the cruelties practised upon him by those demons in human form under whose care he has been placed."

"True! too true!" groaned Harry Bramstone in the bitterness of his remorse. "That was indeed the chief inducement that urged his being sent there; I would have made him mad to obtain possession of his property, the accursed bait that led to all this crime."

"Crime be blowed!" exclaimed Arnold impatiently, "what crime could there be, I should like to know, in sending an old fellow like that to a lunatic asylum, where, if he chose to be quiet, he might have been as comfortable as at his own home! crime, indeed! if we had murdered him, something might have been said, but hang me if worse could have been thought of us than for taking care of the old gentleman when he was too bad to be able to look after his own affairs."

"Upon my word, you seem to take things uncommon cooly!" cried Uncle Sam. "However, I now want to know from your father whether he is willing to lend a helping hand to restore Septimus Bramstone to his home, or whether I and Valentine must be obliged to do it without his assistance?"

"Ha! ha! ha!" chukled Arnold, "you fancy yourself a devilish cunning fellow, I dare say, but it strikes me you've got them to deal with that knows a move or two as well as yourself. You managed, as I found out, to trace the old gentleman down to the cottage in the forest, but since then we've taken good care to remove him to another place where you won't discover him in a hurry, I can tell you."

"Villain!" exclaimed Uncle Sam in a towering pation.

"Ah!" replied Arnold cooly, "it's all very well for you to call me villain, and all that sort of thing, but I happen to be on the on the right side of the hedge, old boy, and hunt about as you will it won't be very easy to track out the den that now hides him."

"I will though," cried Uncle Sam, "I will, if it costs my whole fortune to do it;—an advertisement in the daily papers, and the offer of a handsome reward will soon effect the object we desire."

"Your promised reward will do no good, I can tell you," retorted Arnold,

"and as for advertising him, the chance will be about as good as the other, for it so happens, my cock-o'-wax, that he has been put into the new crib under another name, so that you may hunt all over England and yet be none the wiser."

"But I can afford the clue and will do it too," cried Harry Bramstone, whose eyes flashed fire, and whose whole appearance showed that the frenzy was obtaining a still further mastery over his brain, "I am the monster who thus sought the injury of a brother, and even though a felon's doom should be mine, yet shall he be again free."

"Why, what nonsense are you talking about now?" exclaimed Arnold; "who ever heard a man criminating himself when there's such a good chance of getting over the business so cleverly?"

"I can bear this reproach upon my conscience no longer!" cried the old man passionately. "I feel a load upon my heart that must be removed, or, in my despair I shall, perhaps, lay violent hands upon my own life."

"Bah! and what occasion is there for all this folly?"

"Because he is ever haunting me," exclaimed Harry Bramstone in frenzied accents. "Sleeping or waking, the same form stands reproachingly before me; he admonishes me to make instant reparation or dread the future, and I will do so let the consequences be what they may."

"Did any body ever hear such nonsense?" cried Arnold, pale with apprehension. "What form, I should like to know, would think it worth while to haunt you unless there was something to be got by it?"

"Ah, boy, you may try to jeer me out of it," muttered the old man, "but you cannot convince me that the terrible being does not even at this moment stand before me. See!" he exclaimed yet more furiously, and starting up he pointed to his own shadow in the pier glass before him. "See where he stands yonder!—do you mark his reproachful looks? He glares upon me like some fiend come to bear me to a place of dreadful punishment. But no—I will not hence with him ;—I am yet strong enough to struggle with him and thus do I put to flight the hideous phantom !"

Suiting the action to the word, Harry Bramstone with closed fist rushed towards the glass which he would have demolished at a blow had not all who were present rushed forward and seized him in their arms at the very moment when the work of destruction was about to take place. Upon finding his object thus defeated, he shouted, fought, and cursed those who had interfered, and it was not without considerable difficulty that he was at last forced back to his chair. Valentine and Uncle Sam now tried as much as possible to soothe and allay the irritation under which he laboured, and having succeeded in this they earnestly besought Arnold to restrain himself as much as he could so as to afford no further no further ground for a repetition of the violent scene they had just witnessed. For a wonder, the young man yielded to their solicitations ;—in fact he was alarmed at the old man's outbreak of frenzy, and dreading a second edition of this maniacle exhibition he promised to coax his " old dad," as he called him, into a little more composure.

Having assured themselves that Harry Bramstone was sufficiently quiet to be left, Valentine and Uncle Sam took their departure, though not without assuring Arnold that they should return again in a day or two, when it was hoped the old gentleman would be better able to converse with them, and describe the means by which Septimus was to be released from the wretched abode to which he had been conveyed under an assumed name.

CHAPTER XXXIX.

VALENTINE AND UNCLE SAM ARE HONOURED WITH A VISIT THEY LITTLE EXPECTED. —AN INVITATION TO DINNER, AND AN INTERVIEW WHICH PROVES HIGHLY SATISF TORY TO OUR HERO. —THE LOVERS AND THE STOLEN KISS. —AN AWKWARD INTERRUPTION. —MR. EDWARD SLANLEY'S ODD ANTIPATHY TO RAW LOBSTERS. —THE GHOST OF A POLICEMAN.

WHILST our hero and his kind hearted relative were on the following day concocting various schemes for the immediate schemes for the immediate release of poor Septimus from the clutches of his enemies, they were surprised at hearing a carriage stop at the door, the steps of the aforesaid vehicle were then let down with a tremendous rattling noise that threatened to disturb the whole neighbourhood, and then succeded a thundering rat-tat-tat at the knocker which sent Susan Gabble scampering up the kitchen stairs as if the house was on fire, or some other dreadful calamity had taken place. Even Valentine felt his curiosity excited to know who this unexpected visitor could be, and running to the window he saw a neat looking carriage drawn up to the door, and by the livery of the servants he at once recognized the domestics of his supposed future father-in-law, the wealthy Mr. Edward Stanley, who had no doubt come to enquire the reason of our hero's long absence from his house.

" Well Val., my boy, who is it ?" enquired Uncle Sam, anxious to have his curiosity gratified. " Who is it, you rascal?—tell me this instant, or I'll make 'a new will, and your name shall not be so much as mentioned in it !"

" The gentleman stands before you," answered Valentine, as Mr. Stanley entered the room; " I have the honour, Uncle, of introducing you to my excellent friend, Mr. Edward Stanley ;—Mr. Stanley, allow me to present my Uncle Sam.—a man whom you will be proud to know, and who, I am sure, will be flattered by making your acquaintance."

The two gentlemen bowed to each other in the good old Chesterfield style, and when they had muttered something about the great pleasure they both felt in being introduced to each other. Valentine conducted his visitor to a seat, and then waited patiently till the other should think proper to explain the nature of the business that had brought him there. Most provokingly, however, the conversation was confined for some time to those interesting little bits of common-places for which we English folks are rather celebrated.

"Lovely day, sir," said Mr. Stanley, bowing stiffly, and looking as if he knew not what to say.

"Very," answered Uncle Sam;—"want a little rain, though, for the wheat;—do a deal of good, sir;—do a deal of good."

"No doubt of it," replied the visitor, in a tone of decision, that was meant to show he knew as much about what would do good as the person who had last spoken. And then casting his eye towards the sky,—which by-the-bye, happened to be perfectly clear and cloudless, — he ventured a yet further remark, "that he should not be at all surprised if we had falling weather before long. This was rather a poser to Uncle Sam, who, in reality, saw no reason for making such a prognostication, and then hemming once or twice very loud, just to clear his throat, he enquired the state of the funds,—what railway shares were at a premium, and which at a discount, and whether there was any news on 'Change relative to the alarming quarrel between the tea-growers and the tea-drinkers. All these questions were answered by Mr. Stanley with a great deal of good humour, mixed with an equal proportion of sound knowledge, and at last, when the subject began to flag from utter exhaustion, he skilfully changed the conversation into another, so that Valentine might be able, now and then, to pop in a word or two edgeways.

"Now, perhaps neither of you have a notion of what has brought me round to see you to-day?" said Mr. Stanley, chuckling as if he began to feel a little more at home.

"Can't say, indeed," answered Uncle Sam; "and yet, between ourselves, I should be more than half inclined to guess it was your carriage that brought you."

"Ha ! ha ! ha ! — good ! — very good !" cried Mr. Stanley;—love a joke, I see, my friend ;—merry fellow, like myself—always upon the look out for a bit of fun, eh ?"

"Uncle Sam and you will be the best friends in the world, I can see," exclaimed Valentine, who was exceedingly happy to see the old gentlemen getting to be on such good terms together. "You already seem to understand each other, and if I am not very much mistaken, you will be like a couple of brothers before many hours are over your heads."

"Aye, aye," cried Mr. Stanley ;—"we shall be good friends enough, I'll warrant you; so now hear what I am going to say, and then contradict me at your peril. The fact is, you must dine with me to-day,—won't be refused,—settled thing,—good wine in the cellars,—and the man that says 'nay' to me, must rank me as his foe for the remainder of his life. So, you see, there is no getting off this little affair, unless you would purposely offend me."

"Offend you ! — heaven forbid !" cried Uncle Sam, rising and seizing the old gentleman's hand with the warmth of an old friendship.

"Then you and your nephew will dine with me ?"

"Aye, and sup with you into the bargain," answered Uncle Sam ;—"you are one of the right sort, Mr. Stanley ; — a man exactly after my own heart, and hang me if we wont be like brothers from this time forward."

"So we will," exclaimed Mr. Stanley; "and then there is my daughter Angelina,—as pretty a piece of flesh and blood as any father need be proud of. Kind, affectionate, young, pretty, —But stop,—I am getting on a little too fast here—your nephew, Mr. Valentine Vaux, shall answer for me whether I have exaggerated in describing her affections."

"I fear my powers of description

would fail me," answered our hero; "Miss Stanley is, indeed, all that her father has ——"

"Psha!" interrupted Uncle Sam, "what is the use of your taking the trouble to describe ths girl, when I am so soon to judge for myself? I shall see her, you dog, and old as I am, beware lest I should prove a dangerous rival, and prevail upon the young lady to take pity upon a bachelor of some fifty years standing."

"Well, well," exclaimed Mr. Stanley, rising and shaking hands with the two gentlemen, "I must now leave you to settle that affair between yourselves. Remember, we dine at five precisely, and if you should happen to be half-an-hour before your time, I have a few good paintings, the examination of which to amuse you till dinner is on table. So farewell, my friends, —farewell, till we meet again:"

So saying, the old gentleman took his departure, and hurrying to his carriage, Uncle Sam and our hero fell into a reverie which lasted some time. At last, the elder of the two jumped up from his seat, took three or four turns up and down and the room, and then taking Valentine by the hand, he exclaimed :—

"Val, my boy, I congratulate you with all my heart; you are going to get married, it seems, to this old gentleman's daughter. You have my full concurrence; your mother will, of course, give her consent, and when our poor old friend, Septimus, is fairly out of his trouble, the wedding shall take place, and we shall be as happy as the days are long."

"Ah! sir!" cried Valentine, "if you are thus satisfied with my choice now, what will you say after your interview with the beautiful Angelica Stanley?"

"Say!" exclaimed the old gentleman warmly, "why, I shall say, Valentine my dear fellow, I am perfectl well pleased that you haue been so prudent in your selection of a wife. She is an angel in petticoats—a divinity in perfection, and all I wish is, that she had not a shilling of fortune to ——"

"Would you have her a beggar, sir?"

"Yes, you rascal," exclaimed Uncle Sam, "but only that I might have the pleasure of enriching her as your wife."

"My dear sir," cried Valentine, "your kindness fills my heart with gratitude."

"Fiddlesticks! don't talk to me of gratitude, and all that sort of nonsense," vociferated the old gentleman. "What I say I mean, so now hear what I intend to do for you. I have no notion of a nephew of mine marrying into a wealthy family like a pauper; you must be provided for with some liberality, and, therefore, I purpose making you a present of ten thousand pounds on the day of you marriage with Mr. Stanley's daughter."

"Oh! my dear uncle!"

"Silence, you young jackanapes, will you?" interrupted the old gentleman. "A man may do as he likes with his own, I suppose, and as I intended you to have all I possess at my death, I choose now to let you have a part of it during my life-time. I shall enjoy the remainder of my fortune all the better for it. Of course, there can be no objection to the course I have proposed."

"But this is so unexpected a kindness."

"Perhaps so, but the less you say about it the better," exclaimed the old gentleman. "I never like to be thanked for doing a kind action, and so hold your tongue unless you would offend me for ever."

"Nay," cried Valentine, "that is the last thing I would ever think of doing. It would be but a poor return indeed for the generosity of your conduct."

"Do pray have the goodness to hold your tongue, sirrah, will you?" exclaimed Uncle Sam. "If a man cannot do his own pleasure without all this fuss being made about it, hang me if ever I'll perform another good-natured action as long as 1 live. Let the matter drop, Valentine, I tell you, unless you would put my monkey up altogether."

"I have done, sir," replied our hero, "though it seems a hard thing to be debarred expressing one's gratitude when there is so much reason for it."

"Again!" cried the old gentleman, "will you never hold your tongue, sirrah?"

"This moment, my dear uncle, since you wish it."

"Then now go to your own room and prepare yourself for setting off on this visit, I suppose it will take some time to dress on an occasion like this, whilst an elderly biped like myself, can adonize and prepare myself for company, in the space of a very few minutes."

Smiling at the good natured railery of his uncle, Valentine left the room, thus affording the old gentleman an opportunity to write a letter to Harry Bramstone, urging him to perform an act of justice towards his unfortunate brother, and imploring that he would appoint a meeting for the following day in order that the sufferings of poor Septimus might be brought to as speedy a close as possible. This note being written and sent off to the post office, Uncle Sam proceeded to perform his own toilette, and scarcely had he come down stairs after executing this important duty when he was rejoined by Valentine who was now all hurry to be off on this visit to the house of Mr. Edward Stanley. Upon this a coach was sent for from the nearest stand, and having comfortably ensconsed themselves therein, they soon found themselves at the door of their warm hearted host, who welcomed them to his mansion with all the sincerity of an old established friendship. This done, he led them to the library where Angelica was waiting to receive them, and to whom he presented Uncle Sam as a relative of Valentine's, and therefore, as a matter of course, one whose acquaintances was to be desired and esteemed.

"She'll do, Val, my boy," whispered the old man digging his elbows into the ribs of his nephew; "she is a girl after my own heart, so if you have any notion of crying off the bargain, say the word and I'll take your place in a jiffy."

"Upon my word, sir," answered Valentine, "the young lady would feel deeply honoured if she knew the favour she has so suddenly found in your sight."

"I don't know what you gentlemen are talking about," said Mr. Stanley, "but as dinner is not yet quite ready, suppose we go and have a look at my pictures; there are some good ones among them I can assure you, and the gratification of seeing some of the best works of the most esteemed ancient paintings, will, I hope, amply repay the trouble of following me through two or three rooms."

"But papa," cried Angelica, "you forget that Valentine has seen your pictures over and over again. It would be no treat to him, I dare say, and besides——"

"Aha!" chuckled the old gentleman, "I see how it is, you don't want to part with him; something to say perhaps? Well, well, I won't insist upon the point, so have your own way for once, my child, only don't believe above half the flummery and nonsense he'll be telling you."

"Val, my boy," said Uncle Sam, winking slily at his nephew, "you are a lucky fellow by Jove; the young lady won't part with you even for a moment, whilst an old 'un like me may go as soon as I please, and, between ourselves, perhaps the sooner we interlopers are off, the better you'll like it."

"Nay, sir," answered Angelica, blushing, "I merely proposed Valentine staying here because ——"

"You had no wish to part with him, eh?" exclaimed her father. "Well, well, girl, you need not look so ashamed at being found out, your mother and I were just the same when we were young, we never liked to be troubled with the company of other people, in fact, there are always little soft sayings that pass between lovers which they never wish more rational people to overhear."

"More rational, papa!" cried Angelica, with a roguish look of reproach.

"Aye, those were my words," exclaimed her father, "for I do not consider that when young people are in love they talk altogether as rationally as at other times. All their notions run upon the soft nothings that seem ridiculous to more sober minded people; then they sigh and look at each other, then the lady blushes like a peony, and the gentleman simpers out something or other very fooolish, by way of proving the depth of his passion. Oh, I have no patience with the silly creatures, I have outlived all that sort of thing, and now, believe me, I would rather run a dozen miles than be forced to hear the flummary and nonsense that passes current between a brace of lovers."

"Upon my word, sir, you are very complimentary," exclaimed Valentine laughing at the old man's words.

"At any rate I am very sincere, and that is a great deal more than all lovers can say for themselves," answered Mr. Stanley archly.

"Gadzooks! you don't mean to fancy that my Val is one of that sort?" cried Uncle Sam, somewhat between jest and earnest.

"I believe him to be an honourable and most worthy young fellow," replied Mr. Stanley, "in fact, I have taken a vast liking to him, and as a proof of my esteem, I have promised to give him my daughter's hand, on condition that the match meets the approbation of his own immediate friends."

This was said as the two elderly gentleman were leaving the room, so that neither Angelica nor Valentine overheard that part of their conversation. The latter, indeed, was particularly well pleased to find himself thus left to enjoy a *tete a tete* with the mistress of his affections, and drawing a chair near to the one on which seated, he began to consider within himself how he should best commence the affair nearest to his heart. In the meanwhile, Angelica sat expecting what was to follow, and perceiving how restless and fidgetty he was, she could scarcely forbear giggling outright. At length perceiving that he grew more and more confused at her provoking silence, she said archly:

"Did you speak, Mr. Valentine.

"No, Miss Angelica, but,"—

"For goodness sake don't put that odious Miss before my name," she cried playfully. "There is something so cold and distant about it; and it appears so formal, that it never ought to be used except when one is spoken to by those we don't care about."

"How would you have me address you then?"

"Call me plain Angelica then."

"Nay, *beautiful* Angelina would be far nearer to the mark."

"Ah! now I see you are a going to flatter me."

"Upon my soul I would not," answered Valentine. "Flattery is a meanness I despise, and should never be used except to those whose weakness of intellect render them objects for commisseration."

"Now you are turning moralizer," cried the pouting girl.

"Nay, dearest Angelica"—

"*Dearest* Angelina!" she exclaimed; "there now, that sounds better than your cold *Miss*, and I do not mind listening to what you have to say."

"Then perhaps you will say when I may have the happiness to call you mine?—Nay, do not be angry, sweet girl, for your father has already given his permission for our nuptials to take place whenever you may think proper to name the time. My own family is anxious for the alliance to take place as soon as possible, and therefore I again ask you to name a no' very distant day for the accomplishment of my happiness."

"Let us speak of this some other time," cried Angelica, with downcast eyes. "At present you have taken me somewhat with surprise, and—and—"

"Why now you are as much confounded as I was myself, but a short time since," exclaimed Valentine.

"Dear Valentine, I cry your mercy for the present," returned Angelica, earnestly. "It is a matter that requires some consideration, when a young female has to decide at what

VALENTINE VAUX,

OR THE

TRICKS OF A VENTRILOQUIST

BY TIMOTHY PORTWINE.

moment she will quit the paternal roof, beneath which all the happy days of her early life have been passed. My father, too, will not part from his child without a pang, and I would therefore, consult him ere I give an answer to your question."

"And yet," said Valentine, "it is not long since you promised to bestow yourself upon me at the altar so soon as my friend, Mr. Septimus Bramstone, had been restored to his once peaceful home."

"When that has been done," replied Angelica, "it will be time to remind me of my promise."

No. 27.

"Well then," answered Valentine, "a few days,—nay, perhaps a very few hours, will serve to accomplish the release of the person you speak of. His brother, at last, begins to repent the villanous part he has acted towards him, and I expect by to-morrow at furthest will see him once more restored to his anxious friends."

"Well," returned Angelica smiling, "I am glad to hear that one obstacle is so near being removed. You say to-morrow will see Mr. Septimus Bramstone at liberty; come to me on the next day and assure me that your expectations has been realized, and I will then name the day on which the nuptial ceremony shall be performed."

"Am I to understand that as a promise?"

"Most certainly you are; my word has been passed, Valentine, and I will not break it."

Valentine was in raptures, and edging his chair a little nearer to hers, kissed her ere she was aware of the boldness of the attack he was about to make. Most provokingly, too, at that moment, Uncle Sam, and Mr. Stanley popped into the room, and when Angelica had sufficiently recovered from her surprise to give utterance to her indignation, she perceived, to her own inexpressible mortification, the two elderly gentleman advancing, and grinning at the little scene they had just witnessed.

"Oh, never mind us, Miss Stanley," cried Uncle Sam, good humouredly; "your father and I think nothing of a harmless kiss; in fact, we were admiring the dexterity with which Valentine contrived to snatch it, and, between ourselves, the young dog deserved it for the clever manner in which he pounced upon his fair prize."

Angelica was about to explain that she had given her lover no encouragement for the liberty he had taken, but at that moment the dinner bell rung, and our whole party proceeded down stairs to the dining room. Valentine and Angelica of course sat near each other, the kiss was soon forgotten, and by the time she left the room, while the gentlemen enjoyed themselves over their wine, our hero had completely re-established himself in her favours.

While the bottle circulated, Mr. Stanley began to speak of the new police regulations, and of the antipathy he had formed against those understappers, whom he was pleased to designate as the "raw lobsters." Against one of these in particular, he seemed to have taken a most profound dislike, from the circumstance of the fellow's always keeping up a cry of "keep moving there," whenever anybody stopped to speak to a friend in the street, even though it might only be for a moment. Indeed so great was his dislike towards this man, that he declared his intention, on the very first occasion that offered, to punish the fellow in a way that he least expected. Now, it so happened that Valentine had seen the policeman referred to, and resolving to have a little bit of fun, he imitated the tones of the officer, and dexterously throwing his voice behind a screen that stood near, he exclaimed sharply:—

"Come, I say, move on there, will you!"

"The devil!" exclaimed Mr. Stanley, starting fairly out of his seat, and looking about him with evident alarm. "Who was it that spoke?"

"One that means to worry you as long as ever you live," growled Valentine.

"Oh, oh! we'll see about that," exclaimed the old gentleman wrathfully. "Here, Richard, Simon, Jonathan, William, where are you all!" And then seizing hold of the bell-rope he pulled and tugged away with such violence as to pull the whole concern about his ears. The alarm, however, was soon spread among the servants, and whilst their master was still raving and stamping, the aforesaid Richard, Simon, Jonathan, and William rushed into the room.

"Wh-wh-what's the matter, sir?" demanded all the four.

"Matter!" shouted the old gentleman; "matter enough I think;—you have let that infernal policeman into the house, and if you don't show him into the street through yonder window I shall discharge you all at a minutes' notice.

Hereupon, the four male domestics ran about to different parts of the room, one looking under the tables, one in this place, and one in another; but, of course, without finding any thing like a policeman in the room. Then they all paused, and looked first at one another, and then at their master, wondering what they ought next do.

"Come, keep moving, will you!" again cried Valentine, shifting his voice to another corner of the apartment.

Upon this away they all scampered again round and round the place, upsetting the furniture, and creating a scene of confusion that at any other time would have filled their master with rage and vexation. Sometimes they were poking their heads up the chimney, then they went and looked into the very same places that they had examined half-a-dozen times already, and when at last they found that their search was quite useless, they came to a dead stand-still and told their master that it was their firm belief there was nobody at all in the place. Upon this Mr. Stanley grew excessively enraged, and seizing one of the sofa cushions he hurled it at their heads, and thus sent the four men scampering down stairs as if the devil was at their heels.

All this time Uncle Sam had enjoyed himself amazingly, because he happened to know from what scource the mischief had come; but now when he began to find that their host was growing outrageous, he winked to Valentine, as much as to say that he thought the joke had been now carried quite far enough. Whether our hero thought so too, or whether the presence of Angelica checked him, we know not, but certain it is that he at once set himself to the task of soothing the old gentleman, and so successful was he in this effort, that before many minutes had elapsed, Mr. Stanley began to entertain serious notions that he had been making a bit of a fool of himself. Of course nobody ventured to be so rude as to agree with him in that notion; but Valentine laughed outright at the idea of the policeman getting into the room without any body being aware of it. It was further agreed that all the mistake must have originated in the excellence of the wine they had drank, and as there was no question about the quality of the article that had been consumed, a question was raised by the worthy host whether they should not sit down and drink out another bottle or two, while they talked over the affair and endeavoured in some way or other to account for the singular deception which had been practised.

But Angelica knew very well that this might only lead to a repetition of the same that had just passed, and as coffee had just been prepared for the gentlemen in the drawing-room, she soon prevailed upon them to give up the pleasures of the table and accompany her to where they might drink a more harmless and less exciting beverage. Upon this they all adjourned accordingly, and after a rubber or two at whist to wind up the evening, Valentine and his uncle bade their kind host and his daughter good night, and returned home, both of them full of praises and admiration of the beautiful Angelica.

CHAPTER XL.

FATHER AND SON PROVE TO BE IN EVERY RESPECT WORTHY OF EACH OTHER.—PRIVATE CONFAB IN WHICH THE READER WILL FIND MUCH TO MARVEL AT.—ARNOLD PROVES HIMSELF TO BE A VILLAIN, AND HIS SIRE DROPS A HINT OR TWO THAT SHOWS HIS REPENTANCE TO BE ANYTHING BUT SINCERE.—ARRIVAL OF VISITORS AND WHAT TAKES PLACE CONSEQUENT THEREON.

CONSIDERABLY recovered from the paroxysm of frenzy that had seized him the day before, Harry Bramstone was sitting by himself in his own apartment, when a loud rapping was heard at the room door, and by the impatience which had been manifested by the applicant for admission, there could be no doubt whatever but that it was Arnold, who had come to pay his dutiful respects to the author of his being. Now, Harry had no great desire to see him;—in fact, he would rather just then have avoided the interview, but while he was weighing this matter in his mind the knocking was repeated louder than before, and directly afterwards the door was flung violently open and Arnold, in no very good humour, entered the room.

"Well, old gentleman," he exclaimed with his usual easy tone of impertinence, "I'm blessed if I didn't think something uncommon awful had happened, to you; thought you might have slipped your wind and died in the night just to get out of this horrid scrape your own tom-foolery has brought us into."

"Arnold," cried the other reproachfully, "this is not the language a father should hear from his son. Learn your duty, sir, or leave my house for ever."

"Oh, with all my heart," returned the youngster with careless impudence; "if you are tired of me I can notch my timber as soon as you please, only before I go, it may, perhaps, do you good to hear a little piece of my mind."

"I want none of your advise, sir," answered Harry Bramstone with anger, "your insolence is intolerable, and it is time that it should be checked."

"And how will you hinder it, old chap?"

"By commanding you to leave my house."

"Humph! you would have me to starve then?"

"There's no necessity for that, Arnold; you have your hands to work with, and it only requires a little industry to get a very good living for yourself and wife."

"And you would be barbarous enough to set me to work?"

"Most assuredly I would," answered the old man; "idleness is the parent of every vice, and you have been so long depending upon support from me, that it is time I should now tell you my circumstances are not sufficiently flourishing to allow me to do so any longer."

"Well, I'm blowed if that ain't a good 'un, however!" exclaimed Arnold. "You talk about your circumstances being bad, and yet it was only yesterday that you talked about letting Uncle Septimus loose again, by which you would be completely flummuxed out of every chance of bettering yourself."

"Nevertheless, it must be done, Arnold."

"The devil it must! and why, most sapient dad?"

"Because my own conscience demands it," answered his father; "I have been driven to the verge of madness already, and any longer suspense on that subject would drive me to that asylum to which my own baseness has sent my unfortunate brother Septimus."

"Damn it! you are now going to pitch your gammon about conscience and all that sort of stuff," exclaimed Arnold. "If we have sent the old gentleman to a madhouse it was done for his own good; or, at least, it must be our business to make the world believe so. He took too great a fancy to that young fellow, Valentine; would have left him all his browns, too, I dare say, if it had not been for this bright scheme of ours to prevent it."

"Well, let things take their own course," answered Harry; "for my own part, I would not again endure the past tortures for all the wealth the world contains, and with the view of relieving my conscience I have determined that my brother shall have his liberty."

"Then, down we go, full gallop," replied his hopeful son; "Uncle Sep. won't forget us for what we have done, and away goes all his tin to a fellow that has no business whatever with it."

"Even that I could endure rather than the misery of knowing that I, his own brother, have sent him to suffer the most dreadful agonies, both of mind and body."

"Oh, its all very to talk sentimental and that sort of nonsense sometimes," replied Arnold impatiently, "but do have a little sense for once, and remember what the consequences will be to ourselves if you persist in letting him out of Grabfast's hands. Won't he make a will, think you?—and if he does, do you expect that any of the rowdy will come into our hands?"

"I feel certain it will make no difference," answered his father. "Septimus would not be revengeful, even if he knew the full extent of our guilt. Besides, we have not acted incautiously in this matter; there is the evidence of the two doctors that he was decidedly insane at the time we delivered him up to Grabfast, and the world, my dear boy, will give us the credit of letting him out again as soon as we could do so with safety.

"The world," answered Arnold, "may perhaps say so, but what will the old gentleman himself think?"

"His customary good nature will prompt him not to judge too severely of our motives," replied Harry. "He will blame the doctors for the opinion they gave, and, if we only keep our own counsel, depend upon it every thing will be as right as—as——"

"A trivet!" exclaimed Arnold; "egad, I don't know but what there's some sense in you after all. The world is ready enough to swallow gammon of every description, and why shouldn't Uncle Septimus believe us innocent of any evil intentions against him."

"I can rely upon his goodness of heart, boy."

"I would much rather rely upon the goodness of his purse," retorted Arnold. "Let him do something handsome for us at once, and he'll find me henceforth a most dutiful and affectionate nephew."

"You begin to fall into my views then?"

"Oh, most decidedly so, since they don't involve our ruin to the extent I at first believed. Let the old gentleman out by all means, but we must stand to it like bricks, that all we did was for the best."

"That he will readily believe," answered his father.

"But how about Valentine and that queer old figure of fun, his Uncle Sam?"

"Oh, they will not interfere against us, depend on it," returned Harry. "They'll believe anything we choose to say, and what's better than all, perhaps Valentine may walk himself off when he finds the old man friendly with us, and unlikely to get into trouble again."

"Gad! that would be a capital move!"

"So you see, Arnold, I am not quite such a simpleton as you just now took me for."

"You're a perfect Solomon, by jingo!"

"At any rate you will perceive that cunning may serve us where force could not," replied his father. "Things were getting desperately bad and before long we should have found ourselves in a dilemma not easy to get out of in a hurry. Valentine and his uncle had found out where the old man was carried to, and though they failed in getting him off as they expected, I dare say the whole affair would have been carried before a magistrate, and then where the thing would have ended, no one could possibly foretell. We should have been exposed, however, and, with characters blasted by the exposure, we should have been forced to seek a new home without a chance of ever making it up with your uncle."

"I'm blessed if you don't talk for all the world like an oracle!" exclaimed Arnold, delighted at seeing that his father was not quite so honest in the resolution he had come to as had appeared at first;—"there's something like reason in you yet, old fellow, though yesterday I began to think a straight waistcoat would be the best thing I could get for you."

"Well, the recollection of one thing or other, certainly did make me rather frantic," answered the old man. "I felt for all the world as if I should have liked to rush into the first river I came to, and no doubt I should have done something of the kind if I hadn't have recollected this idea of letting your uncle have his liberty."

"This notion is not such a bad one now you come to explain yourself," observed Arnold. "We have only to pitch it rather strong to the old gentleman you know;—swear how much we love him, and all that sort of thing; throw all the blame upon old Dundizzie and Slop, and wind up with vows of lasting affection and zeal in rendering the rest of his life jolly and contented.—That's the stuff to make trowsers of, eh, old boy."

Harry Bramstone thought exactly as his son did, and he was about to tell him so when their conversation was cut short by the arrival of Valentine and Uncle Sam. The former was still rather reserved in his manner towards those whom he justly regarded as the enemies of his friend Septimus, but the latter put on a 'semblance of good humour, and approaching Mr. Harry Bramstone, he said :—

" Well, sir, Val and myself, you see, have made bold to pay you another visit. Always like to take time by the forelock ;—strike while the iron's hot, and then there's some chance of bringing things to the shape we want them."

" Uncommonly happy to see you gentlemen," exclaimed Arnold, winking roguishly at his father." The old man and I were just talking about you, weren't we dad ?"

" Only the very moment before," answered Harry.

" Very likely," observed Valentine, " but the question is whether you were altogether anxious for this visit ?"

" Anxious, my dear fellow !" exclaimed Arnold, " why of course we were ;—I wanted of all things to see you. There's poor dear Uncle Septimus languishing for want of his liberty, and perhaps if we don't make haste to let him out of that infernal cage, he may pine himself to death."

" There Valentine, my boy, you see how sincere they are," exclaimed Sam. " You would have it there was some artifice behind all this sudden repentance, and now you hear from their own lips how anxious they are to assist us in restoring our friend to his home."

" Humph !,' answered Valentine ;— " repentance, sir, often comes too late, and possibly it may do so in the present case,"

" You still persist in judging thus harshly of our motives !" cried Harry Bramstone.

" Till I see good reason for believing otherwise, I certainly shall do so," answered our hero. " Repentance must show itself in actions, not in mere empty words. My friend Septimus has been cruelly incarcerated in a gloomy dungeon, and if you had the hearts of men you would have rescued him long before this."

" But his being taken to a madhouse was no fault of ours," exclaimed Arnold sharply.

" Perhaps, then," retorted our hero, " you will have the goodness to explain where the blame lies ?"

" With those infernal doctors," replied Arnold.

" And pray who employed them in this dirty work ?"

" How should I know ?" demanded the other. " Dundizzie and Slop were sent to examine the state of Uncle Sep's health, and the result was that they reported him to be labouring under mental derangement. I'm sure poor old dad and I almost cried the eyes out of our heads when we heard that it would be necessary to send him off immediately to a mad-house, and it was not without great difficulty that we were prevailed upon to consent that he should be taken care of for a little while."

" And very prettily he has been taken care of, certainly !" exclaimed Valentine, indignantly. " By constant ill-usage he has been reduced nearly to the state of a maniac, and yet you would now fain convince us that the tearing of him away from home was absolutely necessary."

Arnold was about to make an angry reply to this, but Uncle Sam saw that a storm just then would do them no good, and interposing between the wranglers, he said :

" The fact is, young gentlemen, you are both a great deal too fast in this matter. Mr. Arnold Bramstone is, I dare say, perfectly sincere in his anxiety to liberate our friend from the horrible doom he has been made to undergo ;—and as for my nephew, I can answer for it that his zeal alone prompts his tongue to utter expressions, that I am sure he will afterwards acknowledge were unjust."

" Let them prove their sincerity then, by immediately accompanying us to the place where the old gentleman is so unjustly confined," exclaimed Valentine.

"Oh, if that's all, we are perfectly ready to go with you," said Arnold, nudging his father to agree with him. "In fact, we were expecting you to call, and all that now remains for us to do, is to set off and bring the old man back with us."

"That's what I call coming to the point," exclaimed Uncle Sam. "It's doing the thing that's right, and if you only assist us as you have promised, why I, in return, will do every thing in my power to reconcile Septimus to you and your father, with as little delay as possible."

"You will?"

"Aye, upon the word of an honest man."

"Why, then all I can say is, you are a jolly old cock for your pains! That's doing the thing handsome, and hang me if both the old man and I don't go with you whenever you choose to say the word."

"Then the word is said now," answered Uncle Sam. "We are here for the express purpose of seeing whether you would accompany us, because we neither of us wished to do any thing rashly, for fear we should afterwards be sorry for it."

"What would you have done then if we had refused?" demanded Harry Bramstone eagerly.

"What?" cried Uncle Sam, "why have applied to the magistrate for a warrant against you and your son to be sure. That would have brought matters to an issue, I rather think; and the exposure it must have produced, would have been anything but pleasant to men who have any regard for character."

"That's quite enough, old tar," exclaimed Arnold, putting on his hat and gloves;—"we are both of us quite ready to go with you, so just lead the way, and if we don't bring the ancient veteran back with us, say I'm a know-nothing chap, that's all."

The threat of exposure was equally effective with Harry Bramstone, and having shuffled himself into his great coat, he accompanied the rest to the street door, where a coach was in readiness to convey them on the important mission that was to restore Septimus Bramstone to the world.

CHAPTER XLI.

THE RIDE TO HAINAULT, AND THE SILENT COMPANIONS ARNOLD BRAMSTONE MEETS WITH.—ARRIVAL AT THE LONE COTTAGE, AND A SCENE OF INTEREST. — GRABFAST MANIFESTS SOME RELUCTANCE TO PART WITH HIS VICTIM, BUT IS AT LAST COMPELLED TO YIELD.—SEPTIMUS ONCE MORE ESCAPES.

THE ride was a particularly silent one, for though Arnold tried to be uncommonly loquacious at first, the indifference with which his sallies were received, acted as a complete extinguisher to his wit, and at last, giving up the affair in utter hopelessness, he solaced himself with a cigar, which he smoked away in utter contempt for the stupid dummies, as he mentally called them, among whom it was his present fortune to be cast. Uncle Sam regarded him as a foolish puppy, to whom good words would be thrown away. His father was too full of his own thoughts to bestow any attention upon the chattering of a booby, and as for Valentine, he so utterly despised his younger companion, that nothing could have induced him to enter into conversation till the affair of Septimus had been brought to a satisfactory conclusion. Now and then they stole silent glances at each other, and occasionally expressive glances were exchanged between the sire and son, but still the quiet was undisturbed, and on they went as fast as the horses could trot, without so much as a single syllable being uttered by any of the parties.

At length, having fairly got beyond the suburbs of London, they turned down the bye-road that led towards the lonely cottage where Septimus had been conveyed, and there might be perceived the uneasiness, with which, Harry Bramstone anticipated the coming interview with his deeply injured brother. It was in vain that Arnold trod upon his toes by way of giving a hint that it would be far better to keep up his courage; the old man felt conscience-stricken, and when at last the silence was broken by Uncle Sam declaring that the house was in view, his tortured spirit burst forth, and uttering a heavy groan of anguish he sunk back upon his seat and covered his face with his hands. Arnold was greatly incensed at this; but he could not just then conveniently express his indignation, and when the coach had stopped and the door was thrown open, he hurried out and muttered forth his execrations against all persons who had not fortitude to support themselves. Luckily, however, this was not overheard by any of his companions, and by the time he had reached the door he was joined by the others, when a consultation took place as to whether they should all make their appearance at once, or commission Harry Bramstone to open a communication with the inmates. In the midst of this the window above was heard to open, and remembering the incident of the pistol on a former occasion Uncle Sam caught hold of Valentine and was going to drag him to a place of safety, but this was rendered unnecessary by the tone of conciliation with which the parley was carried on between this man at the window and the elder Bramstone. In fact, when the business had been thoroughly explained the ruffian disappeared from above, and in less than a minute afterwards they could hear the bolts and bars being removed, and when this operation had been completely performed the door was opened and the whole party entered.

"Is Mr. Grabfast here?" asked Harry of the man.

"Yes,—no—that is perhaps he is, and perhaps he aint," answered the fellow sulkily.

"What do you mean, sirrah?" demanded Valentine impatiently;—"we ask a plain straight-forward question, and you answer us with equivocation."

"I answer according to circumstances," replied the fellow gruffly. "Master aint obliged to be at home to every fool as asks for him."

"But I wish to see him," exclaimed Harry Bramstone; "we have an affair of importance to communicate which requires his immediate attention."

"And pray what may the affair of importance be?" demanded Mr. Grabfast, who at that moment made his appearance from an inner room.

"Ah! I thought you were not very far off," cried Harry seizing the hand of his old acquaintance. "The fact is, my dear sir, we have come about your patient,—my poor dear brother Septimus, who we wish to remove for the present in order to try the effect of country air and the society of his friends."

"Indeed!" exclaimed Grabfast, "and are you aware, sir, of the danger to be apprehended from letting a madman lose upon the world. It is a perilous experiment, Mr. Bramstone, and I shall be answerable if any accident should follow so ill-advised a step."

"Oh, never fear for yourself, sir," answered Uncle Sam, "for there are plenty here who will take any blame upon themselves in the event of any being incurred."

"Very likely," replied Grabfast drily; "but I don't choose to take any man's word for that."

"Nay, but in this instance you must do so."

"Must!"

"Aye, or there are enough present to insist upon compliance," answered Uncle Sam. "We have heard of your tricks, sir, and you have already experienced some of our resolution, whenever we have taken any thing into our heads."

"My dear Grabfast, it's no use to offer any resistance," interposed Harry Bramstone. "These two gentlemen threaten to kick up a dust if you don't comply, and it is therefore my request that you immediately deliver my poor afflicted brother into my hands."

"Am I to understand that you insist upon it?"

"Most certainly you are,"

VALENTINE VAUX,

OR THE
TRICKS OF A VENTRILOQUIST.

BY TIMOTHY PORTWINE.

"Then the blame must rest upon your own head," answered Grabfast, and then beckoning to a couple of keepers, he whispered something to them, upon which they raised the trap-door in the middle of the room, descended a flight of stairs, and presently afterwards returned with poor Septimus, in the most abject state of misery and neglect that it is possible to imagine. For a moment the unfortunate man gazed wildly around him, and then rushing forward with a cry of joyful recognition, he threw himself at the feet of Uncle Sam, exclaiming :—

"Thank heaven, you are here at last !—Oh, my dear friend, for mercy's sake release me from the hands of these cruel men, whose object is to destroy me by the most lingering tortures ;—save me,— save me !''

"Aye, my poor friend, or die in your defence," cried Uncle Sam feelingly. "We are here to carry you from this hateful place, and woe to any one who shall dare to offer any resistance, now that we have once more met."

"Am I to understand then that this madman is to be forcibly taken from my care ?" demanded Grabfast, almost choking with rage.

"It matters not what you understand, sir," answered Uncle Sam ;—"the fact is, you have got resolute people to deal with, and I warn you not to offer any opposition, seeing that it must prove perfectly fruitless."

"Not with the assistance I can call if it should happen to be necessary," returned Grabfast. "I am well prepared to resist any violence you may offer, and after this warning let the blame, if any mischief should happen, rest on your own head."

"Mr. Grabfast, you will oblige me by surrendering my brother without any more words," interposed Harry Bramstone.

"And why do you ask it?" demanded the other angrily. "Was he not placed under my charge by yourself, as a man who was unfit to be at large?"

"I acknowledge it was so," replied Harry; "but since then I have reason to believe that I have been grossly imposed upon by the medical man who reported his case. My poor dear brother has already suffered too much, and I would now make all the recompense in my power by rendering his immediate release."

Arnold looked highly delighted as the old man gave utterance to this hypocritical speech, but Septimus turned away with horror from him, and crept still nearer to Uncle Sam and Valentine for protection against those from whose baseness and inhumanity he had already endured so much. Mr. Grabfast observed this, and taking advantage of it he said exultingly:—

"Well, I dare say you may have very good reasons for your present conduct, but it seems your brother has no very great confidence in the repentance you have just expressed. See how he crouches up to yonder old gentleman, as if he would rather place himself under his protection than yours."

"Ah!" groaned Harry, "that is because he knows that the grief with which I reflect upon the sufferings he has been made to endure so unintentionally on my part. Poor dear brother! it only requires that he should know my anxious care for his welfare, and he will forgive all that at present appears so much against me."

"Of course he will," said Arnold,

"he's one of the right sort of chaps, and it will be all settled comfortably enough when he learns to distinguish between his real friends and his enemies."

As he said this he cast a spiteful look towards Valentine and Uncle Sam. This, however, was not taken any notice of by either of them, and during the pause that ensued, the coachman was called to assist in lifting Septimus from the house to the vehicle. To their gratification, no resistance was offered either by Grabfast or his men, and leaving with the former a considerable sum of money, in discharge of his bill for maintenance and medical attendance, they stepped into the coach, and ordered the driver to set off for London with all the dispatch he could. Had Septimus been aware that his brother and Arnold were to accompany them, he would most likely have recoiled from their society; but by the time those two worthies had followed him into the coach, he had fainted from utter exhaustion, and in that state of unconsciousness he was conveyed back to the home where he had spent so many happy hours of his life.

CHAPTER XLII.

SEPTIMUS FINDS HIMSELF AT LAST IN GOOD HANDS.—AN EXCURSION TO GREENWICH, AND THE VARIOUS ADVENTURES THAT HAPPEN THERE. —FORTUNE-TELLING EXTRAORDINARY. — THE FIELD PREACHER'S MISFORTUNES.—A TRIP TO LONDON BY THE RAILWAY.

IT is necessary to relate all that took place during the time that Septimus was recovering from the effects of the cruel treatment he had received. Suffice it to say, that he received by Valentine and Uncle Sam all the tender and affectionate attentions of a son and a brother, and that Mrs. Vaux conduced no little to his recovery, by the zeal with which she watched by his bedside, and ministered to his various wants. In fact, after the first few days of his return, his health and strength began visibly to mend, and by the time a fortnight had passed away, he was able to quit his bed and resume his old seat in the easy chair, where he was surrounded by all those friends who really felt an interest in his restoration to the health and vigour, he had formerly enjoyed.

As for Harry and Arnold Bramstone, however, their conduct had been too malevolent to be easily forgotten, and as their names caused evident uneasiness to the patient, they were never mentioned after that effect had been perceived. Yet both the hypocrites paid daily visits to the house to make enquiries about the old gentleman, a compliment that was coldly acknowledged by Valentine, while he took particular good care that neither of them should see Septimus until he had himself given permission for them to be admitted to his presence. At this they both affected to be very much concerned, declaring that they were extremely repentant for what had taken place, and still persisting in throwing all the blame upon the two doctors, upon whose advice they over and over again declared they had acted. But all this show of kindness was merely assumed, for in their hearts they sincerely wished he might die, and the favourable answers they each day received concerning his health, served only to fill them with despair and disappointment.

Septimus, it is true, gained strength as fast as could be expected, considering the dreadfully emaciated state to which he had been reduced; but yet his mind seemed fixed upon gloomy thoughts; he was constantly looking back to the frightful scenes that were passed in the madhouse, and the only means that seemed to offer to prevent these constantly recurring to his mind, it was proposed by Valentine, that, as he was now considerably better, they should take short excursions out of town, in order to turn his attention from the gloomy subjects that afflicted him. This proposition af-

forded general satisfaction, and as the season happened to be remarkably fine, a trip to Greenwich by the steam boat, and back again by the railway, was suggested as likely to afford a very fair beginning to their excursions. Behold them, therefore, on board one the vessels that are constantly plying between London and their place of destination, on which occasion the old gentleman was accompanied by Valentine and Uncle Sam. It had been proposed that Mrs. Vaux should make one of their party, but that lady happened to entertain an invincible objection to running the risk of being blowed up either by land or by water, and though her son strenuously urged the perfect safety with which these trips might be undertaken, she still persisted in her former resolution of staying at home, and accordingly stay at home she did, no less to her own satisfaction than the disappointment of her friends. Still matters went on pretty smoothly in her absence, for Valentine, with the aid of his ventriloquial powers, made himself merry at the expense of several of his fellow-passengers, some of whom he played off his tricks upon in one way, and some in another, until their arrival at Greenwich, where a white-bait dinner was ordered to be in readiness for them at four o'clock, thus affording them ample time for a stroll through some of the most delightful walks for which that neighbourhood is so justly celebrated. The park, of course, was the great attraction to our visitors, who, wending their way towards the hill, were highly gratified at watching the somewhat boisterous amusement that was taking place among sundry happy groups of cockneys, who had taken advantage of the fine day to breathe an air uncontaminated with the smoke of London. Some of the younger cocknies aforesaid, were running their lasses down the hill, to the very great danger of their necks, and the rather liberal exposure of their legs. But this was taken all in good part by the girls themselves, for though the laugh was against them, they met it with an equal hearty laugh in return, and undeterred by sundry falls, which sent the unlucky tumblers from top to bottom of the hill, they kept the game alive, determined, as they expressed it, to enjoy themselves as much as they could, since these bright moments of their lives were not of very frequent occurrence.

In another place groups of lads and lasses were enjoying themselves at the delectable game of kiss in the ring. Now, this fun Valentine would have liked amazingly, for he saw many a bright eye glancing towards him, and we will not venture to say that he would have resisted the temptation had he been free from the society of the two elderly gentlemen, whose morality would have been shocked at such a proceeding; as it was he overcame the longing he entertained for earning a kiss from some of the pretty wenches before him, but wishing to place himself beyond the reach of temptation, he prevailed upon his friends to continue their walk towards a more retired part of the noble park. Still, however, he could not help regretting the outward circumstance that had marred his wishes, and he had just fallen into a philosophical train of thoughts, in which the marvellous difference that existed between youth and old age, formed the chief ingredient, when he was aroused by the voice of Uncle Sam, who enquired what in the name of fortune a little party of three females could possibly be doing to absorb their attention so closely. Upon hearing this enquiry, our hero directed his attention towards the spot pointed out by the old gentleman, and there, beneath a wide spreading tree, he beheld a couple of buxom lasses earnestly engaged in conversation, of whom they were in all probability enquiring their fortune.

"Well, Valentine," exclaimed Uncle Sam; "you are a man of the world I know, and perhaps you can enlighten me upon this mystery. What in the name of all that's curious, can these two pretty wenches have to say to that dirty looking drab with a child at her back?"

"Oh," laughed our hero, "the two pretty girls that have so greatly taken your fancy, inherit a fair share of mother Eve's curiosity, and are seeking to penetrate the mysteries of the future, through the instrumentality of the dark-eyed daughter of Egypt, who professes to be deeply versed in that lore which enables us to take a peep into the time that is to come."

"Oh! oh! the woman is a fortune-teller then, and the two lasses are weak enough to believe that she can tell them all that is to happen in their after lives. Gad, if they were daughters of mine I would lock them up for a month to come as a cure for their folly."

"Shall I try to cure them of their credulity by less harsh means?" asked Valentine.

"Certainly, if you think remonstrance would have any effect," answered the old gentleman.

"Remonstrance would do very little good in this case," rejoined Valentine; "but as they seem to be very deeply engaged in conversation with the Gipsy, I think I can contrive to place myself behind the trunk of the tree where I can overhear all that passes, and then astonish them a bit with a specimen of ventriloquism."

"Excellent, by Jupiter," exclaimed Uncle Sam; "that would indeed be applying your art to a very good purpose, and for once I don't mind standing by to be a witness of its effects upon those simple minded wenches."

"Have a care young man, have a care!" cried Septimus, "it may be dangerous to trust yourself within the lure of those pretty eyes, and I, for one, will not be a party in any frolic that may chance to win your heart from my young favourite, Miss Stanley."

"Oh, there's no fear of that I can assure you, my dear sir," answered Valentine, laughing at the old man's caution. "I would merely try the effects of ventriloquism upon these two girls, and if I do not sicken them of all taste for diving into the future, say I am no conjurer that's all."

And with these words he walked stealthily away; took a circuitous route, and contrived to place himself behind the trunk of the tree without being observed either by the Gipsy or her fair auditors. By this time one of the girls had had her fortune told, and was about to retire with her companion, when the Bohemian assuming the usual whining drawl of her tribe, said :—

"Heaven speed you young ladies, and may you both have husbands rich, youthful, and handsome."

"I am sure you do not wish it more than we do ourselves," answered the one who had hitherto been a mere spectator of what was going on between her companion and the Gipsy. "We both of us desire that at any rate, and for my own part, I have made up my mind never to marry at all unless I can have for my husband a man that is exceedingly young, exceedingly rich, and exceedingly good-looking in the bargain."

"Cross my hand, lady, with a piece of silver, and you shall know who your future husband will be."

"But will you tell me truly?"

"Aye, unless the stars should for once play me false," answered the woman. "I am known to all the visitors in these parts as the only true prophetess, and even the royal family have done me the honour to come and consult me as to their future destiny.

"Indeed! and did they tell you they belonged to the illustrious class of persons you have named?"

"No lady," answered the Gipsy; "they came disguised, that I should not know them; but I at once discovered who they were by my art, and when they found that they were known, they slipped a purse into my hands and disappeared in an instant."

"But still you might have been mistaken as to their high rank."

"Nay, I had proof of who they were," replied the woman; "for the purse was marked with the royal cypher, and from the time that it came to be known I have been called fortune-teller to the royal family."

"And pray, my good woman, what is all this to lead to?"

"To your having your fortune told if you please Miss," answered the Gipsy with a coaxing whine. "Few ladies refuse me when they know the high patronage I have been honoured with, and sure you will not leave me without knowing what sort of a man you will have for a husband?"

"Well, that knowledge will certainly be cheaply purchased at a shilling," answered the laughing girl, taking the coin she had named and placing it in the hands of the woman. "There is the price of your information, and now, in the first place, I would know whether the gentleman who is to be my husband will be fair or dark?"

"Dark, — decidedly dark!" exclaimed Valentine from his place of concealment, and so exactly imitating the voice of the Bohemian as to defy detection. The Gipsy stood mute with surprise, and the lady supposing her question to be properly answered, proceeded :—

"Well, I have no objection to his being rather dark, but you must promise that he will be moderately so."

"Alas! young lady," continued Valentine in the same drawling tone, "it is not possible to avert what the stars have ordained, and I grieve to say the man to whom you will be wedded has a skin as black as the far-famed Jim Crow."

"Oh!" screamed the maiden with unfeigned horror,—"don't mention the horrible brute to me again, unless you would see me expire with terror at your feet. Ugh!—the very thought of a black-man would almost tempt me to commit suicide."

"Yet what must be, must," answered the supposed Gipsy, who by this time had effectually silenced the Bohemian by slipping a crown-piece into her hand. "The stars have willed it so, and therefore becomes your duty to submit with all the resignation you can."

"Don't talk to me about resignation," cried the terrified girl,—"the bare idea of wedding such a monster is enough to drive one mad,"

"Oh, it will be nothing when you are used to him," replied Valentine, still keeping up his character from the place where he had concealed himself:—"Besides, these lines in your hand tell me that you will be blessed with a numerous family, and when you behold your children around with their happy smiling faces you will forget your husband's colour, and love him as if he was as fair as yourself."

"Children!" cried the girl in a tone of horror.

"Aye, lady, a dozen of them at the very least."

"Oh the little wretches!—I shall die,—I'm sure I shall, at the bare idea of being surrounded with a parcel of whity-brown little objects!"

"Nay, you would regard them as so many sweet pledges of mutual affection."

"Say rather, mutual hatred!" exclaimed the irritated young lady,—"But you are joking now:—you know you are, and this is only said to try me."

"It's true, every word of it," answered the supposed Gipsy.

"Oh, do but say you have been amusing yourself, and I'll—I'll—yes, I'll give you this bran new sovereign that my pa gave me only this morning."

The woman, unable to resist the temptation, held out her hand for the promised reward, and as the girl advanced to give her the bribe she just caught a sight of Valentine's coat-tail, which the wind at that moment most provoking blew up, as if for the express purpose of putting an end to his joking. Upon this she raised a scream of terror, and seizing her companion by the arm she dragged her away from the place vowing that she had been betrayed and that that should be the very last time she would ever be foolish enough to rely upon the promises of an ignorant fortune-teller. As they passed the place, too, where Septimus and Uncle Sam had seated themselves to wait for Valentine's return, they were greeted with a loud laugh from the latter, and then scampering off as fast as their legs

would carry them, they were soon lost among the laughing throng that was assembled on the hill.

The two elderly gentlemen enjoyed the joke amazingly, when Valentine related all that had passed between himself and the young lady. In fact, Uncle Sam absolutely roared himself hoarse at the young lady's horror at having a black husband: and even Septimus was seen to smile for the very first time since he had been dragged away to the mad-house.

When the narrative was finished they all set forward on their return to the town of Greenwich, but as they had nearly an hour to wait for dinner, they strolled towards a crowd which they perceived had collected at the further end of the street, and long before they reached the spot they heard a Methodist preacher dealing forth damnation and all sorts of other pleasant things upon those who ventured to differ from him in religion. The poor fellow was one of those unfortunate maniacs who are allowed to walk at large and disseminate their ignorant rhapsodies among the ignorant, many of whom deride at, while few listen to them with that decency which genuine religion always commands. The poor fellow, who was now holding forth, kindly assured his auditors that nothing could save them from the wrath to come—that they were, in fact, all wretched sinners, and that only a few elect could ever hope to enjoy the blessings of a better world. In truth, the unfortunate madman had worked himself up to such a pitch that he was absolutely foaming at the mouth, and his hands and arms were swung round and round, something like the sails of a windmill in a high breeze of wind.

"My friends," he exclaimed, "take warning from my words, and turn from your wickedness—give up those vile games of Satan that I, with grief unutterably, have just now witnessed in yonder park—sin no more by playing at those unholy games of roly-poly and kiss-in-the-ring. They lead mankind into temptations of the flesh, and lo, we fall, even unto the bottom of the pit that hath no bottom, and ——"

Here his eloquence was cut short by a disaster that he had not anticipated, for some wicked urchins having tied a string to one of the legs of the stool on which he stood, gave it at this moment a sudden pull, and down came the righteous man upon his latter end, to the no small diversion of the greater part of the crowd, and the great consternation of a few pious old ladies who had joined the crowd in order to profit by the outpourings of this wonderful man.

Luckily, however, the preacher had sustained no very great damage, and when the stool had been replaced in its former position, he once more mounted it and began anew the exhortation that had been so suddenly brought to a termination.

"O-h-h-h, my friends," he continued, "I can see that Satan is busy among us here to-day. He is striving to work mischief and to drive me away, lest by my preaching I should save any of you from his clutches ;— he is jealous of me, you see, and has come purposely into the street of this town to hunt up all the souls he can find, to feed his everlasting fire. Yea, he is among us here in this congregation, and woe unto those who are not prepared to wrestle with him as I am."

"He is at this moment at your elbow !" exclaimed Valentine, in a peculiarly solemn tone that made the ranter turn pale with terror, and looking round in the direction from whence the voice came, he beheld a sooty-faced chimney-sweep who stood grinning at him with an ominous leer that seemed to say he was just ready to carry him off on the point of his pitchfork. On perceiving this suspicious-looking figure, the teeth of the preacher chattered in his head, and waving his hand authoratively, he exclaimed with a stentorian voice :—

"Avaunt, Satan!—flee from us, for I am bold of heart; and, lo, with the sword of grace I will fight and defend myself against thy malignant power."

"I'll tell you what, old fellow," retorted the angry sweep, "if you comes any more of that ere chaff, I'm dashed if I don't pitch into you in less than no time. Who do you call Satan, you old leatherlungs?"

"Get thee behind me, Satan !— get thee behind me !" cried the terrified ranter; "thou hast mistaken thine aim for once—for we whom thou see'st here are of the elect. Cast him out, friends—cast him out, or verily he will be presently playing some of his spiteful tricks."

"Take that for your pains, you psalm-grinding son of a tinker !" exclaimed the exasperated chimney-sweep, snatching off his soot-begrimed cap, and aiming it with unerring precision at the head of the offending party, on whose cheek it left a magnificent beauty-spot that remained unmoved in spite of all the attempts that were made to remove it with the aid of a handkerchief. Upon this the crowd grew most riotous in their mirth, upsetting once more the stool on which the preacher had been elevated, and then elbowing him about till he was fain to beat a hasty retreat, lest they should proceed to still further acts of violence. Rushing through the crowd, he darted first down one street, and then another, overturning in his way sundry old apple women and their stalls, and once very narrowly escaping the attack of a tremendous large dog which had rushed out of a neighbouring court, and joined in the hunt after the unfortunate field-preacher. At last, however, a benevolent old lady opened her doors to receive him, and under her protection he remained until the crowd had dispersed, and a free road was open for him to depart.

Of course, neither Valentine nor his friends had joined in the pursuit after the poor devil, who they in reality pitied, lest he should meet rough treatment from the mob which is always so ready to tease and torment those whom they take it into their heads to tyrannize over. Our three friends had in fact hurried off as fast as they could to the tavern where their dinner had been ordered, and as the reader may feel interested in the circumstance, we take it upon ourselves to say—under the rose, of course—that three better trenchermen could hardly have been found, than those who now sat down to enjoy the good things that had been prepared for them. Then followed wine, over which many a joke was passed; and by the time a bottle a-piece had been sacrificed to the honour of Bacchus, our friend Septimus declared that he felt himself far better after it than if he had swallowed the filthy medicine which his doctor poured in upon him with so generous a desire to effect his complete recovery.

As for Uncle Sam, he was in the highest possible state of good humour. His heart grew warmer and his tongue went faster with every glass of wine he swallowed; and having emptied a couple of bottles, he declared that he was just in the humour to sit down and have a right jolly drinking bout. Of this fact there was no doubt; but as he happened to be rather unruly when too far gone, it was thought advisable to break up the party, and call in the waiter for their bill. What the amount was, we will not mention, for fear it should frighten any of our friends from entering one of the Greenwich first-rate taverns. Certain it is, however, that the sum total completely electrified the gentlemen, and paying the amount, together with a liberal gratuity to the waiter, they took their departure, vowing to eschew tip-top houses in Greenwich for the future.

CHAPTER XLIII.

TRICKS UPON TRAVELLERS, OR HOW TO PUNISH SELFISHNESS.—VALENTINE'S IMITATIONS PROVE TO BE A SOURCE OF CONSIDERABLE AMUSEMENT.—A QUARREL, IN WHICH THE SURLY GENTLEMAN COMES OFF SECOND BEST. — A SHORT TRIP IN A STEAM-BOAT, PROVES OF SINGULAR IMPORTANCE TO UNCLE SAM.—AN UNEXPECTED MEETING.

MAKING their way towards the terminus of the Greenwich railway, Valentine and his friends procured seats in one of the carriages, but not before a particularly ill-tempered lump of humanity in the shape of an elderly gentleman of sixty-five, had taken up room enough to have satisfied any person of moderate desires. This proved both annoying and inconvenient to our hero, who at first politely requested the aforesaid elderly biped to edge off a little nearer to his own corner; but as well might he have spoken to a stone wall as to his fellow passenger, for the latter-named personage only answered him with an ill-natured grunt of defiance, and folding his arms across his chest, he settled himself in an attitude that seemed to say he should not give way an inch to oblige even the sovereign of Great Britain.

By this time the train had started, and as it was clearly of no use to kick up a riot in the vehicle, our hero followed the suggestion of his friends, and seated himself as well as he could between them, he began to turn over in his own mind how he might best revenge himself upon the surly gentleman. At first he threw out a variety of hints about the disagreeable qualities of *some people* who never knew how to behave themselves when chance threw them into decent society; but this was thrown away upon the person for whom it was intended, who merely treated his nose to an immense pinch of snuff, and then lolled himself back upon his seat with the very evident intention of enjoying a slight snooze till the end of his journey. When this failed, various other plans were tried with an equal want of success, which so provoked Valentine, that resolving in his own mind to have some sort of satisfaction for the inconvenience he had suffered, he imitated the braying of a jackass in hysterics with so much effect, that the surly gentleman started up, rubbed his eyes, and looking round him with consternation, demanded of his fellow-passengers if they could inform him from whence the terrific sounds had issued.

"What terrific sounds do you mean, sir?" asked our hero, with an air of great surprise.

VALENTINE VAUX,

OR THE
TRICKS OF A VENTRILOQUIST

BY TIMOTHY PORTWINE.

"Good heavens, sir! do you mean to say you heard nothing?" exclaimed the stranger, with the utmost astonishment.

"Really," answered Valentine, "you speak so strangely that no one can understand what is meant.—What sound,—what noises, I ask, have occasioned the alarm you appear to feel?"

"Is it possible that none of you gentlemen heard it?"

"Ridiculous!" exclaimed our hero: "how could we be expected to hear that which never took place?"

"Aye, how indeed," joined in Uncle Sam.

"The man must have taken leave of his senses!" muttered Septimus Bramstone, enjoying the joke.

Believing he must have been in a dream, the surly gentleman made no further reply, but throwing himself once more back in his seat, he soon fell into a second slumber, from which, however, he was quickly roused by a "ee-awing" that was even more terrific than the first. Enraged beyond measure at this repeated interruption of his rest, the old gentleman started on his feet, and was about to indulge in a furious speech against the cause of all this disturbance, when the train suddenly stopped, and he was precipitated upon his latter end, with a violence that threatened to expel all the breath out of his body. But this, instead of quieting the perturbed spirits of the surly gentleman, served to increase his rage more and more, and he was about to pour forth a volley of abuse against the proprietors of the railway for allowing such noisy animals to be conveyed at the same time with human passengers, when the door of the carriage was thrown open and a policeman making his appearance, announced that they had reached the termination of their journey.

"Blood-an'-ouns, man !" roared the incensed passenger, "what is the meaning of the scandalous outrage that has been perpetrated on us?—Speak, sirrah, or dread the wrath that will burst forth."

"Well, I'm blessed if you ain't a rum'un, any how," answered the man, grinning with most provoking indifference. "We do sometimes carry out and out queer characters in these here concerns of ours, but blow me if ever I recollected having to do with such a mad chap as you, either."

"The fact is, the gentleman has been rather troubled in his sleep," replied Valentine. "He has been raving all the way along about being disturbed by the braying of a donkey, as if it was likely such animals would be allowed to travel in one of the company's first class carriages."

"Oh, it's quite preposterous," exclaimed Uncle Sam.

"Perfectly ridiculous !" added Septimus, who was now so far recovered that he could join in a little bit of fun.

"Why, as to that ere," answered the policeman, "I won't say nothin' at all about the thing being impossible. The fact is, our company is far too respectable to carry donkeys, but I've seed a lot o' jackasses go backwards and forwards every day of my life."

"Ha ! ha ! ha !" shouted Valentine, Uncle Sam, and Mr. Septimus Bramstone, in full chorus.

"Perhaps you meant that bit of wit against me?" exclaimed the surly gentleman, in a towering passion. "But the cap don't fit, you rascal, and, if it did, you should soon find out that the ass was not without the power of kicking.—A pretty pass, indeed, that a gentleman like myself is to be insulted by a contemptible fellow that I help to pay."

"Beg pardon, sir," replied the policeman;—"no offence, you know,—you began the chaff, you know, 'else there wouldn't have been a word said about jackasses."

"My fault, eh !" vociferated the passenger :—"well, things are coming to a fine pass, indeed, if a respectable man is to be talked to by a scurvy chap like you."

"Come, I say," retorted the policeman, "don't be chattering too much about your respectability, or I may happen to let a little more out than you'd like to hear. I knows all yer tricks—I do—and mayhap these gentlemen shall learn what sort of a companion they've had with them from Greenwich."

"My good fellow ———"

"Oh, don't be palavering me with your "My good fellow this," and "My good fellow that"—I'm a man that knows what's what, and ever since that last Old Bailey concern—"

"Hush !" interrupted the surly passenger, wishing to put an end to the affair before matters assumed a more serious aspect—"don't say another word about that ugly business, and this sovereign shall be at your service."

"What's all that whispering about?" exclaimed Valentine, who observed the uneasiness of his late fellow-traveller. "Let us have no secrets among friends, but out with the truth at once and shame the devil."

"Aye, aye," interposed Uncle Sam—"if this person is—as I suspect—an impostor, tell what you know of him, that we may take care and shun his society for the future."

"Oh, I've no objection, I'm sure," answered the policeman; "and I should think the gen'l'man himself can't mind it, seeing that he was pretty considerably talked about not long ago, when there was sich a to-do about stealing that bill from Lord Simon Softly—"

"Ho, ho!" interrupted Valentine—"I begin to smell a rat: this would-be gentleman—this surly individual, who must needs occupy one entire side of a carriage to himself, is no less a personage than the renowned Mr. Schemer, who, by turning queen's evidence, saved himself, whilst, at the same time he convicted his associates, and sent them as felons to Botany Bay."

"By goles, you've hit the right nail on the head this time at any rate," cried the policeman. "This is the werry individual you have named, but, perhaps, as he looks a little bit ashamed of himself, he is a-going to take to more honest ways for the future."

"This is all a mistake, I assure you," cried Schemer, with an evident wish to escape as speedily as possible;—"I am not the person you mean:—the—the—the fact is,—my brother,—yes, my brother, gentlemen,—is very much like me in features, and people are apt to mistake one for the other."

Here a loud shout of laughter burst from the crowd by whom they were surrounded, and a shabby-genteel looking young man forcing his way through, regarded Mr. Schemer with a scrutinizing look, and then broke forth in a strain of vituperation and reproach.

"You infernal old villain," he exclaimed. "I don't wonder at your being ashamed to acknowledge yourself. You have been the ruin of others, and whilst they are suffering punishment for their faults, you are left at large to carry on your vile practices and make fresh victims of those that are simple enough to be your dupes. But I have got my eye upon you Mr. Schemer, and as sure as I stand here, it shall not be long before I bring you either to Botany Bay, or the gallows!"

"Go away, fellow, I know you not," cried the swindler, utterly confounded at the turn affairs had taken.

"Oh no, it's not convenient to know me, I dare say," exclaimed the other, placing himself before Schemer so as to prevent his escape. "You it was that induced my brother to join you in robbing the public, and when every thing was found out, you turned round upon your late companions and stood up in the witness-box to procure their conviction. I saw you while sentence of transportation was being pronounced upon them, and as I live, there was a villanous smile on your countenance that betrayed the satisfaction you felt at having thus easily got rid of those who could no longer be of service to you. From that moment I have never ceased to look upon you as my future prey, and mark my words, Robert Schemer, the time is not far distant when I shall stand up in the same witness-box to give evidence that shall satisfy the vengeance that rankles in my heart."

"Gentleman," cried the swindler, looking round upon Valentine and his friends, "will you stand by and see a person used in this infamous manner?"

"Why, for my own part," replied Valentine, "I must needs confess that it appears you richly deserve all the reproaches which have been heaped upon you by this man. His brother has had his character and prospects in life blasted through his unfortunate acquaintance with you, and to me it seems nothing more than natural that he should expose the author of so much mischief, and thus perhaps prevent a great deal more of that mischief which you have it in your power to do."

"Bravo!—that's speaking like a man!" shouted the mob in extacies at the view our hero had taken of the matter;—"the gen'l'man ar' a real gen'l'man, and he aint a going to take part with no vagabones like you."

"Shall we carry him down to the nearest wharf and shove him head foremost into the Thames?" asked a sprightly looking youth in the garb of a costermonger.

"Why that is a proceeding I cannot recommend," answered Valentine. "He might probably lose his life in an event of that sort, and in such a case, your own neck, and those of all others concerned in the affair, would stand but an indifferent chance, if a jury should be called upon to give a verdict according to their conscience."

"Damn it! is the rascal to get off, without any of his deserts then?" asked another of the crowd.

"Who do you call rascal?" exclaimed Schemer plucking up a little courage from the advice which had just been given by Valentine;—I would have you to know, sirrah, that I am a respectable man, and if anybody worth powder and shot, was to make use of such expressions towards me, I would take the law and trounce him as sure as he lived."

"Perhaps you'll take the law on me for that then?" said the costermonger darting forward and giving the bill-stealer a shove that sent him reeling into the arms of a sturdy coal-heaver, who in turn, sent him spinning off in another direction, from whence he was again pushed to a fourth party, and in that way he continued to be driven about until he at last sunk fairly exhausted on the ground.

Thus situated, Valentine could no longer withhold his assistance, and raising the prostrate body of his late fellow-traveller, he was just advising him to make the best of his way home when the costermonger made a sudden rush forward, and raising his huge fist, fetched the unfortunate Mr. Schemer a bonnetter, that knocked his hat over his eyes, and left him to grope his way out the crowd in the best way he could. In this condition he was driven about by the mob till Valentine flew to the assistance, who leading him from the railway terminus saw him safely into a hackney coach, and then left him to return home full of reflections on the salutary lesson he had that day received.

"Well, my boy," exclaimed Uncle Sam, as our hero returned from performing this last act of humanity; "you certainly did well to take care of the poor devil when every body else was against him, but who would ever have thought that the surly old fellow who wanted to occupy one half the carriage for his own convenience,

would turn out to be nothing but a rascally swindler?"

"Ah! who indeed?" cried Septimus Bramstone;—"Egad, the fellow was bounceable enough during our short trip, and would have had it all his own way if it had not been for Valentine's mad prank of rousing him from his slumbers, with that tremendous donkey braying that was enough to rouse the dead from their graves."

"Served the fellow right," exclaimed Uncle Sam bluntly;—"he chose to make himself disagreeable, and was, of course, fair game to those he thought fit to annoy with his selfishness."

"Between ourselves," observed Valentine, "I was determined to have satisfaction somehow or other, and if the delicate braying of a jackass had not been enough, I would have treated him with imitations of a whole herd of wild beasts, by way of testing the sensibility of his nerves."

"So that he would fancied himself in some travelling menagerie," exclaimed Uncle Sam.

"At any rate," answered Valentine, "he might have been assured that while he was in the place our menagerie would not have been without one important animal in the collection."

"And pray nephew what animal would that have been?"

"A bear!"

"Ha! ha! ha!—meaning himself of course.—Well Valentine, you are a bit of a wag I see;—always upon the look out for fun;—wicked dog—sad rascal."

"That I like fun, as you call it, my dear uncle, is not to be denied," answered Valentine; "but you must acknowledge that in seeking it, I always endeavour rather to effect good than harm by it. For instance, my pranks just now with Mr. Schemer could not possibly do any harm, and my recent affair with the Socialists,—as they call themselves, may effect some good results among those who were foolishly wavering towards their pernicious doctrines."

"Aye, aye, there's no doubt you will try to make out a good story for yourself Val," returned Uncle Sam. "Must say something you know, by way of an excuse for all the mischief you have been doing."

"I trust," replied Valentine, "you will not be able to substantiate any very serious charges of mischief against me. My shafts are intended only for the wicked or the foolish ;—those men who are really friendly to their fellow creatures, have nothing to fear from my love of the art I have so often practised with success."

"Valentine is in the right." interposed Mr. Septimus Bramstone. "By the gift he possesses in ventriloquism, he has it in his power to effect a great deal either of good or harm ; fortunately, he possesses sense to guide him, and the consequence is, that he never employs its assistance to the injury of any one. In my own case he has effected considerable service, for had it not been for him I should at this moment have been—"

"Damn it, old friend, never mind where you would have been," interrupted Uncle Sam, "but rather let us enquire where we are now. To my fancy this is a dirty filthy looking place as ever I chanced to find myself in, and as Val has been at the pains to bring us here, perhaps he will have the goodness to explain where we are and the motives he had for introducing us to such a dingy looking place."

"Follow me a little further, and you shall see why I have brought you here," exclaimed Valentine, leading the way down to the waterside, where a number of small steam boats were laying off ready to start with passengers for different parts of the river. Still, however, Uncle Sam was at a loss to to divine the object he could have had in taking them there, and when he had exhausted a variety of useless conjectures, he at last fairly gave in, and demanded what was the next scheme he had in view.

"Why, the fact is," replied Valentine, "you are a bit of a novice in town, and I thought you might as well see all you can before leaving London, to shut yourself up in the country as you propose. From this place, for the moderate charge of fourpence, we can

be conveyed to Westminster Bridge, and at the same time you will have an opportunity of seeing both sides of the river, which in itself is no trifling gratification to the man who feels proud of the country to which he belongs. For my own part, I am fond of these short trips, and believing that you would feel some pleasure in the change, I—"

"Don't say another word about it, Val." interrupted his uncle; "your motive was a good one, and so there's an end of the matter. As a youth, I always loved the water, and even now in my old age, nothing could afford me greater delight than to look upon scenes that I have not had an opportunity of witnessing for many and many a long year."

So saying, he leaped on board the vessel that was lying nearest to the wharf, and being presently followed by Valentine and Mr. Septimus Bramstone, he took an arm of each, strutting up and down the narrow deck, and occasionally glancing towards the company which was by this time thickly crowding into the boat. Our hero, too, was much gratified at observing the number of pretty girls who it seemed were to be his fellow-passengers ; and he was more particularly directing his gaze towards one of them whem his uncle suddenly started back a couple of paces, uttered a cry of astonishment, and instantly turned as pale as a sheet of writing paper.

"Good heavens ! are you ill, sir ?" asked Valentine, in a tone of unfeigned alarm.

"No, no—not exactly ill, my boy," stammered Uncle Sam : "turned a little queer—that's all ; but it will be over presently. Damn it though," he added in a tone of vexation, "I wish we had not come on board this infernal steam boat."

"Indeed ! why just now you appeared to be quite delighted with it.'

"Well, sir, suppose I was, is that any reason why I should not alter my mind ? I tell you it's an infernal boat, and I am a most unlucky old man, even to have stepped a foot on board her."

"If that's the case," observed Septimus, "the sooner we leave it the better—we are not obliged to remain, you know, and particularly as there seems to be people enough already to fill it."

"Don't be in a hurry about going just yet," exclaimed Uncle Sam, whose eyes were fixed towards the after-part of the vessel. "Now, I am here, I'll remain if it's only just to see how she conducts herself, when she knows I am on board."

"Bless me!" cried Valentine, "this is very odd. You really talk quite wildly, sir:—is it of the vessel or some human being that you are speaking of?"

"Do you see yonder portly lady?" demanded Uncle Sam.—"I mean yonder one in the black silk dress and a feather in her bonnet big enough for the plume of a mourning coach?"

"We do—we do," answered Valentine and Septimus Bramstone, both of them wondering what in the name of fortune was coming next.

"Well then, gentlemen, in that lady you behold the Widow Wiggins."

"Indeed!" exclaimed our hero; "and who the devil, my dear uncle, is the Widow Wiggins?"

"An angel, Valentine—an angel!"

"Not an angel of *light*, if I may judge by her present *weight*," observed Valentine, jocosely.

"Ah, my boy!" groaned Uncle Sam, "it's all very well for you to be jesting, but that woman, at one time in her life, had very nearly been your aunt."

"Gad! then chance has thrown us in the way of an old flame of yours, eh?" exclaimed Valentine. "Well, this is lucky at any rate, for of course you mean to introduce me and Mr. Bramstone to the widow."

"Not for worlds," exclaimed Uncle Sam. "During our courtship we had a few words and parted; and from that time to this we have never met till this very moment."

"And you have remained an old bachelor ever since?"

"I have," answered the elderly gentleman.

"And apparently the lady has not altered her state," observed Valentine; "probably she regretted the cause of the rupture between you, and has remained a widow ever since, in hopes that you might one day or other be induced to forget old differences, and make her another offer."

"Valentine!" exclaimed Uncle Sam, sternly, "can you look at me and fancy for a single moment, that I am ever likely to commit matrimony. No, no, my boy, I have got over all that sort of nonsense now; and having lived a life of single blessedness all these years, I mean to die a sturdy old bachelor."

"Hollo!" cried Septimus, at this moment breaking in upon their conversation;—"the widow seems inclined to look out for another chance, at all events, or else I am much mistaken in the motives that induce her to accept a nosegay with such a smile, from the hands of that elderly beau on her left."

"By Jupiter, you are right!" exclaimed Uncle Sam, staring with all his might at the Widow Wiggins, and clenching his teeth like a madman. "She is actually suffering the attentions of that old booby, while I am present to be a witness of their foolery. Valentine, you know something about these matters, — what would you advise me to do?"

"Remain where you are and take no notice," answered our hero.

"And very good advice too, which I cordially join him in urging you to adopt," added Septimus.

"Ah! but flesh and blood won't bear it," cried Uncle Sam; "I'm getting desperate, and if the old fellow don't leave her in less than no time at all, I'll challenge him to meet me with either swords or pistols."

"In which case you would perhaps lose your life," observed Valentine, who, by-the-bye, knew pretty well that there was no fear of matters coming to such an extremity.

"Then I'll go and reproach the widow for her folly." exclaimed Uncle Sam, breaking away from his friends, and proceeding towards that part of the vessel where the widow was seated. Valentine and Septimus Bramstone found it was no use to oppose him, and remaining where they were, they watched Sam as he stealthily approached the party he was about to reprove. In fact, he had advanced very near to them without being observed, and the elderly beau was just in the act of politely handing a peach to the lady, which she, in her turn, was about to receive with equal politeness, when Uncle Sam, in a low sepulchral voice, exclaimed :—

"Widow Wiggins !—Widow Wiggins !"

A cry of terror burst from the lips of the lady,—the elderly beau started back with terror marked in his countenance, and almost at the same moment the widow jumped from her seat and threw herself into the arms of Uncle Sam. Hereupon a scene took place,—the passengers flocked around anxious to discover the cause of such singular conduct, and even Valentine and Septimus Bramstone were drawn to the spot, partly by surprise and partly by curiosity.

"Dear papa," cried a young lady who was leaning on the arm of an elderly gentleman of elephantine proportions, "do see what is the matter with the poor woman :—I declare if she has not fainted away just as I did last Thursday when Horatio Fitzsimon Starchly came unawares into my presence after a painful separation of three weeks and two days."

"Fiddlesticks !—what do you suppose is the matter with her ?" growled the old man. "She seems to have been struck comical all of a sudden, and I must say she might have acted more modestly than to have flopped into a man's arms in the manner she has done."

"Excuse me, sir," said a particularly yellow and wrinkle-skinned old dowager, "but it seems, from your observations, that you are nothing better than a brute! The poor dear creature has no doubt been deluded by that hoary-headed sinner that has got

hold of her ;—and, for my own part, I only wonder she condescended so much as to faint in his arms at all."

"Oh, Samivel, Samivel !" cried the Widow Wiggins, " who'd ever have thought of this meeting between such old sweethearts as you and I ? But it's fate that has done it, I suppose, and so perhaps fate means us to be married, after all the crosses and disappointments we have met with."

" No, I'm damned if fate means any thing of the sort," answered Uncle Sam, willingly transferring his burden to the arms of the elderly beau. " I have reached years of discretion at last, and if you want a husband in your old age, I dare say there's one not very far off."

"Samivel !" shrieked the widow imploringly.

" Ah! that caper won't do now, widow," answered Uncle Sam with cutting frigidity. " There was a time, ma'am, when I worshipped your very footsteps, when, in fact, I would have made a fool of myself by marrying you. But that's all passed now; I've made up my mind to die an old batchelor, and it ain't all the widows in the world that shall ever tempt me to commit matrimony at the wrong side of sixty."

" Hush, sir, for heaven's sake hush !" whispered Valentine. " Remember, we are surrounded with people, and a scene like this is very likely to make you appear ridiculous in their eyes."

"What care I, Valentine, for a parcel of gaping fools, that had much better be looking after their own business ?" exclaimed his uncle. " If they think so much of the Widow Wiggins, let them all marry her at once; they may do it for aught I care, but as to being carnied over by her, I'd sooner suffer my right hand to be cut off; aye, or even my head, if it comes to that !"

Upon this Uncle Sam dashed his hat violently upon the deck, which was almost as quickly picked up by Valentine, and restored to the place for which it was intended.

Still, however, the old gentleman was exceedingly indignant at the murmurs of discontent which he heard around him, and it was by no means certain that he would not commit a breach of the peace, had not the boat at that moment reached the pier at Westminster bridge. Upon this Valentine and Septimus dragged him by force of arms to the shore, but before they had succeeded in completely carrying him up the steps, they were overtaken by the elderly beau, who, quite out of breath with the effort of running, popped a card into Uncle Sam's hand.

"There, sir, that is my card," exclaimed the beau, panting from exertion; "I say, sir, you are no gentleman,—no gentleman, sir, I repeat, and if you think fit to resent what I have said, you have my address, and I shall be willing to meet you when and where you please."

Saying this, the old beau skipped off as nimbly as his legs would carry him, leaving Uncle Sam vociferating and scolding at Valentine and Septimus, because they' would not be civil enough to let go their hold of him, just while he followed the elderly Adonis, to give him one good kick upon the broad seat of honour. Our hero, however, was deaf to his entreaties, and having succeeded in dragging him up the steps of the landing-place, he next led him towards the park, where the frantic gesticulations of his relative were less likely to attract the attention of the public. In a short time Uncle Sam became a little more calm, and vowing vengeance against the ancient beau who had thus excited his wrath, he suffered himself to be led quietly to the house of Septimus Bramstone, where a short period served to restore him to that admirable equanimity of temper for which he was so celebrated.

———

CHAPTER XLIV.

A RECONCILIATION TAKES PLACE BETWEEN SEPTIMUS AND HIS RE-LATIVES.—OUR HERO PAYS A VISIT TO MISS STANLEY.—A MORNING IN THE ZOOLOGICAL GARDENS, AND THE VARIOUS ADVENTURES THAT TAKE PLACE.—A GIRAFFE TAKES AN EXPENSIVE LUNCH.—UNBEAR-ABLE CONDUCT OF THE BEARS.—THE ORANG OTANG AND THE EX-QUISITE, OR RIVAL IN MONKEYANA.

PASSING over a few days subsequent to the events narrated in the foregoing chapter, we have to announce to our readers the gratifying fact of Septimus Bramstone's entire forgiveness of his brother and nephew, who, in spite of the scandalous proceedings they had thought proper to take against him, were now received into as much favour as if nothing had ever occurred to disturb the harmony that had former-ly existed between them. At first Uncle Sam was strongly opposed to this reconciliation, because, he argued, their transgressions had been so heinous, and their conduct altogether so scandalous, that it was impossible to say whether they might not again attempt some similar act of vio-lence if an opportunity should offer for carrying their revengeful designs into execution. But Septimus would not listen to the arguments of Uncle Sam, and, backed by the opinions of Valentine, the good old gentleman stuck hard and fast to his original determination, so that it was arranged a day should be named on which Harry and Arnold Bramstone were to be invited to dinner, so that, over a bottle of wine, all former differences should be entirely forgotten. To Uncle Sam this appeared to be giving way too much to those who deserved no pity or consideration, but as Sep-timus was fixed in his resolution, the point was yielded without much diffi-culty, and the next day was named as that on which the restoration should be effected. Accordingly a note was

VALENTINE VAUX,

OR THE

TRICKS OF A VENTRILOQUIST.

BY TIMOTHY PORTWINE.

despatched to Harry, inviting him and his son to dinner, and excusing extending the invitation to their wives, on the ground that their visit might be made more comfortable on another occasion. When this epistle was despatched to its place of destination, Valentine left his friends for a time, having made up his mind to pay a visit to Miss Stanley, who he had just heard was returned from the country, where she had been staying a few days with some friends. A brief space therefore served to bring our hero to his place of destination, where he was received by Mr. Stanley with his usual friendliness and cordiality :—

"Ah! my dear boy, glad to see

you, glad to see you," exclaimed the old gentleman, cordially shaking him by the hands and regarding his visitor with that look of frankness that is not to be mistaken. "This is kind of you to come and see us, for though Angelica has not said a word upon the subject, I know she was thinking in her own mind how glad she would be if you were here."

"Miss Stanley does me much honour," answered Valentine, "for the fact is, I was thinking whether she would not almost forget such an humble individual as myself during the absence, that to me has been so painful."

"Psha?" cried Mr. Stanley, "how

can the girl forget you when I know she doats on you to distraction; that is,—zounds! what am I talking about? —why, if Angelica was to hear me acknowledge as much, the poor girl would, I believe, never forgive me."

"Well then, my dear sir, suppose you leave me to find out whether I am welcome or not to her by the reception I meet with; though, to confess the truth, I must say Angelica always receives me in a manner most flattering to my vanity. In fact, that I am welcome I have every reason to believe, and——"

"Hush, you dog, here she comes," interrupted the old gentleman. "Poor wench, she will be surprised, no doubt, to see you; that is to say, if those infernal long-tongued servants have not already given her a hint who is here."

"Which they most certainly have," cried Angelica, who happened to over-hear the latter part of her father's speech as she was entering the room. "My waiting-woman was bursting to tell me the news, and no sooner did I hear that Mr. Vaux was with you than I hastened hither to thank him for the politeness of his visit."

"Mercy on me!" exclaimed Mr. Stanley, "why this exactly reminds me of the time when I used to go a courting your poor dear mother. We both of us used to say such fine things to each other, were always so pleased to meet together, and at the same time so loath to part when the period arrived that rendered it necessary to bring my visit to a conclusion."

"Lor' papa, how you talk!" cried Angelica, "what in the name of goodness will Mr. Vaux think?"

"Think?" exclaimed Valentine;— "that you are all goodness and condescension to one who feels but too happy in having secured your respect and esteem."

"Capital!—couldn't have paid a more handsome compliment myself," cried the old gentleman, trotting briskly about the room and rubbing his hands in high glee. "It does one's heart good to hear a sensible fellow talk, and, as I said before, it exactly

puts me in mind of the time when I was paying my attentions to——"

"Aye, aye, dear papa," interrupted the laughing girl, "we have heard that story so often, that we now know it by heart. You are so fond of look-ing back to old times that I am afraid Mr. Vaux will begin to grow tired of stories so many times repeated."

"Hold your tongue, you baggage, and allow my friend to correct me himself if my conversation should prove wearisome," exclaimed Mr. Stanley, good humouredly. "Old folks, you know, have a privilege to bore their friends as much as they please, and if Mr. Vaux does not like my conversation, why I will leave you together, which I suppose is what you want."

"Why, I declare, papa, if you are not growing quite angry with me!" cried the pouting girl.

"Nay, that is impossible," answered the old gentleman, "for the perfect good nature of your remark is of itself sufficient to ensure you from my anger. However, we will now drop the subject, and if you and Mr. Val-entine like to take a stroll with me, I think I have a little project in view that will yield equal satisfaction to all parties."

"Oh, I am sure I shall make no objection," cried Angelica, glad of anything that would change the topic into a more agreeable channel. "I love a stroll of all things, so pray do not keep us any longer in suspense, but let us know at once which way your own views are directed?"

"Guess," exclaimed her father.

"Nay, I declare if you don't grow quite tantalizing!"

"Nevertheless you must do as I have said, or the project will stand a fair chance of being knocked on the head."

"Then allow me to venture the first conjecture," interrupted Valentine, "and in doing so, I could hazard a good round wager that your thoughts are directed towards the parks."

"Aye, but to which of them?" de-manded Mr. Stanley.

"Why to Hyde Park, of course,

where so much company is to be seen."

"No."

"St. James's Park, then ?" cried Angelica.

"Wrong again."

"How provoking!" exclaimed his daughter, and then recollecting herself, she added—"Ah! now I know; you are going to the Regent's Park, and,—and,——"

"Well, child, why do you hesitate ?"

"I was going to say," resumed Angelica, "that it was very likely you are going to fulfil the promise so often made of taking me to the Zoological Gardens, which you know I so much wish to see."

"You have guessed it at last," exclaimed her father. "It is to the Zoological Gardens that I am about to take you, and if Mr. Vaux has no objection, I shall be happy to have his company. There is a seat in the carriage at his service, and I think I know somebody who will be all the better pleased for having him with us."

Valentine, of course, accepted this offer with the greatest pleasure, and as soon as he had signified his acquiescence, Angelica skipped out of the room to dress for the little jaunt. During her absence the carriage was ordered, and whilst that was getting ready, the old gentleman asked our hero a thousand questions, all tending to draw from him what he really thought of Angelica, and whether he thought of bringing their courtship to a speedy termination. To all these questions Valentine returned evasive answers, because, in point of fact, the definitive arrangements were not yet settled between him and Angelica, as to the exact period of their marriage, and he was just beginning to feel uncommonly aukward at the very close questions that were put to him by the old gentleman, when his future bride came tripping into the room, and thus put an end to a conversation that greatly perplexed him. Almost at the same moment, too, a servant came to announce that the carriage was at the door, upon which Mr. Stanley bustled off, leaving our hero to conduct the young lady to the vehicle. In a few seconds, therefore, they were on their route to the Regent's Park, and ere half-an-hour had elapsed they found themselves at the principal carriage entrance belonging to the Zoological Gardens. Here they presently alighted, and then proceeding through the gateway, they found themselves in the splendid grounds devoted to one of the noblest sciences to which man can direct his attention. Enchanted at what they saw, it was some few minutes before they could exactly make up their minds which way to turn their steps; but at length perceiving the tall figures of a couple of Giraffes, they proceeded towards the crowd of people by whom the animals were surrounded.

"Well! if they ain't the beautifullest creatures I ever seed, in all my born days !" exclaimed a fat vulgar-looking woman, whose tawdry dress shewed her to be the wife of some purse-proud citizen, who, like Whittington, had had the good luck to raise himself from the rank of an errand boy to be somebody of consequence in the City of London.

"Hush, mamma !" simpered a softlooking youth, whose arm she had hold of, "it ain't ettykettee to talk out loud when people are near. They'll be taking us for nothing better than hugrubs, unless we behaves ourselves in a manner becoming our station in life."

"Lor' Jack, how you talk to be sure !" cried his affectionate mother, with an evident determination not to be put down. "Ain't we come here to see all the sights as is to be seen, and do you think I can help hollering out when I see such rum-looking animals as them there?"

"Hold your tongue do, and don't make such a fool o' yourself," exclaimed the dutiful youth. "When people are surprised, they shouldn't say any think, and yet here you keep kicking up a shindy, just for all the world as if you wanted everybody in the place to know what an ignoramus you are."

"And so, Jack, I oughtn't to speak when I'm very particularly astonished?"

"Certainly not."

"Well, then, my dear boy, perhaps you'll have the goodness to say what I ought to do now that—that nasty long-necked thing has snatched my bag out o' my hand, and scrunched it every bit up before my face."

"Lor' mother, you don't say so?"

"Only look if it ain't," cried the terrified dame, in a tone of ludicrous agony that set everybody about her laughing.

The youth looked as he had been desired, and there sure enough was the bag in the giraffe's mouth, and before any effort could be made to rescue the property, the reticule and its contents had slipped down the capacious throat of the voracious animal.

"There!" cried the horror-struck dame; "if there ain't a little fortune gone down that nasty creatur's throat, never believe me again as long as I live. Two ten-pun-notes, one five ditto,— four golden sovereigns, a pair of scissors, my last new thimbles, a paper of patent needles, three boxes of Morison's pills, and a clean white cambric handkerchief."

"My goodness!" gasped the astonished youth, "won't he have *sharp* pains in his in'ards after swallowing the scissors and patent needles?"

"Oh, that's nothing to what the poor creature will suffer from his dose of Morison's pills," observed an ancient gentleman, who was standing close by.

"And then what a lot of money he has swallowed into the bargain," interposed another by-stander.

"He'll be ill to a certainty," exclaimed the ancient gentleman.

"Lor', sir!—why do you think so?"

"Because I should say that what he has swallowed will be too *rich* for his stomach."

"Ha! ha! ha!" shouted another, "*that*, I suppose, was intended for a bit of very good wit?"

"Really," exclaimed the unfortunate lady who had lost her property in this unexpected manner, "I can't see what fun people can find in looking on at mischief like this. But there *is* brutes in the world," she added spitefully, "and where should we look for 'em so well as in these here 'logical Gardens?"

Valentine found that words were likely to run rather high, and as no efforts of his could do any good towards making the animal disgorge his expensive lunch, he led Angelica and her father towards that part of the grounds where the bear pit is situated. Here, as in the place they had just left, they found a great many people assembled, all of whom seemed to entertain a vast curiosity to see the bears, though few would venture within a distance that might entail the possibility of procuring for them a hug from friend bruin. Almost everybody had come provided with cakes and buns, with which they plentifully regaled the bears, in hopes that, out of gratitude for favours received, they might climb up the pole and exhibit some of their ursine tricks. But the animals were too wide awake to do any thing of the sort, for they merely eyed their visitors with a look of sovereign contempt, and absolutely refused to move a peg, in spite of all the hallooing and din with which their ears were assailed. There was one person, however, who they appeared to regard with a look of particular dislike;—this was a cockney counter-jumper, who happening to have a holiday on the occasion, seemed to think he had a perfect right to see as much as he could for his money. With this notion he resolved to make the bears go through all their tricks, and in furtherance of this design, he poked his stick at them, and by various hideous noises, endeavoured to set them clambering up the pole. Valentine saw this, and hoping to have a bit of fun at the cockney's expense, he threw his voice towards the bear, who happened just then to be looking towards his tormentor, and exclaimed in a sort of growl:—

"Well, spoony, what are you arter now?"

Upon this the exquisite started back aghast, and would have fled from the spot had he not been detained by the reflection that he would most likely be followed by the laughter and jeers of the assembled multitude.

"I'm blessed if that 'ere animal didn't speak as plain as any human cretur!" cried the keeper, who had just reached the spot at the moment when Valentine had practiced his deception. "I heerd him call that eere gen'l'man *spoony*, and if that don't show the animal's sagacity, I don't know what does, that's all." And then addressing himself more particularly to the bear, who had produced these remarks, he began to talk to him in a gibberish that seemed to be perfectly well understood between them. But the animal was not by any means in a good humour on that occasion, and as he fixed his eyes upon the countenance of the keeper, Valentine again growled:

"What are you playing your tricks with me for?—Ain't I your prisoner; —and oughtn't that to be enough, without sending a parcel of fools to stare at and put me out of countenance?"

"Well, this does beat every thing I ever heered on afore and no mistake!" exclaimed the astonished keeper.

"Marvellous!" ejaculated an antique dowager.

"What is marvellous?" demanded the voice from the bear. "Is it strange that a poor devil like me should speak when he is made to endure more than his patience knows how to put up with?"

"I'll tell you what it is, Mr. Keeper," said an exquisite, who had hitherto been a silent spectator of this curious scene; "that is the most unnatural brute I ever saw in all my life, and my advice is, that you kill him before any further mischief happens."

"Kill me!" exclaimed the bear, after a terrific growl. "I'd like to catch any fellow trying it on, that's all. Kill me, indeed!—drat my old hide, if I haven't half a mind to jump over and see how you'd like killing yourself."

This hint was not lost upon either the exquisite or those by whom he was surrounded, for a general rush was immediately made from the place, many of the people tumbling to the ground in the confusion, and all hallooing and shouting with terror, as if his bearship was in truth following closely at their heels. At this moment Valentine raised a tremendous growl, that was heard all over the gardens, upon which another general exclamation of terror was raised, and away darted the crowd of fugitives without knowing, or, indeed, caring where they went, so long as they escaped the ravenous beast that they supposed was following to devour them all at a mouthful.

At last, however, finding that they were still safe, they came to a dead halt, and began to argue with one another whether they had not greatly magnified the danger, and whether in fact the bear had escaped after all, as had been imagined. Certain it was that no one could say he had seen anything of the much dreaded enemy, and as the keeper, who had by this time joined them, declared that it was quite impossible the bear could escape from the place where he was confined, a pretty general notion was entertained that there were more fools than one in the gardens, and that their conduct held them all in rather a ridiculous light.

The exquisite, in particular, was exceedingly indignant at the precipitate flight he had been induced to make, for a tumble or too that he had received, had very seriously discomposed the arrangement of his dress, and what made the thing still more provoking, was that the young lady he was paying his addresses to, and her mamma, had just arrived in the midst of the confusion, and were witnesses of the scene in which he cut so conspicuous a figure. He, however, endeavoured to laugh it off as a very capital joke, but as the young lady was not inclined to regard it in that light, he was obliged to stammer out the best excuse he could, for the want of courage he had manifested in the affair.

"The fact is, my dear girl," he said, "the bear is a most ferocious animal, and when every body declared that he was going to break loose, I thought of you, and the horrid pain it would give you if the news should be brought that I had fallen a victim to the nasty brute."

"Oh, then it was not on your own account that you fled with such rail-road speed, when a report was raised that the bear had broken loose from his pit?"

"'Pon honour it was not," answered the dandy. "I could have faced even a tiger if it had been myself only that was to suffer; but when my charming, adoroble Augusta was to be left a prey to anguish and despair, I thought the better part of valour was discretion, and preferred running away to falling a victim to my own rash temerity."

"Oh," laughed the young lady, "I believe there is not the least fear of your ever falling a prey to your rash temerity, as you call it. Mamma, to be sure, was terribly frightened when she saw you running as if you would break your neck, but, for my own part, I saw nothing alarming in it, and, to tell you the truth, I could not help laughing to see how famously you could run when once put upon your mettle."

"Did my adorable Augusta laugh to see her own Horatio in such a pickle?" drawled out the exquisite.

"I did indeed, and that most heartily too."

"Cruel, cruel girl——"

"Now do Horatio," interrupted the young lady, "do for goodness sake, condescend to talk sense for a little while; you know how much I dislike all this high-flown stuff, that only ought to be read in novels and ro-mances, and really, if you would not sicken me at once with such folly, you will at once speak to me in the the language of good, plain, common sense."

"Divine creature, I will!" ex-claimed the exquisite in his usual strain of folly; "teach me how I can make myself most agreeable to yourself, and I will so conform my words and ac-tions that you shall acknowledge me for the aptest pupil you ever had to do with."

"Nay, you positively grow worse and worse."

"Am I then disagreeable to you, divine creature?"

"That," replied the laughing girl, "is asking a question that I cannot answer without bringing upon myself a charge of being too forward."

"'Pon honour you're too bad," drawled out the insufferable puppy;—"must say—no—mustn't say yes."

"That's my brother,—I'll swear to him among a thousand," exclaimed a voice from behind, and on looking round to discover who it was that had thus claimed so close a relationship, he discovered a large orang otang seated in his cage and grinning at him with as much familiarity as if he really was as nearly akin as he had said. Horror-struck at such a salutation, and disconcerted by the laugh with which he was saluted on every side, Horatio would have bolted from the spot, had not Augusta held him tightly by the arm in order to prevent his escape, while a chance remained of the joke being carried any further. It was in vain that the exquisite sought to re-lease himself, for the young lady was determined that he should be punished for his insufferable folly, and Valen-tine, who was glad of the opportunity to punish such an empty coxcomb, made his way slily towards the den, and once more threw his voice with such dexterity, that the words he uttered seemed to proceed from the mouth of the orang otang.

"Ah!" he exclaimed, in a mournful tone, "it's easy to see that he wants to cut his own brother because he don't happen to be dressed out in such fine clothes as himself. But I'll expose him to all the world; every body shall know what an unnatural monster he is, and then people shall judge whe-ther he ought not to be shut up in this cage instead of myself."

"Hollo! what's old Peter arter now?" cried one of the keepers, bust-ling up and looking at the baboon as if he began to doubt whether he had heard right.

"Oh, there's no occasion to inter-fere with Peter, as you call him," said a little old gentleman who appeared mightily to enjoy what was going forward. "That baboon is a most sensible animal, and it seems that he has just found a brother that he has lost sight of for some years."

"What do you mean, sir?" exclaimed the exquisite wrathfully, "do you wish to insult me, by insisting upon any relationship existing between that horrid monster and myself?"

"I don't pretend to know anything about family matters," answered the old gentleman, "but I must say there is a remarkably strong likeness between you and the monkey."

A loud laugh followed this sally, and the dandy was about to make his escape with what celerity he could, when the supposed voice of the orang otang again fell upon his ears.

"Don't let him go, gentlemen," exclaimed Valentine, again speaking so as to make the company believe the voice came from the cage; "hold him fast, or he may, like myself, fall into the hands of people who will make a show of him."

"Release me!" roared the exquisite struggling with all his might to get free; "take your hand from me, every one of you, or I'll—I'll——"

"Well, what'll you do?" asked one of the men belonging to the gardens, whose gigantic size bade defiance to all the puny efforts of the dandy, "you threaten a great deal, young feller, now what is it you're a going to do?"

"Why nothing at all," answered the supposed baboon. "Lor' bless you, he's a fellow that can talk like a lawyer about what he'll do, but bring him to the point and you'll find him of no more use than a baby."

"Curse the monkey! will no one kill him for me?" cried the dandy in a tone of despair.

"Which on 'em do you mean, sir?" asked the keeper slily. "Do you mean yourself, or t'other monkey?"

"Am I to be insulted with impunity?" exclaimed the enraged Horatio.

"No, sir," replied the man, "if you're to be insulted at all its to be with *chaff*."

"Fellow!—you are too low for my notice."

"Indeed!—that's lucky however, for I'm blessed if ever I want to be taken notice of by sich as you."

"Bravo!—bravo!" exclaimed the voice from the cage of the orang otang; —"at him again, he's got no friends. Give him another slap good luck to you."

"So I will, Peter," answered the keeper, giving a wink to the baboon, as if he supposed monkies understood anything so vulgar. "He's rayther up in the stirrups just now, but I think he's got where he'll find out his mistake before we've done with him. So now, Mr. What-dye-callum,—if you've got any conceit in you, perhaps you'll like to go outside the gardens and show whether you've got any mettle in you of the right sort."

"Am I to be insulted, fellow?" lisped forth the dandy.

"I don't know what you call an insult," answered his antagonist, "but I like a bit of a shindy now and then, and as you seem to ride rayther rusty, it would perhaps be as well to settle the business now we're both warm."

"Your master shall hear of your blackguard conduct," cried the exquisite, growing more and more incensed.

"Master never interferes with any amusements," answered the keeper, "he knows I take a pleasure in keeping people orderly, and will never be angry with me for having a bit of civil jaw with a chap like you."

"Rascal! these insults will prevent people ever venturing into the gardens."

"It won't keep any body away that we care to see," answered the other.

"At any rate it will keep me away."

"So much the better if it does!"

"Insolent scoundrel!"

"Ah, it's all very well for you to call me an insolent scoundrel, but I can tell you our guv'nors have given strict orders that no stray monkeys are to be let into the grounds on any consideration. They say we've got enough here already, so now you can leave the place as soon as ever you please."

Enraged at this, the exquisite could no longer control his temper, and raising his silver-mounted cain, he was just going to deal his antagonist an awkward wipe across the shoulders, when he was suddenly lifted off the ground, and, to his inconceivable horror, he found himself enfolded in the trunk of a huge elephant, who for a minute or two danced him up and down in the same way that a nurse would dandle a baby. It was in vain that the poor exquisite screamed for help, for just as two or three persons were rushing forward to his rescue, the elephant slowly moved off with his burden towards one of the ponds, into which he quietly dropped the luckless Horatio, amidst the laughter and uproarious shouts of the assembled spectators. This, of course, formed a suitable termination of the day's sport; and as soon as the exquisite had been released from his unpleasant situation, the company separated, leaving him to the care of a good-natured old gentleman, who took him to his house, dried his clothes, and then conveyed him to his own house, where he remained a close prisoner till the noise of his adventure had in some degree died away.

Having seen poor Horatio dragged from the pond where he had been so unceremoniously deposited by the elephant, Valentine and his friends left the garden, from whence they proceeded to the residence of Mr. Stanley, where our hero passed the remainder of the day, no less to his own satisfaction than that of the fair Angelica, who was now growing so attached to him that his absence was the source of the greatest punishment to which she could be subjected.

CHAPTER XLV.

HARRY AND ARNOLD BRAMSTONE HAVE A LITTLE PRIVATE CHAT ABOUT FAMILY AFFAIRS.—MATTERS WEAR RATHER A DARK AND THREATENING ASPECT. — MORE TO BE DONE BY SCHEMING THAN HARD WORK.—THE INVITATION RECEIVED, AND THE JOY IT BRINGS WITH IT.—ARNOLD GETS DRUNK AND SLEEPETH.—OUR HERO'S METHOD OF ROUSING HIM.— A SINGULAR BATTLE WITH ———

THE day following was that which had been appointed for the meeting between Septimus Bramstone, his brother, and Arnold, who, conscience-stricken as they were, had never ventured to call upon their ill-used relative since the period when they had witnessed, and in fact aided, his release from the hands of Mr. Grabfast, the madhouse-keeper. To be sure, it must be confessed, there was a little good generalship in this, for both the father and son reckoned on the extremely easy disposition of their relative for a speedy reconciliation, and they, therefore, determined to wait patiently till he should have got over the first feeling of indignation with which he would be sure to regard their unwarrantable conduct. Now and then Arnold walked before his uncle's house, in hopes that he might be seen and hailed by the old gentleman, but in this he was doomed to be sadly disappointed, for Septimus happened at the time to be confined to his bed, and the consequence was, that the young man's trouble and well-devised scheme, was entirely thrown away.

In this uncertainty several days passed away, and both the old man and his son began to be assured that this time they had offended beyond all hope of forgiveness. Indeed, Harry Bramstone was awaked to a sense of the ruin that stared him in the face, for every day he was called upon, and pressed by unfortunate tradesmen—writs were served, judgments obtained, and a prison appeared to be the only alternative that remained. Nor was

VALENTINE VAUX,

OR THE
TRICKS OF A VENTRILOQUIST.

BY TIMOTHY PORTWINE.

extravagance and idleness had reduced him to a similar hard strait, and he was just making up his mind that nothing now remained for him but to work for his living—a thing never before to be thought of without shuddering at the vile necessity—when the message arrived from Septimus, inviting his father and himself to spend the following day with him. The letter was written with the same cordiality and frankness that had ever been the characteristic of the old gentleman—there was no coolness whatever to be observed from beginning to end; and no sooner had Arnold read the epistle through, than, starting up from his seat, he seized his father round the waist, and waltzed him about the room with so much animation that the old gentleman was at last obliged to cry out for quarters. "Dance, dance, you old buffer—why don't you dance?" exclaimed the younger worthy, as his father sunk exhausted into a chair—"here's news worth the hearing, and yet you take it as coolly as if it wasn't likely to be thousands of pounds in our way."

"Why, for that matter, I am quite as well pleased as yourself," answered Harry Bramstone, endeavouring to recover himself after all this exertion; "there is a heavy stake depending upon this, and perhaps my own personal liberty depends upon the degree of kindness with which I am received by your uncle after the unfortunate affair that had nearly forfeited his friendship."

"Aye, aye, dad—I know all about it," answered Arnold: "you mean to kick him for a few hundreds, just to satisfy some of the hungry sharks of the law, and carry on the war again till better things begin to turn up for us. Zounds! things began to wear an awkward look—duns out of number bothering out our hearts and souls for money that the hungry vagabonds knew we did not possess—everything going wrong; and old uncle, as we supposed, sulking with us, and unlikely to put his hand in his pocket for a single farthing to save us from ruin."

"'Gad! this is more than I expected though," exclaimed Harry Bramstone:—"things began to wear such a threatening aspect that I had made up my mind in a few days to go to prison."

"Confounded unpleasant — wasn't it," cried Arnold. "With poverty staring me in the face I began to tremble for the consequences; and do you know, terrible as the alternative was, I had made up my mind to do a something that my blood now runs cold to think of."

"God bless me, Arnold, you didn't think of committing suicide — did you?"

"No, father—a thousand times worse than that."

"Oh speak, my dear boy," cried the agitated father—"what—what, in heaven's name, did you think of doing?"

"Of going to work for a living!" answered Arnold, with amazing *sang froid*.

"Psha! I thought you really meant something desperate."

"Well, my dear sir," replied Arnold, "and is not that something desperate? Do you suppose a high-spirited young fellow like myself could make up my mind to such a thing without a struggle, as between life and death? Oh,

you have no idea of the trouble *that* reflection brought me. I imagined myself slaving at a desk all day for about a pound or five and twenty shillings a-week at the outside. To be at another man's beck and call—to go out or stay at home just as he might be pleased to order; and then to return to my wife in the evening just in time to get a night's rest, and then go to work again the next morning. The thought was a terrible one, old gentleman, and yet that's what I must have come to if Uncle Septimus had not sent word to say that we were to dine with him to-morrow."

"Nonsense, Arnold," exclaimed his father; "what difference can that make in our present circumstances?"

"A vast deal, if you have but patience to wait for the result," answered Arnold. "The old man will want to soap us down for fear we should serve him in the same way that we've done before :—we must both of us tell him how queerly we're off in the exchequer department, and when he finds how hard up we are, it won't take much trouble to persuade him to lend us a few hundreds."

"LEND!" exclaimed Harry Bramstone—"and how in the name of fortune are we ever to return it again, think you?"

"Ah! you always look forward so much beyond your nose," replied Arnold :—"I said *lend*, of course, and the old buffer must suppose we mean nothing else; because few people like to *give* away a large sum of money, though they think nothing about it so long as they expect the parties mean to return it again. Now, Uncle Septimus is just that sort of chap—he'll lend us the money, no doubt, but I shouldn't like him to have a notion that there's not much chance of his ever seeing a copper of it again."

"Arnold, I am afraid you are a bit of a rogue."

"And if I am," answered the dutiful son, "I learnt the whole art and mystery from yourself. You have always lived by scheming—we have carried on the war by it ever since I can recollect anything, and I suppose it's now too late to think of getting on by any other means."

The old man groaned aloud as he acknowledged to himself the truth of his son's last observation ; he saw but too plainly that he was deeply involved in a labyrinth of his own making, and though he would gladly have retrieved past errors by future amendment, he had not moral courage enough to set about the task boldly and fearlessly. He observed too that his son had not omitted to follow the baneful example that had been set him; and a flood of painful thoughts rushed through his mind as he reflected on the probable fatal consequences which would be sure to follow the heedlessness with which Arnold had started in his career of extravagance. These reflections were too much for him ; and rising hastily from his seat, he paced uneasily up and down the room till his son's voice once more recalled him to his recollection. But Arnold's endeavours to cheer him this time were utterly fruitless; and repelling him with a look of sternness, he hurried from the room and betook himself to his own chamber, where in solitude and quiet he might ruminate over those events which had occasioned him so much uneasiness.

It was not till the next day that Arnold and his father met again, and when they did see each other, the latter had completely recovered from the gloomy fit of the preceding evening, and grasping the hand of his son, he apologized for his harsh conduct, alleging as a reason for it, that his mind was harrassed with the difficulties in which he was involved, and again expressing his determination as soon as possible, to inform Septimus of the strait to which he was reduced, and at the same time, to ask his assistance to extricate himself from it.

Now, to all this, Arnold could not possibly offer any opposition ;—the thing met his own views exactly, and when this had been arranged between them satisfactorily, it was judged high time to set forth on the visit to Septimus, as the old gentlemen was extremely punctual in his habits, and neither the

father nor son thought it would be prudent just at that period, to give him any occasion for finding fault with them. Having therefore got ready, they both of them set out, and so nicely did they manage to time their walk, that they contrived to reach the house of their relative, just as the clock was striking four, which was the hour named at which dinner was to be on the table.

We will not attempt to describe the meeting between Septimus Bramstone and these worthies, for such matters are not over-pleasant to the reader, and we dare say, they will be quite satisfied, if we assure them, that the two visitors were received with far more welcome than they had any right to expect. In fact, Septimus would not allow either of them to revert to past transactions, and when he had assured them of the joy he felt in seeing them once more; he led them into another room where they found Valentine, and Uncle Sam, both of whom received them as if nothing had happened, in deference to their host, whose pleasure they would not mar by any cool deportment to those, who Septimus Bramstone had thought proper once more to receive into his house.

Then followed dinner, and then came wine, which latter article served to remove any stiffness or formality, that might have existed before. As for Arnold, he was determined to show his admiration for the liquors, by the quantity he drank, and accordingly glass after glass disappeared with a magical celerity, that would have amazed any one who was not before acquainted with his peculiar talent for emptying decanters on the shortest and most expeditious terms. The consequence was, that in the course of the first hour he grew very talkative ;—during the next, he became very fuddled, and throughout the succeeding one, he slept and snored away, to the great amusement of Valentine, and the equally great annoyance of the three elder gentlemen.

" I can't think what the deuce ails Arnold to day," said Harry Bramstone, " speaking, as actors say, ' through music." "He used to be a cheerful companion enough, but somehow or other, to day he fallen off asleep, and it seems to me as if the devil himself wouldn't be able to awake him."

"I think if I blew a little of the smoke of this cigar under his nose, it would soon rouse him," observed Valentine, suiting the action to the word, and treating his companion to a fumigation that for few moments completely obscured him from the rest of the company.

But Arnold was not to be cheated of his rest quite so easily, and merely coughing a little to clear his throat, he shifted his position, and then resumed his snoring still more harmoniously than before.

"Shall I have another try?" asked Valentine, addressing himself to Harry Bramstone.

"With all my heart," replied the old man, who feeling rather excited with the wine he had drank, thought it would be highly amusing to see his son writhing and fidgeting to get away from the smoke.

"No, no," interposed Septimus, "let him sleep and recover himself a little,—besides, it seems cruel to torment when he has not the power to protect himself."

"Then he ought to be awake instead of sleeping and snoring before company," answered his father, whose parental affection was not to be doubted. "He has no business to get fuddled in decent company, so go on again Mr. Vaux and see whether you can't rouse him from his slumbers."

Thus invited, Valentine again commenced operations, and after puffing and blowing for some time he succeeded in setting Arnold riggling and fidgetting in his chair, sometimes rubbing his nose with his hands, as if something tickled him, and at others muttering something that nobody could understand, but at which everybody laughed as if what he had said was excessivly funny. When this little bit of pantomime business was over, Valentine re-commenced, and then something of the same kind was acted again, till at last the sleeper could no longer endure the torment, and throwing out both arms and legs with tremendous impetus, our hero would assuredly have been floored had he not been prepared for such an event, and thus got clear off, before the fist of the slumberer was fairly struck out.

"Hollo! what's the row now?" he exclaimed, rolling his head from one side to the other. "Who's been playing their larks with me, eh? Ah! Val.—Val.—you're a funny rascal, damme, a confounded funny rascal, but see if I don't pay you out for this some day or other."

"My dear fellow," said Valentine, "we missed your cheerful conversation, and I merely tried these means of rousing you from your slumbers."

"Funny fellow,—very—a damned funny fellow," muttered Arnold, and then throwing himself once more back in his seat for another snooze he warbled :—

" Oh slumber my darling,
    Thy sire is a knight,
    Thy mo-ther's-a-la——"

Here the song was cut short by another snore, and again the interesting Arnold Bramstone was closely nestled in the arms of Morpheus.

"Drat the fellow, I'll be hanged if he ain't off again," exclaimed his father with unfeigned astonishment. "It's a remarkable fact, but whenever my boy gets a little drop too much, he's sure to go off to sleep just for all the world like a top."

"Well then, there let him sleep for the present," said Septimus. "He may perhaps recover himself after a little while, which will be much better than drinking any more wine for some time to come."

"It's my particular wish that he should be roused up," exclaimed his father, who also, by this time begun to find out that his brother's wines were not of an inferior quality. "I say it's my particular wish that he should be roused up directly. Mr. Vaux, will you have the goodness to give him a dose of ditto repeated?"

"By all means if it is your particular

request," answered Valentine, and drawing his chair a little nearer to the sleeper, he again poured such a volume of smoke under the nostrils of Arnold, that the latter named personage forthwith began to splutter and sneeze after a most surprising fashion.

"Who the devil's playing their confounded larks with me?" he exclaimed, kicking the chair on one side and throwing himself into a fighting posture. "Who was it, I say, was it you old buffer, eh?"

"No," answered his father, to whom this respectful question was put; "I hadn't any thing at all to do with it."

"Then perhaps it was you?" continued Arnold staggering up to Uncle Sam, but on receiving a negative from that worthy, he lumbered towards Septimus, to whom he was about to put the same question, when a wink and a frown from his father had the effect of bringing him to his recollection. As he turned away, however, his eye chanced to alight on a plaster figure of Hercules, towards which he reeled with drunken gravity, and enquired of his godship whether he had had any hand in the fumigation he had received. Of course, Hercules deigned not to make a reply, upon which Arnold became so incensed, that doubling his fist, he fetched the renowned hero of antiquity such a blow, that down he fell from his pedestal, and away flew arms, legs, and head, rolling about the room in "most admired disorder."

This served to bring Arnold to his senses, and being then reminded by his father of the foolish action he had been guilty of, he apologised to Septimus for the mischief he had done, and, on hearing that it was Valentine who had roused him from his slumbers, he laughed heartily at the ridiculous figure he had cut, promising at the same time to be more careful in future, and never again to go to sleep in company.

The remainder of the day passed pleasantly enough, and when at last Harry and Arnold Bramstone took their departure, it was not without gratifying proofs that Septimus had freely forgiven them the injuries which they had inflicted on him.

CHAPTER XLVI.

VALENTINE MAKES ARRANGEMENTS FOR A VERY IMPORTANT AFFAIR.—A SHORT EXCURSION PROJECTED AND PUT INTO EXECUTION.—INCIVILITY OF A COUNTRYMAN.—A VOICE FROM BELOW.—THE HUNT AFTER A BURIED JEW.—LABOUR IN VAIN.— A PUGILISTIC ENCOUNTER INTERRUPTED BY EXTRAORDINARY MEANS.

WITHIN a few days after this reconciliation had taken place, Valentine had an interview with Miss Stanley in which he pleaded his love with such good effect, that the marriage ceremony was appointed to be celebrated at the expiration of a fortnight from that period. Of course the interval was to be occupied by the bride-elect in making preparations for this important event, whilst our hero, on his part, was busily engaged with lawyers and other worthy functionaries in attending to the drawing out and executing certain very necessary documents, y'clept marriage settlements. But this was dry work to Valentine, who had a thorough hatred for law, and no soooner had he got released from further attendance on his attorney, than he resolved to indulge himself with a solitary ramble in order to enjoy once more a sight of the delightful green fields which he had scarcely had a glimpse of since he left his native place to come to London.

A trip to Dulwich was therefore determined on, and having let the two elderly gentlemen into the secret of his intended movements, he set out, and popped into one of the numerous Camberwell "busses" which soon conveyed him to that pretty suburban village, from whence he intended to walk leisurely to the picture gallery, of which he had heard so much talk.

Soon, however, altogether forgetting the object for which he had set out, our hero diverged from the romantic lane down which he had been proceeding, and had crossed several fields before he became aware that he was travelling without exactly knowing whither. This was the more vexing when, after several ineffectual attempts to regain the path he had left, he found that he had completely missed his way, and that in all probability he would have to retrace his way back to London without accomplishing the design with which he had set forth. Unwilling, however, to be defeated, he began to look about him to see if there was any one about of whom he might enquire his way, when a sound as of somebody at work met his ear, and in that direction he accordingly set off, resolving to reach his place of destination if there was a possibility of doing so. Having crossed a pretty wide field he jumped over a stile, and immediately found himself on the brink of a gravel pit, where a labouring rustic was busily employed in digging and delving, whilst two or three idlers were looking on and talking over the important affairs of the neighbourhood.

"My good friend," exclaimed Valentine, to the only industrious man in company, "can you put me in the way for reaching Dulwich?"

"Eh?" returned the party addressed, bringing his body to an upright position and looking quite amazed at seeing a stranger so near.

"Can you direct me the nearest way to Dulwich?" repeated Valentine wondering at the man's stupidity.

A loud laugh was the only reply to this question, and what made it still more provoking, was the fact of all the idlers joining in the shout of merriment. Valentine was quite enraged at being laughed at, and at the moment he felt half inclined to jump down and give the fellow a sound thrashing; but recollecting that in such a case he should most likely bring three or four others upon him, he wisely swallowed his indignation, and, with as much civility as possible, inquired why they laughed at instead of answering a plain, straight-forward question.

"Because," grinned the digger and delver, "I thought as how every fool know'd his way to Dulwich."

"At any rate," retorted Valentine pettishly, "it seems that every fool is not able to give a civil answer."

"May be not," muttered the fellow; "but I aint set here to answer all sorts o' stupid questions, so you must go and ax somebody else your way to Dulwich, for I'm blessed if I aint as downy as yourself, young fellow."

"Why you most incomprehensible ass, what do you take me for?" demanded our hero, wrathful.

"What do I you take you for?" answered the man, "why for one o' them cockney chaps to be sure that comes down here when their mother's don't know they're out, and plays off all sorts o' mad pranks with us. So go to bed with you for I sharn't answer none of your questions."

And with that the fellow set to work with redoubled diligence as if to make up for lost time.

Valentine was enraged at the insolence of the fellow, and the thought struck him that he was a fit object on whom to exercise a little of his own peculiar talent, and taking a convenient position he so managed his voice, as to make it appear to issue in a deep groan from the spot where the rustic was at work.

"Wh-wh-what's that!" exclaimed the man with extreme trepidation, "what n-n-noise was it that seemed to come up from under my feet!"

"I'm blessed if I know, Bill," answered a tall man, taking a short pipe from his mouth, "I heer'd summat like a groan, yet it couldn't be that neither, seeing as how there's oney ourselves and that ere gen'l'man near the place."

Somewhat encouraged by this assurance the man once more resumed his labour, but he had not proceeded far when another groan was heard which was immediately followed by a deep and awful silence.

This was a complete startler for the yokels; they stared at each other with stupid astonishment, and Bill, terrified at what he had heard, threw down his spade, declaring that he would have nothing more to do with a place that was haunted. In fact they were all of them going to make a bolt of it with as little delay as possible, when Valentine, in his own voice, entreated them to stay.

"For heaven's sake," he exclaimed, with apparent earnestness, "do not leave an unfortunate fellow creature to perish for want of a little assistance. It is evident that some one must be underground, and his life will be sacrificed unless something is done to rescue him."

"But how are we to know it's a human being?" asked the tall man with the short pipe;—"mayn't it be a wicked spirit come to do us harm?"

"Nonsense!" exclaimed our hero, determined to give them a little useless labour for their civility; "work away at the spot where you heard the sound, and if you succeed in rescuing a fellow creature from destruction, I will give a couple of sovereigns by way of reward."

This latter hint was not without effect, and to work they all set themselves, as if heart and soul were bent on finding the poor devil who they supposed had been buried in the gravel pit. They had not proceeded very far, however, when another groan was heard louder than any that had preceded it, and immediately afterwards the imaginary buried man exclaimed:—

"Dig away!—Dig away if ye are men, or I must perish before ye get me out!"

"Where be you then?" asked one of the rustics as soon as he could gather courage to put the question.

"Just under the spot where you have been digging," replied Valentine in an assumed voice.

"How deep are you in the ground, old fellow?"

"Can't say, but not very low down though."

"Well, suppose we have another shy, Bill?" exclaimed the tall man. "The poor devil can't be very comfortable, you know and I'm blessed if we shouldn't thank anybody that would get us out of such a hobble if we happened to need it."

"Well said," cried Valentine;—"set about your work cheerfully my friends, and I dare say your toils will soon be rewarded, by seeing an unfortunate sufferer rescued from certain death."

With that the men once more threw down their coats, and seizing hold of their tools they commenced labouring away in good earnest. At last, however, one of them sent his spade to its full depth through the gravel, and as he did so, a loud shriek was heard, that made them all start back with horror.

"Ah!" exclaimed Valentine assuming a voice of terrible agony, "you have nearly cut my arm off with your infernal spade. Quick, quick! my friends, or I shall bleed to death before you get down to the place where I am lying!"

"Consarn it all! how much further have we got to dig?" cried the man who had answered Valentine so roughly.

"Oh, not much further I should think,—not above a foot or so," answered the supposed sufferer.

Hereupon the men began digging away as if for their lives, but when they had dug down to the distance of a foot there was no more sign of any human creature being buried there than when they first commenced their labours.

"I'm blowed if it ain't a very strange thing, that we don't see nothing whatsomedever of this here chap," said the tall man, looking mysteriously at his companions. "Its a most unaccountable thing—mind ye, I make use of a very strong expression;—its a most *unaccountable* thing, I say, that the more we work the more we seem to lose the chance of finding this here chap."

"Depend upon it," observed one of his companions, "the devil is having a lark with us to-day. This here ain't no man at all—because why?—no man could come there no hows, that I can think of."

"Let's ask him who he is before we go any further," exclaimed another of the men.

"Well, ask him yourself then," retorted the first speaker. "It's only one fool's work, and hang me if I'm going to ask questions of an evil spirit—that is, supposing it really is one."

"Aye, aye, ask him who he is," said Valentine, enjoying the consternation he had created among the fellows who had just before so wantonly insulted him.

Upon this the tall man laid aside his pipe for a moment, and then putting his mouth very near to the ground he said :—

"Friend, before we go any further, we want to know who it is that has been buried in this queer outlandish place. My comrades and I ain't half satisfied about it's being all right; so if you want our assistance tell us your name."

"Barney Aarons," answered the voice from below.

"What Barney Aarons?"

"The Jew pedlar that travels the country."

"Oh," exclaimed the tall man, "if it's only a Jew pedlar we may as well let him stay where he is. He's been cheating some of our neighbours I suppose, and so they've put him in here to prevent his doing any more mischief."

"Aye, aye, if it's only the Jew pedlar let him stop where he is," responded every voice.

"Is it possible," exclaimed Valentine, in his own natural voice, "that you can be so base as to leave a fellow-creature to perish, merely because he happens to profess a religion different to your own?"

Struck by the severity with which these words were uttered, the men once more recommenced their labours, and proceeded some distance further before they again left off to express their surprise at not finding the person they were in search of.

"Phew !" exclaimed Bill, leaning upon his spade, " I'm dam'd if I ain't tired o'this sort o'fun, and it's my opinion this 'll turn out to be some o' Satan's doings, just to give us all the trouble he can."

"I'll soon see what sort of a chap it is," said the tall man; and then stooping so as to bring his mouth almost to the ground, he bawled as loudly as he could :—

"If you be Barney Aarons, and nobody else, how came you to get into such uncommon queer quarters?"

"I was last night knocked down by some villains," answered the imaginary Jew ; "and after robbing me, I was thrown into a hole in this gravel pit, where I was left to perish. But I have some gold still left that was saved inside the lining of my coat, and half of that shall be yours as soon as I am released."

Again the men set to work with all their might, and such good use did they make of their time, that three or four feet of gravel had been removed, though still without finding the object of their anxious labours. Indeed Valentine so contrived it, that his voice grew fainter and fainter, till at last the moanings and complaints of the imaginary Israelite were hardly to be heard at all.

"Where the deuce has the fellow got to now?" exclaimed Bill; "just now I fancied we were close to him, and now he seems to be further off than ever."

"Stop a bit and I'll ask him," said his long companion ; and then stepping down he said, as loudly as he could bawl, "I say, Mister What's-your-name, it's all very fine for you to be playing your larks with us, but I'm blow'd if we're going to stand much more of this nonsense. Tell us where you are, and we'll have one more trial for it ; but if that don't do, you must stay where you are and be ——"

"I'm here—a little on one side of where you're working," answered the voice :—"you've been digging down right away from me, and here have I been hallowing till my lungs ache, to let you know that you were labouring in vain."

"Consarn it all ! the feller's a playing his tricks with us," cried the man they called Bill. "He ain't no where, so that's all about it;—'cause if he was, we must have come to his dirty old carcase before now."

"How you talk, Bill," replied his companion; "don't he tell you that he's a leetle a one side of where we've been working, so if we cut away the gravel just hereabouts, it can't be

VALENTINE VAUX,

OR THE
TRICKS OF A VENTRILOQUIST.

BY TIMOTHY PORTWINE.

any great time before we can get to him."

"You mean to have another shy then?"

"In coorse I do, so here goes:—hooraw, my lads, cut away like good uns, and if that don't do, why then the old bloak must take his chance, that's all I know about it."

So saying, they pitched into their work in fine style, and in an inconceivable short space of time the hole was very considerably enlarged, and yet, to their mortification, neither Jew nor Gentile was to be found anywhere.

"Dang my old shoes! this place must be haunted any how," exclaimed No. 32.

Bill, wiping away the perspiration from his brow. "It must be some devil's imp that's been a larking with us all this time, and I shouldn't wonder if he appears presently to carry the whole lot on us off to his infernal hot regions below!"

"Don't be a fool, Bill," answered his quaking comrade. "The devil don't like to be chaffed about, and if you go on at that rate, I'm dashed if I don't cut away like a good un!"

"You're an infernal stupid fool, and a coward into the bargain!" exclaimed Valentine, imitating the voice of Bill, and so managing it that the other should suppose the words were uttered by no other lips but his. "I say you're a great lubberly coward, and ——"

"Do you call me a coward!" roared the lanky yokel, fiercely, and looking unutterable things at his companion.

"I do," answered Valentine, in assumed voice.

"Just say that again, old flick, and see how I'll walk into yer," vociferated the tall 'un. "Only just call me a coward, and if I don't give you summat for yourself never trust me again, that's all."

"And what'll you do?" cried Valentine, longing to bring about a quarrel between these doughty heroes;—"you can bounce pretty well, I know, but as to doing anything with me, that's more than your betters can do, old boy."

"Then I'll tell you what it is, Bill," retorted the other, "perhaps you'll just stand up for a civil fight, I won't be long in taking the conceit out of yer, and then perhaps you'll afterwards know how to treat a better man than yourself with proper respect."

"I never see sich a better man!" exclaimed Valentine, admirably imitating the tone of the digger of gravel. "Because you happen to be the biggest, you think, I s'pose that I'm goin' to be afeard on yer."

"There, then, take the change out o' that!" exclaimed the lanky hero, and at the same time he dealt Bill a touch across the nose that sent the blood spouting forth as if it had been issuing from a fountain. As for Bill, he was utterly astonished at this rough salutation, being perfectly unconscious of having in any way offended the party who had thus unceremoniously assaulted him. However, to do him justice, he was no coward, and doubling his fists he made play with such admirable skill that his antagonist soon found that he had one to deal with who was pretty nearly, if not quite, his match. At this interesting period their companions gathered round, each taking sides to see fair play between the belligerent parties, and there was every prospect of what

the fancy call glorious sport, when Valentine began to think it high time to interfere for the purpose of preventing any further mischief from his pranks.

It was in vain, however, that he tried to soothe the anger of the combatants. They were both of them enraged to the highest pitch, and having once commenced the battle were resolved to settle the differences between them, and prove to their entire satisfaction which was the better man of the two. Accordingly, at it they went for another round, a good deal of sparring and much caution being observed on both sides. At length, however, the little one let fly at the face of his antagonist, but in return he caught it severely from the lanky one, and down they both came together amidst the cheers and hubbub of their companions. Then succeeded a short pause; after which both men stood up prepared for the next round, but so disfigured were their faces by this time, that it would have been difficult for their own mothers to have recognized them. Valentine now thought they had had enough punishment for the ill nature they had exhibited towards him, and once more directing his voice towards the hole they had been digging, he uttered a groan so loud and startling, that the combatants, without stopping to finish their fight, snatched up their garments and fled with all the speed they could muster, and closely followed by their companions, whose terror was at least equal to that of the two principals in the fray. In fact, none of them thought of stopping until they had safely reached the village.

Seeing the ground thus suddenly cleared, and laughing at the terror with which he had inspired these worthies, our hero now pursued his way in the direction they had taken, and shortly afterwards found himself in the romantic little village of Dulwich. But the object for which he had left London was defeated; the hour for closing the College had arrived, and, disappointed at the result of his day's excursion, he returned home, resolving to take some other opportunity to visit a gallery of paintings of which he had heard so much.

CHAPTER XLVII.

PREPARATIONS FOR A MARRIAGE.—
UNCLE SAM'S KINDNESS SHINES
FORTH CONSPICUOUSLY.—GENERAL
SATISFACTION IS GIVEN TO ALL
PARTIES.—MARRIAGE FESTIVITIES.
—CONCLUSION.

AT length arrived the happy day that was to unite Valentine Vaux to the wealthy heiress, Miss Angelica Stanley. Great had been the preparations to give due honour to this important event, and never had Uncle Sam been seen in such a high state of bustle and excitement, as on the occasion alluded to. He was here, there, and every where; running about with a most laudable desire to make himself generally useful, and doing a thousand little kindnesses with all that cheerfulness and good nature for which he was so conspicuous. In fact, the whole arrangements of taking a house and furnishing it in a handsome style, had been entrusted to his well-known taste in such matters, and to do him justice his laudable efforts to please were crowned with deserved success.

Nor was Septimus Bramstone an unconcerned spectator of all that was going forward. He rejoiced exceedingly at the bright prospect that had opened upon his young friend, and it is even stated on undoubted authority, that he proposed to open the ball,

which was to be given after the marriage ceremony, with the widow Vaux, who had happened in his hearing, to express her partiality for the old fashioned minuets which were so fashionable in her younger days.

Nay, even Harry and Arnold Bramstone were observed to grow more cheerful as the all-important day approached; the elder gentleman in particular, was in much higher spirits than he had been seen in for a long time before, a fact that may in some measure be accounted for by his recent restoration to his brother's friendship, and the consequent probability that Arnold would not have his future prospects blighted by the cruel part they had both taken in seeking to immure the old gentleman for the remainder of his life in a madhouse.

It is needless to pursue our narrative any further than to assure our readers that the marriage of our hero and Angelica took place at the appointed time, and that the festivities which ensued were of a description worthy of the happy occasion they were intended to celebrate. Even the minuet of Septimus and his partner was gone through with wonderful eclat, so much so, indeed, that Valentine—by no means a bad judge of such matters—declared that he had never seen any thing more gracefully executed in his life.

And now we will bring our task to a conclusion, merely contenting ourselves with observing that the union of our lovers proved a most happy one in every respect, and, with the ample means at his disposal, Valentine Vaux is now become one of the most esteemed members of the high society he so greatly adorns.

THE END.